"The previo... ...cliff-hangi... ...raced for l... ...oncoming Bugger invasion. In this book, Earth starts falling off the cliff. . . . There is nothing sanitary about the fighting, although the pacing and the vivid action scenes will satisfy hard-core military-SF buffs. At the same time, the characters and the ethical foundations under them are at the high level we have come to associate with Card. Laying their own foundations under Card's Ender Wiggins saga, the Formic Wars promise to add to Card's already high reputation and to his collaborator's as well." —*Booklist* (starred review)

"Scott and Johnston explore human ignorance and compassion through a tapestry of galactic warfare in the second volume of the Formic Wars trilogy, collectively a prequel to *Ender's Game*. . . . Card and Johnston craft cinematically detailed environments for their space miners, thieves, and outcasts, probing the inner mechanics and conflicts of various groups. Social upheavals and political ineptitude are realized through rich characterization and brisk action, marrying the genre staple of alien invasion with conflicts of conscience." —*Publishers Weekly*

"The sections that feature highly intelligent, self-reliant children—Card's trademark—are as excellent as ever. . . . Another solidly engrossing installment, where the aliens are really just a sideshow: What we're witnessing is how and why Ender's child armies came to be." —*Kirkus Reviews*

"Card's strengths lie in his storytelling skill and his ability to create likable, strong, yet flawed characters, and fans of his Ender stories should flock to this prequel series." —*Library Journal*

BY ORSON SCOTT CARD FROM TOM DOHERTY ASSOCIATES

ENDER UNIVERSE

Ender Series
Ender's Game
Ender in Exile
Speaker for the Dead
Xenocide
Children of the Mind

Ender's Shadow Series
Ender's Shadow
Shadow of the Hegemon
Shadow Puppets
Shadow of the Giant
Shadows in Flight

The First Formic War
(with Aaron Johnston)
Earth Unaware
Earth Afire
Earth Awakens

Ender Novellas
A War of Gifts
First Meetings

THE MITHERMAGES
The Lost Gate
The Gate Thief

THE TALES OF ALVIN MAKER
Seventh Son
Red Prophet
Prentice Alvin
Alvin Journeyman
Heartfire
The Crystal City

HOMECOMING
The Memory of Earth
The Call of Earth
The Ships of Earth
Earthfall
Earthborn

WOMEN OF GENESIS
Sarah
Rebekah
Rachel & Leah

THE COLLECTED SHORT FICTION OF ORSON SCOTT CARD
Maps in a Mirror: The Short Fiction of Orson Scott Card
Keeper of Dreams

STAND-ALONE FICTION
Invasive Procedures (with Aaron Johnston)
Empire
Hidden Empire
The Folk of the Fringe
Hart's Hope
Lovelock (with Kathryn Kidd)
Pastwatch: The Redemption of Christopher Columbus
Saints
Songmaster
Treason
The Worthing Saga
Wyrms
Zanna's Gift

ORSON SCOTT CARD

and Aaron Johnston

EARTH
AWAKENS

—◆—

THE FIRST FORMIC WAR

Volume Three of the Formic Wars

A TOM DOHERTY ASSOCIATES BOOK | NEW YORK

EARTH AWAKENS

Copyright © 2014 by Orson Scott Card and Aaron Johnston

All rights reserved.

A Tor Book
Published by Tom Doherty Associates, LLC
175 Fifth Avenue
New York, NY 10010

www.tor-forge.com

Tor® is a registered trademark of Tom Doherty Associates, LLC.

ISBN 978-0-7653-6738-9

Tor books may be purchased for educational, business, or promotional use. For information on bulk purchases, please contact the Macmillan Corporate and Premium Sales Department at 1-800-221-7945, extension 5442, or write to specialmarkets@macmillan.com.

First Edition: June 2014
First Mass Market Edition: May 2015

Printed in the United States of America

0 9 8 7 6 5 4 3 2 1

To Scott Brick,
reader, writer, actor, storyteller, and first-rate wizard

CONTENTS

1.	Code	1
2.	Glow Bugs	9
3.	Drones	23
4.	Gravity	50
5.	Alliance	63
6.	Reinforcements	84
7.	Dozers	102
8.	Secrets	128
9.	Goo Guns	154
10.	Shield	174
11.	Options	197
12.	Rena	207
13.	India	219
14.	Dragon's Den	238
15.	Reunion	260
16.	Holopad	276
17.	Cocoons	289
18.	Soldier Boy	305
19.	Despoina	318
20.	Train	335
21.	Strike Team	354
22.	Nozzles	372
23.	Casualties	383
24.	Landers	411

25. International Fleet   435
26. Kim   455
27. Belt   460
     Epilogue   465
     Acknowledgments   469

EARTH
AWAKENS

CHAPTER 1

Code

Changing the course of a war for the survival of the human race doesn't often come to anyone, but it's especially rare for eight-year-olds to have the opportunity. Yet when Bingwen saw that it was within his grasp, he didn't hesitate. He was as respectful of authority as any child could be—but he was also keenly aware when he was right, and those in authority were either wrong or uncertain.

Uncertainty was what surrounded Bingwen now, in a barracks building of an abandoned military base in southeast China. The men around him were Mobile Operations Police—MOPs—and Bingwen knew that, as an eight-year-old Chinese boy, he was only with them because Mazer Rackham had adopted him.

How long would they allow him to remain with them, now that Mazer Rackham was gone?

Gone and probably dead.

Bingwen had seen plenty of death since the Formics first began spraying the fields of his homeland with a gas that turned all living tissues, plant and animal, into rotting jelly, breaking down into their constituent organic molecules. Turning back into fertile soil. A vast compost heap, ready for whatever the Formics intended to plant in their place.

The Formics killed indiscriminately. They slew harmless people at their labors, terrified people fleeing from them, and soldiers firing at them, all with the same implacable efficiency. Bingwen had seen so much death he was glutted with it. He was no fool. He knew that just because he needed Mazer Rackham to be alive did not mean that the Formics would not kill him.

Here's why he was so certain that Mazer was alive: The team had succeeded in its mission. The plan was good. And if something had gone wrong, Mazer was the kind of resourceful, quick-thinking soldier who would see a way out and lead his men through it. Whether he was the commander or not.

That was what Bingwen had learned from watching Mazer Rackham. Mazer wasn't the leader of the MOPs team. But the MOPs soldiers were trained to think for themselves and to listen to good ideas no matter whether they came from leaders, eight-year-old Chinese orphans who happened to be very, very good with computers, or a half-Maori New Zealander who had been rejected for MOPs training on the first go-round but who persisted until he practically forced his way onto the team.

Mazer Rackham was with the MOPs in China only because he was the kind of man who never, never, never gave up.

I'm going to be that kind of man, too, thought Bingwen. No.

I *am* that kind of man. I'm small, young, untrained as a soldier, and as a child I'm someone these men expect to protect but never listen to. But they never expected to listen to Mazer Rackham, either, never expected him to be one of them. I'm going to find him, and if he needs saving I'm going to save him, and then he can go back to taking care of me.

Bingwen had been watching the monitor with the rest of them, when the lens on the barracks roof showed the impossibly bright flare of the nuclear explosion, followed by the mushroom cloud. They all knew what it meant. The team consisting of Captain Wit O'Toole, Mazer Rackham, and Calinga had succeeded in piloting their Chinese drill sledges *under* the impenetrable shield that surrounded the lander, and then set off the nuclear device. If they had not reached their objective, they wouldn't have set off the nuke.

But did they set it off as planned, with a timer that allowed them time to dive back into the earth on their drill sledges and get clear of the blast zone? Or did they set it off as a suicidal act of desperation, barely managing to do it as the Formics prevented them from getting away?

That was the uncertainty that filled the barracks now, six hours after the explosion. Should they wait for O'Toole, Calinga, and Rackham to return? Or should they assume they were dead and go forward to try to assess the effectiveness of the attack?

Bingwen would be useless on such a reconnaissance mission. His radiation suit had been designed for a small adult, which meant it hung on Bingwen's eight-year-old frame like an oversized sleeping bag. He had scrunched up the arms and legs in order to reach the feet and gloves, but the accordion effect forced him to stand bowlegged and waddle when he walked. When it was time for the MOPs to leave the barracks, Bingwen would be left behind—and they would be right to leave him.

Meanwhile, though, Bingwen was useful for the only kind of recon that was possible right now—by radio and computer. All the MOPs were trained on all their hardware, and were very good at improvising with whatever was at hand. They had antennas on the roof as soon as the explosion was confirmed, as well as a small sat dish.

Already they were getting confirmation from their own sources in faraway places that all Formic activity around the nuked lander had ceased.

What Bingwen was good for was monitoring the Chinese radio frequencies. As the only native speaker of the southern Chinese dialect and the best speaker of the official Mandarin tongue, Bingwen was the one most likely to make sense of the fragments of language they were picking up.

And even as he listened, he was using one of the holodesks they had found at this base to scan the available networks to see what was being said among the various Chinese military groups.

Anything official, any orders from central command, would be encoded. Anything not encoded was likely to be of the "What's happening? Who set off that explosion? Was it nuclear?" variety—questions to which MOPs already knew the answers.

But Bingwen was deft at finding his way into computer networks that didn't want to admit him. The computer he was using was in the office where official communiqués would have been received. The computer had been wiped before being abandoned, but it wasn't a real wipe, it was just a superficial erasure. They had left in a hurry and who did they expect to come in after them? Formics—and Formics completely ignored human computers and other communications, that was well known. So the computer wipe had been cursory, and it had taken Bingwen only a few minutes to unwipe everything.

That meant that while Bingwen couldn't possibly decode anything himself, the decoding software was in place, and after several false starts and reboots he had managed to get in using the password of a junior officer.

Unfortunately, the junior officer had been *so* junior that he was only able to decode fairly routine messages, which meant that Bingwen had to labor under the same restrictions. Routine *encoded* messages were still a huge step up from panicked queries and radio rumors, so while Bingwen continued to listen to the radio chatter that the MOPs operatives were locating for him, he opened message after message as each emerged from the decoding software.

Finally he found something useful. "Deen!" he called out.

Deen, an Englishman, was acting CO in O'Toole's absence. Everyone knew Bingwen would not have called out to him for anything less than definitive information. So it wasn't just Deen who came, it was everyone who was not actively engaged in an assignment at the moment.

Naturally, the computer message was in Chinese, so nobody could read over Bingwen's shoulder. Still, he ran his fingers along the Pinyin text as he interpreted on the fly. "Two soldiers in MOPs uniforms," said Bingwen. "Held at General Sima's headquarters."

"So the Chinese are taking them seriously," said Lobo. "Sima's the big guy."

"Sima's the guy who had absolutely no interest in cooperating with MOPs," pointed out Cocktail.

"So they're alive," said Bolshakov, "but they've been taken to the guy who is most likely to resent their presence here."

"Two soldiers," said Deen. "Not three."

They all knew that meant that either one of the team had been a casualty during the operation, or three had made it out alive but only two had been taken by the Chinese.

By now the decoder had spat out two more messages, and one of them was a follow-up that contained names. "Prisoners identified as O'Toole and Rackham," said Bingwen.

"Have they contacted our people at all?" asked Deen. "Are there negotiations going on for release?"

Bingwen scanned the message. "No. Sima's people are reporting that they have them, but nothing else. They're not asking what to do with them, and they're not reporting what they plan to do."

"Sima wouldn't ask anybody, and nobody would have the gall to make suggestions," said Bolshakov. "Even at the highest levels of the civilian government, they tread lightly when they're dealing with Sima."

Silence for a few moments.

"Extraction would be a bad idea," said Deen. "But all the other ideas I can think of are worse."

"Even if we can figure out exactly where Sima's base is, we won't know how to get in," said ZZ. "Or out again."

"I just love winging it in the middle of foreign military bases," said Lobo.

"And when we succeed in getting them out," said Deen, "we will have alienated one of the most powerful men in the Chinese military, right when we *ought* to be getting credit for saving millions of Chinese lives."

"I have an idea," said Bingwen.

He waited for them to dismiss him, to tell him to be quiet, to remind him that he was a child. He expected this because it's what adults always did. But they were MOPs. They listened to anybody who might have useful intelligence or offer alternative plans.

Bingwen began to type into a message window. He was writing in Pinyin, because that was his native language, but he translated as he went. "MOPs team headed by Captain Wit O'Toole gives all honor and thanks to glorious General Sima for providing MOPs with drilling sledges to carry MOPs nuclear device under Formic defenses."

"We didn't get the sledges from Sima," said Cocktail.

"We got them in spite of his opposition, didn't we?" said Bolshakov.

"Let the kid write in peace," said Deen.

Bingwen was still typing, interpreting into English as he went. "All credit to glorious General Sima of People's Liberation Army for coming up with plan to destroy Formic lander from inside. All thanks to him for allowing MOPs soldiers to have great honor of carrying out his plan using nuclear device General Sima requested. Proud to report complete success of nuclear venture. Surviving MOPs soldiers have returned to General Sima to report complete success of his brilliant and daring plan."

"What a pack of crap," said Bungy.

"Brilliant crap," said Deen. "Crap that might get the Captain and Rackham out of jail."

"This little orphan boy is playing international politics better than most grown-ups," said Bolshakov. "Don't ask Sima anything, don't beg, don't extract. Just give him all the credit and announce to everybody that our men are in his headquarters. He's not going to *deny* any of this. We did this without his consent and it worked, but by giving him credit for it we take away all his embarrassment and give him every incentive to treat our guys like heroes."

"I wrote it in Chinese because I know how to make it sound formal and proper," said Bingwen. "But now I need somebody with better English to write it so it will sound right in the international version."

For the next fifteen minutes, Deen and Bolshakov helped Bingwen make a credible sentence-by-sentence translation into credible English that sounded as if it might be the original from which Bingwen's announcement had been translated. Meanwhile, ZZ and Cocktail came up with a recipient list that included high Chinese government offices, MOPs' own headquarters, and news nets around the world. "One more thing," said Deen. "Sign Captain O'Toole's name to it."

"He won't like that," said ZZ.

"He'll love it, if it gets him away from the Chinese," said Deen.

A few moments later, Deen reached down into the holodisplay and twisted send.

"If this doesn't work," said Cocktail, "we can still go in and kill a lot of people and drag our guys out like in an action movie."

"What Cocktail is saying," ZZ translated to Bingwen, "is that if this works, you saved a lot of people's lives and got us out of a jam."

What Bingwen was thinking was: Mazer wasn't killed by the nuke or the Formics, and maybe I just saved him from the Chinese.

CHAPTER 2

Glow Bugs

Victor cut into the Formic ship knowing full well that he would likely never come out again. There were simply too many variables beyond his control, too many unknowns. What was beyond the metal wall in front of him, for example? A squadron of Formics waiting with weapons drawn? An automated security system that would incinerate him the moment he stepped inside?

He had no way of knowing. The ship was the largest structure he had ever seen, bigger even than most asteroids his family had mined in the Kuiper Belt. And every square meter of it inside was a mystery. How could he possibly find the helm and plant the explosive if he had no idea where the helm was located? There might not even be a helm, for that matter. And even if there was, how could he reach it undetected?

He pushed such thoughts out of his mind and focused on the wall in front of him, turning his head from left to right so that the beams of light from his helmet could illuminate its surface and show him every detail.

He had reached a dead end, or more accurately the bottom of the hole he had climbed into, a hole on the side of the ship so deep and dark and narrow that it reminded him of the mine shafts his family had dug into asteroids. *Pajitas por las piedras,* Father had called them. Straws through the rock.

Father. The thought of him was still like a knife inside Victor.

Even now, weeks after learning of Father's death, Victor still couldn't fully grasp the idea. Father was gone. The one constant in Victor's life, the one unshakable foundation Victor had always clung to was gone.

It was Father who had always been the steady voice of reason during a family crisis. If there was a mechanical breakdown on the ship, for example, if life-support was failing, Father never panicked, he never lost faith, he never doubted for an instant that a solution could be reached, even when Victor saw no possible outcome. Father's calm, set expression of absolute confidence seemed to say, We can solve this, son. We can fix it.

And somehow, despite the odds against them, despite having hardly any replaceable parts, Father had always been right. They *had* fixed it, whatever it was, a busted coupler, a faulty water purifier, a damaged heating coil. Somehow, with a bit of luck and ingenuity and prayers to the saints, Victor and Father had set everything right again. The solution was rarely pretty—a jury-rigged, make-do repair that would only last them long enough to reach the nearest depot or weigh station—but it was always enough.

And now that pillar of confidence was gone, leaving Victor feeling untethered from the only anchor he had ever known.

A voice sounded in Victor's earpiece. "Are you sure you want to go through with this, Vico?"

It was Imala. She was outside in the shuttle, hovering a few hundred meters from the Formic ship. She and Victor had flown the shuttle from Luna, moving at a slow, drifting pace so as not to alert the Formics' collision-avoidance system. Victor was now sending her a live feed from his helmetcam.

"If you want to pull out now, I won't think any less of you," said Imala.

"You said it yourself, Imala. We can't sit idly by. If we can do something, we should do it."

She knew the risks as well as he did, and yet she had insisted on accompanying him.

"We don't know what we're getting into," said Imala. "I'm not saying we shouldn't help. I'm saying we should be certain. If you start cutting there, there's no turning back."

"This is the only place I *can* cut, Imala. I can't cut through the hull outside. It's covered with those plate-sized apertures, any one of which could open while I'm hovering above it and unleash laserized material directly into my handsome face. Cutting out there would be like cutting into the barrel of a loaded gun."

"Keep telling yourself your face is handsome and it might come true," said Imala.

Victor smiled. She was making light, breaking up the tension like Alejandra used to do.

Alejandra, his cousin and dearest friend back on his family's ship, El Cavador. She and Victor had teased each other like this constantly. She, telling him that he was knobby kneed or laughing at him for squeaking like a girl whenever she or Mono had jumped out of a hiding place and startled him. And he, mimicking her whenever he caught her humming while she worked. Hers were pleasant little melodies that seemed to sway back and forth like a swing. "What are you humming about any-way?" he had asked her once. "What's so pleasant about doing the laundry?"

"I'm telling myself a story," she had said.

"A story? With hums? Stories require words, Janda."

"The story is in my head, genius. The humming is . . . like the soundtrack."

"So you're telling yourself a story and making up the music while you're washing other people's clothing. You're quite the multitasker, Janda. And these stories, let me guess, they're about a handsome, teenage mechanic who can fix anything and build anything and smells as sweet as roses."

She had looked at him with such a start, with such an expression of surprise on her face, that at first he had thought he had offended her. But the look had vanished an instant later, and Janda had returned to smiling and scrubbing the clothes again, with her hands in the dry gloves box where the sudsy water was contained. "Victor Delgado," she had said. "Don't you know? If I ever created a story about you, I would make it a true story. You wouldn't smell like roses, you would smell like farts." Then she had flung open the dry gloves box and threw a soaked shirt in his face. And the next moment she was roaring with laughter because in his surprise, in his twisting to avoid the soaked fabric, he *had* farted. Accidently of course, something he would never do in front of her, but there it was.

And she was still laughing when he finally got his feet anchored to something and grabbed the shirt and flung it back at her. She had dodged it easily, and a heartbeat later he was flying away up the corridor of the ship, humiliated and yet laughing inside as well.

She had gotten in trouble for that, he remembered. Water had leaked out of the scrubbing box, and it had taken four women a good twenty minutes to collect it from the air and the crevices in the wall.

He should have seen it then. He should have known that the friendship they shared was something more than that. Why hadn't he recognized what those feelings truly were?

Because he had never experienced them before, he told himself. Because they had come on so gradually all his life that by the time he recognized them for what they were, it was too late to stop them.

It made little difference now. Janda was gone. Just like Father.

And here he was talking to Imala the same way. Why? Because it was natural? Because he missed that part of himself, the part that could tease a friend? It wasn't flirtatious. Or at least he hoped it didn't seem that way. He was eighteen. Imala was . . . what? Twenty-two? Twenty-three? He was a child to her. Did she *think* him flirtatious?

Imala's face appeared in Victor's HUD, snapping him from his reverie. "If you're having doubts, Vico, then let's rethink this."

She had mistaken his hesitation for fear. "I'm fine, Imala. I'm just taking a moment to consider how best to do this."

He unstrapped the duffel bag from around his back and pulled out the bubble, an inflatable dome designed to form an airtight seal on the side of the ship. With Victor inside the bubble, he could cut a hole into the ship without exposing it to the vacuum of space.

Victor pulled the ripcord, and the bubble filled with air and assumed its domed shape. He climbed under the dome with his duffel bag of tools and sealed the bubble to the wall. "Whatever happens, Imala, don't stop recording."

They had agreed that Imala would record everything Victor captured with his helmetcam. If he didn't make it back, they needed to share what they had found with whoever would listen. "Don't just give it to Lem," Victor had said. "Upload it on the nets. Broadcast it to the world. If enough people know what's inside that ship, maybe someone will see a way to end this war."

He unzipped the duffel bag and dug around the tools, looking for the laser cutter. His gloved hand found it and pulled it out. Victor set it to a low setting, pressed it against the wall, and waited for the beam to punch through. Father had taught him this technique years ago. The two of them out in the Kuiper Belt had cut into a dozen derelict ships over the years. Most had been grisly scenes: free miners hit by pirates; ships with mechanical failures that had stranded the crew and starved them out. Whoever they were, they were almost always dead by the time El Cavador arrived.

Mother had tried to protect Victor from participating, arguing about it with Father one night when they thought Victor was asleep in his hammock. "Anyone in the family can do that job," Mother had said in a hushed tone. "It doesn't have to be Vico."

"No one uses these tools as often as he and I do," Father had said. "I trust him with a cutter more than anyone. I don't want someone doing this who isn't experienced with the equipment. Anything could go wrong."

"Which is why our *son* shouldn't be the one to go."

"He's a member of this family, Rena. Everyone has their duty."

"He's just a boy, *mi amor. Un niño.*" A child.

"*Cierto,*" Father had said, falling into Spanish alongside her, the way he always did whenever a disagreement escalated. "*Un niño que hace su parte en esa familia, tal como tí y tal como yo.*" A child who does his part in this family, just like you and just like me.

In the end, they had compromised. Victor would help cut, but he wouldn't go inside the ship and assess the damage. "Leave that to the men of the crew," Mother had said. Father hadn't argued, and so Victor had been spared the worst of it. But *not* seeing what was inside the ships was perhaps worse than actually seeing them since Victor's mind always painted the worst possible picture.

He wondered then, as he often did, where Mother was now. Lem had said that the women and children on El Cavador had left the ship and boarded a WU-HU vessel, but Lem had no idea where the vessel was or if it had even survived the attack. It had been heading for the Asteroid Belt, so in all likelihood Mother was there now, perhaps at a depot or outpost where other survivors were gathering. She wasn't dead. Victor refused to even consider it. Losing Father had been grief enough. No, Mother was safe somewhere, tending to the women and children, comforting them, strengthening them, protecting them as she had always done on El Cavador. He had to believe that.

The laser punched through.

Victor stopped the beam and checked the readings. "The wall's only four inches thick, Imala. I can cut through this easily."

"Be careful, Vico."

He intensified the laser, set it to the proper depth, and quickly cut out a small hole no bigger than his finger. Then he inserted the snake camera through the hole to see what was on the other side. He couldn't see much. The space was dark and empty, a crawlspace perhaps, or a shaft of some sort. Whatever it was it was clearly big enough for him to climb into. And more importantly, it was free of Formics.

He retracted the snake, cut a hole large enough for his body to pass through, pushed the cut piece into the ship, and shined his light inside.

The shaft was a meter high and four meters wide. It extended to his right and left as far as he could see, sloping downward in either direction, matching the bulbous curvature of the ship. The walls were discolored and unattractive, covered with rust, blemishes, bumps, and imperfections, like scrap metal left to oxidize in a damp place for a few hundred years. It was almost as if the interior of the ship had been built with crude, unrefined ore, creating an ugly canvas of browns and grays and touches of black that felt dingy and ancient and long ignored.

The air in the shaft was no cleaner. Dust motes and clumps of small, misshapen brown matter floated everywhere. Victor looked at his wrist pad and read the sensors. "Air is twenty-four percent oxygen. That's only slightly higher than Earth, Imala. The rest is nitrogen, argon, and a touch of carbon dioxide. I could breathe this if I wanted to."

"I wouldn't," said Imala. "There could be traces of other elements in the air that we can't detect but are lethal, even in small doses."

"I wasn't planning on taking my helmet off, Imala. Not with all this dung in the air."

"Dung?"

He delicately poked a clump of brown matter hovering nearby, pushing it away. "I'm guessing that's not mud."

"Gross. What is this place? A sewer line?"

"Either that or the Formics don't have a good waste-disposal system. Maybe the whole ship's this way." He climbed through the hole and into the shaft, pulling his duffel bag in behind him. Then he grabbed the circle of wall he had cut out and pressed it back into place, using magnets to hold it tight. The hole he had cut for the snake camera was still uncovered, so he capped it with a metal patch from his duffel bag. If someone came along and studied the hole, they would see something was amiss, but the walls were so discolored and random that the magnets and patch were fairly camouflaged.

He stuffed his tools back into his bag and slung the bag back over his shoulder. The lights from his helmet moved around the shaft, taking in his surroundings.

"There are grooves in the floor, Imala, like tracks. Maybe two inches deep, running the length of the shaft. I count three of them. The Formics must have equipment that runs on them."

"How do you know which wall is the floor?"

"Educated guess," he said. "The Formics can walk upright, but they're tunnel dwellers. They prefer to crawl and don't require a lot of headroom. So width is more important than height. You could fit four Formics abreast in here. That would allow for several lanes of traffic and tracks for moving equipment."

"So where do you go now?"

Victor looked to his right and left. Neither way gave any hint as to where it might lead. "There are fewer floaties in the air to the right," he said. "I take this as a good sign."

He rotated his body to the right, placed his feet on opposite walls and pushed off, shooting upward. As the shaft curved, he pushed lightly off the walls to course correct himself, keeping his forward momentum, the wall inches from his face.

"It's good you're not claustrophobic," said Imala.

"I was born and raised on a mining ship, Imala. I was a mechanic like my father. He used to send me into HVAC ducts and tight spaces when I was four years old to reach things he couldn't. I've spent half my life crammed into places much narrower than—"

He grabbed the wall and stopped himself; then he blinked out a command and killed his helmet lights.

"What's wrong?" asked Imala.

Victor lowered his voice. "Ahead. I saw light."

It had appeared for only an instant, a faint green dot of light that had zipped from one side of the tunnel to the other before disappearing. Victor hovered there, squinting into the blackness, looking for it. Had he imagined it? A trick of the eye?

No, there it was again, a circle of light no bigger than his thumb twenty meters ahead of him. It shot back across the width of the passage and came to rest on the opposite side, glowing softly.

"What is that?" Imala said. "A firefly?"

Victor zoomed in with his visor and got a better look. The bug was perched on a mud nest built onto the side of the wall, its bulbous belly pulsing with light, filling that section of the shaft with a greenish hue. Its body was small, maybe four centimeters long—yellow and brown flecked with spots of red. Its four legs clung to the nest as it lazily flapped its two sets of wings. The hind wings were transparent and three times as long as its body. They glimmered and shone in the light of its bioluminescence. The forewings were much shorter and shell-like, as if they provided protection to the thorax and abdomen whenever they were pulled in flat across the back.

"I think we just discovered another alien species," said Imala.

"Let's hope it's not as nasty as the Formics," said Victor.

"I don't see any stingers or pincers."

"Even so, I'll give it a wide berth and hope it ignores us." He pushed off the wall and continued forward, steering toward the side of the shaft opposite the bug. When he was level with it, a second glow bug appeared to his right, crawling out of another nest Victor hadn't noticed.

Victor caught himself on the wall again and froze, hoping it would ignore him.

The bug, seemingly oblivious to him, launched from the nest and flew directly to a small clump of Formic dung in the air. It seized the dung with its legs, tucked it tight to its body, and flew back to the nest.

Curious, Victor drifted closer.

The bug pulsed with light as it fed the dung into a hole in the nest where several larvae lay packed together wiggling.

"It's coprophagic," said Imala.

"Meaning what?" said Victor.

"Meaning it eats dung. Or at least its infants do."

"That's disgusting."

"They have to get minerals from somewhere, Vico. This is its habitat. I don't see any other food source."

"There are minerals in dung?"

"You've never heard of fertilizer?"

"For plants maybe. Feeding it to your babies is something else entirely."

"The nests are probably made of the same material," said Imala.

"Poop nests. I'm liking this ship less and less by the minute."

"That's ecology, Vico. That's how species coexist. Every creature making do with what it's given. Maybe the glow bugs and Formics have a symbiotic relationship. The bugs clear the air and provide light for the tunnels. And the Formics provide them dinner."

"Must we call it dinner?"

He pushed off again, continuing upward, the glow from the bugs behind him slowly fading. After another fifty meters, the external mike on his helmet picked up a faint buzzing noise. As he continued, the buzzing grew louder.

Then he saw the light.

Ahead in the distance were hundreds of glow bugs concentrated in the shaft. They zipped back and forth between nests on the wall, harvesting matter from the air, buzzing and darting about in a frantic flurry of activity.

Victor stopped. "Looks like a swarm, Imala."

"You can't get through there without disturbing them," she said. "It's too tight of a space."

Victor moved closer. "Lem said this suit was tough. Even if they attack, they probably won't penetrate it."

Lem had outfitted them with all of their equipment, including new suits developed by Juke Limited that were designed to withstand the rigors of asteroid mining and yet were sensitive enough to measure all their biometrics.

"You can't be sure of the suit's durability," said Imala. "I say we try the other way."

"We're just as likely to find them in the other direction, Imala. And we've already come this far. If I go slow enough, maybe they won't bother—"

A high-pitched scraping sound echoed through the shaft, like an old rusty gate swinging open. The glow bugs all stopped instantly, a hundred dots of light, coming to rest midflight, wings fluttering, listening.

"What was that?" asked Imala.

Another scraping sound, louder this time. The glow bugs zipped to their nests and clung to the sides, filling the shaft with light and leaving a wide open space in the middle.

"That sound has them spooked," said Imala.

"I've got a hole," said Victor. "I'm going for it."

"Vico, wait!"

But he was already moving, shooting forward, trying to take advantage of the opening. He twisted his body as he flew, hoping to squeeze through the space without disturbing the nests.

But he got it wrong. The suit was bulkier and bigger than what he was used to, and some of the nests extended farther out into the middle of the shaft than he had expected. His left shoulder struck a nest, breaking off a chunk and sending a handful of glow bugs scatter-

ing and buzzing with agitation. Victor spun away, trying to avoid the bugs, and hit another nest in the process;
then a third and a fourth. He couldn't avoid them. They
were all packed too tightly together.

He tried spinning to his left to reorient himself, but
his forward motion was already carrying him upward,
and his twisting only set him farther off course. He
reached out with his feet to catch himself and felt the
squish of wings and bodies as his boots took out a
whole swath of nests below him.

The other bugs leaped from their nests, rushing to
him, fluttering all around him, landing on his arms and
legs, buzzing in front of his helmet, blocking his view,
filling his ears with the collective roar of their wings. He
had been wrong: there were not hundreds, there were
thousands.

Imala was shouting over the radio. "Get out of there!"

He twisted again, getting his bearings, finding the wall
with his feet, and pushed off, shooting away. He couldn't
see. His visor was a wall of wings and bioluminescence
and tiny, wiggling, frantic legs. The light in his eyes was
blinding, like a hundred lit bulbs thrown in his face.

His body slowed. He pushed off again, crushing more
nests. He flew ten more meters. Then twenty. He could
feel the pinching and marching of feet all over him, even
through the thick layers of his suit. Were they eating
their way inside? Were they burning their way through?
Would his suit self-seal if they tore a hole? Panic seized
him. He shook himself, throwing off his forward momentum. He careened into the wall to his right, crushing glow
bugs and nests in the impact. He got his footing, pushed
off again, flailing his arms as if they were on fire, knocking glow bugs free and leaving a wake of broken wings
and smeared bioluminescence behind him.

Then his arm brushed a wall and he felt solid metal.
No nests. He was clear.

He reached out again and yes, the walls were clean. The nests were behind him. He pushed off again, launching hard. One by one the remaining bugs peeled away, falling from his suit, disappearing from view. He didn't stop, but pushed off again, inspecting himself as he flew, shaking his legs and arms and brushing the remaining glow bugs away.

His attention was so focused on clearing his suit that he didn't see the Formic until it was right in front of him.

CHAPTER 3

Drones

Lem Jukes sat in the living room of his penthouse apartment on Luna, smiling his way through another interview and pretending not to notice the cameras. The reporter sitting opposite was a young Danish woman named Unna, with short pink hair, big silver loop earrings, and a tight-fitting, low-cut white jumpsuit that exposed as much skin as the networks would allow. The producers had sat her only inches away on the loveseat, her knees nearly touching Lem's.

Unna pursed her lips, furrowed her brow, and placed a hand gently atop Lem's own. "You must have been terribly afraid, Lem. What was going through your mind when the Formics poured out of their ship?"

The battle in the Kuiper Belt. It was all the media wanted to talk about: how Lem and the crew of his asteroid-mining ship had gallantly attacked the Formics out beyond Neptune in an attempt to stop them from reaching Earth. Lem, you must have been so afraid. Lem, where did you find the courage? Lem, how did you muster the strength?

Lem had told the story and answered those questions in so many interviews in the last few days that he could put his brain on autopilot and regurgitate every detail without giving it any thought. Yet he knew that if he wanted to come off as sincere, if he wanted the vid to get traction on the nets, his words couldn't come off as rote.

Lem nodded thoughtfully, as if no one had ever asked that question before. He angled his face slightly to the side, giving one of the cameras a nice profile. "I *was* afraid, Unna. Terrified." He paused for dramatic effect. "I had men down on the surface of that ship who were in danger. I felt helpless. I wouldn't wish that experience on anyone. Nothing is more painful than to watch your friends die."

"You call them your friends?"

"A mining ship is very close quarters. I had traveled with these men and women for a year at that point. We knew each other intimately. We were like family."

"Speaking of families, you started a foundation to support the families of the crewmembers you lost."

Lem nodded. "I felt the need to honor those men and women, to remember their sacrifice. And I wanted to ensure that the needs of their loved ones would be met. Juke Limited takes care of its own, Unna. Our company feels a responsibility to its people. I've always respected my father for his belief in that regard."

She was asking all the right questions, giving him a chance to make a plug for the company whenever it seemed natural and unscripted. The PR team, who had arranged this interview, would no doubt be grateful. It had been their idea to conduct the interview here in Lem's apartment. "People want to see where you live, Mr. Jukes, what you eat, where you sleep, the design of your furniture. It's real, it's intimate. It will humanize you."

Meaning what? Lem had wanted to ask. That I'm not human enough already?

But he had kept his quips to himself.

In some respects, Lem found it all exhilarating and familiar. Before leaving for the Kuiper Belt, he had often had a camera shoved in his face, snapping photos and recording vids of him as he stepped out of his skimmer at some red-carpet affair. He was not a celebrity in the traditional sense. He had first gained notoriety as the handsome son of Ukko Jukes, the asteroid-mining tycoon and wealthiest man alive. But later, as Lem had made his own fortune independent of his father, proving he could be just as aggressive an entrepreneur as his father had ever been, Lem's face had appeared on more reputable, business-oriented sites. Suddenly he was not only known, but also respected.

And now here he was, reinventing himself yet again. Lem Jukes, war hero.

Unna's questions then went to the Battle of the Belt. "You and your crew found footage of the battle."

"That's correct," said Lem. "We didn't participate in the attack. It happened away from our position, but we were able to recover a beacon that recorded the events. We brought that footage back to Luna so that Earth would know what sacrifices had been made to protect us. It was the largest coordinated assault that anyone has made against the Formics to date."

"Free miners and corporate miners fighting side by side," said Unna. "Two groups that don't normally get along, am I right?"

"We've had our differences in the past, yes," said Lem. "Corporations are typically more stringent adherents to the laws of the space trade. We pay tariffs, taxes. We cooperate in all respects with STASA, or the Space Trade and Security Authority. We don't shy away from federal oversight. Free miners, on the other hand, take a more liberal approach to the economy of space. They see it as a frontier, where families should be able to establish their own rules and operate however they see fit. Naturally, those two disparate economical philosophies are going to collide when they're forced to occupy the same space. But those days are over. We can no longer act independently. We're stronger together than we are alone."

"Would you say the same to the nations of Earth?" asked Unna. "Are we stronger together than we are alone? There have been very few alliances formed since this war began, and not a single significant coalition. China refuses to allow outside military assistance, despite the fact that the Formics are killing millions of their people. What's your reaction to that?"

"Earth is our nation now," said Lem. "Earth is our borders. The *them*, the enemy, is out there now. It's not Russia or the U.S. or the Middle East. It's the Formics. And it's going to take all of us working together and combining all of our talents and resources to incinerate them. Until the world wakes up and recognizes that, until we all agree that we can't operate independent of each other, defending only our little corner of the globe and nothing else, then we're going to continue to lose this war. Sadly, that's a lesson China has learned the hard way. I was elated to hear the news this morning that Chinese troops conducted a joint operation with the Mobile Operations Police and destroyed one of the Formic landers, but China must accept more help than that. I recognize that the Formics landed on Chinese soil, but China is not the only nation threatened here. The entire human race is in danger. We must put national security behind global security. Using MOPs is a step in the right direction, but we're talking about twenty to thirty men, barely a platoon, hardly enough troops to stop the waves of Formic foot soldiers armed with bioweapons marching across southeast China. The Russians stand ready to help. So do the Americans and Australians and Indians. All China needs to do is open its borders and let its neighbors come to its aid."

"We're told Russian troops are crossing the border as we speak," said Unna.

"Yes, in isolated places. And at every location, the Chinese are pushing them back, fighting them tooth and nail. The fear is that the Russians are really an invading force, that they won't leave once the Formics are defeated, and frankly that's a legitimate concern. Were I China, I'd be nervous as well. But China's allies can help. NATO can offer assurances. The Americans can broker a pullout of troops. Let's work together. Let's unite against a common enemy. Otherwise we don't stand a chance."

"One more question, Lem. You stared into the face of a Formic. In the heat of battle, out there in the Kuiper Belt, you looked deep into a Formic's eyes. What did you see there?"

"Their eyes aren't like ours, Unna. They aren't windows to their souls. Or if they are, they have no soul. Because there is nothing there, no compassion, no remorse, no friendship, no desire to understand us. There is only blackness, a deep, empty, vacant blackness."

Unna thanked him for his time and the use of his home and wrapped up the interview. The producer stepped in and gave the order to kill the cameras.

The bright lights dimmed, and the camera operators began packing up their equipment. Simona was at Lem's side with her holopad an instant later, gently taking his arm and leading him away from the bustle of the crew.

"Well done," she said. "I liked the part at the end about the eyes. Very spooky. I got goose bumps." She looked down at her holopad. "You only mentioned the company by name twice, but I'll tell the PR people to get over it. You can't be a robot. If you say Juke Limited too often, you'll sound like you're shilling."

"I *am* shilling."

"What you're saying is important, Lem. It's giving

people hope. And right now people need all the hope they can get." She typed something on her pad. "We'll have to edit out all that talk about China, though. That can't air."

That annoyed him. "Why not? Because we have customers in China?"

She looked up at him, tired. "Do you have any idea how much ore the Chinese government buys from us every year, Lem? They're not just a customer. They're our third *largest* customer. It's an important relationship to maintain. Angering the Chinese would send the Board into a tailspin."

"Everything I said is true."

She tucked her holopad under her arm and straightened his tie. "Be that as it may, these interviews are not podiums for geopoliticking. Focus on your story. That's what people want to hear. Let the governments of the world focus on China."

She was Father's personal assistant, but she had offered to be on hand for all of Lem's interviews for "moral support." Lem knew full well that she was here on assignment from Father to ensure that Lem didn't screw up, but he enjoyed having her around nonetheless.

"If I go on camera again, Simona, I want it to be with a real news outlet, not with a pink-haired bimbo. Please, for my own dignity."

"Unna isn't a bimbo, Lem. She's huge all over Europe, particularly with eighteen- to thirty-five-year-olds. We're hitting all demographics here. If we stick with traditional news networks, we'd be speaking only to geriatrics." She straightened his suit coat and brushed off his lapel. "Now, you've got another interview in four hours. This one's in Finnish, but don't think that means you can say anything you want. I'll have every word translated and approved before it airs."

Lem smiled. "Don't you think it's sexy when I speak in Finnish?"

She rolled her eyes. "You also have a message from Dr. Benyawe. She called from your warehouse while you were in the interview. She wants you to call her immediately."

Lem started moving for the door. "Cancel my next interview."

Simona hurried to keep up. "He's a celebrity reporter out of Helsinki, Lem. You'll be doing it by holo. That's your home country. You're a national hero there. We can't miss this one."

"Cancel it."

She caught his arm, stopping him. "Why? What does Benyawe want?" She studied his face. "Is she helping you send a team to the Formic ship? Is that what this is about?"

He pulled her to the side, out of earshot of the film crew, and lowered his voice. "Just cancel the interview. Please."

In exchange for information, Lem had told Simona that he was preparing to send a small strike team to the Formic mothership. He hadn't given her any of the details, but now he wished he hadn't mentioned it at all.

Before she could object, he was out the door and making his way down to his skimmer. The warehouse was in a different dome on the other side of Imbrium, so it took Lem over an hour to get there. He parked on the launch pad beside the warehouse and moon-jumped to the entrance. Once inside, he turned on his magnetic greaves and walked across the warehouse floor, weaving his way through the piles of space junk. A few of the piles were as tall as he was, stacked with busted satellite parts and scraps of salvaged mining vessels. Victor and Imala had left it here unused, and it annoyed Lem that someone hadn't cleaned it up.

He reached the far end of the warehouse and entered the conference room, surprised to find the overhead lights off. Dr. Benyawe was at the holotable, a half dozen screens floating in front of her, her face illuminated by their bluish glow. She was thin and lithe, even for a Nigerian, and although she was approaching her sixties, the years had been kind. Her hair was gray, but her skin was smooth and youthful. Dr. Dublin was asleep on a cot in the corner, still wearing his company jumpsuit, hair unkempt and mouth half open. He probably hadn't showered in days. He and Benyawe had been taking shifts ever since Victor and Imala left.

Lem approached her and kept his voice just above a whisper. "Please tell me they're not dead."

She smiled, and in that single expression, all of Lem's anxiety melted away. "I thought you would call first," she said.

"I wanted to see for myself." He turned to the screens in front of her. The largest showed the Formic ship, a giant red teardrop in geosynchronous orbit, silent and lethal and still. Another screen showed a three-dimensional rendering of Victor and Imala's shuttle, with its current operations and functionality.

The plan had sounded brilliant when Lem had first heard it. Victor and Imala would camouflage a small shuttle, covering every inch of it with scraps of space junk to make it look like a useless piece of wreckage. Then they would drift toward the Formic ship and hope the Formics dismissed them as debris. If so, Victor and Imala could reach the ship without being vaporized by the Formics' defenses and then enter the ship and sabotage the helm.

Lem had financed the whole thing, but now that Victor and Imala were underway and the money was all spent, the entire enterprise seemed ludicrous.

"Their shuttle reached the Formic ship an hour ago," Benyawe said. "Victor has left the shuttle and flown untethered to the hull. He found a recessed area in the side of the ship where a cannon is normally stored, and he's going to attempt to cut his way inside." She moved her stylus through the holoscreens and brought one forward. It showed a rendering of Victor's spacesuit. All of the data was at zero.

"Why aren't we getting his biometrics?" Lem asked.

"We got some interference when he went into the ship. Imala still has contact with him. She's recording everything on her end."

"Can we see his helmetcam?"

"That's an enormous amount of data to send. We're keeping our contact with them to a minimum. If the Formics can detect communications, we don't want to draw attention to the shuttle."

"What's Imala's status?"

"She's still in the shuttle, holding its position. She's a better pilot than I thought."

"They drifted like a hunk of debris, Benyawe. Anyone can fly a shuttle that slowly."

"Drifting is the easy part. Keeping the shuttle close enough to the Formic ship that Victor can leap to it, and yet not so close that the shuttle threatens to touch the ship and alert the Formics, that's hard."

Lem turned to the screen showing Victor's suit. "Can they hear us?" he asked. "Are we transmitting audio to them?"

She pocketed her stylus. "No. Why?"

He hesitated. It would be better to discuss this outside, alone. "Wake Dublin. Have him relieve you. Then meet me out in the warehouse."

He walked out and stood by a pile of circuits and waited.

The warehouse was quiet and cool and smelled of rust and oil and old scraps of metal. All of the workers were elsewhere—probably making repairs to the structure and getting it back up to code. The warehouse manager had assured Lem when they moved into the building that it was safe to use for the time being, but he recommended they make drastic improvements as soon as possible.

That had been the first clear sign that Father had screwed Lem with this assignment.

At first Lem had been flattered by the position. "Executive Director of Mining Innovation, Kuiper Belt Division" was a lengthy title and—more importantly—had a ring of authority to it. It sounded like a hop, skip, and a jump away from a seat at the Board of Directors. And it seemed like a natural fit for Lem, who had just experienced firsthand all the challenges and opportunities of the Kuiper Belt.

But it had quickly become apparent that the position was worthless. The company had no plans to push into the Kuiper Belt. It took Lem all of twenty minutes to discover that. There were no plans to establish supply routes that far out, no plans to build more mining vessels that could endure those conditions and distances, no plans for establishing an economic infrastructure whatsoever. If anything, there was deep-seated resistance to the idea, especially from the finance division.

The final nail in the coffin came when Lem received a list of engineers assigned to his team: Benyawe, Dublin, everyone who had accompanied him to the Kuiper Belt, and not a soul more.

No doubt Father would argue that this was smart management—everyone on the team already knew each other and could therefore get to work immediately.

But Lem knew the truth of it. Father was clearly isolating him. He was keeping Lem as an employee as the media expected but not allowing Lem to interact with any executives and build any alliances. Even the warehouse Father had given him was isolated, far from the underground tunnels that were the bulk of corporate headquarters.

Father's true intentions were made particularly plain when Lem realized how low his security clearance was. Most of the doors in the company's tunnels would not open when he approached. When he removed the proximity chip from his wristpad that the company had issued him and compared its code with others, he learned that his clearance level was no better than the lowliest of employees.

Not very subtle, Father. You're not even trying to conceal your contempt.

Benyawe came out of the conference room, squinting at the overhead lights. She saw his humorless expression and said, "Why do I have a feeling I'm not going to like what you have to say?"

"You're not," said Lem. "I've been withholding something from you, and it's time I told you. My father is preparing to launch an attack on the Formic ship."

She looked surprised. "When?"

"In three days."

"With what, mining ships?"

"With the new Vanguard drones."

Benyawe looked taken aback. "The drones? Those are still on the assembly line. They haven't even been field-tested yet."

The prospecting drones were Father's newest industry innovation, a way to evaluate the economic viability of asteroids without the need of an expensive crew. Father had announced them to the world just before learning of the Formics.

"The drones have been rushed through production," said Lem. "And that's not the worst of it. My father is arming each of them with a glaser."

She stared at him, too shocked to speak. Lem didn't

blame her. The glaser—or gravity laser—made mining asteroids as easy as pulling a trigger. It shaped gravity in much the same way a laser shaped light, ripping apart asteroids using tidal forces.

"My father's under the impression that if a glaser can vaporize a giant asteroid, why not let it do the same to a giant alien ship."

"You have to stop him, Lem. The glaser is too unstable, too destructive. He can't fire one this close to Earth."

"He's not firing *one*, Benyawe. He intends to fire fifty."

"Fifty?"

"That's how many drones are scheduled to launch."

"How long have you known about this?"

Lem sighed. "A few days."

"And you didn't tell us immediately?"

"I'm telling you now."

She narrowed her eyes. "Did you know about this before we sent off Victor and Imala?"

"Yes," he said without hesitation. He had decided that he wasn't going to lie to her. "I found out right before they left."

Benyawe raised her voice. "And you let them go? You sent them on their way knowing your father was going to fire on the vessel? You put them in harm's way."

Lem kept his voice calm. "They're at the Formic ship, Benyawe. They *went* to harm's way. They *walked* into danger. And anyway, before they left Victor assured me that they could leave Luna and get back here in four days time. That would have been a full day before my father plans to launch. I thought this was a nonissue. I didn't expect Victor and Imala to be so far behind schedule."

"Victor is a kid, Lem. He was giving you a ballpark estimate. You can't bet his life on that. Of course there would be delays. There always are." She shook her head.

"I can't believe you would endanger them like this. Did you even tell them what your father was planning? Do *they* know drones might be coming?"

He hadn't told them of course. He had worried they might abort. "I wasn't going to burden them with that knowledge. They were already worried enough about the Formics' defenses."

Benyawe waved a dismissive hand. "Spare me, Lem. Don't pretend you kept this from us for any reason other than your own self-interest. This is you and your father playing war games, desperately trying to outdo the other with no regard for the people caught in the middle."

"You're forgetting this whole escapade wasn't my idea, Benyawe. It was Victor's and Imala's. I brought it to you, I asked for your opinion, I got you involved."

"Yes, and you left out that crucial bit of information about a fleet of drones potentially firing on the mothership and ripping Victor and Imala apart."

Lem put up his hands, stopping her, his voice even. "Are you done vilifying me? I just told you, the drones don't launch for three days. That gives us plenty of time to remove Victor and Imala from harm."

"Why didn't you tell me this earlier, Lem? At the very least, you should have told me about the drones the instant it became apparent that Victor and Imala would arrive behind schedule."

"I didn't tell you because I was afraid you would abort the mission and pull them back immediately, before they reached the Formic ship."

"You're right. I would have."

"Then I made the right decision to keep it from you," said Lem. "We had to know if this tactical approach would work. No one has reached the Formic ship until now. Every military that has approached it has been obliterated. Even nukes can't get within a thousand klicks of the thing. And if we can't touch it, we can't stop it. This entire war hinges on that single objective: Getting in that ship and cracking it wide open. That's why I kept the drone attack from you. Victor and Imala had to reach the ship. And if they die today, if all we learn from them is that there's a way to reach that ship, then that's knowledge worth dying for. Victor and Imala would agree with me."

She shook her head and was quiet a long moment, not looking at him. Finally she said, "So now what? We pull them out? Tell them to turn back?"

"No, we tell them nothing. They're at the ship. That's the first big hurdle. They actually might sabotage it. And if they do, my father will have no need to launch the drones. In the meantime, you will help me convince him to postpone his attack."

"How?"

"We'll go to my father and tell him about Victor and Imala, show him they've reached the ship, and ask that he postpone."

"He won't listen," said Benyawe. "You know him as well as I do. He'll see Victor and Imala as unfortunate casualties and he'll launch anyway."

"Which is why you and I are going to prove to him that attacking the mothership with glasers is a dangerous idea."

"That won't take three days," said Benyawe. "That's an easy argument to make. I'll talk to him myself."

Lem shook his head. "It's not that simple. The glaser my father is using with the drones is not like the prototype you and Dublin developed. It's smaller, more compact. A different team of engineers has been developing it for over a year now based on your and Dublin's original designs. They started as soon as we sent word from the Kuiper Belt that the glaser was operational."

She looked affronted. "Why aren't Dublin and I consulting with these people? We spent six years designing the prototype. We know the tech better than anyone. We could point out flaws, suggest refinements, help them avoid the same mistakes we made."

"Because when you say 'flaws,' or 'refinements,' all my father hears is 'delays delays delays.' You're not consulting because you'd muck up his production schedule. You'd slow everything down."

"Yes, but going to market too soon, hurrying a glaser into production before it's ready, that's far more dangerous. This doesn't make sense, Lem. This isn't like your father. He's never reckless."

"My father is eager to end a war, Benyawe. The glasers are his answer, whether they're ready or not."

"They can't possibly be ready. A year isn't enough time. How could they have made the necessary modifications that fast without encountering glitches?"

"That's what you and I must prove."

"Fine. Take me to them. Dublin can come as well. We'll inspect them. If there's anything amiss, we'll detect it."

Lem shook his head. "Close, but no. *I'm* going to inspect the glaser, and *you're* going to stay here, watch a live feed from my camera, and tell me what I'm looking at. The glasers are being assembled in a manufacturing plant that isn't on the company map. High-level clearance. You don't have access. They'd frog-march you out of there before you got within a hundred meters of the place."

"You don't have clearance either."

"I'm the son of the CEO. Everyone knows my face. They'll assume I have clearance. And even if they *are* suspicious, even if they *want* to approach me and question my presence, they'll be too afraid of offending Father to say a word. I'll be fine."

"How will you get in the doors?"

Lem pulled a small proximity chip from his pocket. "With this." He slipped it into his wrist pad. "It will open every door in the company."

"I'm not going to ask where you got that or how much it cost."

"I bought it from one of Father's former security officers."

"Former?"

"He suddenly came into some money and decided to retire." Lem rebooted his wrist pad so it would recognize the chip. "Watch the feed and walk me through the inspection. I'm going there now." He turned and moved toward the exit.

"You should have told me about the drones sooner, Lem."

He didn't answer. He pushed open the door, deactivated his greaves, and leaped to his skimmer.

He flew out of the dome and headed east, putting the city behind him. Father built the company's tunnels outside of Imbrium in a wide intricate web far from the prying eyes of regulators. The plant where the drones were being prepped was down in the easternmost tunnels, where security was especially tight. Lem had visited it once before when he weaseled his way onto a tour the plant manager was giving Father. What Lem saw had impressed him: dozens of drones being armed with glasers, hundreds of assembly bots welding and cutting and drilling, an army of workers frantically trying to make Father's deadline. It was a clear testament to how determined Father was in his cause.

Lem's guidance system spotted the landing pad, and he brought the skimmer down dead center. The pad sank below the surface and into the docking bay, where the docking bots grabbed the skimmer and slid it into a holding container. A tube encircled the cockpit and allowed Lem to exit.

His earpiece was synched with his wrist pad, and he listened as it gave him directions from the bay to the foot tunnels. Dozens of employees were in the tunnels, going about their business. Lem walked down the center of the main passageway, head high, being as conspicuous as possible, moving with confidence, as if he had every right to be there.

Ahead of him was the first automated security gate. Foot traffic moved through it uninterrupted, the scanners silently identifying every proximity chip that passed. Lem wondered what would happen if his chip proved to be a dud. Alarms? Sirens? Armed men suddenly at his side?

He walked through without incident.

He continued on, following the wayfinding signs to the manufacturing plant. When he stepped through the entrance, he walked out onto a platform that overlooked the assembly line where the drones were being prepped.

Only, the drones weren't there. The plant was empty. All of the worker bots had been pushed up against the side walls, leaving the floor clean and bare. Lem stared, his mind racing. Had Father moved up the schedule? Had they already launched? Should he rush out and warn Victor and Imala?

He hurried to his right and took the stairs down to the plant floor, desperate to find a computer terminal. There would be tracking records, work orders, launch clearances. He booted up one of the worker bots, plugged in his holopad, and slid on his goggles. Benyawe was waiting for him on his HUD.

"Show me one of the drones," she said.

"I can't. They're gone."

"Gone? Where?"

"That's what I'm trying to find out."

Lem poked his stylus through the holos in front of him, maneuvering through the operating system, clicking

through files, not sure where to find what he was looking for.

"You need the production schedules," said Benyawe.
"You're digging around in the wrong places. These are
system files."

"I don't know this OS."

"Then stop and let me drive."

He passed control over to her and watched as the files
zipped by. After a moment she pulled up a schematic of
the new glaser, spun it around, and dove inside it, flying
through its circuitry, pausing every now and then to examine some chip, component, or mechanism.

Lem said nothing, letting her concentrate, though inside he felt a tightening grip of panic. After two minutes
Benyawe said, "I need to see the stability readouts and
precision reports. They've made all sorts of crazy tweaks,
some of them brilliant, some of them asinine. If I had to
guess, I'd say these smaller models have a faster fire rate,
which, considering their diminished size, would make
them prone to vibrate and overheat."

"Can I help you?" A voice behind Lem startled him.

Lem spun around and removed his goggles. Benyawe
disappeared, and her audio cut from his earpiece. A
short stocky man in a static suit was regarding Lem with
an air of suspicion. Half a second later, before Lem could
even speak, the man's face brightened. "Mr. Jukes. We
weren't expecting you."

Lem smiled, nonchalant. "Yes, well, my father says
you've been doing great things here. I came to see the
drones, but it appears I'm too late."

"Cleared them out hours ago. I didn't think we would
make the new deadline, but when your father makes a
request, we do our best to meet it."

Lem dropped the act, his expression serious. "Hours
ago? Where are the drones now?"

The man retreated a step, his smile fading, sensing

Lem's panic. "Gone, Mr. Jukes. Launched. On their way to the Formic ship."

Lem flew west in his skimmer, soaring over the pock-marked surface of Luna, putting the drone plant behind him. He called Father directly, but there was no answer. He called Simona, and the music played for a full minute before he gave up and disconnected. She was either avoiding him or on another holo.

Who else could he contact? Who else would have answers? The worker at the plant had been useless. "How much time do I have before the drones reach the Formic ship?" Lem had asked. "Hours? A day? What's their speed, what's their angle of approach?"

"I don't know, Mr. Jukes. We only prepped them for delivery. They didn't tell us the intended flight path."

"What about the pilots who are operating them? Where are they? Here on Luna? Where's the command center?"

The man had cowered, backing up into a worker bot. "I don't know, Mr. Jukes. I swear. They don't tell me those things."

"Where's the foreman? You have a foreman, right? Someone in charge? Someone who actually *does* know something."

But the foreman knew nothing. Or at least he claimed to know nothing. And Lem had left at a run.

He tried Simona again, and this time she answered, her head appearing in the holo above the dash, her face flat and without emotion. Lem didn't wait for her to speak first. "Why didn't you tell me the drones had launched?"

She seemed unsurprised by the question and unfazed by his tone. "I don't work for you, Lem. I'm your father's assistant. My job is to keep *him* informed."

"You told me I had three more days."

"I didn't lie. When I gave you that information, that was the schedule."

"You knew I had people heading toward the Formics. I told you that."

"No, you told me you had a team *preparing* to go. You didn't tell me when they were leaving."

"They've already left. They're at the ship now, Simona. My father has to abort. If the drones fire on the ship, my people are dead."

"Can't you contact them?"

"Of course I can."

"Then call them yourself and have them pull out. The drones won't reach the ship for another few hours."

Lem's voice rose. "They can't pull out that fast, Simona. If they rush away from the ship, the Formics will detect their movements and blow them away. They have to move slowly, at a drift. And even if they started drifting now, they wouldn't be far enough away by the time the drones arrived. If the glasers fire on the Formic ship, the subsequent gravity field will expand outward and consume my people and their shuttle. Are you following me here? They die if they run, they die if they drift. There's no scenario in which they survive if the drones attack. Father has to postpone. My people need days to get clear."

"They don't have days, Lem. They have hours."

"Are you listening to me? Is your mind processing the words I'm forming into sentences? The drones can't attack." The casual way she was regarding him was infuriating, as if she already knew every one of his arguments and simply didn't care.

"Where is my father?"

"In a very important meeting. He can't be disturbed."

"He's about to be disturbed. Where is he?"

"He's inaccessible, Lem. I'm sorry."

"We're talking about people's lives, Simona. My father can afford a momentary interruption."

"No, he can't. Not in this meeting anyway. I'm sorry, Lem. I wish I could do more. Now you answer a question for me: How did you get inside the drone plant? I just spoke with the foreman. Who let you inside?"

Lem disconnected, and Simona's head winked out. She wasn't going to help.

He debated calling Benyawe but then decided against it. If she knew about the launch she'd fly into a panic, insisting that they contact Victor and Imala, which would only put them into a panic as well. No, Lem would handle this. He didn't need Benyawe barking her disapproval. That wouldn't help his anxiety or the situation.

He made another holo call, this time to Father's office. No one answered, which was odd since Father had a team of secretaries on staff around the clock. It meant Simona had gotten to them already and told them to avoid his calls, or she had put a block on his holo signature. Either way, it meant she was sandbagging him. He would have to find Father himself.

But where? The tunnel system was extensive, stretching for several kilometers in every direction, a labyrinth with secret wings and levels not found on any map. Father could be anywhere. Or he may not be in the tunnels at all. He could be dining with a potential client in Imbrium. Or visiting one of the shipyards, or a hundred other places.

Who are you meeting with, Father? What could be so important?

The skimmer Lem was flying was a company vessel, he remembered. It was connected to the company's data system. It knew all, saw all. It was better than Simona.

"Computer, access today's meeting schedule for Ukko Jukes."

"I'm sorry," the woman's voice said. "You do not have access privileges."

Of course I don't. Father's security restrictions on me saw to that.

"Access the meeting schedule for Simona Moratti," he said.

"I'm sorry. You do not have access privileges."

He exhaled. This wasn't going to work. The answer was there in front of him; he just couldn't reach it.

"Computer, check dinner reservations throughout Imbrium in the name of Ukko Jukes." He doubted the company's data system could access every restaurant in the city, but he knew the company had relationships with the finer establishments, the kind of places Father would go. He had seen Simona make reservations with her holopad.

"No matches found," said the computer.

"What about reservations in the name of Simona Moratti?"

"No matches found."

Again, another strike out. There had to be another way.

"Computer, can you access the security cameras throughout headquarters?"

"Affirmative."

"Can you identify the location of a specific employee?"

"Only if the employee's face is currently within view. Otherwise I can only approximate a location based on the last recorded sighting or based on the last use of the employee's proximity chip."

"Can you identify the location of my father Ukko Jukes?"

"Affirmative."

"Where he is?"

"You do not have clearance for that information."

Lem swore. "Override clearance restriction."

"Permission denied."

Lem was ready to hit the dash when he remembered that he *did* have clearance. He had purchased it. "Computer, how are you identifying me right now?"

"Voice recognition. Lem Jukes. Executive Director of Mining Innovation, Kuiper Belt Division."

"Cancel voice recognition. Identify me based on my proximity chip only."

"Done. May I be of further assistance?"

"Give me the current location of Ukko Jukes?"

"Ukko Jukes is in the executive dining room, C Gate access, room 1345."

Lem changed course and accelerated toward C Gate. He arrived moments later, parked the skimmer, and took back passages toward the dining room. Knowing Simona, she would have taken every precaution. If she had alerted the secretaries at Father's office, she had likely sent similar warnings to Father's security detail. Keep your eyes open for Lem. If he shows up, politely deny him access.

Or, knowing Simona's dark mood at the moment, maybe she had ordered them *not* to be polite. Either way, Lem wasn't going through the front door.

The staff entrance was at the back of the kitchen, accessible via a side corridor off the main tunnel. A crowd of chefs in stiff white uniforms looked up from their work when Lem entered. Lem smiled and sidled past them, heading for the double doors that led to the dining room. No one spoke or tried to stop him.

The company had spared no expense on the dining room, a lavishly decorated space with a vaulted ceiling and chandeliers. There were over a dozen tables, but only one of them was occupied. Father sat across from a woman in conservative business attire. Lem didn't recognize her, but he knew at once that she was here on business and not as Father's date. Father would never pursue a woman so close to his own age and with such plain features.

Lem squared his shoulders, buttoned his suit coat, and approached them, smiling pleasantly. "Father, I'm so glad I found you. Could you and I speak in private for a moment regarding a most urgent matter?"

The surprise on Father's face was replaced with a forced smile of barely contained fury. "Lem. This is very unexpected."

Lem turned to the woman. She had a pin of the American flag on the lapel of her jacket. A politician most likely, though Lem had no idea who. A congresswoman, perhaps. Or someone from the current administration. Why was Father meeting with the Americans?

He extended a hand. "Lem Jukes."

She took his hand, showing no signs of irritation. "Margaret Hopkins. U.S. State Department. And you hardly need introduce yourself to me, Mr. Jukes. I've seen several of the interviews you've given on the nets. That must have been a harrowing experience to face the Formics in the Kuiper Belt."

"I don't recommend it," said Lem. "A summer cabin with a nice mountain breeze is more to my liking." He turned to Father, impatient. "A moment, Father?"

Ukko Jukes dabbed at the corner of his mouth with a napkin and leaned forward in his seat. "Ms. Hopkins and I were having a private conversation, Lem. Perhaps you and I can talk after."

"It can't wait. Would you excuse us, Ms. Hopkins?" Lem gestured to a door across the room that led into a parlor.

Father considered a moment, forced a polite smile, then stood and followed.

The parlor was four times the size of the dining room. Rustic leather furniture, Persian rugs, shelves filled with antique paper books. When the doors were closed behind them Father said, "You have ten seconds to explain yourself."

"You launched drones at the Formic mothership. You need to recall them. I have people there now."

Father showed no surprise. "I know about Victor and Imala, Lem. And I'm not recalling the drones."

It took a moment for Lem to find words. "You know about them? And you're going to let them die?"

"They died the moment they launched, son. They're taking on an alien ship with tech far greater than anything the human mind has ever conceived. Victor is eighteen years old, practically a child. Imala's an auditor. These aren't soldiers, Lem."

"Victor is intelligent, Father. He's resourceful."

"Simona is resourceful. A three-legged dog is resourceful. That doesn't mean we should launch them into space and expect them to defeat an army. Victor has a personal vendetta against us. Imala Bootstamp is no better. She threw away her career to go to war against me. And you want to *protect* these people?"

"Does it matter who they are if they defeat the Formics?"

Father laughed. "Do you honestly think that's even possible? They're fools if they think they can take out that ship, and you're a bigger fool for believing them."

"At least let them try. What have we got to lose?"

Father looked incredulous. "Do you watch the news, Lem? Are you even aware of what's going on in the world? People are dying by the millions. Old, young, women, children. They're hit with the Formic gases, and their flesh melts off their bones. Guangzhou, Foshan, all along southeast China. How long do you want me to wait exactly? Because every second I do, for every minute I keep those drones waiting, more people are going to die. Scientists, doctors, engineers, people a hell of a lot more resourceful than Victor Delgado. Is that what you're proposing to me? That I sit back and let that happen, let thousands and maybe tens of thousands of people on Earth die so I can give more time to *two* people who have no chance of getting out of that Formic ship alive anyway? Is that what you're suggesting? Am I reading your logic right? Because if so, than I wasted a hell of a lot of money on your education, because that's bad math. Two people are not greater than thousands."

Lem said nothing.

Ukko exhaled and ran a hand through his hair. "I'm proud of you for taking the initiative, son. You had good intentions. But this problem is bigger than you think."

"I know how big the problem is, Father. And saving Victor and Imala isn't the only reason why I'm here. The glaser is unstable. You can't fire it this close to Earth."

Father rolled his eyes. "This again."

"Benyawe has seen the schematics. The design is flawed. Blowing up Earth won't exactly save us from the Formics."

Father was suddenly angry. "Do you take me for a fool, Lem? Do you have such a low impression of my intelligence that you think I would not take precautions? If one of the glasers were to misfire, we would terminate the drone from our position here on Luna. They're not on preprogrammed flights. We control them here."

"The misfires aren't the real problem," said Lem. "It's the *well-aimed* firings I'm worried about. We have no idea what will happen if we hit the Formic ship. It has mass. The resultant gravity field will expand outward exponentially, consuming everything in its path. I saw it happen. We blasted an asteroid in the Kuiper Belt much smaller than the Formic ship, and the subsequent gravity field grew so fast and so large that it nearly consumed our ship and killed us all. The Formic ship will likely react the same way. If you hit it with fifty glasers, it could create a gravity field that reaches Earth and rips the planet apart."

"You're describing highly unlikely probabilities, Lem. You're pulling at straws."

"Talk to Dr. Benyawe if you don't believe me. Or to Dublin. Get their opinion, if you don't want mine."

Father was quiet a moment. "Are you finished? Because I have a meeting to return to."

He wasn't going to abort, Lem realized. He was going to do what he always did, ignore anyone who disagreed with him.

"And let me give you some unsolicited advice, Lem. Don't send a message to Victor and Imala. Don't warn them. That would be cruel. You'd essentially be telling them they have a few hours to live."

"*Not* telling them is cruel as well."

"*Dying* is what's cruel, son. Protecting someone from the knowledge of their own death is a mercy. Stay silent. For their sake. You may think that monstrous, but it's a kindness."

Ukko turned and walked out.

Lem stood there, considering, alone. He pulled his holopad from his pocket and prepared to call Benyawe, imagining how the conversation would go. Then he pocketed the pad and looked for another exit. Father was right. He couldn't save Victor and Imala. Silence was the only kindness he had left to give.

CHAPTER 4

Gravity

The Formic was down on its arms and legs inside the shaft, pulling a metal cart behind it. Victor caught himself on the walls before colliding with it, his helmet less than a meter from the creature's face. Victor rolled to the side to avoid it, fumbling for his weapon. The gun was up and in his hand an instant later, but his finger paused on the trigger. The Formic wasn't paying him any attention, Victor realized. It hadn't so much as flinched or turned in his direction. Instead, it continued down the shaft, moving past him with slow methodical steps, showing no signs of alarm.

It was then that Victor noticed the metal plate over the Formic's eyes, a sort of half helmet that obstructed its vision like blinders.

It didn't see me, Victor realized. I was simply in its path over the track.

The cart was an odd thing: boxy, metallic, and covered with rust, without any lights or visible tech along its surface. Its four sets of ancient, corroded wheels fit snugly into the recessed grooves of the floor and ceiling, keeping the cart securely locked on the track. The wheels squeaked and jostled as they rolled over minor bumps and imperfections on the surface.

A harness around the Formic's midsection locked into the track beneath it and prevented the creature from going anywhere but forward. Two poles extended back from the sides of the harness and fastened to the cart like traces. One of the Formic's hind legs was injured, Victor noticed. It bent outward instead of inward, forcing the Formic to walk with an awkward limping gait that made Victor almost pity the thing.

When it had moved on and Victor had lowered the gun, Imala whispered, "Are you hurt?"

Victor holstered the weapon. "Scared witless maybe. But unhurt."

"What was it pulling? Could you see in the cart?"

"No. All the sides were sealed. At least we know now what the tracks are for and what was making the squeaking noise."

"I don't get it, Vico. Where's the tech? These are supposed to be an advanced species, and yet so far all we've seen is floating excrement and carts that would predate our Industrial Revolution."

"It didn't see us, Imala. That's all I care about."

"The blinders over its eyes, though. That doesn't make sense. It's as if it were a beast of burden."

"Maybe it *is*," said Victor. "Did you notice it limping? Maybe maimed Formics are relegated to manual-labor jobs. Maybe everyone has a duty, and if you're injured and can no longer perform your duty, they turn you into a mule."

"That hardly sounds like a civilized society."

"Who said they were civilized? They're murdering planet thieves, Imala. You've seen the vids. They don't care about their own well-being. They only act in the interest of the group, the many. If he's told to be a mule, he'll be a mule."

"How do you know it was a *he*? Maybe that was a she."

Victor smiled. "I'm perfectly aware that women can do manual labor, Imala. I'm not sexist." He pushed off again, continuing up the shaft, putting the Formic behind him.

"I'm not suggesting that you are, Vico. I'm making a point about the Formics. They all look the same to me. Male, female. I can't tell the difference."

"Maybe we haven't seen any females yet. Maybe all of the soldier Formics sent to Earth were males."

"Why males?" said Imala. "Females can be warriors, too. In fact, from a biological perspective, the female is more often the protector of the young. The male usually does his business in the mating process and leaves."

"Well, you know men, Imala. Only good for one thing."

"I'm serious, Vico. Your family called the Formics *hormigas*. Ants. And who leads an ant colony? A queen. The males are merely her workers. Same with bees and wasps."

"Just because they loosely resemble ants, Imala—and I emphasis the word 'loosely'—that hardly means they function like an ant colony. Maybe all the Formics we've seen are females. Or maybe they have seven sexes. Or just one. Who cares? What does it matter?"

"Of course it matters. It absolutely matters. If you don't understand your enemy how can you possibly hope to defeat him? What is the hierarchy here, for example? Who relegated that Formic to cart work? Who gives the orders? We're here to take out the leader if we can, and yet we have no way of identifying him or her. They don't wear uniforms, so there's no visible rank classification. How are we supposed to fulfill our objective if we haven't the foggiest idea what we're looking for?"

"The leader will be at the helm," said Victor.

"Maybe," said Imala. "We're not even sure if there is a helm. We know next to nothing."

"We know they're killing people on Earth, Imala. That's information enough for me."

She didn't argue further, but Victor knew her well enough to know she had plenty more to say.

After another ten minutes, the curvature of the floor leveled off, and the end of the tunnel came into view. Victor couldn't see much of what was beyond the shaft other than bright light, crossbeams, and a hint of the wall on the opposite side a hundred meters away. Whatever the room was, it was wide and colossal.

"Is that the helm?" Imala asked.

"Doubt it," said Victor. "I've been moving parallel to the hull toward the back of the ship, not toward the center."

His external mike was picking up noise now. At first he thought it might be mechanical—bots perhaps or machines pumping and hammering, working in unison. But the more he listened, the more he realized there was no order to the noise, no rhythm of operations, no repeated sequence of sounds that come from machines doing a task over and over again. No, this noise was too random, too scattered—like the sound of people at work—the clang of metal, the hiss of saws, the grinding and turning of heavy equipment. There were Formics in that space, he realized. And lots of them.

He inched his way forward toward the end of the shaft. The lip of the shaft was rounded, and the track ran over the lip and downward, disappearing from view. Victor reached out, grabbed the edge, and pulled himself forward just as—

Another Formic appeared, crawling up into the shaft in front of him, barreling its way inside, changing its orientation ninety degrees to enter the shaft. Victor had only a moment to push off the floor at an angle and get clear. He initiated his glove and toe magnets midflight and stuck to the opposite wall. The Formic clawed its way farther into the shaft, feet scrabbling at the divots beside the track to get purchase. The cart followed it in, metal squeaking and screaming as the anchor rod scraped against the inside of the track. Like the other Formic, this one wore blinders over its face and continued into the darkness without seeming to notice Victor was there.

Victor clung to the wall and waited until the creature was out of sight before crawling back to the lip of the shaft. The room that opened up before him was larger than any enclosed space he had ever been in, like the vast domed stadiums of Earth. It was oval in shape—like the inside of an egg—and its walls were lined with cart tracks that led to dozens of different shafts much like his own. Cart-pulling Formics were everywhere, moving along the tracks, all held in place by their harnesses and anchor rods.

The center of the room was a massive space filled with large chunks of ship wreckage. Victor's heart sank when he realized what it was. It was the Italians all over again. A nightmare revisited. Cabins, engines, helms, cockpits, fuselages, fuel tanks. All twisted and broken and ripped apart.

Imala sounded nervous. "What is that, Vico?"

"It's wreckage, Imala. It's the debris of destroyed human ships."

She was quiet a moment. "How is that even possible?"

Victor turned to the left and saw a massive aperture on the wall, currently closed. "They must have brought the big pieces in from outside through that aperture."

"Yes, but where did the *debris* come from? How could they recover it? Is this from the ships that attacked them here in orbit? The cannons destroyed those ships. They obliterated them. The pieces exploded and flew off into space."

"Well, they obviously recovered some of the pieces, Imala. Look at that chunk of hull plating there? It has the American flag on the side. That's from the American fleet." He zoomed in with his visor to show her. The flag was scorched and the metal was twisted, but there was no denying the red and white stripes and blue box of stars.

"Not all of these are military vessels, though," said Victor. "Look. See those pieces there?" He zoomed in on another hunk of debris. "That's free-miner design. That's from a digger, Imala. That's a clan ship."

"I don't understand," said Imala. "Free miners haven't attacked the Formics."

"Not *here* they haven't. Not in near-Earth orbit."

"What are you saying? That some of these ships are from the Belt?"

"And the Kuiper Belt," said Victor. "They have to be."

"That's not possible, Vico. The Formics were coming in hot. They were decelerating the whole time, but they were never slow enough to recover anything."

"They didn't have to, Imala. The pieces followed them in. Remember the vids Lem showed us of the Battle of the Belt? When the Formics destroyed some of the ships, several pieces of the wreckage got caught in a magnetic field behind the ship. The field wasn't strong enough to seize the pieces and pull them behind the ship like the tail of a comet, but the field was strong enough to influence the trajectory of the wreckage and put it on the same course as the Formic ship."

"So this wreckage followed the Formics to Earth? They've been dragging debris across the entire system?"

Victor didn't answer. The full implication of what he was saying had just taken root in his mind. "What if a piece of El Cavador is here, Imala? What if part of my family's ship got caught in that field and pulled to Earth? Or worse, what if some*one* from El Cavador is here?"

It was unlikely, he knew, but he couldn't deny the

possibility. Lem had said that during the battle in the Kuiper Belt the Formics had flung the men of El Cavador away from the Formic ship and out into space. That wouldn't put them behind the ship and anywhere near the magnetic field, but what if the Formics had thrown at least one person in that direction? And what if that one person had been Father?

No, it wasn't possible. The Formic ship was moving too quickly. Even if a scrap of El Cavador or someone from the ship *had* been snagged, course-corrected by the field, and sent toward Earth, that scrap or person would still be in space and moving in this direction, months or years behind the Formics. Plus, the farther away they were when the magnetic field pulled them, the less likely they were to hit Earth. Any deviation in their course, however minute, would send them millions of klicks from here.

No, Father was *not* in this wreckage. Nothing from El Cavador was. The free-miner scraps here had to be from ships in the inner Belt. Nothing else would have reached Earth this soon.

And yet despite that, despite the logic of it, Victor wanted to leap out from his concealed position and rummage through every scrap of wreckage he could find just to prove to himself that he was right.

The Formics put an end to that notion. There were six of them to his far left clinging to a chunk of debris. Three more were attached to a bigger piece below his position—hammering, cutting, inspecting, disassembling. And those were the ones he could see. There were likely others, hidden among the various pieces.

"What are they doing?" asked Imala.

"Salvaging anything useful," said Victor. "Looking for parts, hunting for metals that they can melt down and forge differently, exactly what humans do when we find a derelict ship."

Ahead of him, a large chunk of wreckage rotated, revealing two Formics clinging to the back side. They crawled along it, spinning it in zero-G, until they revealed a small cockpit with a dead human pilot inside.

"Victor—"

"I see it."

The man was slumped forward in his seat, his helmet obscuring his face. The Formics scurried to the cockpit and began cutting the canopy away using small devices concealed in their grip. When the canopy was free, they cut the man's straps and restraints and pulled him from the cockpit. The back of the man's helmet had an oxygen tube tethered to the ship, and one of the Formics severed it with a single swipe of his cutting tool. The other Formic removed the man's helmet. The pilot was young, with close-cropped hair and a small frame. The Formics removed his flight suit as quickly as someone peeling a fruit, as if they had done this many times before. Next came his inner garment until they had his chest and stomach exposed. Before Victor knew what was happening, the Formics cut the pilot open across his lower abdomen and reached up inside him. Imala gave a sharp intake of breath.

Globules of blood seeped out and floated in the air. The Formics rooted around for a moment, then removed their bloody hands and pushed the man aside, done with him. They scurried away until they found something else that caught their interest. Then they hunkered down and began cutting again.

"What just happened?" said Imala.

Victor watched the limp, eviscerated body of the pilot float away from the wreckage. "They were looking for something," he said. "When they didn't find it, they moved on."

"Get back to the shuttle, Vico. This is too big for us. It's too dangerous."

"I'm already here, Imala."

"You don't even know where *here* is."

Victor looked to his right. "Those shafts up there, they point toward the center of the ship. If I can get to one of them—"

"You can't," said Imala. "It's too bright in here. You'll be exposed. There are at least twenty Formics who could see you. You'd never reach the shaft. And even if you did, you have no idea where it leads. Also, they're eviscerating people in there. So, I'd say it's a lost cause."

Victor poked his head out of the shaft and looked down. A few meters below him a Formic pulled a cart to the right, heading toward the distant shafts. "I could hitch a ride, Imala. I could grab on to a cart, use it as a shield, and let the Formic pull me to the shaft."

"Listen to me, Vico. We did our best here. We got some intel, and now it's time to take it to those who can use it. We've gone as far as we can."

"We've got nothing, Imala. We found some glow bugs and the cargo bay. That's strategically useless. We need intel with military significance, something that a strike team can use to disable the ship."

"I thought we were the strike team."

"We are. But if we fail—"

"We won't fail if we survive. Now turn your butt around and get to the shuttle before you're seen."

He looked below him again. The Formic and its cart were almost past him. His window of opportunity was closing. "I'm going for it, Imala." He muted her audio before she could object, then he scanned the debris in front of him. The Formics were busy at their tasks, not looking in his direction.

Victor took two quick breaths, found his courage, and then crawled out of the shaft and down toward the cart like a spider, clinging to the wall with his toe and glove magnets. For one terrifying moment, the duffel bag on this back caught up with him and shifted his momentum just as he was reaching out with his hand and foot. He instinctively blinked out a command to increase the magnet's power, and his hand and foot slammed into the wall with a deafening clang. He clung there a moment, his heart hammering, not moving, praying that no one had heard. If so, all was lost. He was in plain sight, a sitting duck.

He relaxed the power to the magnets and got moving again, scurrying now, eager for the partial concealment of the cart.

Seconds later he reached it. He grabbed the front of it on the right side and then brought his knees up to his chest in a fetal position to make himself as small as possible. It wasn't enough, though. The cart was only two thirds his size, and his shoulder and buttocks and the top of his helmet were sticking out for all to see. The duffel bag on his back wasn't helping, jutting out behind him like a turtle's shell. If seen from the other side of the cart, he might go unnoticed, but if anyone looked in his direction from a high angle, it was over. They would come for him—cutters out, maws open, hands bloody.

The Formic pulling the cart paused, and for a terrifying heartbeat Victor thought it had detected him. Then it lowered its head and pulled harder, as if adjusting to the nearly imperceptible increase in mass of its cargo.

It was not a fast Formic, Victor soon discovered. Each step was deliberate and labored. Victor's eyes traced the track in front of him, calculating the distance to the shaft far ahead. At this rate, they wouldn't reach it for another ten minutes or more. That was too much time. He wouldn't go unnoticed for that long.

A light on his HUD was flashing. It was Imala, trying to get his attention. He debated keeping her muted until he reached the shaft, but the flashing light became more insistent, and eventually he gave in and reopened her audio.

She was yelling, frantic, midsentence "—extended all the way! They've all extended!"

"Imala, slow down. What's extended?"

"The cannons! I see eight of them extended. No, nine."

"Cannons?"

"Formic cannons, Vico. Outside the ship. The one over the hole, it's extended, too. Something is coming. I've got movement on my Eye. Over forty contacts, heading toward us."

"You mean ships?"

"Fanned out, coming from multiple angles. A hundred and sixty klicks out and moving in fast."

A fleet, Victor realized. An attack. But who would be attacking? The Americans had already lost their fleet. Who else had that many weaponized fighters?

"The Formics are firing!" said Imala.

"Show me," said Victor.

A vid feed appeared on his HUD. A half dozen of the Formic cannons were in view, each of them slinging pellets of green plasma into space in a steady stream of glowing destruction.

"Show me the contacts," said Victor.

A second window appeared on his HUD showing blinking dots moving toward a center target. The fighters were coming in hot, but the cannons were picking them off easily. Two of the dots winked out, then three, six. They were nimble things, Victor saw. They juked right, then left, spinning and dodging in a way Victor didn't think possible. But the pellets persisted, and one by one the dots on his screen winked out until only six remained.

"Who are they, Imala?"

"No idea. The Eye can't identify them."

On Victor's HUD, one of the remaining six fighters

disappeared, destroyed. Then another, then another, leaving only three.

"What do we do?" asked Imala. The panic in her voice had been replaced with a calm resignation. Victor would never make it to the shuttle in time, and they both knew it. The fighters would fire on the ship with their nukes long before Victor was halfway up the shaft. And if he ran for it and the fighters failed, then he would have revealed himself to the Formics in the cargo bay for no reason.

No, if he moved he was dead.

And anyway even if he could make it to the shuttle, it would only be to die with Imala instead of alone; any blast from the Formic ship would kill them both.

He wanted to say something comforting to Imala, an expression of gratitude perhaps, or an apology for dragging her into this, the kind of parting words that people share when death was imminent. He owed her that much. But every sentence that formed in his head felt trite and awkward and overly dramatic, so he said nothing.

On the vid feed, one of the Formic cannons slammed into the hull in a twisted heap, like a metal can suddenly crushed by a giant invisible boot. Then another cannon crumpled. And another.

"What's happening, Imala?"

"I don't know. The cannons are collapsing."

"They can't collapse. There's no gravity."

And then there *was* gravity. All around him. One second he was weightless, the next he was pressed flat against the side of the cart, heavy and disoriented, the weight of the duffel bag and all of the tools crushing him. The debris in the center of the room fell all at once, a mountain of wreckage crashing down, crushing Formics, banging and colliding in a deafening boom. The Formic pulling the cart was now tipped far to one side away from the wall, nearly upside down, its legs flailing, trying to get purchase. If not for the anchor bar still locking it to the track, it would have plummeted downward.

Every part of Victor felt as if it were being crushed. His organs were heavy in his gut; his muscles were pressing down upon his bones; his helmet, his suit, everything was smothering him, squeezing him. The world became fuzzy and dark at the edges. He was blacking out. Imala was yelling in his ear.

The cart suddenly shifted, bending downward, tilting to the side, nearly dumping him off. Victor scrambled to hold on, suddenly awake, the impossibly heavy mass that was his body sliding toward the edge. His hands clung to one of the cart's traces, his feet dangling, his grip sliding downward inch by inch. He could see far below him. Fifty meters down the ship debris had clustered into a pile of twisted metal and jagged points, like a mountain of dirty knives waiting to receive him.

The duffel bag, by some miracle, had snagged on a corner of the cart and now rested on the cart's side above him. The strap of the bag, tight around Victor's chest, was all that kept him from falling off. He needed to secure himself another way, he realized, get a better grip on the traces, lock himself into the wall somehow. If the bag tore loose, the weight of the tools would pull him down like a stone.

He tried readjusting his grip so he could free his other hand to reach back and unstrap the bag.

But then the anchor rod bent again with a screech of twisting metal and the cart tipped downward. The duffel bag slipped free and slammed into him, knocking Victor free. Arms flailing, he reached out, grabbed nothing but air, and fell.

CHAPTER 5

Alliance

Just outside the city of Lianzhou, at the foothills of the Nanling Mountains in southeast China, Mazer Rackham sat cross-legged on the dirt floor of his tent, eyes closed, back straight, deep in meditation. He was aware of everything around him. The cot to his right. The wind on his face and bare chest—blowing in gently from the open tent flap. The warmth of the sun. The dirt and grass and pebbles beneath him. The soldiers and vehicles moving about the camp. The four armed Chinese guards outside the tent, each ready to shoot him should he try to escape.

Mazer inhaled deep, exhaled slowly. His Maori mother had taught him to believe in Te Kore, the void, the place unseen, the realm beyond the world of everyday experience, an existence between nonbeing and being. The realm of *potential* being.

Mazer knew he was well below his potential at the moment. His body was not as strong as it had been— his abdominal wound had sapped him of energy and strength. Nor was his mind as clear as it should be. The deaths of his crew and companions still swirled in his mind like a storm. Patu, Fatani, and Reinhardt—killed when the Formics shot down their HERC. Then Danwen, the grandfather who had tended Mazer's wounds. And now Calinga was gone as well, vaporized in the nuke detonation.

The loss of them all left an emptiness inside him, as if a plug had been pulled from his foot and a portion of his soul had drained out of him like water.

No, not soul. *Mana.* Energy, essence, power, the presences of the natural world. That's what had flowed out of him. That's what the *whakapapa* taught, what Mother had whispered in his ears at night as a child as she tucked him into bed. "We are all brothers and sisters, Mazer. People, birds, the fishes, trees. All of this is family. All of this is *whānau.*"

His Father had called it nonsense. He had never said so while Mother was still fighting cancer, but Father had made his feelings plain enough after she had died. He never forbade Mazer from believing, but Father's skepticism and disdain for it was so thick and bitter and obvious that Mazer had abandoned it for no other reason than to remove anything in their lives that might keep him and Father apart.

But now here Mazer was, drained of *mana,* sapped of his essence.

The rational, educated side of his mind—the side shaped by Father and books and computers—said that such thoughts were ridiculous. The mystical Maori *mana* was a thing of fiction. A fool's hope, a religion born of ignorance.

Yet there was a stronger voice inside Mazer. A voice that clung to the notion. Mother's voice. Soft and gentle and layered in love. A voice that told him to believe.

He had not entertained such thoughts for many years. Mazer's faith had died when Mother did. And yet he couldn't deny that something had leaked out of him. He could feel the vacancy as assuredly as he felt the ground beneath him. And until *mana* flowed back into him, he could not be who he was, who he should be. His mind was clear on that point. Unless he found *mana,* unless it flowed back into him, he would continue as a lesser form of himself.

He opened his eyes and dug at the dirt. He found a pebble just below the surface no bigger than a pill. He lifted his canteen off the cot and poured water over the small stone, rubbing it between his fingers to clean it of dirt. In the school of learning, the *whare wānanga,* a student swallowed a small pebble, a *whatu,* in the initiation ceremony. It was believed that by swallowing the stone, a student established the conditions whereby *mana* could flow into that person in the form of knowledge.

Mazer placed the stone on his tongue, took a drink of water, and swallowed.

It was not foolishness, he told himself. He had done this eagerly as a child, swallowing the water so quickly that some of it had gone down the wrong pipe and sent him into a fit of coughing. Mother had watched from the front row of the cultural center, beaming with pride. And hadn't he felt stronger after the ceremony? Hadn't he flexed his arms and told Mother that, yes, he *could* feel it now. He *was* stronger. And she had laughed and taken a knee in front of him and told him how proud she was of her little warrior. Mazer had felt such a rush of love in that moment, that the memory of it, even now, caused his cheeks to burn. If that wasn't *mana,* he didn't know what was.

A jeep came to a stop in front of his tent, tires squishing in the mud. Mazer watched as Captain Shenzu of the People's Liberation Army got down from the driver's seat, approached Mazer's tent, and stepped inside. Shenzu's camouflaged field uniform was a mottled mix of browns and greens with his rank on his collar and the red star of the Chinese military embroidered on his upper right sleeve. He looked as if he hadn't slept in days.

"General Sima requests your presence," Shenzu said in English. "Please put on a shirt and come with me."

Mazer's shirt lay on his cot. He had removed it before his meditation and exercise. Prior to the crash, he could do a hundred push-ups without slowing his pace or breaking much of a sweat, but now he could barely do twenty without the pain in his abdomen lighting up like a flare.

He got to his feet and picked up the shirt.

Shenzu winced and gestured to the red, jagged scar across Mazer's midsection. "That's a nasty cut, Captain. And recent by the look of it."

Mazer pulled the shirt down over his head and covered the scar. "Our HERC was shot down near Dawanzhen by a swarm of Formic fighters. I was the lucky one."

Shenzu's expression softened. "And your crew? Patu, Fatani, and Reinhardt?"

Shenzu knew their names of course. It was Shenzu who had come to New Zealand before the war and convinced Mazer's superiors at the New Zealand Special Air Service to conduct a joint training exercise with the Chinese military. And it was Shenzu who had hand-picked Mazer and his crew for the task. The deal was simple. Mazer and his team would teach Chinese pilots how to fly the HERC—a new experimental anti-grav aircraft—and the NZSAS would get a few free aircraft for their trouble.

"My crew died on impact," said Mazer.

Shenzu looked genuinely regretful. "You have my condolences, Captain. They were good soldiers."

"Thank you," said Mazer. "And yes, they were."

A silence stretched between them until Shenzu said, "I suppose I am partly responsible for their deaths. I brought them to China, after all."

"You didn't know what was coming," said Mazer. "The Formics killed them, not you. Though you did threaten to shoot us down."

Shenzu nodded. "You and your team had stolen a HERC, expensive government property you had no authority to fly off base."

"We were helping civilians," said Mazer.

"My superiors were afraid your flight path would be seen as an act of aggression against the Formics and instigate a conflict. There are still some officers who believe that's what happened."

"Is that what you think?" Mazer asked.

Shenzu hesitated then shook his head. "No. The Formics had already killed hundreds of civilians when they landed. Threatening to shoot you down was a mistake."

"What about arresting me and Captain O'Toole?" asked Mazer. "Was that a mistake as well? Are you intending to punish us for destroying one of the Formic landers? For helping your people?"

Shenzu turned his body toward the open tent flap and gestured toward the jeep. "General Sima is the man to answer that question. Shall we?"

They climbed up into the jeep and drove north through camp, maneuvering through a sea of tents, the bustle of camp all around them. Trucks and four-wheelers slogged through the mud. A team of mechanics huddled around a half-disassembled transport. Medics treated the wounded at a field hospital. Soldiers formed lines at mess halls and latrines. Trucks were being fueled and serviced. Equipment was being checked and rechecked. Loads were being tied down. They even passed a pickup game of baseball, where soldiers swung a broomstick bat at a wadded ball of socks.

"How many men are here?" asked Mazer.

"Close to eleven thousand," said Shenzu. "The camp extends for almost two kilometers west of us, all the way to the Qinglian Expressway." He pointed to their right. "The easternmost boundary of camp is the Lianjiang River. And just beyond that is the city of Lianzhou, where General Sima has established his command post."

It wasn't much of a city in Mazer's opinion. There were no high-rises, no industrial complexes, at least not along the western bank of the river. Nor were there any people, from what Mazer could see. All the streets and shops along the river were vacant and quiet.

"Has the city been evacuated?" Mazer asked.

"The military ordered them north shortly after the invasion," said Shenzu. "It wasn't safe for them here, and the city is an important strategic position. The Qinglian Expressway is a supply line from the north. It's one of the few highways that has been cleared of abandoned vehicles for the army's use. It takes a lot of vehicles to move an army this size. Plus the city itself is a good source of food, blankets, communication devices, and other supplies. General Sima has crews collecting anything that might be useful as we speak."

"He's plundering the city?"

"General Sima's actions are in the best interest of the people," said Shenzu. "If the military isn't equipped, it can't protect the citizenry. And remember, this is China, Captain. Everything belongs to the republic anyway."

Ethics aside, it was a smart strategy, Mazer had to admit. Traditional supply lines weren't an option at the moment. Roads were out. The army was fragmented. Sima couldn't count on resupply trucks reaching him, particularly if he intended to move south, where the Formics were aggressively gassing cities. Those sites would be quarantined. Everything would be contaminated. Water, food, and supplies found there would be worthless. Stocking up in Lianzhou was necessary.

Shenzu stopped the jeep outside a tent where four armed guards stood at attention. "Stay here," he said.

He hopped out, approached the guards, and presented his credentials. The lieutenant stepped aside, and Shenzu entered the tent. A moment later he returned with Captain Wit O'Toole, who looked unhurt but in desperate need of a shave.

"I'm glad to see you still alive," said Mazer.

"That makes two of us," said Wit. He climbed into the backseat, and Shenzu was off again.

"General Sima was insistent that we separate you two," said Shenzu. "I apologize for the inconvenience."

"Arresting us is what's inconvenient," said Wit. "We're wasting precious time, Captain. We should be attacking the other two landers. Once the Formics figure out how we destroyed the first one, once they realize the underside of the lander is their weak spot, they will take steps to shield it. And if they do, we're back to square one. We can't penetrate their shields. They'd be unstoppable."

"Duly noted," said Shenzu. "As for the other two landers, you need not worry. We have drill-sledge teams prepping to attack as we speak."

"With nukes?" asked Wit.

"I don't know the details of the op," said Shenzu.

"The drill sledges won't be able to drill into the underside of the landers," said Wit. "The Formics are tunnel dwellers. The area immediately below the landers will be dug out. We had to shoot molten ejecta at the hull and burn our way in. Captain Rackham and I should debrief whoever is leading the op."

"General Tang has that duty," said Shenzu. "And knowing General Tang, he will not want your assistance. Our orders are to take out the Formic death squads gassing cities in the south."

Shenzu reached the main road and turned east, heading toward the bridge that traversed the Lianjiang River and led into the city.

"How is General Sima intending to take down the

death squads?" asked Mazer. "Each Formic is armed with a sprayer, and you need not inhale the gas for it to be fatal. If it merely touches your exposed skin you're dead."

"We learned that the hard way," said Shenzu. "We lost thousands of soldiers at the beginning. Beijing has now given the order that no soldier should engage the Formics without a full biosuit and oxygen. In theory that's a good policy, but it's unrealistic. There aren't enough suits and O_2 to go around. Not even close. We can't even outfit twenty percent of our army. The suits simply don't exist. That many were never manufactured. No one ever imagined we would need that many."

"What about the Formic gas?" asked Mazer. "If we can find a way to neutralize it, we would remove the threat entirely."

"We're working on a counteragent," said Shenzu. "The military established a level-four containment facility here in Lianzhou. General Sima has a team of bioengineers there studying samples of the gas."

"Who are the researchers?" asked Wit. "Military?"

"Mostly. There are a few civilians as well, specialists brought in from Hong Kong at the Politburo's insistence."

"Where did they get samples of the gas?" asked Mazer.

"Initially we had bioweapons experts collecting gas in the field," said Shenzu. "They sucked up pockets of it from the air or wiped up residue that had settled onto surfaces or standing water." He shook his head. "It didn't work, though. The collected samples were too dissipated at that point, too mixed with our airborne molecules, making it near impossible to isolate the alien compounds. They needed the gas in a more condensed form, they realized."

"You went after the goo guns," said Mazer. "The sprayers the Formic death squads carry."

The weapons were of a simple design. Each consisted of a tube-shaped backpack attached to a long metal wand the Formic swung lazily back and forth, killing everything in its path. It was not unlike the sprayers pest controllers used, a fact Mazer had found morbidly ironic. Now the bugs were spraying us.

"Taking them hasn't been easy," said Shenzu. "The Formics collect their dead. As soon as we kill one, a swarm of them sweep in on skimmers and gather up the corpse and its weapons. It's almost as if they know instantly when one of their kind falls."

"How many goo guns have you collected?" asked Mazer.

"Not enough," said Shenzu.

The jeep reached a checkpoint at the bridge's entrance, and the soldier on duty waved them through. They crossed the bridge and made their way into Lianzhou. The city was empty and eerily quiet. The people had left in a hurry, abandoning everything. An overturned stroller lay on the sidewalk. A food truck was parked at the corner, its side window open as if ready for business.

Shenzu ignored the blinking traffic lights and drove four blocks east to the municipal building, a bland, two-story concrete structure. He parked and led them up to the second floor.

General Sima had commandeered a corner office with windows that afforded him a view of his camp across the river. He stood at a holotable, studying a series of maps projected in front of him. He wiped the map's contents away as soon as Mazer and the others entered.

Shenzu approached the table, snapped to attention, saluted, and spoke in Chinese. "General Sima, I present captains Wit O'Toole and Mazer Rackham."

Sima came around the table and regarded Wit and Mazer coolly. He was older than Mazer expected. Mid-sixties perhaps, well past retirement. His eyes were dark and full of suspicion. His brown wool uniform was stiff and unadorned save for a single rank insignia on his right shoulder.

"The American and the Maori," said General Sima. He spoke in English with a heavy accent. "I have read your service records. You both have quite the impressive list of accomplishments. Even you, Captain Rackham, whose service has been relatively short." He turned back to the table, made a hand gesture in the holofield, and Wit's and Mazer's records appeared.

General Sima scanned the documents. "Captain O'Toole, former U.S. Navy SEAL. Highly decorated. More successful ops on your record than most special-ops soldiers have in a lifetime. And you, Captain Rackham. Pilot. Commendations. Test scores off the charts." He turned back to them. "Soldiers to the core, the both of you. And yet, despite this overwhelming evidence of heightened intelligence, you both seem to believe you can come to my country and do whatever the hell you want." He flicked his wrist and their records disappeared, replaced with a large photo of a black crater in the earth. It took Mazer a moment to understand what he was looking at—the landscape was so different from how he had seen it last. The Formic lander and adjacent mountain of biomass were obliterated. Nothing remained save for a few scraps and pieces no bigger than Mazer's hand.

General Sima faced them. "You both stand accused of detonating a nuclear device on Chinese soil without the consent of this government. A capital offense. How do you plead?"

"Is this a court-martial?" asked Wit.

"Of sorts."

"Mazer Rackham and I were acting in the best interest of China, sir. The lander was slaughtering your people. Our tactics were extreme, yes, but only because they were necessary. The lander had to be obliterated. It was a base of operations for many of the Formic transports and flyers. It was full of enemy combatants. There was a mountain of rotting corpses beside it. The whole area was an environmental disaster."

"You *created* an environmental disaster," said Sima, gesturing to the crater.

"It was a contained nuke, sir," said Wit. "The structure took most of the blast. There will be minimal fallout. Our hope was that you would mimic our tactics and take out the other two landers."

"We will," said Sima. "We have drill-sledge teams prepping as we speak."

"I'm glad to hear it," said Wit. "If we can be of any assistance—"

General Sima glowered. "Do you think we would use you after you showed such contempt for our government?"

"Contempt, sir?" said Wit.

"Did you seek permission from the Politburo or the CMC? No. Did you defer to the military and allow us to conduct our own operations? No. Did you steal a nuclear armament from the PLA? Yes."

"We did not steal the nuke, sir. On that point, and others, I must respectfully disagree."

"You collaborated with traitors in our military to acquire the nuke. That person or persons stole it from our arsenal and placed it in your hands. That makes you guilty of espionage, theft, handling a weapon of mass destruction with the intent to kill, and about ten other national and international laws. You have spit in the face of the UN Security Council, the People's Republic of China, and my superiors."

"We made our intentions known on the nets," said Wit. "We were never secret about our plans to take out the lander. That has been our practice from the moment we entered China—"

"Which you also did illegally," said Sima.

"We have always been transparent, sir," said Wit. "We have constantly shared our tactics in the hope that the military would adopt our tactics that work and avoid the mistakes we've made. I am proud to say that many units in your military, including some under your command, have employed our tactics to great success. They in turn have shared their tactics with us, and we have executed their tactics to equal success. This has been a collaboration from the beginning."

"An unsanctioned collaboration," snapped Sima.

Wit's voice was calm and even. "Would you rather we had not killed the Formics we have, sir? Would you rather we had not destroyed the lander, with its fighters and skimmers and soldiers inside?"

General Sima ignored the question. "Who gave you the nuke? I want names."

"I can't give you names," said Wit. "The people who helped us remained anonymous."

"How did they communicate with you?"

"Through our site. Their messages self-erased after viewing. Their delivery paths were encrypted. Their log-in names were randomly generated. There are no bread crumbs for you to track, sir. These people are invisible."

Sima gave Wit an icy stare for a moment. Then he swiped his hand through the holofield, rummaged through a few files and brought up a grainy satellite photo. They were looking down on a small camp near a lush jungle forest. A skimmer was parked nearby. People were gathered together in a group.

"Someone flew to your camp and delivered the nuke,"

said Sima. "We have the sat photos to prove it. Who was it?"

"I cannot say," said Wit.

"Can't or won't?" asked Sima.

"No name was given, sir."

"A description perhaps."

"There are over four million active personnel in the PLA, sir," said Wit. "I doubt I can describe one man's features so clearly that you'll find him based on that description alone."

It was a subtle bit of deception, Mazer knew. The person who had delivered the nuke was actually a woman. Wit was leading the general well off her path.

"We are allies in this war, General," said Wit. "Not enemies. You need all hands on this. The civilian casualty reports are in the tens of millions. I'm thrilled to hear there are drill-sledge teams prepped to strike the landers, but even if they succeed, this war is far from over. MOPs can help. We can offer training, tactical advice, intel on Formic behavior and combat. We know how they attack, retreat, regroup. Their movements may appear random, sir, but Captain Rackham and I have recognized patterns in how they swarm. Let us combine our resources and skills, sir. We will work under your command."

"Under my command, you say?" General Sima turned to the holofield and flicked his fingers in a preprogrammed pattern. "According to the news nets, you MOPs have been doing that all along."

Several vids began playing: news feeds from around the world. Reporters and anchors of various nationalities were speaking to camera, their voices muted. They showed aerial footage of the black crater where the Formic lander had stood. Then they cut to photos and vids of General Sima.

Mazer understood at once. "They're giving you credit for the blast."

General Sima flicked his hand and stopped the vids. "Your fellow MOPs issued a communiqué to every major news organization in the world claiming that MOPs have been operating under my command all along. They say I devised every detail of the mission and supplied you with the drill sledges and the nuke. They claim the whole op was my idea."

"The MOPs must have learned that Mazer and I were in your custody," said Wit. "They did what they thought was necessary to ensure our safety."

"Your safety was never threatened."

"My men didn't know that," said Wit. "All they knew was that their commanding officer and fellow soldier had been arrested. By giving you the credit and painting us as allies, they made it impossible for you to harm us."

Sima grit his teeth. "They lied to the world and made me look like a fool in front of my men, all of whom know perfectly well that I had nothing to do with the destruction of the lander."

"If you're displeased with the communiqué, sir," said Wit, "all you need do is deny it. Go on record with the press that it's false. Call it what it is. A lie. Tell the world you had nothing to do with the lander's destruction. In fact, were it up to you, the lander would still be standing because you would have arrested every MOP at the border who dared to stick his nose in your country's business."

Sima glared at him but said nothing.

"But before you make such an announcement," said Wit, "consider what will happen if you corroborate their story. You will be an international hero, sir. The world would forever remember you as the commander who struck the first blow against the Formics."

"The world would remember a lie," said Sima.

"The world will remember what it *needs* to remember, sir. We are losing this war. Global morale could not be lower. Earth needed this victory if for no other reason than to reestablish confidence in the human race. By taking responsibility, you would be doing your country and the people of Earth a great service. If you are worried about saving face with your men, tell them you had to keep the op a secret. Tell them even your closest senior officers were unaware of your plans. Tell them you *had* to conduct the op this way. You knew the use of nukes was illegal, you knew it would take your government far too long to approve such a strategy. Yet you couldn't stand idly by while your own people suffered. You did what you knew you must. You worked with us privately and told us your plan. You couldn't supply your own men to conduct the op—doing so would make them complicit in your plans, which you knew were illegal. And you refused to order your men to do anything that might lead to their imprisonment.

"But MOPs . . . well MOPs were another matter. They were already here illegally. They were already taking great risk and demonstrating tactical expertise. Them you could use. They could execute your master plan."

Sima glanced at Shenzu, as if taking note that Shenzu was hearing all of this as well. "You're suggesting I tell my men I blatantly disregarded my superiors and committed a treasonous act?" said Sima. He scoffed. "Yes, what a brilliant way to teach them discipline."

"You're teaching them what you value, sir," said Wit. "You're placing the lives of your people far above your career. Your men will love you for it."

"I do not need to curry allegiance from my men, Captain O'Toole. Nor do I need leadership advice from you. You seem to forget that I had you both arrested. How am I to explain that in this elaborate farce of yours?"

"Say you staged our arrest because you were unsure

how the Politburo or CMC would react to the nuclear
blast. By publicly arresting us, you were able to take us
under your protection without arousing suspicion. Had
you openly harbored us, it could have been seen as an
act of defiance. Arresting us is precisely what a brilliant
commander who had orchestrated this whole operation
would do, sir. It allows the government to calmly consider the situation and believe you are still their man."

"I *am* still their man," said Sima.

"Of course you are, sir. That's my point. They now see
the wisdom of your actions." He gestured to the holofield. "One of those vids is your own state news site.
The Politburo is already getting behind this. This is the
event they have been waiting for. It sends a message to
the world: China is still strong. China can win. They are
making you a national hero. I suspect you have already
received e-mails from Beijing praising you for your actions."

General Sima pursed his lips and considered, a gesture that seemed to confirm Wit's suspicion.

Shenzu stepped forward, bowed slightly, and directed
his eyes at the floor. "General Sima, your humble servant
requests permission to speak freely, sir."

General Sima sighed and regarded Shenzu with a tired
expression. "Say what you will, Captain."

Shenzu stood erect. "General, you are more than justified in feeling wronged, sir. The lie the MOPs have
broadcast is deceptive and unconscionable. It makes a
mockery of our military and our dedication to integrity
and personal ethics. I might also add, sir, that your devotion to the laws of our country is a great inspiration
to this your humble servant and all those under your
command who—"

"Get to the point, Captain," said Sima.

Shenzu nodded. "Sir, what these men propose sounds

wise to me. This gives China the victory we need. The militaries of the world regard us as weak and disorganized. Unless we prove them otherwise, their disregard for us will increase and morale will continue to decline. Taking this recognition is not a selfish act, sir. It would be the opposite. You would be doing it for the glory of China. It would be the greatest service you have rendered in a lifetime of selfless acts and accomplishments."

"My greatest act would be something I had no part in?" said Sima. "Your flattery falls flat, Captain."

Shenzu bowed, eyeing the floor again. "If I may also add, General, I would be happy to corroborate your story. If asked, you can claim I was your liaison to the MOPs. That would add credibility to the account. The idea that you contacted the MOPs and coordinated with them without any assistance strains believability, sir, not because you are incapable, but because your movements and communications are so closely watched. You would need help within the military to pull this off, sir. An accomplice. Preferably someone of my rank. As a captain I am high enough in rank to go where I please, yet low enough in rank that my movements would largely go unnoticed. Your more senior officers do not have that luxury."

"You would lie under oath?" said Sima. "You would perjure yourself? Is that how little you regard your own honor?"

"My honor is my most valued possession, sir," said Shenzu. "Greater even than my life. By validating your story, sir, I am protecting China. Is that dishonor? To preserve one's homeland? To aid one's general? I think not. I would consider it my highest honor to stand with you and protect your good name."

General Sima rubbed at his chin and was quiet a moment. "And why would I choose you as my liaison?"

Shenzu kept his eyes down. "I have worked closely with the drill-sledge teams for over a year, sir. I know the tech. I also have a history with Captain Mazer Rackham, whom I brought from New Zealand to train our HERC pilots. Mine is a face he trusts. You of course knew all of these details, and thus called me into your office and gave me this top-secret assignment."

Shenzu bowed again and took a step back.

General Sima turned to the vids still hovering above the table. After a long moment he turned back to Wit. "What of the traitors who gave you the nuke? They will obviously know I'm lying. They could come forward and contradict my story."

"They won't," said Wit. "They were never going to come forward in the first place, but they certainly can't do so now. MOPs have given you the credit. This is your victory to claim."

General Sima studied each of their faces then came to a decision. "Very well. MOPs have been under my command for five days now. Captain Shenzu has been serving as my liaison." He turned to Shenzu. "You will prepare a full report of the activity of those five days, Captain, with minutes from our meetings and details of my plans to destroy the lander."

"Yes, sir," said Shenzu.

"Make sure those meetings do not contradict my actual itinerary. I don't want our fiction to have historical inaccuracies." He turned to Wit and Mazer. "In the meantime, we need to find a place for you and your men in my army. How many men are in your unit?"

"Eighteen when we left them, sir," said Wit. "Plus we have an eight-year-old boy in our company. An orphan. He sort of attached himself to our unit. We'd like to find him safe passage to a secure location away from the fighting if possible."

Sima raised a disapproving eyebrow. "You've been fighting Formics with an eight-year-old child?"

"He's safer with us than he would be on his own, sir," said Mazer. "We don't involve him in the fighting directly. We've done our best to protect him."

"My army is not a daycare," said Sima. "He has no place here. Nor can I afford to send a transport. The best I can do is find a place for him at Dragon's Den, which may be safer than going north anyway."

"Dragon's Den?" asked Mazer.

"An underground facility a hundred klicks from here. It was originally designed as a safe house for senior Party officials and their families in the event of a global war. Several thousand refugees have already gathered there. Local villagers mostly. The facility is well beyond capacity, but we'll find your orphan boy a cot to sleep on and food to eat."

Mazer nodded. A wave of relief swelled inside him. They were going to get Bingwen to a safe place. "Thank you, sir," he said.

"I'm sending you there as well," said Sima. "Both of you." He looked to Wit and then back to Mazer. "If you're truly under my command now, as you say, you will follow my orders to the letter. Is that clear?"

"Yes, sir."

"We have a team of bioengineers here in Lianzhou developing a counteragent for the Formic gas. The CMC is of the opinion that the team is too exposed here. Their lab isn't designed to withstand a direct attack. If the Formics learned of their intentions and swarmed the facility, Beijing doubts we could adequately defend them. I have therefore been ordered to move our bioengineers, their equipment, and all hazardous material to a lab at Dragon's Den. The bioengineers will continue their work there, underground."

"You said there were civilians there," said Wit. "Is it wise to bring a lethal substance inside an enclosed space where civilians are being housed?"

"The tunnels are vast," said General Sima. "Civilians are kept in an area apart from the military and far from the lab. In the event of an emergency, the various wings can be sealed off from one another. It's not an ideal situation, I agree, but this is hardly an ideal existence we're living. You and Captain Rackham will join the armed escort taking the bioengineers to Dragon's Den. The convoy leaves tomorrow morning at 0600. You will rendezvous with the other MOPs at Dragon's Den and await further orders. Captain Shenzu, you will accompany the escort as well. Isn't that what a MOPs liaison would do?"

"Yes, sir," said Shenzu.

"In the meantime, escort these men to the hotel where the other officers are staying. Give them each a vacant room and a fresh uniform." General Sima turned to Mazer and Wit. "The hotel has hot water. It's fresh and uncontaminated. I suspect you haven't had a shower and a good night's sleep in quite some time. I suggest you take advantage."

He crossed to the glass window and stood there, hands clasped behind him, looking west toward the river and the camp beyond it. Mazer was beginning to think they had been dismissed when Sima said, "Have you ever lost soldiers under your command, Captain O'Toole?"

"Yes, sir," said Wit. "More than I care to admit."

"And what about you, Captain Rackham?" asked Sima. "You're young. Perhaps fate has been kinder to you."

Mazer's thoughts went to Patu, Fatani, and Reinhardt. Somehow he got the words out. "I have lost soldiers as well, sir."

Sima nodded. "To lose a soldier is a type of death. A lesser death than the one that will take us all, but a death nonetheless. If we did not feel so, I suppose we would be unfit for command." He turned and faced them. "I have lost upwards of ten thousand since this war began. All of them sons and daughters to me. If we do not stop this gas, this weapon of the enemy, I will lose them all. See to it that I don't."

CHAPTER 6

Reinforcements

When Victor awoke in the cargo bay he was weightless again, his arms floating out beside him in the air, his feet anchored firmly to the wall.

"Victor, can you hear me?"

A voice in his ear, over the radio. He blinked again, his mind still in a fog. "Imala?"

"You blacked out. Are you hurt?"

She was out in the shuttle. He remembered now. He had fallen from the cart, and his boot magnets had saved him. He had initiated them as he was falling, and he had kicked out frantically toward the wall until one of the boot soles had snapped against the surface and held. Gravity had swung the rest of his body downward like a pendulum, and he had slammed into the side of the wall with such force that he was certain he had broken something.

"Answer me, Vico. Are you hurt?"

"My ankle," he said. "I think I sprained it." The pain was throbbing and hot.

"Yes, it's starting to swell," said Imala. "I have your biometrics here in front of me. I'll inflate and cool the area."

Victor winced as the suit around his ankle filled with air and dropped in temperature.

"You're in the open, Vico. You need to move. There's a shaft near you. Can you reach it?"

Victor reoriented himself and took in his surroundings. The shaft was fifteen meters to his right. "Yes. I can make it."

"Then move," said Imala. "You're near the debris, and one of the Formics may have survived the fall."

Victor turned and looked in the direction he had fallen, shocked to see how close he had come to death. The wreckage from the human ships had scrunched together into a giant mangled heap, only ten meters from his current position. Had he fallen any farther, he would have impaled himself on a jagged piece of metal protruding from the pile.

Imala was wrong, though. If there were Formics in that heap, none of them could have survived.

Even so, he needed to get out of the open. He bent forward, attached his glove magnets to the wall, and began to climb, wincing in pain whenever he pushed off with his left foot. He reached the shaft, climbed inside, and concealed himself in the shadows.

From here he had a good view of the cargo bay. The inner wall of the bay had taken a beating from the gravity. Whole sections of wall had crumpled inward and broken free, exposing rows of tightly packed pipes underneath. The pipes all seemed to be running in the same direction from the front of the ship toward the rear. There were valves and fasteners on the pipes every few meters, and to Victor's surprise none of the pipes appeared damaged.

Elsewhere, where the inner wall had held, cart-pulling Formics had gone back to work, pulling their cargo on the tracks as if nothing had happened. A few had stopped at places where the inner wall in front of them had been ripped away, leaving them no more track to walk on. They stood there, stuck, unable to advance.

"What happened, Imala?" Victor asked. "Why did we suddenly have gravity in here?"

"The ships that attacked must have fired a weapon that somehow created gravity inside the ship."

"How is that possible?"

"No idea," said Imala. "But all of the cannons on the surface of the Formic ship were crushed against the hull like tinfoil. That's why you blacked out. You were feeling too many Gs. It's a miracle your boot magnets held."

"What happened to the attacking ships?"

"Destroyed as well. Once the cannons were gone, the irises on the hull of the Formic ship opened and unleashed the plasma. The attacking ships were vaporized in an instant. I recorded the whole thing. That's why you're weightless again. The gravity weapons were destroyed."

"Where did these ships come from? Who has a fleet that large?"

"They weren't ships, Vico. These things were too small to be ships. They were drones."

"Drones? If Earth had drones, why did we launch manned fighters? Why risk pilots' lives if you didn't have to?"

"Because these drones aren't from Earth," said Imala. "I just backtracked their flight path. They came from Luna."

"Luna?"

"And that's not the worst of it. All of our com lines with Luna went dark right before the attack."

It all became clear to Victor in an instant. "Lem. That bastard sent a drone fleet to kill us."

"But why?" said Imala. "He financed our attack, Vico. He gave us the shuttle, our gear."

"Of course he did," said Victor. "This was his golden

opportunity. We put our heads on the chopping block and placed an ax in his hands. Don't you see? We went to him for help, and he saw it as an opportunity to silence us. Think, Imala. Lem and Ukko both want us gone. You're a whistleblower, I'm a witness to a crime Lem committed. What better way to make those two problems go away than to erase us."

"It doesn't make sense, Vico. You're suggesting Lem invested all this money into this operation just to bump us off? There are far less expensive ways to kill people. If he had wanted to silence us he could've done that on Luna."

"Then why did we lose contact with Luna right before the attack?" said Victor. "And no, Lem couldn't have dealt with us on Luna. There was too much attention on him. He was dogged by the paparazzi. And Ukko wouldn't take that risk anyway. A scandal like that would topple the company. This is cleaner. No witnesses. No one knows we're even out here. No one would connect us with Lem."

"Benyawe could," said Imala. "She was helping us, Vico. I can't imagine she would be a part of this."

"Maybe she didn't know. Maybe she thought Lem was legitimate."

"But then she and Dublin and the others at the warehouse who all saw us preparing for this would be loose ends. Are you suggesting Lem would silence them as well?"

"I'm suggesting they're all corporates, Imala, and they'll do whatever is necessary to protect the corporation."

"I can't believe that, Vico. Benyawe and Dublin are good people. They worked hard to help us."

"Who else would send drones from Luna, Imala? Who else has the capability to build a fleet like this?"

"I'm not saying these aren't Juke made, Vico. I'm

saying we don't know the circumstances. Maybe Juke sold the drones to the Americans. Or to China, or to NATO."

"Even if that's the case, Imala, Lem could've told the buyer, 'Oh, by the way, we have a strike team at the ship at the moment. Be a lamb and don't blast it to hell just yet, if you don't mind.'"

Imala said nothing.

"They cut all communication, Imala. They cut us loose. If it wasn't Jukes, why didn't they send a warning? The drones came from Luna. They would have seen them long before we did."

Imala said nothing.

"They knew we were here, Imala. They knew I was inside. So they attacked the ship to destroy it and counted our corpses as a consolation prize. Then they become world heroes, and all their problems go adios. The money Lem put into this is nothing to them, Imala. They were willing to pay twice that just to dump me out in the Belt, remember?"

"But Benyawe—"

"Is one of them," Victor interrupted. "They may have kept her out of the loop, but you can be sure she's toeing the line now."

Imala was silent a moment. "So what do we do now?"

"When we're done here we go back to Luna and jettison Lem Jukes into space without a helmet. That's what we do."

"What do you mean, *when* we're done here. We *are* done here, Vico. We lost the duffel bag. It's under a mountain of debris. And even if you could reach it, the bomb and equipment will have been crushed. You're lucky it didn't detonate already. We're through here."

She was right. The whole plan had been in that duffel bag. Victor peeked over the lip at the wreckage. There was no sign of the bag anywhere, and Victor doubted he could separate any of the pieces that had been crushed together. Plus, if the bomb *was* damaged, it would be dangerous to try to recover it. Still, they couldn't leave empty-handed.

"I still have my helmetcam, Imala. And Earth still needs information about this ship. I'm going to the helm to gather what intel I can. If anything happens to me, you know what to do."

He waited for her to object, but she said nothing.

"You're not going to argue?" he said.

"Why waste my breath?" said Imala. "You're more bullheaded than I am. You'll go regardless of what I think."

He smiled. "Turn off all communication equipment with Benyawe in case they attempt to reconnect with us and confirm we're dead. Suit biometrics, ship monitoring, cut it all. We go totally black. Let them think we *are* dead. Then redirect all my helmetcam data somewhere else, a private cloud account, maybe. Somewhere Lem can't access it. Because if he has it, he'll bury it. The last thing he wants is the world knowing he tried to erase us."

"There are data satellites I can use," said Imala. "I'll program a timer and a fail-safe into the account, with instructions to forward everything to the nets if we don't log in every twenty-four hours. That way, if something happens to us, the data doesn't go undiscovered."

"Good," said Victor. He repositioned himself and zoomed his visor binocs to a space across the room where the inner wall had fallen and pipes lay exposed. "I want to check those pipes out first. They must carry the plasma to the irises."

He crawled to the edge of the shaft, made sure no one was looking, aimed his body, and launched. The kick with his left foot sent a stab of pain through him, but he tried to ignore it, soaring across the room, aiming for a spot on the wall to the left of where the pipes were exposed. He twisted his body at the last moment and landed expertly, his ankle blossoming with pain.

He crawled toward the pipes using his hand magnets. When he was within a few meters, alarms on his suit went haywire, screaming in his ears.

Bweep. Bweep. Bweep.

A message flashed on his HUD. WARNING. RADIATION.

"The pipes," he said. "They're radioactive."

"Get out of there!" shouted Imala.

Victor recoiled and launched again. He landed on the opposite wall, turned and launched a third time, this time aiming for a shaft that led toward the center of the ship. He landed near the shaft entrance and crawled inside.

"Are you all right?" asked Imala.

"I think so," said Victor.

"Do you feel light-headed at all? Nauseated?"

"I didn't get radiation poisoning, Imala. I wasn't exposed long enough. I should have known they'd be radioactive. They're funneling gamma plasma. The ship has a ramscoop drive. It collects hydrogen atoms as it flies through space and uses the subsequent gamma radiation both for fuel and as a weapon. Did you see the nozzles? Every few feet there are T-shaped nozzles on the back of the pipes that extend up to the hull and the irises. If we had a way to close off those nozzles, the plasma couldn't fire. We'd render the ship defenseless."

"There are tens of thousands of irises, Vico. Thus tens of thousands of nozzles. You couldn't close them all even if you had an army of helpers. And you can't access most of them anyway. They're behind the inner wall and run the length of the ship."

"I didn't say it was possible, Imala. I'm making an observation."

Victor froze. A half dozen Formics in heavy, protective suits had just crawled out of a large shaft across the room, pushing two massive carts. The shaft was at least four times the width and height of the shaft Victor was in.

Four of the Formics removed a large sheet of metal from one of the carts and carried it to where a portion of the inner wall had fallen away. They positioned the sheet over the exposed pipes, and the other two Formics sealed the metal plate into place.

"A repair crew," said Victor. "To cover the pipes. They must know when radiation leaks into the ship."

"You'll need to find another way out," said Imala. "You can't get back to the original shaft this way without being seen."

"First the helm," said Victor.

He turned away from the cargo bay and headed up into the shaft. It was dark and narrow and littered with dung and dust. Victor blinked out a command and his suit began to create a map of his progress. He passed glow bugs and intersections and side passages. At times the shaft widened to accommodate another track, but Victor stayed true to his original course, heading toward what he hoped was the heart of the ship. He had expected to encounter more cart Formics, but he saw none. His ankle had swollen despite the cool pack and increased pressure, and the pain had settled into a dull, throbbing ache.

Soon the path began to clutter with discarded carts, all anchored to the track in a long continuous row on the right side of the shaft, with no harnesses or Formics attached. Victor maneuvered around them, squinting into the blackness ahead of him. He had decided it was too risky to use any artificial light and had thus been relying on the glow bugs for any illumination. The bugs had thinned in number recently, however, and the way before him now was as black as space. He slid his hands along the wall, feeling his way forward.

And then the shaft ended, opening up into a much wider but darker space. Far in the distance was a small circle of light, like the end of a long tunnel. Victor strained to see anything in the room, but he saw little definition in the blackness.

He risked a beam of light from his glove and shined it on the walls just ahead. The room was like a circular cave lined with honeycomb, with each cell as wide as Victor's shoulders and a meter and a half deep. All of the cells near the entrance were empty save for grime and dirt and dung. Between the rows of cells were narrow ladders that extended the length of the room toward the distant light.

"What is this place, Vico?"

"Not sure," Victor said. "Food storage maybe. A hatching site."

"I say we turn back," said Imala. "I don't like surprises."

"This whole ship is a surprise, Imala. I say we push on and get past this as quickly as we can."

He maneuvered to one of the ladders and began to climb, listening for any sounds of movement ahead of him. The rungs were too narrow and close together to fit the toes of his bulky boots, but he was able to pull himself along with his hands.

When the shaft was a distance behind him, he paused to catch his breath and turned to his immediate right, where a Formic's face was inches from his own.

Imala cried out and Victor recoiled, pushing off and kicking away from the ladder, shooting backward, all control lost. He crashed into the honeycomb on the opposite wall behind him, the waxy substance crushing inward on impact. His hand wrenched his gun free and brought it up, ready to fire on the attacking creature.

Only, no Formic came.

He waited, finger on the trigger, heart pounding, but

nothing lurched at him from the darkness. Finally he pointed his light and found the Formic across the room where he had left it, still tucked in its cell, unmoved.

"Is it dead?" Imala asked.

Victor looked to his right and left. Around him were other Formics, all in the same state of repose, their large black eyes staring outward. Victor reached out and scanned the nearest one with the sensors in his glove. "It has a heat signature, Imala," he whispered. "It's alive." He shined his light ahead of him and saw that between him and the light at the end of the chamber were dozens of Formics tucked into their cells. "This is a sleep chamber, Imala."

"Get out, Vico. Now."

Calmly, slowly, wincing at every sound he made, Victor freed himself from the damaged honeycomb and made his way to the nearest ladder. Shards of honeycomb floated in the air around the crater he had made in the wall, and Victor saw that by some miracle, he had landed in a cluster of empty cells surrounded by sleeping Formics.

He turned back to the ladder, feeling sick.

He looked ahead of him and behind him, judging the distance to the nearest exit. Instinct told him to flee back to the relative safety of the shaft. That was the quickest way out and the one with the fewest Formics in his path. And yet he found himself putting one hand over the other, continuing his climb toward the unknown, moving quickly now. Imala remained silent, and for that he was grateful. He wanted to be able to hear any rustling or movement, however slight, around him. He passed Formics on all sides, their faces near his own, their vacant eyes staring outward. One of them could be awake and he wouldn't even know it, he realized. He pushed the thought away, focusing on the next rung in front of him. And the next. And the next.

Minutes passed and then he was clear, drifting up and out of the chamber, exhaling deep, his arms tingling with exertion. Bright light was ahead of him, and he floated forward, shielding his eyes. He caught himself on a mesh netting in front of him and blinked, letting his eyes adjust. The sight before him made him almost forget the room he had just left. Beyond the netting was a lush, dense garden four times the size of the cargo bay and as wide as the middle of the ship. It was spherical in shape, and the inner wall was lined with thick jungle vegetation growing inward toward the center. The exception was a wide, circular section of wall on one side that glowed like a sun, bathing the garden in a hard white light.

It was like nothing Victor had ever seen. Trees with massive branches twisted and reached outward, their long wispy leaves floating about them like a woman's head of hair. Oddly shaped flowers with petals as broad as Victor's arm span and stems as thick as his legs. Massive pillars of lichen stretched from floor to ceiling at various angles like stalactites and stalagmites that had met in the middle, thick and solid and covered with mosses. Bushes and fernlike plants with leaves that fanned out in every direction. Grasses tall and short. Ivy that twisted around tree trunks and snaked up branches and then extended their reach beyond the treetops to wrap around the pillars or trees on the opposite side, creating a latticework of green and gold that moved slightly with the currents of air, as gentle as a spider's web.

And creatures. The garden was crawling with insects and alien animal life. Large beetles scurried along the lichen pillars, feasting on the mosses. These were followed by crablike creatures that bit at the lichen wherever the moss had been pulled away. On the ground, two-legged animals that looked like the offspring of an ostrich and an iguana clung to roots and extended their necks, nipping at whatever fruit was nearest.

As a boy Victor had dreamed of such places. Many times on his family's mining ship in the Kuiper Belt, he had brought up images of the jungles of Earth and imagined himself standing beneath their thick canopies, breathing in the crisp, pure oxygen, inhaling deep their damp, green smells. Father had been a boy in Venezuela, and as a child Victor would ask him again and again to describe a rainstorm in the Amazon or the sounds and smells of a world thick with life.

"What is this, Vico?" Imala asked. "Their food supply?"

"It's their life support, Imala. It's how they generate oxygen."

There were holes in the garden floor in random places, each covered with mesh netting to allow oxygen to circulate throughout the ship without releasing the animals from the habitat.

Victor watched a pair of lichen eaters chip away at one of the pillars. He was zooming in with his visor to get a better look when a Formic scurried around the pillar, seized one of the lichen eaters, and snapped its neck. Then the Formic stuffed the creature into a pouch strapped to its back and was off again, disappearing beneath the canopy.

"Scavenger Formics," said Victor. "They must feed off the lichen eaters." With his visor still zoomed in he tried tracking the Formic. Instead the binocs found a cluster of Formic corpses gathered at the base of a tree, their bodies mostly decomposed and crawling with insects. "They use their dead to fertilize the plants," said Victor. "Nothing wasted."

To Victor's right and left, outside the garden, a corridor curved around the spherical habitat. "I'm going around it, Imala, see if the helm's on the opposite side." He pushed off and moved to his right, launching from wall to wall to move up the corridor. Once he reached the other side he quickly concealed himself. A handful of scavenger Formics were outside the garden sphere, removing dead lichen eaters from their pouches and pushing them down tubes into giant steaming vats. Pipes extended from the vats that led to a feeding station where a row of spigots were positioned. Dozens of Formics were gathered at the spigots. They each came forward in turn, drank their fill from the spigot, then moved on.

"This is how they feed?" asked Imala. "A liquefied slurry of melted crab creatures from a community spigot? How is this an advanced species?"

"I need to find another way around, Imala. I can't go through here."

He backtracked in the corridor until he found a groove in the floor. He followed it into a narrow shaft that bypassed the feeding station. That shaft connected with a much larger one, not unlike the giant shaft he had seen empty into the cargo bay.

The shaft ended shortly thereafter at a room as wide as the ship and shaped like a giant wheel. The center or hub of the wheel had consoles and equipment all around it, presumably for operating the spokes of the wheel, which were massive transparent tubes sixty or seventy meters high that extended all the way up to the hull of the ship on all sides. Each tube was over ten meters wide and had a troop carrier at its bottom, nose pointed upward, ready to launch. Hundreds of Formics were climbing up into the bottom of the tubes and loading into the small ships, with wand sprayers in hand and gas packs on their backs.

"What's happening?" asked Imala.

"They're sending down reinforcements," said Victor. "They're launching more ships and troops. They're retaliating for the gravity attack."

The last of the soldier Formics climbed up into the tubes and sealed the door behind them. The Formics manning the consoles outside the tubes spun giant wheels, and the irises at the end of the tubes opened, exposing the blackness of space beyond.

Without warning or countdown, the launch mechanism shot the troop carriers upward like the contents of a giant pneumatic tube, slinging them out into space with such speed that Victor guessed the Formics inside were feeling five or six Gs. The decking beneath Victor shook from the force, and then all was still again. The Formics at the consoles closed the launch tubes, reset the launch mechanisms, and then exited the room, leaving it unoccupied. Victor waited a few minutes to ensure no one returned and then launched down to the equipment, Imala cursing him the whole way for taking yet another risk.

"A *needed* risk, Imala. This is how they replenish their forces. If we can find a way to sabotage the tubes, then we can cut off their line of troops and supplies, we can weaken them by attrition."

He caught himself on the consoles, eager to see the tech. But just like the Formic pod he and Father had boarded in the Kuiper Belt, the console here had no markings whatsoever. "Look at this, Imala. Nothing is labeled. There's no language, no numbers, no symbols of any kind. No instructions whatsoever on how to operate this thing."

"Maybe they don't need symbols. Maybe they know the equipment perfectly."

"Everything has symbols, Imala. Humans would be lost without labels on our buttons. We'd be operating blind. How do they measure anything without numbers? Speed, intake, fuel, weight, navigation. How can they be precise about what they're doing? This is like a keyboard without letters. And look at the setup. It's entirely mechanical. No screens, no readouts. There have to be computer elements to this, but I can't see them."

He flew to one of the tubes and examined the launch mechanism. It took him over an hour to determine how it operated. Imala kept pestering him about time and his oxygen levels and the need to get moving. Finally he heeded her and moved on, taking another passageway behind the hub and launch tubes. He maneuvered through the tunnels for another half hour—doubling back at a few places and taking different routes—before he finally found the helm, positioned as he had expected in the center of the ship. Victor hid himself inside the door and recorded everything with his helmetcam.

The helm was a compact space only big enough to accommodate eight Formic workers, all of them buckled to poles that extended from the floor or ceiling. They hovered before a series of screens showing the blackness of space from various angles. Tiny objects on the screen were drifting, and the computer tracked each one with a dot of light.

"This must be their collision-avoidance system, Imala. This is how they track any approaching ship."

"If they're tracking movement here," said Imala, "they probably open the irises and fire the weapon from here as well."

Victor watched the Formics work, recording their every move. He had hoped to find a leader here, someone giving orders to the crew or, even better, commanding the troops on Earth. A general, a king, a ruler, anything. Victor no longer had the explosive device, but he still had his sidearm. If he killed the leader, the others in the helm would overwhelm him, but wasn't that a sacrifice he should be willing to make? Wasn't that his duty as a human being, to strike a heavy blow even if it cost him his life?

A part of him had worried that once he reached the helm his courage would fail him, that he would freeze again like he had done the first time he saw a Formic.

But now that he was here, now that his hand was on his sidearm and the opportunity was before him, the doubt was replaced with a surprisingly steady calm. He *was* ready to die, he realized. They had killed Alejandra and Concepción and Toron and Father. They had destroyed his ship, his only home, everything he had ever owned and cared about. Maybe Mother as well.

Yes, he could kill. And gladly.

But as he watched those on the helm, it quickly became apparent that no one was in charge. No one relayed any orders, no one shared any intel, no one sought instructions from a superior. Nor were there any written messages being shared, or gestures, or communication of any kind.

It all became clear to Victor then.

He removed his helmetcam and positioned it up in the corner near the ceiling, giving him a clear view of the console and main instrument panel. Then he backed out of the helm and hid himself in the shaft. "Have you ever been inside the helm of a big ship, Imala? Especially when there's a threat nearby?"

"No."

"It's chaos. People yelling across the room, passing intel, sharing computer readouts. It's loud, fast-paced, and highly collaborative. Everyone is making sure everyone else has all the information they need to do their jobs right."

"And yet the Formics at the helm act like the others don't even exist," said Imala.

"None of them talk at all," said Victor. "It's completely silent. We knew the soldier Formics on Earth were silent, but I had always assumed that was because they were so focused on the business of killing. But *these* Formics here, they should be in crisis mode. They were just attacked. They would be on high alert. And did you watch them? Did you notice how they did things simultaneously, even when they weren't looking at one another?"

"It was almost as if they *were* speaking to each other," said Imala.

"Exactly. In fact, I think they *are* speaking to each other. Only they do it in a way we can't see. Mind to mind."

"You mean telepathy?"

"I know it sounds absurd, Imala, but they respond instantly to stimuli that they can't possibly have known about unless someone told them. And yet no one tells them anything." He crawled out of his hiding place. "I left my helmetcam in the helm. Keep recording everything. I'm coming back your way. We're returning to Luna. I've learned everything I can here."

"Hallelujah. Be careful."

He made his way back, retracing his route, staying in the shadows and avoiding being seen. The wide shaft by the garden went directly to the cargo bay as he had hoped. The flotsam from the human ships had drifted back up into the center of the room. The repair crew was nowhere in sight. Victor made his way to the shaft he had first used and followed it back to where he had cut his way into the ship. He crawled outside, sealed the hole, removed the bubble, and flew back up to where the Formic cannon lay crushed against the side of the hull. There was a hole among the wreckage large enough for him to crawl through, and he wiggled out, free of the ship.

He spotted the shuttle, aimed his body, and pushed off lightly, exerting just enough force to move at a slow drift. It took him over an hour to reach the shuttle at that pace. When he crawled back into the cockpit, he was so happy to see Imala that he extended his arms to embrace her. She made a face and held up a hand, stopping him. "You've got Formic dung and glow-bug juice all over your suit. Don't even think about touching me."

Victor wiped a speck of gunk off his chest and wiggled the soiled finger in front of her.

Imala was not amused. "Any closer and I will break that finger."

He smiled, grabbed the wipes from their compartment, and began cleaning himself. "I'm alive, Imala. I didn't think I would be, but here I am, kicking and breathing. It's going to take more than your sour grumpiness to dampen this mood."

"We've made a video, Vico. That's it. We haven't ended the war."

"Focus too closely on the goal you haven't accomplished, and you'll fail to notice the victories you achieve along the way."

"Who said that?" Imala asked. "Churchill? Sun Tzu?"

"No," said Victor. "My father."

Imala looked up from the console, smiling. "You're right. This is a victory, isn't it? A big one. Maybe someone will see this vid and know how to destroy the ship."

A wide grin broke across Victor's face. "But Imala, my sweet, that someone is me. I know precisely how to destroy this ship."

She stared at him. "Then why are we leaving?"

"Because we can't do it alone. We need the right crew. When we have them, we'll come back and finish this."

"We're coming back?"

Victor pulled himself into his seat and began buckling up. "Never leave a job unfinished, Imala."

She turned back to the flight controls. "More quotes from your father?"

"No. That one is all me."

CHAPTER 7

Dozers

A pounding on the door woke Mazer with a start. He sat up in bed in the dark, remembering where he was. The hotel room. Lianzhou. A safe place. He checked the time on the wrist pad Shenzu had given him the night before. It was just past three in the morning.

He threw back the sheet and swung out of bed, the images of his dream slowly fading like vapor. He had been with Kim at the salt marshes of Manukau Harbor. They had come to watch the godwits wade in the marshes and jab their long needlelike beaks into the mud searching for food. There had been tens of thousands of the birds, all squawking and chirping and taking to flight like a swarm, moving as one.

Only, the godwits had changed. One moment they were fat, long-beaked birds, the next they were Formics, miniature in size, scuttling through the water on all six appendages, scampering across the mud and then onto dry land, rushing toward Mazer and Kim like a wave, thousands of them, each growing larger with every step until the Formics were actual size and then twice their size. And Kim had grabbed Mazer's arm and screamed, and an instant later her scream was a high-pitched clicking noise, and she was wasn't Kim after all, she was a Formic, with her maw wide open, ready to envelop him.

Three more knocks on the door. Hard and insistent.

Mazer found his pants, dressed, and made his way through the dark to the door. Two Chinese soldiers with flashlights were standing in the hall. One was a *lie bing*, the other a *zhongzhi*, or the Chinese equivalent of a private and a sergeant.

"Please come with us," said the *zhongzhi* in Chinese. "You and Captain O'Toole are wanted downstairs immediately."

Mazer finished dressing and grabbed what little gear he had. They stopped at Wit's room on the way and roused him. "What's this about?" Wit asked.

The Chinese soldiers didn't answer.

"I don't think they speak English," said Mazer. He translated Wit's question into Chinese, and the soldiers responded.

"Captain Shenzu will explain," said the *zhongzhi*.

They reached the lobby and found Shenzu conferring with a young officer in a biosuit. Shenzu motioned them over and gestured to the man opposite. "Captain Rackham, Captain O'Toole, this is Lieutenant Hunyan. He'll be leading the convoy to Dragon's Den. We've had a slight change of plans."

Hunyan held up his wrist pad and projected a map in the air in front of them. "This is the route the convoy will take. Most of it is a straight shot west across this state highway here. We sent out dozer crews two days ago to clear the road, and they've been pushing aside abandoned cars and obstructions ever since. That is, until four hours ago. We lost contact with them here." Hunyan tapped a spot on the route about sixty klicks out. "They were hit by a swarm of Formic skimmers. We have satellite images of the aftermath."

Hunyan brought up one of the infrared images. The

devastation was obvious. Three dozers lay in ruins. They were massive, bulky vehicles, not street dozers or land-scapers, but the large industrial breed, with impenetra-ble cabs and wheels three meters high. Each dozer had a long, V-shaped blade that jutted out from the front like a spearhead. The blades were almost twice as wide as the vehicle and nearly as long—giving the dozer a threat-ening aspect, like a giant iron arrow. One of the dozers was burning, smoke billowing up from its cabin, obscur-ing the image somewhat. Another dozer lay on its side, the left half of it crunched inward. A third had a gaping hole in the center where a blast of plasma had seared straight through.

"Any survivors?" asked Wit.

"One of the drivers," said Hunyan. "This dozer here, the one turned on its side. The driver's stuck in the cab. We sent an armored vehicle to rescue him."

"Judging by the look on your face and the fact that you pulled us out of bed," said Wit, "I'm guessing your armored vehicle never reached its destination."

"Sadly no," said Hunyan. He swiped through the holofield and a new sat image appeared. It showed a different stretch of road, the features all outlined in varying shades of gray. An armored vehicle lay in two pieces on the asphalt, the edges jagged and twisted as if it had been ripped in half. A tire engulfed in flames was burning in the grass nearby. A Chinese soldier lay on his back in the middle of the road, a pool of blood beneath him. Two shapes that appeared to be For-mics were standing beside the man's body, hovering over him.

Wit reached into the holofield and spread his thumb and index finger apart, zooming in on the Formics. The move didn't help; the image was still fuzzy. "What are the Formics doing to him?"

"They pulled him from the wreckage," said Hunyan.

He made another gesture in the field, and a vid began. It was the driver's helmet feed, from immediately after the crash. The video was dark and green, with lines of interference and static dancing across the screen. The man was on his side. His biometrics in the corner of the vid suggested serious injury. His blood pressure was dropping. His breathing was labored.

Dark shapes appeared, pulling the metal of the cabin back. Two Formics, bug-eyed and calm, equipment in their hands. The soldier gave a weak protestation. His heart rate accelerated. He tried backing away, but there was nowhere to go. Hands reached in and lifted him out. The man cried out in pain. A small silhouette of the soldier's body in the upper right corner of the feed began flashing red over the leg. There was serious trauma to the man's femur.

The image shook as the Formics carried the man out and laid him on the asphalt. One of the Formics reached in and removed the helmet. The world spun. The helmet was set on the ground, pointing away from the man now, back at the wreckage.

"There's a full minute of silence here," said Hunyan. "We don't know what transpires. The driver's blood pressure continues to drop until he flatlines. We think he bled out. We don't know if the Formics did anything to him." Hunyan reached in and switched off the vid. "After that the Formics left."

"What do you want us to do?" said Wit.

"The driver of the overturned dozer at the site of the first attack is still stuck in his cab, alive," said Hunyan. "And we still have five kilometers of road to clear. I need you and Captain Rackham to free the driver. Then you'll provide cover while the driver clears the rest of the road. Otherwise, our convoy can't get through."

"The dozers are all damaged," said Wit. "Unless you have another one, no one's clearing anything."

Hunyan turned to Mazer. "I'm told you're a HERC pilot."

"He's the best HERC pilot," said Wit. "What you are thinking? Flying a dozer out there?"

"It's faster than driving one," said Hunyan. Then to Mazer, "Have you ever carried a load that heavy?"

"Weight isn't an issue," said Mazer. "The grav lenses deflect gravity waves from Earth, sending them around the aircraft. All I need to do is adjust the lenses to perfectly balance with the landforms and maintain a constant distance."

"What if the driver is too injured to finish the job?" said Wit.

"Then I'll drive the dozer," said Shenzu. "I'm coming with you. You just make sure a skimmer doesn't drop a plasma slug in my lap."

"Dragon's Den is much closer to the damaged dozers than we are," said Mazer. "Why not send a rescue team from their end?"

"They can't reach our man," said Hunyan. "They don't have dozers to get through the obstructions."

"So much for a full night's sleep," said Mazer. "Where's the airfield?"

Hunyan led them outside where a truck was waiting. Shenzu, Wit, and Mazer climbed up into the bed, and Hunyan got behind the wheel. They drove west through the city, the truck's headlights cutting through the darkness. The night air was cool and damp, and Mazer pulled his jacket tight around him. They saw no one and heard nothing. The buildings stood like giant hovering shadows, dark and vacant and eerily quiet. A stale, rotting smell permeated the streets: uncollected trash, perhaps, or the stagnant water of the sewer lines, kept still because the power was out.

On the outskirts of town, the buildings gave way to

large industrial complexes, with their oddly shaped pipes, towers, and silos. Next came the flat rice fields, which to Mazer's surprise were still alive, the tall grass swaying in the dark like the surface of the sea.

Hunyan turned onto a service road, passed through an open security fence, and drove up onto the tarmac at a small airfield. A HERC sat parked outside a hangar, where a team of technicians with lights on their helmets were giving it a once-over. Beside the HERC was an armored spearhead dozer, its massive blade extending outward like a wedge. The satellite image hadn't done the spearhead justice. It was twice as large as Mazer thought it would be. Each wheel was taller than the truck.

"You sure that little aircraft can pick up that thing?" said Wit. "That's like an orange lifting a pineapple."

"We'll be fine," said Mazer. "Science is on our side."

Hunyan parked the truck inside the hangar beside three large crates. He hopped out, opened the crates, and began distributing the gear. "You'll wear these biosuits at all times. Each can carry four mini tanks of O_2. There's extra oxygen in the HERC. I'd advise you to keep at least two cans on your person at all times." He handed Wit an assault rifle. "It has built-in smart targeting. Pick your Formic with your HUD, and the smart munitions do the rest. If the target's within a thousand meters, it's a near guaranteed kill. Snap on this secondary barrel here for the grenade launcher."

Wit snapped on the barrel and removed it, getting a feel for the mechanism. Mazer took a rifle and a box of grenade rounds then unwrapped the biosuit and pulled it on over his clothing.

"We'll be tracking your progress from here," said Hunyan. "Good luck."

Shenzu, Wit, and Mazer zipped up their biosuits,

donned their helmets, and loaded into the HERC. Shenzu sat in the copilot's seat while Wit buckled into a jump seat back in the main cabin.

"You give the word to go, Shenzu," said Wit. "This is your op."

"I'm just the liaison officer," said Shenzu. "You're the experienced field commander. I say you're in charge."

"Very well," said Wit. "Mazer, take us up."

"Yes, sir."

Mazer lifted off, maneuvered the HERC over the dozer, and turned on the talons, which unfolded from the side of the HERC and descended to the dozer like giant spider legs. Four of the talons gripped the dozer's side and lifted it off the ground to allow the last two talons to extend underneath and lock in place beneath it. Mazer ran a few tests to ensure the load was secure, then he adjusted the lenses and slowly lifted off.

They picked up the highway south of Lianzhou and flew straight up the center of the road, low and fast, the bottom of the dozer just a few meters off the ground.

"Watch the skies," said Wit. "With a load like this, we're easy targets. We'll have very little maneuverability."

"If something zeroes in on us," said Mazer, "we should set the dozer down, land fast, abandon the HERC, and make for cover."

"Why not drop the dozer and fight?" asked Shenzu.

"Because dying doesn't accomplish anything," said Mazer. "This isn't a combat aircraft. It's a load carrier. It's not nimble. The Formics can dance around us. I learned that the hard way. Plus we're not armed for a fight. We've got a few rockets and a laser. That hardly makes us battle-ready. If we fight, we lose."

"He's right," said Wit. "If the bugs close in, we bail or we fail."

They flew in silence, Mazer watching the radar screen for Formics. It felt strange to fly without Patu, Fatani, and Reinhardt beside him. They had been with him through thousands of flight hours, every takeoff, every maneuver.

And now they were gone.

Mazer had played the crash over and over again in his mind. The HERC had fallen in a dead drop from a low altitude. The chutes had failed, and the rotor blades hadn't deployed fast enough. All things considered, Mazer should have died also, and yet somehow here he was, saved by airbags and luck with nothing more than an ugly gut wound to show for it.

It was the angle at which the HERC had landed that had saved him. Fatani was heavy and sitting on the opposite side and in the rear, and perhaps that was what had tipped the HERC just enough to have it land the way it did, with Mazer farther from the ground than the others at the moment of impact, giving his airbags a microsecond more time to deploy.

He never saw what punctured his lower abdomen. A torn section from the front console perhaps. Or a flying piece of shrapnel. Whatever it was, he was lucky it hadn't torn him in half. Perhaps he had removed it immediately after the crash, yanking it out in some survival reflex. He couldn't remember. Everything was hazy at that point, a murky blur of noise and heat and pain.

His teammates had made no sounds after the impact, and he hoped they hadn't felt the flames that had followed. That was something he could not forget: the raw heat of it, like the air itself was on fire. He had lain in the dirt a short distance away, breathing smoke and the pungent fumes of melting plastic and seared human flesh as the aircraft popped and crackled and sizzled in the fire.

He had been their leader. It had been his duty to protect them. And he had failed them; failed their families.

"We're coming up on the armored vehicle," said Shenzu.

Mazer slowed their approach and hovered over the site when they reached it, shining his spotlights down on the wreck. The two halves of the vehicle lay on the asphalt twisted apart like thin scraps of aluminum. The driver was still on his back in the center of the road where the Formics had left him.

Wit moved up into the cockpit. "Can we get a close visual on the driver?"

Mazer entered the command, and the image of the dead driver appeared in the holofield above the dash, the bright lights from the HERC giving the corpse a pale, ghostly appearance. The Formics had eviscerated him. A gash stretched across the full width of his stomach just above the navel, opening him like a sack. Much of his small intestines had slid out like a slick pink rope, hanging loosely at his side and atop his groin.

Shenzu turned away.

"Zoom in on his stomach," said Wit.

Mazer complied. It was a ghastly sight. The blood-stained uniform looked almost black in the harsh light.

"He couldn't have sustained that injury in the wreck," said Mazer. "It's too straight of a cut. And he was alive for too long after the fact. With a wound like that he would have bled out immediately."

"Meaning what?" said Shenzu.

"Meaning he likely didn't die from the abdominal wound," said Wit. "The Formics eviscerated him after he was dead."

Mazer zoomed in further, focusing on the abdominal skin flap. "Look at the incision. It appears cauterized."

"A laser?" said Wit.

"That would be my guess," said Mazer.

"Wait," said Shenzu. "You're saying the Formics waited until he was dead and then cut him open with a laser?"

"They didn't just cut him open," said Wit. "They

reached inside him and dislodged a lot of his small intestines."

"Why?" said Shenzu.

Mazer shrugged. "Maybe it's their religion. A sort of death ritual. Maybe this is their way of honoring a fallen enemy."

"Then why haven't we seen them do this before?" said Wit. "They've done nothing to suggest they honor us at all."

"Maybe they've recognized we're a formidable enemy," said Mazer. "Maybe they underestimated us before and now they see we won't welcome extinction so easily."

"Or it could be the opposite," said Shenzu. "Maybe this is how they desecrate the dead. A show of dishonor, contempt, like pissing on a grave."

Wit inserted his wrist pad into the holofield and uploaded the images. "I'll send these back to General Sima and Strategos. Maybe they can make sense of it. Let's keep moving."

Mazer took off again, and they made good time. They spotted a few Formic fighters high overhead, but the fighters maintained their altitude and made no move to approach them. Ten minutes later, a half dozen skimmers popped up on the radar several klicks ahead of them, crossing their path and moving north. Mazer landed quickly near a cluster of trees and killed all power until the skimmers had moved on and were well out of range. Then he powered up again and pushed on.

When they reached the three demolished dozers, the edge of the horizon was just beginning to brighten with the arrival of dawn.

Mazer set the new dozer down on the highway and disengaged the talons.

The overturned dozer lay on its side slightly off the road, its bulky mass traversing a drainage ditch. A huge dent in its side suggested that something had hit it, crushing the main cabin partially inward. Mazer landed the HERC beside the dozer, then exited the aircraft behind Wit and Shenzu. The three of them climbed up onto the overturned dozer and found the driver still alive in the cabin. Other than a gash on his head he appeared unharmed.

"The door's crushed," the driver said in Chinese. "I can't open it."

It was true. The frame had twisted and folded inward. If not for the bracing bars inside the cabin, the man would have been crushed as well.

"We need to cut him out," said Wit.

Mazer retrieved a laser cutter from the gearbox and sliced the door free. The driver crawled out and thanked them profusely. His hair and shirt were stained with blood.

"What happened?" said Shenzu.

The driver answered in Chinese. "Troop transports. Three of them. They dropped out of nowhere, gentle as a leaf, no sound at all. Formics poured out and climbed up onto my dozer, right up to the cabin. There were six of them directly in front of me, right there on the other side of the glass. I thought they were going to smash their way inside, but they just stood there staring at me, as if they were waiting for me to invite them in."

"What did the other drivers do?" asked Shenzu.

"They had the same problem. Formics had crawled up to their cabins, too. We all had bugs on us."

"This is before they attacked?" asked Shenzu.

"Before anything," said the driver. "No one had so much as shown a weapon. Then Corporal Jijeng, one of the drivers, got spooked and began screaming, panicked. We told him over the radio to calm down, and maybe they would go away. But he wouldn't listen. He drew his pistol and shot two of them through the glass. Then everything went bad. The Formics rushed back to their transports and opened fire. They killed Jijeng first. Incinerated him. I'm not even sure what they hit him with. One moment his dozer is there, the next moment, there's so much fire, I thought the whole world was burning."

"What about the other dozer?" asked Shenzu.

"They hit it with something else. Not fire. Something thick, like a jelly. It went straight through the cabin."

"And you?" said Shenzu. "It looks like they rammed you."

"One of the transports," said the driver. "It hit me so hard I thought my insides had snapped. I still don't know why. It would have been easier to shoot me with the jelly."

"You were lucky," said Shenzu.

Wit asked Shenzu to translate what the driver had said. When Shenzu finished, Wit said, "Ask him if he can still drive a dozer."

Shenzu translated, and the man nodded. "The Formics aren't stopping me, sir."

Mazer bandaged the man's head, then the driver climbed up into the cabin of the new dozer and fired up the engines. As he pushed the wrecked dozers off the road, Shenzu read a message off his wrist pad. "The convoy has already left Lianzhou. They said we better have the road cleared by the time they reach us."

"No pressure," said Mazer.

The three of them hustled back to the HERC and got airborne. Wit took the copilot's seat, and Shenzu buckled up in a jump seat in the main cabin. They followed just behind the dozer as it continued down the highway, clearing the road of obstructions.

They made slow progress for several kilometers without meeting any resistance. Mazer was beginning to think they might actually complete the mission when Lieutenant Hunyan's head appeared in the HERC's holofield above the dash.

"We have a situation," said Hunyan. "Over sixty troop transports just launched from the Formic mothership. They've spread out over a distance of three hundred kilometers and are descending through the atmosphere now. Beijing is tracking them, and we've calculated their projected trajectories. Several of them are heading toward our position. I'm sending you the data now."

A series of images and maps appeared in the holofield.

Mazer studied them, saw where the reinforcements were entering the atmosphere, and turned to Wit. "We should get up there and gather what intel we can."

"Agreed. Shenzu, tell the dozer driver to stay the course and clear the road at all costs. Mazer, take us up."

Mazer spun the HERC 180 degrees, then shot straight up into the air. Wit grabbed a handhold to steady himself, and Mazer felt his stomach drop. They ascended at a steady rate, scanning as they went, and stopped at seven thousand meters. At first the sensors detected nothing, then the instruments started blipping and dozens of dots of light popped up on radar.

"We see them," Mazer said to Hunyan. "They're coming in hot. I count four transports dropping to the convoy's position." He read off the distances, speeds, and angles of approach.

"Lieutenant," said Wit. "Can you turn the convoy around and return to Lianzhou?"

"Negative," said Hunyan. "We're twenty klicks outside the city. The path is barely wide enough for the vehicles to get through. There's no place to turn around."

"Who is with you?" asked Wit.

"The science team, a few dozen officers, and over three hundred enlisted men."

"What about firepower?" asked Wit.

"We've got antiaircraft missiles and four heavily armed VTOLs giving us air support. We've stopped and are forming a perimeter."

Far in the distance, Mazer saw four white flashes of light high in the atmosphere. The lights descended, streaking downward at hypersonic speed, leaving puffy contrails behind them.

There was another flash of light to Mazer's left, far to the south, heading in their direction.

"Nine o'clock," said Wit.

"I see it," said Mazer. He swiveled the HERC to the left and angled it upward to allow the sensors to get a better read on the incoming ship.

"Can we get a visual?" asked Wit.

Mazer blinked the command in his HUD, and the transport appeared in the holofield in front of them. There wasn't much to see; a searing heat enveloped the transport, obscuring its nose from view.

"Where is it headed?" asked Wit.

"Already working on it," said Mazer. His hands flew inside the holofield, quickly gathering the data and slinging it into the correct receptacles for processing. The answer appeared on the map, and Mazer's heart sank. "Its trajectory puts it very near Dragon's Den."

"How near is very near?" said Wit. "Near enough that Dragon's Den is clearly its target or far enough away that it could be only a coincidence?"

"Both," said Mazer. "It might be gunning for Dragon's Den. It might not."

"There are civilians down there."

"Thousands of them. Probably mostly women and children."

"Any ideas?" asked Wit.

"We get the transport out of the sky a little sooner than it expected."

"You said this wasn't a combat aircraft," said Wit. "You said we weren't nimble enough."

"All true," said Mazer. "So let's use it for what it was made for."

Mazer's hand quickly moved through the holofield. He had the AI verify the transporter's trajectory and pinpoint its exact position at various points in time. Then he entered a series of commands and the HERC shot forward, slamming him and Wit back against their seats. The altimeter numbers spun as the HERC climbed.

"If there's a plan," said Wit, "now would be a good time to share."

"We can't fire on the transport," said Mazer. "It's shielded. That's how they managed atmospheric entry."

Wit gripped the handhold above his head, his knuckles white. "So we can't shoot it down. Great. That's not a plan."

"We wouldn't want to shoot at it anyway," said Mazer. "Even if it didn't have the shield. Unless you're right on top of them, they can dodge whatever you throw at them. I say we take it down the same way we've taken out other transports. We fill it with grenades."

"Every transport we've disabled was on the ground," said Wit. "We tricked them into landing, then we jumped from the bushes. I fail to see any bushes here at forty thousand feet."

"I'll get above it and seize it with the talons. As soon as the Formics disengage the shield, you cut your way in and toss in the grenades."

"What makes you certain they'll disengage their shields?"

"They'll be threatened. They can't defend themselves with their shields engaged. You know how they are, they retaliate with blind ferocity, even if that puts them at greater risk. Once we clamp on, they'll do anything to lose us, including dropping their shields. And if they don't drop them immediately, they'll drop them when they land. Otherwise they can't disembark from the aircraft. We'll destroy them then."

"I liked it better when I didn't know your plan," said Wit.

"Move back to the main cabin," said Mazer. "The drop door is in the center of the floor. I'll open it when the time is right. Strap yourself into the winch in the ceiling. There are boot anchors in the floor. Lock yourself in tight. Once I open the door, the transport hull will be directly below you. Cut your way in with the laser. Once you drop in the grenades, we detach, get clear, and they become shrapnel in the sky."

"You want to grab an alien spacecraft moving at hypersonic speed?"

"It's not moving at hypersonic speed anymore. It's slowed down drastically. It'll be even slower when we reach it."

"How slow is slow?"

"A few hundred kilometers an hour?"

"Naturally," said Wit. He began unstrapping his harness. "How much time do I have?"

"Under two minutes. I suggest you pick up the pace."

Wit wiggled out of the harness and got to his feet. "How are you going to get close enough to grab them without them shooting us down?"

"We'll come at them from above. They won't be looking in that direction. Probably. Plus these are transports. They're not made for deep space travel. They don't have collision avoidance systems. At least the ones we've destroyed in the past didn't, and this one looks no different. Also, they don't yet know we're a threat."

"Of course we're a threat. We're an armed aircraft."

"Formics ignore us until we pose a threat. Think about the Formics that stormed the dozers. They killed the crew after our man attacked. It's only when we confront them, when we resist, that they retaliate. Otherwise, we're not worth their notice."

"What about the armored vehicle that was ripped in half, the man eviscerated on the asphalt?"

"Maybe he fired first. Maybe his gunner engaged them."

"And maybe you're full of it."

"Maybe," said Mazer. "And maybe I'm right. Either way you've got about sixty seconds until we intercept them. Are we doing this or not?"

Wit considered a moment then nodded. "How do I hook myself to the winch cable?"

"There's a body harness in a compartment in the main cabin, directly behind me. Slip it on and tighten the straps around your thighs, chest, and shoulders. Then attach the carabiner on the chest of the harness to the matching carabiner on the pulley cable. There's a screw lock on each. Righty tighty, lefty loosey."

"I know how to tighten a screw lock," said Wit. He left the cockpit and moved back to the cabin.

Mazer heard him rummaging through the compartment, grabbing the gear. They were high above the transport now. It had drastically decelerated. Mazer couldn't tell if the shield was still engaged or not. He called back to Wit. "Are you harnessed in?"

"I've got a harness on. Heaven knows if I strapped it on right."

"Does it feel like the worst wedgie of your life?" asked Mazer.

"The strap's so far up my crack, it's part of my digestive system," said Wit.

"Then you're wearing it correctly. Pull some slack on the cable and buckle in to one of the jump seats. Once we're in position, I'll open the door and you can get up."

A moment later Wit said, "I'm buckled. And I'm already regretting this."

Mazer started blinking out commands, getting ready for the drop. "Hold on to something. Our forward thrusters will still be open, but once I disengage the grav lens, we'll lose altitude fast. The less time they have to react the better."

He put his hand in the holofield where the virtual knob for the grav lens had appeared. "Here we go!"

He cranked the knob hard to the right, and the HERC dropped like a stone.

The straps on Mazer's lap and chest pulled taut as he was lifted off his seat. He gripped the stick tight, breathing evenly, staying calm.

The transport was two hundred meters below them.

One hundred and fifty.

One hundred.

Mazer didn't slow. His stomach was in his throat. He watched the transport with the external cameras, their feeds projected in the holofield in front of him. The transport could react at any moment, he knew. It could spin, flip over, rocket forward to evade them.

Fifty meters.

The transport didn't flinch.

Forty meters.

No movement.

"Brace for impact!" said Mazer.

At ten meters, the transport jinked to the left to avoid a collision, but Mazer reacted instantly, adjusted their approach, and threw down the talons right before impact.

The two aircraft collided violently—the bottom of the HERC slamming into the roof of the transport with a bone-rattling jolt. The HERC would have bounced off had the talons not seized the side of the transport and gripped it tight. Mazer was thrown hard against his harness as alarms went off in the cockpit.

The transport dipped momentarily, then it righted itself and wiggled side to side, trying to shake loose its new cargo. Mazer shifted violently back and forth in his harness, the talons creaking and straining.

Wit called up from the back. "We can't do this if they treat this like a rodeo. Are their shields on?"

Mazer flipped through the exterior camera feeds and saw that the talons were a few inches away from the transport's hull. "Affirmative. Shields are still up."

"We can't hold on forever," said Wit.

"Then we convince them to turn off their shields. Are you still strapped in?"

"Yes, but what you are planning? I've had enough aerial maneuvers."

"Last one," said Mazer.

He shut off the forward thrusters. At once he felt the increased drag and decreased velocity. Now they were dead weight. The transport was pulling them through the air, the HERC held in place by the biting grip of the talons, like a spider clinging to the back of a sparrow. Mazer reached into the holofield and rotated the HERC's two jet engines: one ninety degrees to the right, the other ninety degrees to the left. Now both intakes pointed inward, perpendicular to their flight direction.

"We're going to roll. Hang on."

Mazer tapped the throttle on the left engine, and the sideways thrust put the HERC and transport into a barrel roll, rotating them 180 degrees. Now the HERC was upside down, with the transport upside down and above them. Mazer equalized the thrust on the two engines so they exerted thrust in opposite directions and held the HERC in that position.

"Get ready," said Mazer. "If I'm right, they'll deactivate their shields any moment now."

"We're upside down!" said Wit.

"The plan's the same. I open the hole in the floor, now the ceiling, you cut through and pop in grenades."

"They'll deactivate their shields because they're upside down?" Wit shouted.

"No, they'll deactivate because I'm taking away their gravity."

Mazer rotated the direction of the grav lenses 180 degrees and switched it to full power. Whenever the HERC flew upright, everything above it had less gravity because it deflected the gravity waves from Earth. Now that they were inverted, he had to flip the lenses to achieve the same effect. It also meant the grav lens could once again keep them aloft.

He imagined what was happening inside the transport, with the Formics suddenly experiencing less gravity. Were they strapped down? Were they standing in the cabin? Either way, he'd give them a shake and return the favor. He tapped the two throttles back and forth, rocking the transport from side to side.

The Formics didn't disappoint. Suddenly the HERC flew backward and then caught itself at the rear of the transport, jolting Mazer violently. For a terrifying instant he thought they had been hit with something. Then he realized that the Formics had disengaged their shields and the HERC's talons had clung to nothing for a fraction of a second until they had pinched inward and gripped the hull.

"Shields are down!" Mazer shouted. "Opening door."

The door in the floor of the cabin opened, filling the HERC with the roar of the wind. Mazer watched in his helmet feed as Wit moved to the hole, reached upward with the laser, and cut into the transport's hull.

It was going to work, Mazer thought. It was a ridiculous, half-baked idea, but it was going to work.

Then he saw the Formics.

There were three of them—there in front of him, outside the windshield, clinging to the hull of their transport, flat on their stomachs, looking right at him. They wore gloves on the end of their appendages shaped like flat discs that clung to the surface of their ship. Magnets perhaps.

They scurried forward, rushing toward him, and Mazer saw that his initial assessment was wrong. Only four of their appendages clung to the transport. The other pair held a weapon, short and cylindrical like a dirty metal jar.

One of the Formics rose up and fired. A glob of thick mucus shot forth and splattered against the windshield in front of the copilot's seat, creating a circle of goo half a meter in diameter. Inside the goo was a paper-thin, symmetrical weblike membrane—like a delicately crocheted doily.

The membrane flashed with white light, and the windshield exploded, showering Mazer with tiny shards of glass. Pain hit Mazer, hot and searing, and his HUD started flashing a warning. There were holes in his suit.

The Formics rushed forward, surging for the cockpit.

Mazer had his pistol up in his hands an instant later, firing.

The head of the lead Formic snapped back and its body went limp, still clinging to the hull. The other Formics were undeterred. They scurried forward with unnatural speed. Mazer shot one in the throat and the second in the arm. The latter kept coming, its arm half severed. Mazer put three more rounds in its chest as it tried to crawl into the cockpit, finally killing it.

But that was only the first wave.

Four more were coming, all of them scurrying down the transport with an even greater sense of urgency. One of them fired. The doily glob struck the front of the HERC beneath the windshield. Mazer didn't see where it landed exactly, but the explosion followed an instant later, and then everything went wrong.

Alarms. Smoke. Vibrations. Spots of light twinkling in his vision. A garble of sounds swirled in his head; one moment they were a thousand miles away; a half second later they were deafening. He couldn't see, couldn't think, couldn't make sense of any of it. It was as if the world had been thrown inside a rattle and shaken vigorously.

His vision cleared. He blinked, shook his head. His ears were ringing.

Where was he?

The HERC.

Something was wrong with the HERC. Why was he upside down?

The pistol. He needed the pistol. He looked at his hands and found them empty.

Something hit him in the chest, knocking the wind out of him. It fell to the ceiling in front of him. A Formic. Heavy and hairy, its limbs tangled and scrabbling for purchase, furious, desperate, flopping around in the tight space as it tried to right itself. Mazer couldn't breathe. His chest was empty, his diaphragm flat. All the blood had rushed to his head. He sucked in air, filling his lungs.

The Formic got its footing and came at him, its maw biting at the hard plastic of his visor. Two of its hands—still in their disc-shaped gloves—pounded him, hitting him like fist-sized balls of lead. His shoulders, helmet, chest, arms. Mazer grabbed the creature's forelimbs to try to wrestle it away, but the Formic, despite its size, was as strong as he was.

He almost didn't notice the weapon in its secondary hands, compact and gleaming, aimed at his center mass. Mazer only had time to swat it to the side. The barrel swung wide, and when it discharged, the glob fired out the windshield, hit the transport near its nose, and exploded outward.

Mazer was thrown against his seat. The Formic slammed into him again. Everything started to spin. Outside the windshield the world flashed past like an amusement ride. Earth, sky, earth, sky. He had no sense of direction, no idea what was up and down anymore. He heard a voice. Calm and clear. A woman's, speaking in Chinese. Pleasant but insistent. What was it? Who was she?

It was the HERC's AI, he realized, calmly reading off a litany of system failures.

Mazer pushed the Formic's limp body off him. A shard of shrapnel protruded from its back.

He steadied himself against the wall. His equilibrium was shot. He was going to be sick.

"Get ready," shouted Wit.

For a moment the words meant nothing to him. Get ready? Then it came him. Wit. The hole. The grenades. His asinine, half-baked plan. They were still connected to the transport, both ships spinning and plummeting together.

"Hole is cut," shouted Wit. "I'm punching through."

There was a clang and then Mazer heard three deep pops in quick succession. *Thoop thoop thoop.*

"Cut us loose!" Wit shouted. "Fire in the hole!"

A Formic crawled over the lip of the windshield, its hind legs clinging to the HERC with its magnet discs. It looked at Mazer and raised its jar weapon. Light swirled inside it as it prepared to fire.

Mazer blinked the command, and three things happened in quick succession: the talons disengaged, the HERC shot free as if slung from a catapult, and everyone on board was thrown violently to the side.

If they had been spinning before, they were in a vortex now. The Formic was no longer at the windshield.

The world outside was a blur. They were falling. Twisting. Rolling. The dash was beeping. The numbers in his HUD from the instruments were spinning or changing or gone completely. The female AI was slowly, methodically, ticking off the reasons why they were about to die.

He had to adjust the grav lens. He had to reorient them, stop them, steady them, save them.

But he couldn't. His head was in a blender, thrown every way imaginable as his orientation shifted, spun, flipped.

He couldn't blink the commands. He couldn't steady his eyes and focus on his HUD. He tried raising his hands to the holofield, but as soon as he moved his arm, the centripetal force threw it elsewhere.

It was happening again. He was killing everyone aboard.

Somewhere far away—below them, above them, Mazer couldn't be sure—three grenades detonated, and a fireball lit up the sky then was gone, ripped from his vision as the HERC continued to spin.

Mazer tightened his grip on the stick and centered himself. Blackness was appearing at the edges of his vision. He was going to pass out. He blinked, fighting back, trying to focus.

Down, up, right, left. None of it was clear to him.

The stone, he reminded himself. I swallowed the stone.

He was *tangata whenua,* he told himself, person of the land, born of the earth, voice of the earth, made strong by the earth. Air, mountains, insects, all bound by *mauri.* Only the *tangata whenua* could control that energy.

Father didn't believe it. Father cursed it all.

But Mother believed it.

And Mother was stronger.

He stopped fighting the centripetal forces. He stopped trying to right himself, to be rigid, to control it. Instead he let go. He closed his eyes. His arms went limp, his mind as well. The ringing and alarms and violent rush of air blowing through the hole where the windshield had been. All of that was somewhere else. That was a different power. A weaker one. He was the son of Papatūānuku. Mother Earth. And all that belonged to her belonged to him. Even gravity itself.

He opened his eyes. The readings on his HUD should have alarmed him. They were dropping too fast, spinning too wildly. The grav lenses were damaged, flashing SYSTEM FAILURE. He wouldn't be able to stop the HERC with the lenses. His heart should have sunk. Despair should have settled in.

But instead he felt a great calm. A gathering of his senses. A focusing of his mind.

He had the rotor blades. If he could stop the spinning, the blades would deploy.

But how to stop the spinning? The jet engines wouldn't help, he had no wings for lift, and engaging them might only sling them faster down to the earth.

The solution came at once. Clear and precise. A definitive course of action. And yet it wasn't born from any previous experience or something he had read or studied on the subject. As far as he knew, it had never been attempted. And yet it was glaringly obvious.

There were emergency chutes of course, but he couldn't deploy them all at once in a spin. They would tangle, collapse, be worthless.

But . . . if he deployed them one at a time, in quick succession, each at a moment when the spin was angled in such a way to allow the chute to fully extend and fill with air—even for only a moment. And if he then detached the chute, a second or two later, before the continuing rotation entangled the ropes and made it impossible for the blades to deploy—then maybe, just maybe, each chute could slow the spinning and stabilize the HERC just enough for the blades to deploy.

His hands—shaking and yet somehow steady—reached into the holofield. It was instinct now. Honed by hundreds of simulations, thousands of flight hours, and a lifetime of reading his gut.

Calmly, resolutely, as his body was slung back and forth in his harness, he waited, focusing his equilibrium to a single point in space, sensing the forces around him, seeing a pattern in the randomness of the spins. Then he felt it coming, the right twist, the right angle.

He released the first chute.

There was a pop, a violent jolt as the chute filled, and then Mazer cut it loose. They were still spinning, but slower now.

The second chute deployed, caught, and detached.

Then the third.

A jolt. Detached.

Then the sweetest sound he had ever heard. A bang, like a starter pistol, as the charges blew and the rotor blades that were folded back like cockroach wings snapped forward into place and began to sing.

CHAPTER 8

Secrets

Lem Jukes woke in a bed that was not his own with a woman's arm draped across his chest. Slowly, gently, so as not to wake her, he lifted the arm, set it aside, and slid off the mattress, making as little sound as possible. He tiptoed out of the bedroom a moment later in his T-shirt and boxers and made his way to the kitchen where he had seen a small vid screen the night before. The screen hung beneath the kitchen cabinets. Lem turned it on, put the volume on low, and flipped through the channels until he found a news feed.

He had expected the worst. The coverage would no doubt be about the failed drone attack. Economic pundits would make lofty estimations about how much each drone was worth and how quickly Juke Limited would file for bankruptcy. They would call it the end of the Ukko Jukes era, the beginning of the company's decline. The market would be in a tizzy. Juke stock would drop. The Board would be in a panic. It would be chaos at headquarters.

Well, Father, you dug your own grave. Now you can sleep in it.

But the drone attack wasn't getting any coverage. Instead, a British news anchor in a tight navy suit stood in front of a giant map of southeast China like a miscast meteorologist. With stylus in hand, the anchor tapped the map, leaving blinking red dots behind. "More of the Formic reinforcements were reported to have made landfall in this area here," he said, "gassing the cities of Hezhou, Yangshan, Liannan, and Lianshan." There were blinking red lights everywhere. Southeast China was lit up like a Christmas tree.

The reporter tapped a spot slightly northeast of the others, faced the camera, and put on a grave expression. "Four other transports landed here in Lianzhou, where several thousand Chinese troops had encamped. Sources inform us that this was the camp of General Sima Jinping, who recently destroyed one of the Formic landers with the help of the Mobile Operations Police. The casualty estimates are in the thousands. Our satellites picked up these images. We warn our audience that what you are about to see may not be suitable for children."

Lem's mind was reeling. Reinforcements? He flipped through the channels to another feed and started putting the pieces together. There was mention of a secret attack on the Formic ship, but no one seemed to know what country was responsible. The investigation was ongoing. The Russians were already denying responsibility, as were the Italians, which Lem found laughable. Yes, like anyone even suspected you, Italy.

Despoina shuffled into the kitchen wearing Lem's oxford shirt from the day before and her undergarments. Lem tensed. He was not in the mood for an awkward morning-after conversation. He focused on the screen, while cabinet doors opened behind him and pots were moved around.

A hand briefly rubbed his back. "Good morning," she said groggily.

He turned and faced her, as he knew he must, and

she stood on her tiptoes and gave him a brief kiss on the cheek. Then she turned back to the stovetop and started making breakfast. The casualness of it all bothered him, as if his being here was the most natural thing in the world, as if this was how every morning started: with him, focused on the news; and her, shuffling about, hair unkempt, half dressed, making their breakfast. Just another day in paradise. The thought made him more than a little uneasy. He had not intended things to go this far, and it worried him that she didn't seem to exhibit the least bit of regret.

He couldn't let that distract him, however. He went back to the news feeds, flipping between three different reports, catching snippets here and there. They were calling it the second wave. There were no landers this time, and for that everyone was grateful, but there was little else to be happy about. The Formics had adopted far more aggressive tactics. And the transports that had descended in the second wave were not the only ones suddenly attacking cities. Several transports that had come in the first wave, and whose troops had been gassing uninhabited rural areas, abandoned those places to target populated areas.

It was worse than Lem had imagined. The drones had initiated a counterattack that the Chinese would pay for in blood. Father hadn't just failed in his drone strike, he had kicked the war into overdrive; he had made everything ten times worse.

Lem suddenly felt sick. He could see it in his mind. He could picture a Chinese family, a father, mother, two young children, already fearful of the Formics, worried that their city might be next, huddled in their living room as the mother sings a reassuring song. The father gets up, parts the curtain at the window, and sees a transport alight on his lawn. A rush of Formics disembark, sprayers in hand. The father runs to his family, pushing them toward the back door, which flies open an instant later as the Formics rush in, spraying the gas that will melt the children's faces.

A hand touched Lem's forearm, and he recoiled.

Despoina laughed. "Sorry. I didn't mean to scare you. Here." She held up a mug capped with a lid and straw. "Do you like hot cocoa? It's my mother's recipe. Well actually it's my great-great-great"—she waved a dismissive hand—"well, I don't know how many greats—my super-great-grandmother's recipe. But everyone after her has claimed it as her own, so in that sense it's my mother's, too." She held the mug closer to his face, smiling.

Lem took it and forced a smile. "Thanks."

She stood there watching him in anticipation, waiting for him to try it.

He took a sip. It tasted like every other hot cocoa he had ever had. "Wow. That's great."

She brightened. "It's the chocolate bar chunks." She reached to her left and grabbed the wrapper off the counter. "You chop up these chocolate chunks, melt them down, and mix it in. It's from this chocolatier in southern France. My mother buys a box and has it shipped over every Thanksgiving so she can have it in time for her Christmas parties." She turned over the wrapper and looked at the label. "Isn't it crazy to think that people are still chocolatiers?" She broke off one of the remaining squares of chocolate and popped it in her mouth. "I mean, how does someone even decide they want to be a chocolatier?"

There was a pause, and then Lem tore his eyes away from the screen. She had asked him a question. "Chocolatiers? Uh, I'm guessing every kid in the world would want to be one if they knew such a thing was possible."

"Exactly. I know I would have. You wonder though, is there a school for chocolatiers?" She laughed. "My word, can you imagine? I would get so fat." She popped another chocolate square in her mouth. "And the curriculum. What do you minor in? Nuts?" She held up the wrapper to him and turned her head away. "Take this evil away from me. It's too delicious."

Lem had no choice but to take it.

Her hands were suddenly on his chest. "Delicious like you." Her voice was just above a whisper. She closed her eyes, head back, lips puckered.

Lem winced. How had this gone so wrong so quickly? Despoina was the most restrained of Father's secretaries, the most demure. In the office she rarely said a word.

She had been that way when he had shown up at Father's office the day before and asked her out. She was so surprised by his invitation, so taken aback, that she had assumed she had misunderstood.

"Are you saying you want me to reserve dinner for you and your father?" she had said. "Because Simona typically handles his dinner reservations."

Lem had looked at her with mild amusement, standing beside her desk, leaning on the door frame of her glass cubicle. "No. I'm asking you to come have dinner with me. The two of us. Alone. At a restaurant."

She had blinked, not sure how to respond.

Her reaction hadn't surprised him. She was not the kind of woman who drew a man's eye. Simple haircut, modest conservative wardrobe, a small frame that made her seem younger than she probably was. She was not unattractive, really, but she wasn't exactly glamorous either. Which, combined with her shyness, meant she probably wasn't getting a lot of attention from the menfolk.

Lem had come because he had needed a distraction. He had followed Father's advice and cut the communication lines to Victor and Imala's shuttle. The drones were on their way; there was nothing Lem could do.

But as he had flown around in his skimmer, waiting

for the inevitable to happen, avoiding going back to the warehouse, where he would have to face Dr. Benyawe and explain his actions, the thought had occurred to him to go to Father's office. There were questions that still needed answering, after all. Why had Father met with someone from the U.S. State Department, for example? Who else was he meeting with? What was he planning?

And who better to have the answers to those questions and the willingness to share them than an ignored young secretary low on male companionship?

"I have a lot of work to do," Despoina had said. "Files to prepare for your father, memos to write." She had blushed. "Besides, it might not be . . . you know, appropriate."

Lem laughed. "Not appropriate? Why, because you work for my father and I'm his son?"

"Because you and I both work for the company." She could hardly look at him she was so embarrassed.

"Why does that matter?" Lem had said. "Three-quarters of the people on this rock work for Juke. You think that precludes you from having dinner with any of them?"

"Isn't that against the company policy or something?" she had said. "Not that this is a date or anything, but, you know, the appearance of a date."

This was just sad. "First of all, this is absolutely a date. No question. Full-fledged date. Second, this can't be the first time a coworker has asked you out."

She brushed a speck of dust off her desk. "I stay very busy, Mr. Jukes."

"Mr. Jukes is my father. I'm Lem. Can you say that? Lem. It's not a difficult word. One brief syllable. The first half of 'lemon.' Or 'lemmings.'"

She had smiled at that, looking down at her keyboard, tracing the edge of it with her finger. "I know how to say your name."

"Prove it."

She had laughed awkwardly and shrugged. "Lem."

"You say it like it's a joke. Like it's a punch line. My feelings are hurt."

She had sighed, rolled her eyes, tossed a hand. "Lem."

"Now you say it like I'm an annoyance."

"That's not far from the truth," she said. But she was smiling.

Now he was getting somewhere. "Just say it normal. Like we're friends. Like we've known each other for years, and I've been away, and you're happy to see me."

"This is silly."

"Of course it's silly. It's utterly ridiculous. But that's why we're doing it. You haven't done anything utterly ridiculous, I bet, since you were in diapers. And I'm not leaving until you say it."

"I could call security, you know."

"Yes. That's good. You'd have to say my name. Let's do that." He reached across to hit the call button.

She swatted his hand lightly. "Hey. Nobody touches my buttons but me."

"There you go. A little backbone. I knew you had it in you. Just say my name one more time, and I'll leave you alone. You won't have to go to dinner with me."

"I say it and you'll go away?"

"I'll vanish like a genie. Poof. Chimes will play. Smoke will appear. You'll love it. I do it at parties. But you have to say it right."

She exhaled and settled back in her chair, giving in. "Like we're old friends. Like you've been away awhile."

"Which I have been, you know. Two years in the Kuiper Belt."

"Yes. I know."

"Did you miss me while I was gone?"

"I didn't know you. I wasn't working for your father when you left. I'm relatively new."

"But you *would* have missed me. We're old friends, remember?" He was kneeling at her desk now, his elbows on the desktop, his chin in his hands.

A shy smile. "I suppose."

"You suppose? Des, we're old friends."

"My name's Despoina."

"I know what your name is, Des. I'm using the shortened version. It's snappier. Close friends have shortened versions of each other's names. Like Lem. Do you know what Lem is short for?"

"Lemminkainen."

He raised his eyebrows. "Whoa, you didn't even have to think about that one."

She blushed.

"I usually have to give lots of clues, and people still don't get it. We need to put you on a quiz show. How did you know that?"

She brushed the hair out of her face, shrugged. "I don't know. I've seen you on the nets."

"So we *are* old friends. Good, you don't have to pretend to be happy to see me. I'm certainly not pretending." He pointed at his smile. "This is one hundred percent genuine, Des-induced glee."

Later, after dinner, as they rode in his skimmer around the surface of Luna, he had learned everything he needed to know about her. She was the daughter of the CEO of a big avionics company based out of San Diego that had a longstanding relationship with Juke Limited. Ukko and her father were friends apparently.

"You can probably fill in the blanks," she had said. "My father calls in a favor. 'Ukko, she's my girl,' he says. 'College degree. Good school. Very smart. She's got job offers, but I'd like someone I trust watching over her.'"

"That's sweet," Lem had said.

"No it isn't. My father's overprotective."

"It's better than overbearing. Trust me, I speak from experience."

"Anyway, your father was kind. I was mortified that my dad even asked. I really didn't have any other job offers. Not good ones anyway. But I didn't want a job as a favor. I was tired of my life being handed to me. Does that make sense?"

"More than you know."

"Anyway, your father said, 'She'll be one of my office assistants. It doesn't sound like much, but it's a great way for her to meet the senior VPs. They're always pilfering from my office staff. I don't force them to hire anyone. I simply give my office staff a chance to shine, and the VPs come begging for them in short order.'"

"Sounds like a respectable opportunity."

"I thought so, too. So I took it. And here I am."

Her bashfulness had eroded, and after another hour she had invited him to her place. Lem hadn't thought this through very well. He could have said no. Sleeping with her was not on the agenda. Despoina was just out of college. He was seven, eight years her senior. Maybe more. And despite his reputation on the gossip nets, he did not sleep with every woman he met. With Despoina, he had anticipated a nice dinner, some helpful, revealing conversation, and that would be the end of it.

And yet here they were, lip-locked in the kitchen the morning after with Despoina as giddy as a schoolgirl.

She broke off the kiss and wrapped her arms around his waist. "Let's do something fun today, go somewhere. I'll call in sick. You can, too. We'll take the skimmer out."

He didn't know what to say. "Where would we go?"

"I don't know. Where do couples go on Luna?"

Couples? This was veering into dangerous waters. Over wine, as he had expected, she had told him everything she knew about the State Department visit. The Americans wanted to purchase some of Father's fleet, weaponize them, and use them to attack the Formic ship. Father, according to Despoina, had named an exorbitant price he knew the Americans couldn't afford, and that had been the end of it.

It was nothing Lem could use against Father, and it wasn't even particularly interesting. All things considered, it was hardly worth the price of dinner. And yet, Lem had stayed the night anyway.

The thought suddenly repulsed him. While Victor's and Imala's corpses floated in space, while Chinese families burned under the onslaught, Lem had drunk himself silly and rolled in the sheets.

He reached back, gently took her arms from around his waist, and put her at arm's length. "This is not a good day to call in sick, Des."

"Why not?"

He gestured to the vid screen. "Formic reinforcements landed in China. They've killed millions more people."

She put a hand to her mouth. "That's awful." She looked back at him. "But—"

"What does that have to do with us?"

She nodded.

Was she really that naïve? Were the numbers so big that they lost all meaning to her?

He didn't want to mention the drones. He wasn't sure what she knew. "I need to see my father immediately," said Lem.

"Of course. Yes. That makes sense."

They left the building at different times. Lem first went home to shower and change. There were several messages from Benyawe. She was furious. Where was he? They had lost contact with Victor and Imala. Radio, biometrics, everything. The drones had attacked. Why?

Ask my father, Lem thought.

There were messages from Simona as well. Urgent ones. He was to call her. He ignored those as well.

He returned to his skimmer and left the city, heading out toward Father's office at company headquarters. He brought the skimmer down on the landing pad, and it descended below the surface. A moment later in the docking bay, the bots grabbed the skimmer and slid it into one of the parking tubes. When Lem got out, he was surprised to find Simona waiting for him, holopad held tight to her chest, lips pressed together in a hard line.

"Who was the lucky girl this time?" she said.

He gave her his warmest smile. "Simona, shouldn't you be getting coffee for my father? I'll take one as well. Sugar. Cream. Oh and a shoulder massage."

"I called your apartment last night. I called the warehouse. I called your wrist pad."

"That's a lot of calling. I hope you didn't overexert your fingertips."

"You didn't answer or return my holos."

Lem adjusted his cuff links. "I was indisposed."

"Indisposed or inverted?"

He looked perplexed. "Are you calling me a vampire, Simona, or was that supposed to be vulgar?"

She brushed it aside, tapped at her holopad. "Forget it. I don't want to know."

"Really? You seem quite interested to be uninterested."

She gave him a "spare me" look. "Discovering your perverse exploits is the last thing on my mind, Lem."

"So it *is* on your mind somewhere. I'm flattered."

She hugged her holopad again and sighed. "Perhaps you haven't noticed we have a crisis on our hands here."

Lem tapped his cheek with his index finger, pretending to be deep in thought. "Crisis, crisis, hmm, nothing's ringing a bell. Oh wait, do you mean that my father singlehandedly flushed the company down the toilet by doing exactly what I told him not to? Or is there some other crisis I haven't heard about?"

She rolled her eyes and turned away. "Just get in the shuttle."

He noticed the shuttle then, parked off to the side of the terminal. One of Father's security men opened the back door, and Simona climbed inside. Lem followed her in and sat beside her. They took off a moment later, zipping through the vehicular traffic tunnels, which meant they obviously weren't going to Father's office.

Lem took in the interior of the shuttle and bounced a little in the posh seats. "Since when do I get the executive treatment? Maybe you've forgotten I've been demoted. I thought these digs were for people my father liked?"

She was tapping at her pad and didn't look up. "Will you stop being a child for once?"

He spoke in a pouty voice. "Someone rolled off the wrong side of the bed this morning and fell in a bucket of sourpuss."

Simona made no reply.

"How did you know I was going to be at the parking tubes?" Lem asked. "I know you haven't been waiting there all morning. I wasn't scheduled to be here at all."

"Do you really have to ask?"

"I have a hunch, but I'd like to hear it from you."

She looked up at him. "Next time you steal a proximity chip, be a little more discreet about how you use it. And try an erasing program so no one can backtrack all your movements and know where you are at all times."

"If you've been able to track me why did you call my apartment and the warehouse last night? You would have known I wasn't there."

"Because I didn't think you'd be stupid enough to keep the proximity chip after such flagrant abuse of it. I thought you would have dumped it or traded it. We picked up the signal south of town, but I didn't think it was you. Why would you go down there? I was giving you the benefit of the doubt. Silly me."

"Well don't I feel like the village idiot." He was quiet a moment. "So you know where I went last night? You have an address?"

"Who you spend your recreational time with is your business, Lem. I've already erased the address from the memory banks. Believe me, I'm not particularly eager to find out whoever it was who gave you an STD last night."

"You're really annoyed about this, aren't you?"

"Damn right I am. I couldn't get you when I needed you."

The bite in her tone angered him. "Well I'm sorry if I'm not at your every beck and call, Simona. But if you turn back the dials of your memory just a hair, you'll recall that I asked for your help to stop my father and this drone attack, and you didn't exactly spring to my side."

Her voice was calm, but there was steel behind it. "Let's not point fingers, Lem. What's done is done. My loyalty is with your father. I've been clear on that. He pays my salary."

"Are you really that cheap, Simona? Is that all that matters to you? A paycheck? Well, let's hope the Formics don't make you a better offer."

He regretted saying it as soon as the words came out, and he could see that they had stung. She stared at him, jaw set, then turned away, shaking her head.

He should apologize.

There was a line, and he had crossed it.

She tapped at her holopad, her head bowed, her long hair obscuring her face from him.

He was on the verge of apologizing when he recalled that she had kept information from him. He wasn't the bad guy here. He had needed critical information about the drone launch dates, and she had knowingly kept him in the dark. Where were the apologies she owed *him*, huh?

And ever since he had come back from the Kuiper Belt, she had snapped at him and ordered him around like a dog, like some mindless mutt. Go here, Lem. Say this, Lem. Don't say that, Lem. Follow me, Lem. Smile for the cameras, Lem. Double time, hurry up. Snap, snap.

She was Father's puppet, and he had been hers, jumping from one PR interview to the next, playing his part like the trick dog he was.

And Simona, always in her laughably long, modest skirts and high necklines and self-righteous holier-than-thou attitude. It was so infuriating, so condescending, so—

Simona sniffed.

He looked at her. She rotated farther away from him, hiding her face.

Was she . . . crying?

Suddenly he felt guilty. He had never seen her exude any emotion other than impatience and annoyance.

He should say something.

"Simona—"

She cut him off, her voice like a dagger. "Do. Not. Speak to me." She *was* crying. There was a crack in her voice. She didn't look at him. "Say one more word, one word, and I will scream rape and tell Charles to pull over and knock your teeth out. And don't think he won't. Charles knows who signs the checks."

She spat out the last words like venom.

Lem said nothing, not because he thought she'd make a scene, but because whatever he said would only make it worse.

They rode in silence for another minute. When they stopped, Charles, the driver, got out and opened the door for them. Simona exited first, then Lem.

An iron grip seized Lem by the forearm and suddenly Charles was at his ear, whispering. "She doesn't have to tell me to knock your teeth out, amigo. I'll do it because I want to. Make her cry again and see if I don't."

The man's viselike grip released, and Charles casually got into the shuttle and drove away. Lem watched him go, rubbing his forearm.

Fingers snapped behind him, and Lem turned. Simona was at the double doors, holding them open. "Your father is waiting, Lem."

She was her old self again, all business, perfectly poised, showing no sign of having just shed a tear. He followed her into a lobby. Lem didn't know the place, but it didn't look particularly special. Everything seemed dated, in fact. Old furniture. Old décor. An empty receptionist desk. Even the paintings on the walls were from ten years ago.

"Time for an upgrade, wouldn't you say?" Lem said. "This place is like a museum."

Simona didn't reply. She approached a door, and it unlocked automatically. When she pulled it open, it was thick and heavy like a bank vault. They stepped into a pristine white corridor, and Simona pulled the door closed behind them with an echoing clang.

"Okay. I'll bite," Lem said. "Where are we?"

"A place that doesn't exist," said Simona. She started walking briskly, and Lem had to hurry to keep up.

"That's a little cryptic. What is this nonexistent place?"

She didn't look at him. "Are you prepared to sign a nondisclosure agreement?"

"I signed one of those when I joined the company."

"This is different. This is special. You'll sign or you won't leave this facility."

He laughed. "Well now. There's a threat. Is there a dungeon in here for people who refuse? I've always suspected Father had a dungeon. Stone walls; rusty shackles; long-haired, toothless crazy old men as cell-mates."

She didn't look at him or so much as crack a smile.

They walked in silence a moment. Whatever working relationship they had developed since his return from the Kuiper Belt was gone now. He could see that. He had shattered that in the car.

He cleared his throat and lost the flippant tone. "I'll sign whatever you want me to sign."

She stopped, faced him, and held out her holopad. It was a white screen with a black line at the bottom.

"What, now?" he said.

"Just sign it."

"I don't know what I'm signing."

"The document is two hundred and eighty pages long. Shall we have a seat on the floor so you can read all the legal language you don't understand?"

He let the insult pass. He probably deserved it. "In a sentence can you at least tell me what I'm signing?"

"And you'll believe me?"

"I was an ass to you in the car, so you certainly have every right to screw me over right now. But I also know that you're a good person with a conscience. Yes, I trust you."

She brushed the hair out of her face. "Is that an apology?"

"An attempt at an apology."

She exhaled. "You were more than an ass."

"Yes. That's true. I was worse than that."

"A troll."

"Okay. Not where I would go. A little too mythical for me, but yes, I was a troll."

She stared at him for a long moment, the holopad in the air between them, then she gave an exasperated sigh. "This is typical nondisclosure. Whatever you see in this facility can never be spoken of to anyone outside this facility. Even to me or to your father. It says if you break that agreement, we can sue you for all the money in the world and cut off your testicles."

He raised an eyebrow. "Really?"

"Except in your case, since you don't have any testicles, we would probably just sue you." She held up her stylus.

He took it, signed, and gave the stylus back to her.

Simona tucked her pad under her arm and started walking again.

Lem kept step beside her. "So what is this place and why am I here?"

"You're here at your father's insistence. As for why it's secret, it involves, like most things in this company, very proprietary tech. Have you ever heard of Project Parallax?"

"Should I have?"

"Only if you're an academic. An astrophysicist, say. Or a cosmologist. Project Parallax began eight years ago. It was an attempt to position satellites with high-powered telescopes at the outer edge of the solar system. Without the debris of our system clouding their views, the parallax satellites could give scientists a better look at the deep reaches of the universe."

"The Parallax Nexus," Lem said. "The database at universities. I have heard of this. We did that?"

"We *do* that. The nexus is still in operation, though it's managed through a subsidiary. The satellites, however, still belong to corporate and are still functional. They feed data back to the system continually. Research facilities, universities, space agencies like STASA. They all pay us a subscription fee to get data from the satellites."

"Subscription fees? That sounds like chump change. Is this profitable?"

"Hardly. But we enjoy very generous tax and tariff breaks from agencies with oversight of the space trade. That helps immensely."

Lem looked at the white walls. "So this is Project Parallax. I don't get it. What's so secretive about it? Every college kid who walks into a university library can log in to the Parallax Nexus. The data is there for all to see. We're wide open on this."

"I'll let your father explain that part."

She stopped at a place in the wall with an outline of a door. Lem would have walked right by it had she not stopped. A small, pink, cubed holofield appeared above a white shelf to their right. Simona inserted her hand into the field and did an intricate series of movements, as if she were spelling a lengthy word in sign language. There was a quiet click as the locks disengaged, and the door swung inward.

They stepped across the threshold and into . . . the solar system.

Lem stopped. He was standing in outer space—or so it seemed, although he could still feel the floor beneath him. Before him were planets, asteroids, moons, all in miniature, all emitting a little light, floating at chest height. Simona walked past him, passing through a few asteroids, then the sun, to reach Father, who was standing on the opposite side of the dark room, speaking with a technician.

Brief words were exchanged, and then Simona and Father crossed back to Lem.

"Have you heard anything from Victor or Imala?" Father asked.

The fake concern on Father's face was infuriating. *You were the one who told me to cut them off, Father,* Lem wanted to say. *You were the one who sent the drones that likely killed them, after I begged you not to. And now you have the gall to act like you care?*

With Simona present, however, Lem only said, "We lost contact when the drones attacked."

Father exhaled deeply and put his hands on his hips. "It's my fault."

Lem said nothing. If Father was waiting for him to argue the point, he was in for a disappointment.

"Are you all right?" Father asked.

"Me?" said Lem.

"They were your friends. I know this can't be easy. This wasn't your fault, son. I bear all the blame."

Damn right it wasn't my fault, thought Lem.

His father's words had struck him, though. *Were* Victor and Imala his friends? No, theirs had been a working relationship, nothing more. Victor despised Lem. Imala had been warmer, but not by much.

"You've seen the news," said Father. "About China."

"They'll blame you when they learn where the drone attack came from. They'll say you provoked the Formics and cost millions of lives."

"That's ridiculous," said Simona. "Militaries have been attacking the mothership since the beginning. Ukko was trying to protect Earth. Why would they blame him?"

It bothered Lem that Simona had referred to Father by his first name. It was too casual, unlike her.

"Lem's right," said Father. "This is what news programming does, Simona. They vilify people. And nobody's easier to hate than the wealthiest man alive."

"What are you going to do about it?" asked Lem. "The company might not survive this."

"The company, the company. I don't care about the company, Lem. I thought I was clear on that. If the human race goes the way of the dinosaurs, it won't matter if we hit our quarterly earnings goals. Our job is to end this." He put an arm around Lem's shoulder and gestured to the solar system. "So tell me, what do you think of our holofield?"

"Why am I looking at the solar system?"

"Why indeed," said Father. "We call this the Big Room. It's not an original name, I admit, but it's appropriate. This—" He made a sweeping gesture of the space. "This is like a screensaver. It's not to scale obviously. Nothing is actually this close together. But now that you're here, we can get started." He tapped his wrist pad, and the solar system disappeared. Light filled the room, revealing a massive, empty white space half the size of a gymnasium. The floor was transparent, with hundreds of holoprojectors positioned beneath it.

Above Lem, suspended from the ceiling, was a square light rig holding as many holoprojectors as there were below him.

Three squares in the floor began to rise like towers. They stopped half a meter off the ground, forming three cubes, close together.

"Sit," said Father, gesturing to the cubes.

Lem sat.

Father took the cube opposite, and Simona sat at the third.

"There was a technician here a moment ago," said Lem. "He disappeared."

"There are close to a hundred technicians in this facility, Lem," said Father, "all behind these walls. They come and go through the doors as needed. Simona calls them the elves."

"What do they do exactly? These technicians. What is this?"

"This, son, is the business we are in."

"Holoprojection?"

Father laughed. "No. Information, Lem." He waved a hand at the empty room. "Project Parallax has always been about information. Seeing what no one else can see."

Father tapped his wrist pad, and the room went dark again. A white light appeared in the center of the three cubes, floating in the air between them like a tiny hovering campfire. The light changed, took shape, and became the flat ecliptic plane: the sun, the planets, the solar system. Two dots of light on the plane of the ecliptic beyond the edge of the system and directly opposite each other began to orbit the solar system.

"The Parallax satellites," said Lem. "Simona explained this already."

"I didn't tell you how many satellites there were," said Simona.

As Victor watched, another orbit ring appeared with two more satellites—this plane perpendicular to the ecliptic—the galactic plane. A third orbit ring, at a thirty-degree angle: the galactic celestial plane. Then a fourth ring, at sixty degrees: the galactic equatorial plane. All formed a gyroscope of satellites orbiting the system.

"There are eight satellites," said Father, "all with telescopes looking outward into deep space."

"And these satellites are functioning?" said Lem. "They work properly?"

"Very well," said Father.

"Then why didn't they see the Formics coming?"

Father smiled and shook a finger. "An excellent question. The short answer is, the Parallax satellites weren't designed as an alien warning system. They're made for research and for detecting collision threats. And when I say research, I mean they're looking way out there at a specific object or cluster of galaxies, holding a very tight field of view, like a laser dot in the sky, whatever it is that sparks the astrophysicist's fancy. When the satellites aren't doing that, they're flagging light-reflection objects moving in normal parabolic patterns that pose a threat to Earth."

"But the Formic ship *is* a threat to Earth."

"Yes, we know that now, but it wasn't moving in a way that the Parallax computers recognized. We program it to look for very specific things. Giant alien ships moving in ways no one thought possible was not one of those things. And keep in mind, the space between these satellites is tremendous. Opposing satellites on the same plane could be ten billion kilometers away from each other or more. Nor are they fast moving. For satellites they're extremely slow. So no, they didn't see the Formics coming, and frankly I'm not at all surprised. Space is very big, son."

"This is all very fascinating," said Lem. "And I commend you for building your satellite telescope thingies that *didn't* actually prove very useful when we needed them to. But I fail to see the relevancy here. We lost the drones, Father. You may not care about the company. But everyone who works for this company does. You need a game plan. You need to prepare a response. Ukko Jukes kicked the hornets' nest. Ukko Jukes aggravated Formics and incited a second wave. The headlines write themselves."

Father frowned. "I'm disappointed, Lem. I thought for sure you would see the possibilities a configuration like the Parallax would provide."

"Really? We're still on this Parallax thing? The future of this company is hanging by a thread, Father. And that thread is suspended over the crapper. So unless these Parallax satellites are also time machines that allow us to go back and have a do-over with the drones, I don't see the point."

Father sighed wearily and tapped his wrist pad. The original screensaver solar system returned, filling the room. "Information, Lem. That's why Parallax matters. The possibilities for useful, profitable information."

Lem scrunched up his shoulders. "Sorry. If we're playing a guessing game here, I fold. What am I not seeing?"

"If the Parallax satellites can carry scopes that look outward, they can also carry scopes that look inward." Father tapped the wrist pad, and hundreds of additional objects appeared in the room, scattered across the solar system within the ecliptic. Lem stood and walked to one near him. He leaned down to get a better look at it. It was a ship, a digger, no larger than his fingertip. He reached out, touched it, and it ballooned in size to be as large as he was. Lem recoiled a step, startled. Windows of data popped up around the ship, identifying it as a MineTek asteroid digger, C-class—a competitor's vessel. There was a list of all the asteroids it had visited and mined from, as well as a complete ship manifest: the captain's name and photo, the full crew, equipment, weapons, drive system; it was all there.

Lem turned and looked back at his father. "You're spying on the solar system?"

"Not spying, Lem. Observing. Gathering information. With the gyroscope we can see everything we need to know to improve our operations. We can avoid the asteroids that are already occupied by a competitor's vessel, for example. Or we can identify new, potentially viable asteroids—"

"Or you can track competitors' trade routes," said Lem. "You can know everything the other guys are doing and then sabotage and obstruct their operations. You can know who to buy off, who to avoid, where the real money is."

"You make it sound devious, Lem," said Father. "But this is how a company operates. I'm not doing anything illegal here."

"Illegal, no. Unethical, maybe."

Father looked annoyed. "This is why we succeed, Lem. This is why we have the market share we do. Every company in the world does this. They gather and use information. We just do it better than anyone else."

"This doesn't reek of privacy issues to you?"

Father laughed. "Privacy? Are you telling me a CEO on Earth can't stand on the roof of his building and look down at the street and count how many of his competitor's trucks drive by?"

"That's different."

"No. It isn't. Scale doesn't matter. Just because we've got a taller building, so to speak, doesn't make it suddenly wrong."

Lem shook his head. "So you knew. As soon as the Formic ship came into system, you knew what it was, and yet you pretended not to."

"No, I didn't know what it was, Lem. The interference from the Formic ship disrupted the Parallax satellites as much as any other. We went dark for several months. The satellites continued to collect images, but they couldn't transmit. Now that the radiation has dissipated, and transmission lines are reopening, we're slowly coming back online. Now the satellites are inundating us with every image they've taken since they transmitted the last time, before the interference."

"This all has a point, I'm sure," said Lem.

"When you attacked the Formic ship in the Kuiper Belt, Lem, who joined you?"

The question was such a non sequitur that it took Lem a moment to respond. "A free-miner ship. El Cavador. Why?"

"There was a third ship," said Father. "One that didn't participate in the actual attack."

"A WU-HU ship," said Lem. "It took all the women and children from El Cavador. We never saw what happened to it. We couldn't radio it. Everything was chaos."

"The ship survived, Lem."

For a moment, Lem was speechless. "How do you know that?"

Father smiled. "That unethical information is suddenly quite useful, isn't it?"

"These were innocent people, Father. This isn't a game. What happened to them?"

Father tapped his wrist pad, and the solar system disappeared save for a single yellow dot of light, floating in the black expanse. Lem approached it and touched it. The yellow dot ballooned outward until it was a WU-HU outpost two meters across.

"It's in the Asteroid Belt," said Father. "One of several outposts WU-HU has in that sector. This is a computer-generated model based on schematics. The color might be wrong, but this is essentially what it looks like. According to Parallax, this is where your WU-HU ship went. There would be food there, Lem. The captain there is a good woman. If we're reading her profile right, she would have taken them in. Fed them. Sheltered them. I thought you would want to know."

Lem stared at the outpost. Relief welled up inside him like a wave. He didn't know why exactly. These were not his people. They were strangers to him, really. Most of them probably still hated him for bumping their ship off the asteroid in the Kuiper Belt, a move that had gone terribly wrong and resulted in the death of one of their crew.

And yet, it didn't matter if they hated Lem. They were right to hate him. He didn't want their acceptance. He only wanted them to be alive. And now they were. They had suffered, yes. They had lost their husbands and fathers, their livelihood, their home. But at least they still had each other. At least they had someone to lean on in their grief.

Father was behind him, his voice soft. "I've watched

these interviews you've done, son. I've seen you tell your story about what happened out there. It had a profound effect on you. I see that now. I thought it might bring you some comfort to know that a few more made it out alive."

Lem turned and faced him. "This is why you brought me here? This is why you showed me Parallax?"

"I should have shown it to you a long time ago. You're my son, Lem. I've kept too many secrets from you for too long. I regret that. I'm not saying this makes me a good father suddenly. I know what I am. But if I can do something to alleviate any pain my son is carrying, then I'm going to do it."

Lem was at a loss. Was Father actually doing something kind? Was he actually giving without an ulterior motive?

"I don't want you doing these interviews anymore," said Father. "You're not to be paraded around. The PR team will object, but I'll tell them to deal with it. I want you focusing on destroying the mothership."

Lem was taken aback.

Father smiled. "Don't look so surprised. I've learned my lesson, Lem. You have good ideas. Your strategies are better than mine. I ruined what you had planned with Victor and Imala. I take full responsibility. Their deaths are on my hands. I don't expect you to forgive me for that. I only expect you to keep going. Your plan worked, or at least as much as I allowed it to. Your team got to the Formic ship. That's more than I've accomplished. Now you need to do it again. And this time, I assure you, I won't get in your way."

CHAPTER 9

Goo Guns

Mazer lay on his back in the mud beneath the fuselage of the HERC, twisting two wires together, trying to make a spark. They had landed in a rice field
southwest of Lechang, with the nose of the fuselage
resting on an embankment between two paddies. That
left a narrow space beneath the HERC at the edge of the
embankment where Mazer could crawl in, remove some
of the hull plates, and access the main electrical system.
The two wires touched, there was a crack of electricity,
a small motor whirred to life, then something popped
inside the circuit boards and a puff of acrid smoke wafted
out into Mazer's face.

"That doesn't sound promising," said Wit. He was
kneeling at the bottom of the embankment, bending low
to look under the fuselage where Mazer was working.

"I think I just cooked the avionics," Mazer said. "Plus
the lenses are inoperative, and I can't reboot the system.
The only way this thing is flying again is if we launch it
from a giant slingshot."

"I'm not heartbroken," said Wit. "I didn't want to get
back in that thing anyway."

It had been a rough landing. The rotor blades had

slowed the HERC's descent, but they hadn't stopped it. Mazer had brought it down as best as he knew how, but the landing had rattled everyone on board.

Mazer turned over onto his stomach, commando-crawled out from under the HERC, got to his feet, and squinted at the sun. He was covered in mud, and his wet uniform clung to his body. He had shed the biosuit after they had landed. It wasn't much use at this point; the glass shards from the windshield had left gaping holes in it. As for the cuts, Mazer had come out better than he had expected. Two shards of glass had imbedded into his skin, the worse of which was on the back of his right forearm. It had just missed the ulnar artery. Wit had pulled the shard out using tweezers from the med kit, then he had put a few stitches in the wound and covered the area with a liquid bandage. The paste had dried hard and created a sort of vambrace on Mazer's arm.

Mazer walked up the embankment that separated the paddy from the one adjacent and got one of the water bottles from the emergency kit. He unscrewed the top, took a long drink, then poured water into his hand and cleaned the mud from his face.

"Any sign of Shenzu?" he asked.

Wit put the binoculars to his eyes and looked west toward the mountains. Shenzu had gone in that direction a few hours ago with the antenna to try to get a radio signal. "Here he comes now."

Far in the distance, Shenzu stepped from the jungle and made his way across the field toward them. When he arrived Mazer could see it wasn't good news.

"The dozer got through to Dragon's Den, but it makes no difference. The entire convoy from Lianzhou was destroyed. Most of the camp at Lianzhou as well. A small group got out and have regrouped north of the city, but General Sima's army is essentially annihilated."

"That was eleven thousand men," said Wit.

"It gets worse," said Shenzu. "The transports are more aggressive now than they have been. All of them are targeting populated areas now. And I don't just mean the new transports from the second wave. I mean all of them, including the death squads that were in rural areas spraying rice fields and livestock. They're all targeting cities now."

"Which cities?" asked Wit.

"Every city in southeast China, including the big ones. Hong Kong, Shenzhen, Guangzhou, Dongguan. Many of these had already been evacuated, but there are millions of people who hadn't left. Other transports are hitting villages and cities as far north as Linwu County. I can't imagine what the casualty estimates might be." He took a water bottle and downed half of it. Then he wiped his mouth and said, "That's not all. I also got word on the attacks Sima coordinated against the landers."

"The drill-sledge teams?" asked Mazer.

"They failed," said Shenzu. "The sledges waited too long. The underside of the landers were shielded when the teams arrived. Formics wiped out the two teams and destroyed the drill sledges."

"So the landers still stand," said Wit. "And the Formic army is larger and more aggressive than it ever was before. Do you have any good news?"

"I wish I did."

Wit sighed and thought for a moment. "If the convoy at Lianzhou was taken out, then the science team is lost. That means no one is working on stopping the gas. That should be our priority."

"We're not scientists," said Shenzu. "We can't develop a counteragent."

"No, but we can take goo guns to scientists who can."

"Who?" said Shenzu. "China had assembled its strongest team. How will we find replacements? The best universities and research facilities are south along the coast where the death squads are attacking. Those people will be scattered."

"We don't look in China," said Wit. "We take the goo guns to New Delhi. There's a bioengineer there. A man named Pavar Gadhavi, the world's leading authority on defining the folding mechanisms of protein structures. MOPs have used him before to counter bioweapons. He knows me. If anyone can decipher the liquid it's Gadhavi."

"You're proposing we take an alien bioweapon across the border into India?" said Shenzu. "China would never allow this. India either."

"We can't bring Gadhavi to us," said Wit. "It's not safe. Even if we had a second Chinese team, I'd suggest moving them out of country. Besides, we don't have the equipment Gadhavi will need. We have to go to him."

"You speak as if the military and government have no say in the matter," said Shenzu.

"They don't," said Wit. "Not as far as I'm concerned. Mazer and I were under General Sima's command. That command structure has broken. If you want to help, I could certainly use it. We need your expertise, but I'm not waiting for the CMC or Politburo to debate the matter. They would never approve it anyway. Are you in or out?"

"How do you propose getting to New Delhi? Even if the HERC could fly, it would never make that distance. New Delhi is over thirty-five hundred kilometers away."

"We'll find another aircraft. Airports will have abandoned planes."

Shenzu scoffed. "So you'll steal one."

"'Commandeer' is a more polite term," said Wit.

"What about fuel?" asked Shenzu.

"This is why I need you," said Wit. "You're already making a list of everything we'll require."

"If you try to cross the border illegally, India will

shoot you down. They're extremely protective of the border because of the war."

"They won't shoot us down," said Wit. "That would release the Formic gas into their country."

"They won't know you have Formic gas," said Shenzu.

"They will because I'll tell them. Once I do that, whatever fighters they scramble to shoot us down will be ordered to escort us wherever we need to go."

"You've thought this out, haven't you?"

"Actually no, we're making it up together, but it's a beginning. Is there an airfield near here?"

Shenzu was quiet a moment. "They'll arrest you the moment you land in India."

"We've been arrested before. It didn't stick. And anyway Dr. Gadhavi will vouch for us."

"Oh yes, I'm sure a scientist has enough clout to make the government forget you dragged them into an interstellar war. That's a misdemeanor at most. Easily overlooked."

"India is eager to enter this war," said Wit. "They're as determined to wipe out the Formics as you are. China is eager for a solution to the gas. Having India develop the counteragent without China asking allows China to gain an ally without appearing weak. We didn't go begging to India, China can say. They proactively came to us. We didn't need their help, per se, but we'll gladly take it as a show of goodwill. This could birth a coalition, Shenzu."

"Be that as it may," said Shenzu, "if I help you, I would be going outside my chain of command. I would be court-martialed for treason. And if I accompany you to India, I would be tried for desertion as well. I would never see my family again."

"Then point us toward an airfield, and we'll be on our way," said Wit. "We'll say you tried to stop us, but we subdued you and escaped."

Shenzu said nothing for a moment. He looked down at his wrist pad and tapped at it for a moment. When he finished, he looked up and exhaled, as if coming to a decision. "Shaoguan Air Base is thirty kilometers southeast of us. It's a dual-use military, civilian airport in the town of Guitou. We will likely find a plane there."

"We?" said Wit. "You have a family, Shenzu. I don't want to be responsible for keeping you from them."

"If we don't stop the gas, my family won't live long enough to see me anyway. I'd rather they live and I go to prison than I do nothing and let them die."

"We'll tell the Chinese we took you kicking and screaming," said Mazer. "We'll say we had to gag you and bind you because you fought us every step of the way."

"And I never stopped singing the national anthem," said Shenzu.

"Or waving a little Chinese flag," said Mazer.

"How do we get to this airfield?" asked Wit.

"The Wujiang River," said Shenzu, pointing east. "We're close. The river runs straight southeast to the airport. I say we commandeer a boat and avoid the roads until we get Mazer another biosuit."

"If it's a military airfield," said Mazer, "how do we commandeer an aircraft without causing a scene?"

"No one will resist us," said Shenzu. "The airport fell five days ago. One of the hangars wasn't damaged in the attack, and my database indicates there is an aircraft still inside it." He looked uncomfortable. "But I should forewarn you. The army hasn't returned to the site since the attack. It won't be pleasant."

He meant corpses. Carnage. Bodies bloating in the sun for five days. The military was so overwhelmed with the fighting and so depleted of its resources that it couldn't even spare personnel to bury the dead.

They loaded their packs, grabbed their weapons, and

hiked to the river. There were several large homes along the waterway with boathouses. Wit kicked in the door to one of the boathouses, and they found a small fishing boat with a decent-sized engine inside. Wit checked the fuel cell, judged it sufficient, then they loaded their gear, climbed aboard, and cast off.

They heard Chinese aircraft soaring by overhead and later spotted several Formic troop transports as well. But everything remained a few hundred meters up, and nothing dipped in their direction.

Mazer felt exposed without a biosuit. He was keenly aware that at any moment, a cloud of gas could drift into their path and envelop the boat.

He imagined, as he often did, two military officers going to Kim's home in New Zealand, their faces solemn, their hats tucked under their arms. They would be strangers to her, but she would know at once why they were there. We're so sorry, they would say. And Kim would stare at them and lean against the door frame to keep from collapsing.

Mazer should not have listed her as his next of kin. That had been a mistake. They were not married. He had wanted to leave the space blank, but the clerk doing the paperwork had insisted that he list someone. There were uncles and aunts and cousins, of course. Mother had family all over New Zealand. But they were strangers to Mazer now. After he and Father had moved to London following Mother's death, Father had made no effort to maintain contact with Mother's side. That had ended badly. Mazer's grandfather had insisted that Father give Mother a traditional Maori funeral, and Father had flatly refused. There were arguments, raised voices, harsh words, one of Mazer's uncles had moved to hit Father before being restrained. It was as vivid in Mazer's memory as the simple ceremony Father had held. It was just the two of them at the grave site. No minister, no words, no flowers. Just Father's cold hand in his and the silence between them and the smell of fresh-turned earth.

They docked the boat at a jetty at Guitou. The airport was close to the water. A faint, rancid, rotting smell permeated the air. It worsened as Mazer left the boat and approached the shore. When the airport came into view, he saw two long narrow runways, several hangars, and a control tower. To the east of the runways, the military had set up enough tents to house over one thousand men. There were tanks, ATVs, antiaircraft lasers, heavy-equipment transporters, EMP trucks, all the firepower needed to conduct a small offensive.

And all of it lay in ruins.

Corpses were scattered across the camp and airfield. Vehicles were overturned, burned out, and half melted. The runway was pockmarked with craters as big as a truck. The tower had burned down, leaving only its steel skeletal structure leaning dangerously to one side. Two of the hangars had completely collapsed.

No one spoke for a long moment. The smell was so strong Mazer thought he might be sick.

"They came at night," said Shenzu. "One of our anti-aircraft gunners shot down a transporter, and the Formics retaliated minutes later with a swarm. The air was so thick with them at one point that in some of the satellite photos, you can barely see the ground."

"Did they gas this place?" asked Wit. "Is it safe for Mazer to even approach the hangar?"

Shenzu was holding a device in the air. "The gas has long since dissipated. All I'm getting are elevated traces of hydrogen sulfide and methane, both likely from the decomposition. As long as he doesn't touch anything, he should be okay. There are resupply trucks in the camp. We'll find an unopened biosuit there."

They made their way through the labyrinth of tents, heading toward the resupply trucks. Some of the tents had burned down; others had blown over in the wind and rain. Debris was everywhere. Pots, plates, helmets, weapons. Many of the soldiers had been roused from sleep during the attack and had run out of their tents in their undergarments. They lay in the mud among the soldiers in uniform, bloated and pasty and bleached by the sun.

All of the pathways were thick with mud. There were puddles with standing water everywhere, all of them coated with a thin layer of chemical scum.

They passed vehicles that had burned out, some with the driver still at the wheel. They passed downed Formic aircraft, a few of which had crashed into the tents, leaving a swath of destruction in their wake.

Finally they reached the supply trucks. Shenzu used his wrist pad to scan the codes on the side of each truck to check the truck's inventory. They found a truck with biosuits minutes later.

The lock on the back of the truck was still intact, but Wit found an iron bar on the ground, and beat at the lock until it broke free. They dug around inside until they found a biosuit and four cases of decontaminant wipes.

Mazer stripped off his clothes and wiped himself down with the decontaminant right there in the truck. Wit and Shenzu waited outside. The decon wipes were cold and foamy and smelled stronger than bleach. The vapors burned Mazer's eyes. The chemical dried out his skin. The instructions told him to wipe down three times, and he hated the process more each time. When he was done, his skin felt raw and chafed and sore at the crevices. He ripped open the plastic bag that contained his biosuit and put it on. The suit was cold and tight-fitting, but the fabric was pliable and offered plenty of mobility.

When he stepped outside, he adjusted his radio to the right frequency, and the three of them headed for the hangar.

Other than a few holes in the metal wall where shrapnel had punched through, the hangar appeared un-scathed. They all pushed hard against the two main doors and slid them open. Mazer was relieved to find a large Goshawk C14 sitting inside. He had worried that they'd find an aircraft he didn't know how to fly.

The Goshawk was a sturdy VTOL twenty-passenger troop transport with a chin-mounted cannon and a four-engine design. It was much bigger than they would need, and it would take a lot of fuel, but it had some punch to it in case they met any resistance.

"Can you fly it?" Wit asked.

"If it checks out," said Mazer. "I've never taken one up, but it's not unlike the British VTOLs I trained on. And it's a Juke ship with Juke avionics and holocontrols. I know that system better than any other."

"Give it a once-over. Shenzu and I are going to raid the trucks for more supplies."

Mazer spent the next two hours going over the Gos-hawk as thoroughly as he knew how. He used the loader to pull it out onto the tarmac. He fired up the engines, lifted off, checked flight controls, ran tests. Then he plugged it into the power station and charged its fuel cell. By then, Wit and Shenzu had returned with a pickup truck full of equipment. Wit parked it by the Goshawk and started loading supplies into the aircraft.

"What's with the shotguns?" asked Mazer, gesturing to the weapon in Wit's hand.

Wit set it down and picked up a box of odd-looking

shotgun shells. "Shocker rounds, high-voltage neuro-muscular incapacitators, or NMIs. We've got to collect a few goo guns before we head to India. With the shocker round we can incapacitate the Formics without puncturing their goo backpacks. We aim for center mass. Once the projectile pierces the skin, it will deliver two hundred milliamps of juice for thirty seconds. That's enough to stop a human heart. Hopefully it will do the same to the Formics. If not, we also have this." He patted the laser mount on top of the barrel. "When the Formic drops from the shocker round, we close the distance, and put a laser through its head. Then we remove the goo gun from the Formic, which will include the wand sprayer and the backpack, and seal it in one of these containers." He gestured to one of the large biohazard containers in the bed of the truck. "We'll strap down the containers in the Goshawk and we'll carry them to India."

"We'll need to move fast," said Mazer. "In and out. The quicker we recover the goo guns the better. We want to be long gone before any Formic reinforcements arrive."

"That's your job," said Wit. "Shenzu and I will get the goo guns. You remain in the cockpit and take off the moment we're back on board." He looked at Mazer expectantly. "Unless you see a flaw in this plan."

It was a test, Mazer realized.

"With all due respect, sir," said Mazer. "I do have a few concerns."

Wit smiled. "Show me."

Mazer took the box of shotgun shells and dumped them on the tarmac. Then he kneeled down and stood each of them on end. He set the empty box beside them and touched it with his finger. "This is a Formic transport. You're forgetting that every death squad has one. It will be armed to the teeth, and unless we destroy it, it will give chase. That's problem number one." He pointed to the shotgun shells. "The shells are the Formics. Each transport can carry as many as twenty. If you and Shenzu take them on individually, that's two against twenty. If you were mowing them down with heavy machinegun fire or cutting them in half with a swipe of a powerful laser, I might think those odds were possible. But you're not. What you're suggesting requires two shots for each Formic: the shotgun followed by a kill shot at point-blank range. There's no way you can take out that many before they retaliate. You'd have to get off ten shots each and hit every one of your targets before any of them returned fire. Then you'd have to run around to each for the second shot. You don't have time for that. That's problem number two."

Wit was still smiling. "Go on."

"Problem number three is the goo guns. We have no idea how easy it will be to remove the backpack from a dead Formic. The straps fasten around the shoulders and lock across the chest. I've never examined one up close, but we've seen plenty of them from a distance. The straps don't look like fabric. They look metallic. It will take time to cut through that. You don't want to puncture the tank in the backpack, so if you use a laser to cut through, which is what I'd recommend, it will be a delicate procedure. If you and Shenzu do that there at the site, on the ground, before we take off, reinforcements will be all over us before you've gotten one goo gun free. We'd be dead meat."

"Dead meat is bad," said Wit. "We should definitely avoid becoming dead meat. What are you suggesting?"

"Extreme violence," said Mazer. He scooped up all the shotgun shells and put them back in the box. "We follow a transport from a safe distance. The moment it lands, we move in. We attack before all of the Formics have disembarked." He removed three shotgun shells and put them on the tarmac. "Maybe we wait until three Formics are out. Then we obliterate the transport on our descent. We've got a forty-millimeter grenade launcher on the nose turret, two-tube rocket launchers on the sides, and two NATO miniguns mounted in the door gunner position. I suggest we use the miniguns. That's Shenzu's job. I come in low, right up to the open door of the transport, and Shenzu unleashes with the guns. The ricochets should kill everyone inside. The grenade launcher and rockets are too much firepower. The transport would explode, and the blast would annihilate the three Formics outside as well as their goo tanks. We'd have nothing to recover at that point."

"And what am I doing while this is going on?" said Wit.

"When we descend, you're on the other side of the Goshawk with the second sliding door open, picking off the three Formics on the ground. Head shots. Three quick pops. I'd suggest your rifle with smart targeting. Or, if you think your aim is good enough from a moving aircraft, you can use the shotguns. But that's riskier and far less accurate."

"Okay," said Wit. "The transport is now Swiss cheese. I've sunk a few rounds in the Formics' heads. Now what?"

"You and Shenzu are out the doors the moment the landing skids touch down. You rush to the nearest dead Formic with a goo gun and grab him, backpack and all. One of you grabs his forelimbs, the other grabs his hind limbs. Then you toss him into the Goshawk, climb aboard, and I take off. Once we're safely in the air, you can figure out how to remove the backpack and take as long as necessary. When the backpack's off we throw the body over the side and store the goo gun in the container."

"That only gives us one goo gun," said Shenzu.

"One's enough," said Wit. "The tanks are translucent. If it's more than half full, we should be fine. That's enough for Gadhavi to work with."

"If we're only getting one Formic," said Shenzu, "why wait until three Formics have disembarked from their transport? Why not hit it as soon as the first Formic steps off?"

"Because when their transport goes," said Mazer, "there will be all kinds of shrapnel. We can't risk puncturing the backpack. With three, we're playing it safe. At least one backpack should come out of that unscathed."

"Anything else we should consider, Mazer?" asked Wit.

Mazer tapped the box of shotgun shells. "If we wipe out the transport with most of the Formics inside, we'll break open all of their goo tanks and unleash the gas. That's unavoidable. But if the transport is in a populated area, we would be putting a lot of people at risk. I suggest we find a transport headed to either a sparsely populated area or a city or town that's already been given an evacuation order."

"They'll be spraying that gas anyway," said Shenzu. "Does it matter?"

"It matters if we're the ones releasing the gas," said Mazer. "It matters to me."

"The CMC is tracking the transports via satellite," said Shenzu. "And we know which cities and villages have been evacuated. We could probably find a match."

"It also needs to be a transport that's alone," said Mazer. "If it's near other transports, we're inviting a dogfight."

"Anything else?" said Wit.

"We'll be enveloped in the gas during the raid," said

Mazer. "Everything will be contaminated. The entire aircraft inside and out. There's no way we can decontaminate it before we reach India. If we successfully cross the border, we should warn the Indians and offer to burn the aircraft as soon as we land."

"Seems extreme," said Shenzu.

"It's a polite gesture," said Mazer. "If they refuse and offer to clean it, fine. Otherwise, we will have shown them we value their safety more than the Goshawk."

"Which isn't cheap," said Shenzu.

"Add it to my bill," said Mazer.

"Is that all?" asked Wit.

"You tell me," said Mazer. "Did I pass your test?"

Wit smiled. "I'll tell you when we land in India." He picked up the box of shocker rounds and placed them in the aircraft.

"So you're sticking to the shotguns?" said Mazer.

"There's never a single plan, Mazer. You plan for every contingency." He snapped open the action, looked inside the empty barrel, and snapped it closed again. "Besides, I like shotguns."

They loaded the biohazard containers and other supplies into the Goshawk and took off. Mazer followed the Yangxi River through the mountains, staying low and out of sight. They flew west for several hours before Shenzu found their target.

"There's a Formic transport ten kilometers ahead of us, moving north up the Menghe River. All the towns along the river were given an evacuation order. If the transport stops at one of them, we should make our move."

"What's the next closest transport?" Wit asked.

"Twenty-four kilometers away," said Shenzu.

"We're not going to find a better window than that. Track them. Mazer, follow at a distance and stay out of sight."

Mazer turned north slightly and made his way toward the Menghe River. They tracked the Formic transport with a sat feed, watching the map in the holofield. Mazer flew low. Ten minutes passed. Then twenty. The transport skipped over every town along the river.

"It's leaving the river and moving north into the mountains," said Shenzu.

"Heading where?" asked Wit. "There's nothing in these mountains."

"We can't keep this up," said Mazer. "We're losing daylight. And other transports are getting closer."

It was true. On the map, three transports were converging on a point north of them, in the same direction their transport was heading.

"They're moving toward something," said Wit. He tapped each of the four transports in the holofield with his stylus. "Computer, trace these trajectories. Where do they intersect?"

Lines from the various transports were drawn. They intersected at a point on the map north of them.

Wit said, "Shenzu, what's at that location?"

Shenzu was busy a moment with the map. "A mountain. The highest peak in Lipu County. It's called Mount Pig."

"Possible Formic targets?" asked Wit. "Is there a village up there? A town? Anything?"

"Nothing," said Shenzu.

"Can you get us a visual?"

Shenzu went back to the holofield. A moment later a sat feed appeared, replacing the map. There was the mountain peak, and there at its highest point was a round bulbous structure.

"What is that?" said Shenzu. "A water tower?"

"Why would you have a water tower on the top of an uninhabited mountain?" said Wit. "Zoom in."

The image tightened and clarified.

"That's not human engineering," said Wit. "That's Formic."

He was right. They were looking from above, but Mazer could see even from that angle that the design was alien. A round, doughnut-shaped structure stood high above the peak with a flat porch encircling it like a giant wide-brimmed hat. The surface was metallic and crude, as if assembled from hundreds of pieces of scrap.

"What are those strings on the porch?" said Wit. "Zoom in further."

Mazer hadn't noticed them at first, but as Shenzu zoomed in, he saw what Wit was referring to. Only they weren't strings. They were hoses.

"It's a refueling station," said Mazer. "For the transports. Either that or it's where they refill their goo guns."

They watched as the first transport arrived and alighted on the porch. Two Formics exited the transport and grabbed one of the larger hoses and pulled the end of it into the transport, where they disappeared. A crowd of Formics climbed out the other side of the transport and retrieved the small hoses. Working in pairs, the Formics lifted the hoses and attached them to the tanks of their goo backpacks.

"We just hit the mother lode," said Shenzu. "That doughnut thing is full of liquid goo."

"There must be an auxiliary tank in each transport," said Wit. "They fill that up as well as their individual tanks and rely on the auxiliary once their personal supplies deplete. They can stay in the field longer that way."

"Now what do we do?" said Mazer. "We still need a goo gun. We can't just climb up there with a jug after the Formics leave and fill it with a hose. We need a proper receptacle for the stuff. The goo becomes gas as soon as it touches the air."

"We'll take a goo gun," said Wit. "But we need to reevaluate. We obviously can't hit a transport on its way here because it doesn't have any goo left. It's on empty."

"If we hit it when it leaves, though," said Shenzu, "we'll blow its auxiliary tank, which will unleash a massive amount of gas."

"Better to release that gas here in the mountains, far from human habitation, than in the middle of some city," said Mazer.

"Agreed," said Wit. "But maybe we don't have to. What if we hit a transport crew while they're filling up?"

"Risky," said Mazer. "If you fire on the transport, you might puncture the doughnut."

"What if we don't fire a weapon at all?" He reached to his left, dug through one of the crates of equipment, and found a box of the odd-looking NMI shotgun shells. Wit took one of the shells from the box and unscrewed the shell casing. It slid off like a sleeve, revealing a tube of electronics capped by a small dome with four electrodes. "These electrodes are what pierce the skin when the round is fired. They're connected to the base, which consists of a battery, a transformer, and a microprocessor." He gently pulled the electrodes free of the base, and a thin wire uncoiled. "Each of these has three meters of Kevlar-coated wiring in them. When the round strikes the individual, the electrodes pierce them, and the base falls to the ground. Then the electrical charge hits. We have several boxes of rounds. It will take a little work, and a lot of wire splicing, but we could create a decent-sized chain with these. We set that chain on the surface of the porch, and we're in business."

"How would you trigger the electricity?" asked Mazer.

"We wire them all to a single microprocessor. I trigger it with a transmitter."

"The porch is metallic," said Mazer, "but that doesn't mean it conducts electricity."

"We'll test it," said Wit. "I'll set the charge to low."

Shenzu waved his hands. "I'm sorry. Is this a plan? Because I'm not following you."

"We're going to booby-trap the porch of the tower," said Mazer. "We take apart the shocker rounds, wire the electrodes into a chain, and set them on the porch. As soon as the next group of Formics have filled up their goo guns, we electrify the porch and stun them all at once. Then we rush in, finish them off and take a goo gun."

Shenzu looked at them each in turn. "Seems like a lot of work for a single goo gun."

"It's the safest option," said Wit.

"Assuming we don't electrocute ourselves in the process," said Mazer.

They waited until the four transports had come and gone; then Mazer flew them up to the peak of the mountain and hovered over the porch of the tower. Wit and Shenzu hopped out, and Wit handed Shenzu the disassembled shocker round.

"Walk over there and set the electrodes facedown on the surface. Then hold up the base and push your finger into this groove until you feel the pins break."

"What are you going to do?" asked Shenzu.

"Put my hand on the surface," said Wit. "If it shocks me, throw the base over the side immediately. Don't hesitate. And don't touch the electrodes."

"I'll be standing on the surface. Won't it shock me, too?"

"You have rubber soles. You should be fine."

"*Should?*" said Shenzu. "I need better than a 'should.'"

"Fine. I one-hundred-percent guarantee you won't get shocked."

Shenzu frowned.

"Time is of the essence, Shenzu."

Shenzu walked to the far side of the porch and got

into position. Wit bent his knees, placed his palm flat on the floor of the porch, and nodded for Shenzu to proceed.

A moment later, Wit was falling onto his back and Shenzu was throwing the whole contraption over the side. When they climbed back into the aircraft, Mazer said, "I thought you were going to set it on low."

"I did," said Wit.

They found a small clearing nearby surrounded by dense jungle. Mazer landed the Goshawk, and they got to work. It took most of the night to build the chain, with each of them helping in some capacity. When they finished it was several hours before dawn.

Mazer flew them up to the tower. Shenzu held the flashlight while Wit carefully unspooled the wire and laid the chain around the inner edge of the porch, like the band of the hat's brim. Then they flew to the base of the mountain and waited.

Not long after dawn, the first transport alighted on the porch of the tower. Wit, Mazer, and Shenzu watched the satellite feed. As soon as the first few Formics had filled their goo tanks, Wit hit the transmitter. On screen the Formics began to twitch and fall and convulse and die.

CHAPTER 10

Shield

The lobster was excellent, and the creamy burrata as an accompaniment was inspired, but Lem was finding it hard to enjoy either. Across from him, inside their private booth at La Bella Luna, one of the more expensive restaurants on the east side of Imbrium, Norja Ramdakan was attacking his pasta like a man coming off a three-day fast.

"Seventeen percent," Ramdakan said. He stabbed his fusilli with his fork and shoved the noodles into his mouth. "Our stock is down seventeen percent in a single day." He shook his head, disgusted.

As Father's chief financial adviser, Ramdakan was one of the most influential members of the Board. He had been with the company since the beginning, and his iron grip on its purse strings was legendary. He had even flown with Father in the early days, back when Father had captained a small digger in the Belt and made ends meet scraping away at surface rock. Lem couldn't imagine it. Sitting in a booth with Ramdakan for a single meal was bad enough. Living with him in a cramped ship for months on end would be intolerable.

"The company is resilient, Norja," said Lem. "The stock will rebound."

Ramdakan wiped a dollop of tomato ragout from the corner of his mouth. "How, Lem? Do you have any idea how much capital we sunk into the Vanguard drones? Any idea whatsoever?"

Lem knew exactly how much had been invested—down to the decimal place—but he dared not admit that to Ramdakan. That might lead to questions Lem didn't want to answer. Like who in Father's office had given him the information. It wouldn't be difficult to figure that out—several people had seen Lem talking to Despoina that day. And the two of them had spent a considerable amount of time together in the days since. Lem had been careful to keep their interactions out of the public eye, but that didn't necessarily mean their meetings had gone unnoticed.

It made Lem a little uneasy. If Ramdakan knew that Despoina was loose-lipped with Father's business, it would be the end of her. Ramdakan would fire her in an instant and put her on the first shuttle back to Earth. He might even slap her with a lawsuit for good measure. Or drag her through the press and paint her as a floozy. Such tactics weren't below the man. He had used them before to great effect. And it wouldn't matter to Ramdakan that Despoina's father was a personal friend of Ukko Jukes. Business was war. And in war there were no friends.

Lem felt a twinge of guilt. Des didn't know she was doing anything wrong. Lem was Ukko Jukes's son. What harm was there in telling him anything? And it's not like Lem was fishing for information. Anything she told him came out in the natural progression of their conversations. How was your day? What did you work on? Did anything interesting happen? Sure, Lem might ask a follow-up question or two. But it's not like he was probing. He wasn't using her. He was just making conversation. He was giving Des a listening ear. It wasn't his fault that she tended to be a little gossipy—a fact that had surprised him considering how quiet and shy she had been before their first date.

He could tell her that she was divulging secret information, of course. He could suggest she be more tight-lipped. But she seemed so happy to share it, so eager to give him something that pleased him, that Lem didn't want to disappoint her.

Was she doing it to keep him close? he wondered. Was she trying to establish his need for her?

Lem tried not to think about it. And in the meantime, he had enjoyed their additional time together. She was not as insufferable as he had thought she might be. The exuberance she had demonstrated after their first night together had settled down considerably. She was almost normal now. Her giddiness had mellowed into a sweet admiration for him. And hey, was it a crime to be admired by a woman? Was he hurting anything really? Lem couldn't say he found her attractive necessarily, but there was something charming about her. Her naïveté was almost endearing. He had even found himself looking forward to their get-togethers.

How strange, he thought. She was not his type. Not even remotely. And yet he couldn't deny that he felt comfortable when they were together.

"Did you hear what I said?" Ramdakan asked.

Lem looked up from his lobster. "Sorry?"

"I said we've lost enough money to buy a small country, Lem. Enough to buy *several*. It's like we gathered our assets into a giant mountain and set the whole thing ablaze." He dove back in to his fusilli.

"I'm sorry about your stock options, Norja. It was a blow to all of us."

The media had finally picked up on the failed drone attack, and the company stock, as Lem had predicted, was in a tailspin. Lem had wisely sold several thousand shares in anticipation of the news breaking, and he had maneuvered his other holdings into safer waters. So it hadn't been as devastating a blow for him as it had been for others. Ramdakan, on the other hand, had likely lost his shirt.

"Your father doesn't even seem upset about it," said Ramdakan. "That's what kills me. The old Ukko would have been incensed. Now it's all about the war. It's all he thinks about."

"Not without reason," said Lem. "If we lose Earth, it won't matter what the company does."

Ramdakan rolled his eyes. "I'm sick of this. The sensationalism of it all. Earth isn't falling, all right? This isn't the end of the human race. The Formics are in China. That's one country. One." He shrugged. "China is overpopulated anyway."

Lem raised his eyebrows.

Ramdakan put up his hands, palms out. "Don't get me wrong. It's awful what's happening down there. It's terrible. No excuse for it. But the press is acting like we could go the way of the dodo bird at any moment now. How many people are on this planet? Ten billion? Twelve billion? We've got the Formics outnumbered a million to one."

"We haven't stopped them yet. We've failed every attempt, in fact."

"You have to break a few eggs to make an omelet, Lem. That's how it works. You try a few strategies until one sticks. It's only a matter of time."

"That's what Father would say about the drones."

Ramdakan shook his head. "I'm talking about the military, Lem. This is their problem. Not ours. We're a company. Our job is to strengthen the company. And those drones were the future of this company. That was our golden goose. Now they're ashes. The largest single investment this company has ever made in tech, and poof, it's gone. It's hard to bounce back from something like this, Lem. Hard. Nothing makes investors more skittish than a stain on your record with a lot of zeroes after it."

"A kinder man would avoid saying I told you so," said Lem. "But I am my father's son. I told you so, Norja. I told you this business with the drones was a mistake. My father wouldn't see sense either."

Ramdakan grabbed his wineglass. "I've known your father for over thirty years, Lem. He's made mistakes like any man, but I've never known him to be reckless. And this was reckless."

Lem liked the sound of that. It had the ring of doubt to it. Ramdakan was more loyal to Father than most, and if Ramdakan's confidence was starting to crack, it meant others were thinking the same. And if you gently tapped a crack long enough, the whole thing would split wide open.

"Dr. Benyawe used the same term," said Lem. "'Reckless.'"

Ramdakan nodded.

There was a part of Lem that wanted to believe that Father had changed. And for a moment, there at Project Parallax, as Father had told him about the survivors from El Cavador, Lem had actually believed it.

But later, as Lem had sat alone in his apartment considering the events, reality had settled in. Father wanted something. What exactly, Lem didn't know, but he wasn't foolish enough to think that Father had done a kindness without expecting something in return. A lifetime of experience had taught Lem better.

"How are we spinning this with the press?" asked Lem.

"The truth for once," said Ramdakan. "We'll say your father was driven to protect the people of Earth, that ending this war and restoring peace is his highest priority. He's a man possessed." He waved a hand back and forth. "No, possessed is the wrong word. Determined, maybe. Vengeful." He shrugged. "I don't know the language. The PR people are putting it together. It's a nice package. Vids of suffering children in China, the Formics gassing villages, your father from humble beginnings, rising from nothing, a fighter, scrappy. Nice heroic vibe to it. Very globally patriotic. It turns a corporate disaster into a good image piece. Your father hates it. He threatened to fire the entire PR department. He said he wouldn't be made into a sideshow. I talked him down off that cliff, thank you very much." He poured himself more wine. Then he looked at his hand and held it out to Lem, palm down. "Look at that. You see that? Tremors. I'm shaking like a leaf these days. My blood pressure is through the ceiling. I tell my therapist I need to change to different medications; he tells me to get more rest."

"Rest is a good prescription."

"Our stock out of the toilet is a good prescription," said Ramdakan. "We're a mining corporation, Lem. We mine rocks. You know how many rocks we're mining these days? Zippo. Every available ship in the Belt is doing recovery and rescue. And you know how much revenue that brings in."

"The Formics cut through the Belt like a sword, Norja. We lost a lot of ships. We lost a whole settlement at Kleopatra. There's cleanup to do."

Ramdakan rolled his eyes. "Don't get me started on Kleopatra. I never wanted to build a station on that rock to begin with. I was opposed to it from the beginning. And did you hear? The families of the deceased are forming a foundation now. The Families of Kleopatra, they're calling themselves. We haven't even recovered all the bodies yet, and they've formed a damn foundation."

"They're searching for support. Healing."

"They're searching for a class-action suit is what they're searching for. You think these people want to sit around, sing 'Kumbaya,' and cry on each other's shoulders? No, they want to suck us dry like leeches. Lawyers feed off this kind of thing. They'll swarm to these people."

"The company didn't destroy the base," said Lem. "The Formics did."

Ramdakan laughed. "You think that makes any difference? They'll say we didn't build the base sturdy enough, that we didn't provide adequate defenses."

"You're overreacting," said Lem. "It was an act of war. Corporate law gives us immunity."

"You're young, Lem. Once your backside has been singed by a few lawsuits, you'll remember this conversation and know that I'm right."

"We have very good lawyers, Norja."

"The best in the world," Ramdakan agreed. "But that may not be enough. They're saying the drone attack is what caused the second wave, Lem. All those ships in China, all those cities being gassed, all those people being turned into a gooey paste, they're saying that's our fault. They're saying we poked the sleeping giant and the blood is on our hands. For a lawyer, it's a feeding frenzy. This is Christmas come early. They hardly have to lift a finger to make bank on this. Just put the right person on the witness stand, and it's like printing your own money. Kid with an eye patch. Old lady with a missing limb. Juries eat that crap with a spoon. It doesn't matter who's at fault, Lem. We have the money, so we're the bad guys."

"Maybe I can help," said Lem.

Ramdakan looked dubious. "We're not taking another loan from you, Lem. Your father nearly removed my head the last time you did that. Forget it."

"Not a loan. A repurposing of resources."

Ramdakan took a bite of his fusilli and narrowed his eyes, skeptical. "What resources?"

"We've got forty ships docked at Kotka right now with their crews and pilots sitting on their hands doing nothing."

Kotka was the company's largest docking station, positioned just beyond Luna. Asteroid mining ships on the Belt routes would dock there to refuel, restock, complete repairs, whatever. It had congested in recent weeks as ships came limping in from the Belt.

"Are you trying to raise my anxiety?" said Ramdakan. "Do you *want* to give me heart palpitations? Just hearing the word 'Kotka' grows an ulcer on my ulcer. The station is a bleeding wound right now. Money is pouring out of there like water. Food, salaries, heat. It's doing nothing but draining us."

"So why not turn it into revenue?" said Lem.

Ramdakan put down his fork and wiped his mouth. "You've got my attention."

"We know that the Formics can send reinforcements from their ship now," said Lem. "Who's to say they won't send more? Who's to say they don't have ten times that number ready to launch right now? And who's to say those reinforcements will land in China next time? Couldn't they just as easily drop into Europe, America, the Middle East?"

"The media is already saying that," said Ramdakan. "What's your point?"

"My point is this is a business opportunity if I ever saw one. Earth needs a shield, Norja, a defensive wall between it and the Formic ship. That way, if another round of Formic reinforcements is deployed, we'll blast them before they reach the atmosphere. No military has done this yet because a) we didn't know the Formics *had* reinforcements, and b) everyone has been too busy attacking the mothership. We've been playing offense when we should have been playing defense. And now, since every military spacecraft in the world has been destroyed in fruitless attacks, there's no one else out here to provide this shield but us."

"Our pilots aren't soldiers, Lem."

"Of course they are. I was out there, Norja. I saw normal people like you and me take on these bastards toe-to-toe. We're miners, yes, but that doesn't mean we don't want to defend our planet. Look at the Battle of the Belt, Norja. Do you think any of those ships were crewed by soldiers? No, they were manned by average people— people like the crews we have right now at Kotka."

"Yes, and every single one of those ships in the Battle of the Belt was destroyed, Lem. You want to send our boys out there to die?"

"That's just it. We're not sending them to *attack*. We're not putting them up against the mothership. We're sending them to form a wall to stop additional reinforcements. We're waiting for troop transports to come to *us*. And let's not forget that these are *transports,* tiny ships. Our PKs could take them out easily."

"Where's the revenue generation? What you're proposing would drive us into bankruptcy."

"Every nation on Earth will pay through the nose for us to provide this wall. They don't have a choice. Either they finance it or they have nothing between them and Formics raining down on their cities and gassing their civilians. We have relationships with these countries. Most of them are our clients already. Tell them we only ask that they help cover the cost of ship maintenance, fuel, supplies, and salaries. Then we inflate those expenses and pocket the difference. And if they don't want to unite and form a single, global shield directly between Earth and the ship, we do it on a country-by-country basis. So the U.S. buys a shield to protect U.S. airspace. And Russia buys a shield for Russian airspace. Et cetera. In the absence of a fleet, I guarantee you these countries will pay through the nose. And if they don't, we go to the private sector. Companies with large, valuable real-estate holdings will pay to have those properties protected, even from near-Earth orbit. The business model works regardless of the client. We're giving people what no one else can, Norja. Peace of mind."

"And what about the pilots and crew?" asked Ramdakan. "How do you know they'll agree to something like this? Right now they're getting paid for doing nothing."

"The ship I captained to the Kuiper Belt is docked at Kotka. It's called the Makarhu. The current captain, Chubs, is a friend of mine. He would jump at the chance. The rest of the crew would as well. I know them. They want this. And Chubs is a respected captain among the other crews. He can sway them. And if that doesn't work, we'll dangle the money carrot. Everyone will get double time plus hazard pay. "

Ramdakan scoffed. "How could we afford that?"

"We won't have to," said Lem. "Earth will foot the bill a hundred times over. Best of all, the company looks like the savior and shield of the world."

Ramdakan was quiet a moment, his fusilli long forgotten. Finally he said, "Why are you coming to me with this? Why not go to your father?"

Because I need the Board to see I have value, Lem might have said. Because I'm not about to throw Father a lifeline and pull him out of the grave he's dug himself. Because I need to bring the company success while it still feels the sting of Father's failure.

But aloud Lem said what Ramdakan needed to hear. "Because I trust you, Norja. Because you understand finances and profit potential better than anyone. Even better than Father. You can build the model for this in your sleep. You could sell it to the Board today if you wanted to."

Ramdakan nodded. He liked the sound of that. He pushed his plate away. "Have you written this up, given it a framework?"

Lem tapped his wrist pad. "I just put it in your in-box."

Ramdakan nodded again. "I'll talk to some people and get back to you. We'd need to move on this quickly."

"I agree."

Ramdakan made a move to leave but then hesitated and looked back. "Your father won't run this company forever, Lem. There are some who say he shouldn't be running it now, particularly after this business with the drones. But I'm not one of them. Ornery and headstrong as he is, I'm with him to the bitter end. You can count on me for that."

"I'm glad to hear it," said Lem.

"But when the day of his departure does come, I hope you'll stay with us, Lem. Even if the company goes in a different direction. We can always use someone with your skills."

Lem kept his face unreadable but inside alarms were going off. "What do you mean a different direction?"

"I know you, Lem. I've known you since you were a bump in your mother's belly. You're ambitious, just like your father. You're so much like him when he was your age, it's frightening. But there are those on the Board who want nothing to do with you. They know you want to run this company, and they'll fight you tooth and nail for it."

It took a moment for Lem to find words and when he did he tried making a joke of it. "I'm not sure which is more surprising, that there are people who think I'm gunning for the company or that I have enemies on the Board."

"Don't play innocent, Lem. I know you want your father's position. Everyone knows it. Hell you probably deserve it. But it's not going to happen. Ever. It's not good for business."

Lem blinked. And then quickly recovered, smiling again, appearing blasé. "And pray tell, Norja, why am I bad for business?"

"Because you're a shadow of your father, Lem. You're brilliant, don't get me wrong. You're savvy, educated, innovative, a real entrepreneur. You'd be a better CEO than most. But you're not your father."

"Of course I'm not my father," Lem said. "No one is my father but him. Are you suggesting only a clone of him can run this company once he's gone?"

"If you were CEO, Lem, the world wouldn't give you a fair shake. They wouldn't see you for the great man that you are. They would see you as a lesser version of your father. That's all. Why did Lem get that position, they'll say? Because he earned it? Because he deserved it? No, because of nepotism. Because Daddy dearest is tossing junior a bone. He's no Ukko Jukes, they'll say. He's a child of privilege who only earned his success because his father helped him every step of the way, clearing the path before him."

It was such an unfair thing to say, such an infuriating notion, such a flat-out lie, that Lem had to grip the table to control himself. If anything, Father had hedged up his way, dropped obstacles in his path, made him scrabble and fight and claw his way to every success. He was a child of privilege, yes, but that didn't mean he *had* any privileges. In Father's school of parenting it meant the opposite.

"I know that's a hard thing to hear, Lem. I know that sounds cruel. But that's the heart of it. And it would be unwise for the company to appoint a CEO who creates that kind of impression. It makes the company look weak. Like we've taken a step backward. It would be an invitation to our competitors to come at us claws out, fangs bared. You know why we squash MineTek and WU-HU and the others right now? You know why we have the market share we do? Because your father haunts their dreams, that's why. Because he's Ukko 'Iron Balls' Jukes. Because whatever they're cooking, they know Ukko is cooking something better. You're a pretty boy, Lem. It's not your fault. Your father married well, and you got your mother's genes. Your face is on the nets. Women swoon over you. Juke Limited can't have a CEO that makes women weak in the knees. We need a CEO that makes competitors wet their pants."

"So you want a tyrant?" Lem asked. "A Genghis Khan? That management approach died a long time ago."

"You're not hearing what I'm saying," said Ramdakan. "If you weren't your father's son, this wouldn't be an issue. If your last name wasn't Jukes, you would probably be on the shortlist. You've accomplished great things, Lem. But since you *are* the son, the world would put you up to greater scrutiny and find you wanting."

He made a sympathetic face and reached across the table and patted Lem's hand like a parent comforting a grieving child. Lem almost recoiled at the touch. It was such a condescending thing to do.

"I tell you this because I care about you and your father," said Ramdakan. "The Board is already doing everything it can to keep you out, Lem, despite your father's protestations, and they're not going to stop. In the end they will win."

"What do you mean, despite my father's protestations?"

Ramdakan seemed surprised by the question. "Do you

think your father wanted to send you to the Kuiper Belt?
No. He wanted you here on Luna with the company,
close to him, shadowing him. But there were those on
the Board who saw you as a threat. They knew Ukko
would give you more attention than he would give to
them, and they feared they'd eventually lose their seat
on the Board to you. So they lobbied that your father
send you to the Kuiper Belt for two years. It will give
him leadership experience, they said. It will give him a
chance at command. They hoped you'd fail, of course.
They hoped you'd get whacked with a giant asteroid.
And now that you're back, they lobbied to have you sent
to Earth as a partner in one of our failing subsidiaries.
A death sentence. They wanted to exile you, Lem. Send
you into obscurity. So your father gave you the nothing
job you have to simply keep you in the company. He
wasn't going to overrule them and force them to hire
you. That would be hell for you. So he protected you by
creating an assignment away from them with your own
people who knew your value and who would follow
your leadership. Whether he did you a favor is still to
be seen."

Ramdakan pushed back the curtain and stepped out
of the booth. "I'm sorry I'm the one telling you this,
Lem. But you deserve to know the truth. I'll take your
idea to the Board. We'll build this shield. Who knows?
Maybe that will cause some on the Board to warm to
you. But don't hold your breath."

And with that he was gone.

Lem paid for the meal and left the restaurant in a
daze. The magnetic sidewalk outside in the French Quarter was as busy as ever: window-shoppers, couples in
arms, street performers and vendors; as if nothing were
amiss in the world. Everyone's living a lie, Lem thought.
Including me.

He breezed by the crowds, took the tube to where his skimmer was docked, and then flew west toward the warehouse.

Everything he knew about Father had been flipped on its head. Was it true? Had Father wanted him to stay on Luna? Lem had always assumed that Father had sent him to the Kuiper Belt because *Father* had felt threatened by him. It had never occurred to Lem that there were other wolves at play here. And yet hadn't Father spoken to Dublin and Chubs in private and asked them both to protect Lem? Lem had assumed that Father had done so to assert his control over Lem, to diminish Lem in the minds of his crew. But maybe Father had done so because he knew there were those in the company eager to keep the prince from reaching the throne. Maybe he genuinely feared for Lem's safety.

And his current assignment. Had Father actually done him a favor by keeping him outside of headquarters in a newly created position? Was everyone on the Board *that* vehemently opposed to Lem, *that* threatened by him?

He found it hard to believe. He knew all the Board members on a superficial level; he had met them all casually at various events. But other than Norja, who Lem had known all his life, most on the Board had joined the company or risen up from the ranks while Lem was off making his fortune elsewhere. Lem knew their résumés, of course, he knew their skills and education and expertise, but he didn't know them personally. He didn't know their hearts. Maybe they were as devious and scheming as Norja had suggested.

But if so, why would Father keep them on? Why tolerate that level of infighting?

Because Father would say a little feverish competition was good for business. He'd say it keeps everyone sharp. Plus there was the fact that every member of the Board was extremely accomplished and highly valuable. Any CEO would want their counsel. They could have horns and forked tongues and tails out their backsides, and still Lem would be reluctant to let them go. In fact, any one of them could easily be Father's replacement. No one in the business world would bat an eye if the company were to appoint any one of them to that position.

But would the business world react the same way to me? he wondered. Or would they, as Ramdakan suggested, balk and turn up a nose of scorn? Suddenly Lem was unsure.

He arrived at the warehouse to find Dr. Benyawe and the rest of the engineers hard at work on the prototypes. Benyawe still hadn't spoken to him since the drone attack. Lem had been back at the warehouse for a few days now, but she continued to avoid him.

Lem was pleased to see that someone had finally hauled away the leftover space junk that Victor and Imala had left unused, thus removing a visual reminder of the events. Not that anyone was likely to forget, of course. Wherever Lem went in the warehouse these days he could feel workers' eyes boring into him. There goes the man who let Victor and Imala die. There goes the callous snake who cut all communication to the shuttle before the drones attacked.

Lem stepped out onto the warehouse floor and sensed the same scorn from everyone. The room fell quiet, and suddenly the entire staff was intensely focused on their work in front of them.

What do you expect of me? he wanted to ask them. A confession? A mournful cry of regret? You want me to flog myself? Weep and wail and gnash my teeth? Subject myself to sackcloth and ashes? Of course I'm sorry it happened. Of course I hated having to do it. But there was nothing I could do. *Not* warning them was a kindness, people. A mercy. Can't you see that?

No, they wouldn't see that. They only saw that he had deserted two of their own. And yes, that's how they saw Victor and Imala now. Not as outsiders. But as members of the team. It was ludicrous. Victor and Imala had been among them for only a few days, and yet by the way everyone was acting, you would have thought the two were close personal friends with everyone on staff.

This is how martyrs get their fame, Lem thought. As soon as you die, you're suddenly a hero.

Benyawe called to him from the center worktable. "Mr. Jukes. Could I have a moment of your time, please?"

Mr. Jukes. She was being formal with him. That would only make things more awkward. But he smiled pleasantly and joined her.

On top of the table were two metal cubes, each a meter square on all sides. A narrow cable ran between them, connecting them like giant bolas. In the middle of the cable was a reel with at least fifty additional meters of cable, suggesting that the two cubes could be stretched apart for quite a distance without severing the connection. It was a modified design of an idea that Lem had pitched to Benyawe almost a year ago, a replacement for the glaser; using the same tech, but safer. She called them shatter boxes.

"We conducted the first test today with a prototype," said Benyawe. "I thought you might want to see it." She made a hand gesture above the worktable, and a holovid appeared. In it, a small mining vessel in space approached a second larger ship that had been stripped of parts so severely that only its skeletal structure remained. Benyawe paused the vid. "We're nowhere near an asteroid big enough to conduct a real test obviously, so we found a decommissioned ship listed for recycling and hauled it a few thousand klicks away from Luna."

She started the vid again. The smaller ship slung two shatter boxes toward the skeleton ship at high speed. As

the shatter boxes spun toward their target, the reel between them unspooled more cable and the distance
between the boxes grew. Then suddenly the boxes
converged on the ship, attaching themselves to opposite
ends. An instant later the skeleton ship was ripped apart,
not in a single explosion but in a series of lightning-fast
explosions in which every piece broke into smaller and
smaller constituent pieces again and again until there
was nothing left. No ship, no shatter boxes, just fast-
moving dust that was gone an instant later, flying off in
every direction into the vacuum of space.

"Quite the disappearing act," said Lem. He asked
them questions after that. How did the sling mechanism
work? How easily could the shatter boxes be aimed?
Could they hit a moving target traveling at a high velocity? And what about safety, could these be used in
near-Earth orbit without endangering the planet?

Benyawe understood why he was asking. "You want
to use these against the Formics."

"You just proved to me what the shatter boxes can
do to a ship," said Lem. "This is far more destructive and
effective than our lasers, which are the only weapons our
ships have and which were never designed as weapons
in the first place. I don't want to damage the troop transports, Benyawe. I want to obliterate them."

"Transports?" Benyawe said.

He told her what he had proposed to Ramdakan. The
shield. Using Juke ships and crews to stop additional
Formic reinforcements. "I want to arm every one of our
ships with shatter boxes, Benyawe. I want our crews
proficient in their use. That means the sling mechanism
must be able to hold several rounds of shatter boxes at
once or there must be some system for quickly reloading
the sling. I don't want our ships armed with only one
shot. I want them picking targets and taking down as
many as they see."

"We've only conducted a single test, Lem."

She wasn't calling him "Mr. Jukes" now. That was an improvement. "We don't have time for lengthy field tests, Benyawe. I see that it works. I'm sold. I want this moved into production now, today, as soon as possible."

"Today? The Board hasn't even approved the shield yet, much less this tech."

"They will," said Lem. "They'll approve both. As far as they're concerned, this is a financial no-brainer."

"And if you're wrong? If they don't approve?"

"We'll do it anyway. I'll finance it myself. And you can be sure that Chubs and his crew and plenty of the other ships will join us in the fight, regardless of what the Board decides."

She considered that and nodded. She knew Chubs as well as he did. All of the workers had gathered now. The mood of the room had shifted. There was an excitement among them. Lem could feel it.

"How do we move this into production?" said Benyawe. "We need facilities, crews, raw materials, bots."

"We'll use the drone production facility to build the shatter boxes. They're not doing anything at the moment. That whole division is a sunken ship. They'll be eager for the work. Then we move the shatter boxes and drone crews to Kotka and retrofit all the ships there. We'll need every engineer here as well," Lem said, looking around the room at their faces. "The ships at Kotka are of various sizes and shapes, with differing drive systems. We'll have to custom-make the fittings for the sling mechanisms for each ship, placing the sling wherever it will give the crews the most accurate targeting." He turned back to Benyawe. "So I repeat my final question to you: Do these pose a threat to Earth? We fretted over the glasers misfiring and hitting the planet. Is that a problem here?"

"No," said Benyawe. "The shatter boxes only emit the tidal forces once they've attached to their target and confirmed that their positions are polar opposites. There's no chance of them firing as they're rotating through space. I made certain of that. You don't want them misfiring and hitting the ship that launched them."

"What if they miss?" asked Lem. "What if one is slung down toward Earth?"

She shrugged. "It will burn up on reentry. It will never get near the surface."

Lem nodded. "That's good enough for me. Let's get busy. And Dr. Benyawe, a word in private please."

She followed him into his office, a cramped space with bare walls and two old, mismatched office chairs he had found discarded in the warehouse. He motioned Benyawe to one, and he sat opposite. He tapped his wrist pad, and the walls and ceiling went black, dotted with stars and vibrant nebulae, giving Lem and Benyawe the sensation of sitting on a platform in the immensity of space.

"Trying to set a mood?" she asked.

He nestled back into his chair, a musty threadbare thing that smelled like an attic. "It's funny. I hated every moment of our trip to the Kuiper Belt. The cramped spaces, the food, the inconvenience, the confinement. And yet I do miss this." He gestured around him. "There is nothing more peaceful than space."

"Is that what this is?" she asked. "An attempt at peace?"

"Between us?" he said. "I hope so. You're angry that I severed communications with Victor and Imala. But you have to understand—"

She cut him off. "I know why you made the decision you did, Lem. You don't have to justify your actions to me. You tried to stop your father. He had his reasons for moving forward. My issue is that you made that decision without consulting me or anyone else on the team."

"You would have objected," Lem said. "And if you had, I couldn't have stopped you from making a transmission. The only way to ensure that no transmission was sent was to keep you in the dark and pull the plug myself. I did this for their sake, Benyawe. As a kindness, a mercy."

She looked sad. "One day, Lem, you're going to wake up and realize how arrogant you are and how lonely your world is as a result."

He raised an eyebrow. "So much for passing the peace pipe. How am I being arrogant here? Please, I'd be fascinated to hear."

"You assume you're the only person intelligent enough to make a rational decision."

"That's not true. I ask for your counsel all the time."

"No, you ask that I advise you on how to achieve the decision *you've* already made. You don't ask what we should be doing in the first place. And what's ironic is that your father has this same trait and you find it maddening."

"Is this what this is about, Benyawe? You feeling slighted? You not having enough authority?"

She laughed. "Is that what you think? That I want *authority*?" She practically spit the word out. "I would have told Victor and Imala that drones were coming, yes. But I also would have done everything in my power to save their lives."

"There was no way to save them."

"This is my point. *You* decided it was hopeless. And if *you* couldn't think of a solution, then there must not be one."

"Are you saying you had a solution?"

"As impossible as that might seem to you, yes. I would

have told them both to get as far inside the Formic ship as possible."

"Inside the target? The thing the drones were sent to destroy? That would've been your plan?"

"Yes. And if they had followed it they might have survived. We didn't know the strength of the hull. There was a good chance it could withstand the glasers. Which it did. So instead of relaying lifesaving instruction to the people under our care, the people we were responsible for, we did nothing." She stood. "What saddens me most is not that they died, Lem. It's that they died thinking we abandoned them, thinking we betrayed them. That's not a kindness. Or a mercy. That's anything but." She walked out.

He wanted to throw something. Nothing he did could please this woman. She was worse than Father.

Or was he angry because he knew she was right? He hadn't thought to have them hide inside the ship. He *wouldn't* have thought of that. It seemed absurd. And yet in hindsight it would have worked, maybe. It might have saved them.

He couldn't stay here. He had nothing to do but sit in his office and brood while everyone out in the warehouse chatted and twittered about what a monster he was. Thanks, Benyawe. Just as I feel a jolt of optimism, just as I'm rising out of the funk Ramdakan put me in, you have to throw the proffered olive branch back in my face.

He left his office, left the warehouse, not looking anyone in the eye. He climbed into his skimmer without knowing where he was going. The AI told him he had a message from Despoina. It started playing before Lem could object.

"It's me," she said, her voice just above a whisper. "Your father had a conference call today with several delegates from the European Union. Thought you might want to know. Also, I'm making lemon chicken tonight. Tell me what time you're coming."

Great, he thought. Now she wasn't even inviting him. He was expected to come over. And was she calling him from the office? Didn't she realize that all of those holo records were likely recorded?

He erased the message, flew back to his apartment, and threw his jacket to the floor. Let the cleaning crew pick it up. He went to the dispenser in the kitchen and poured himself a drink.

Father, Benyawe, Ramdakan, Des. To hell with them.

He downed the drink and replayed in his mind his conversation with Ramdakan. You're arrogant, Lem. You're too handsome, Lem. You're not your father, Lem. If you only had a different last name, Lem.

A child of privilege, they say. Ha. A child of a curse, is more like it.

Lem turned around, glass in hand, and stopped cold. The gun was an inch from his face.

"Welcome home," said Victor. "We've been waiting."

CHAPTER 11

Options

Victor got no pleasure from the look of surprise and shock on Lem's face. If anything, Victor felt only shame. *Mother would never approve of something like this*, he thought. *Father neither. Waving a gun in someone's face, breaking into his home, frightening him, threatening him. This wasn't the family way. You're better than this, Vico*, he could hear Mother say. *We* taught *you better than this. The Lord said to turn the other cheek.*

Yes, well, both my cheeks have been slapped so many times, Victor thought, *they're red and tender and ready to do a little slapping of their own.*

Yet even as he clung to that thought and *wanted* to seem menacing, the tightness in Victor's face relaxed and the gun lowered to his side.

"Go sit on the sofa," Victor said, gesturing back to the living room with the gun. "And if you so much as twitch in a way that I don't like, I will shoot you in the kneecap." He sounded tired and not altogether threatening, but Lem did as he was told.

Imala was sitting by the hearth with her back against the stone chimney, arms folded across her chest. It had been her idea to confront Lem before they uploaded the vid onto the nets. She and Victor had read the news reports as soon as they were within range of Luna: Ukko Jukes had fired the drones, not Lem. The company's drone fleet was destroyed, and the market was in a panic. "Just because the press doesn't mention Lem doesn't mean he's innocent," Victor had said. "His father could be taking the fall to protect him." But even as Victor said it, he knew it probably wasn't true.

"There are still unanswered questions," Imala had said. "Until we get those answers, we should give Lem and Benyawe the benefit of the doubt."

Victor hadn't liked it. He had argued the matter repeatedly as they had returned to Luna, but Imala had persisted.

Lem sat on the couch. "I see you both raided my closet."

"We needed to shower and change," said Victor. "And since you have more clothes in your closet than my entire family did on El Cavador, we didn't think you'd miss two outfits."

"Be my guest," said Lem. "Take ten. Although I'm not exactly your size."

It was true. Lem was much taller than both of them, and Victor and Imala had rolled up the sleeves and pant legs.

"Let me bring someone up here to get you clothes that fit," said Lem.

Victor sneered. "Do you take us for idiots? You're not calling anyone. Take off your wrist pad and throw it to me. If you touch the screen at all, I'll shoot you in the kneecap."

"You're determined to shoot my kneecaps," said Lem, unfastening his wrist pad and tossing it over.

Victor caught it easily in the lesser gravity. "The kneecaps are where I would start. Then I move my way up."

"Can we dial back the testosterone please?" said Imala. "We came here for answers, Lem. If we like them, Victor doesn't put holes in your legs. If we don't like them, I make no promises."

"I didn't launch the drones," said Lem. "That was my father's doing. If you want to be angry at someone, go shove a gun in *his* face. I tried to stop him, he wouldn't listen."

"Prove it," said Victor. "I find it hard to believe you weren't working with dear old Dad on this one."

Lem scoffed. "You and *your* father might have been all chummy chum, Victor, but my dear old dad and I don't particularly see eye to eye on much of anything. He can't stand to be in the same room with me."

"Then he and I have more in common than I thought," said Victor.

"Ask Benyawe if you don't believe me," said Lem. "I fought to protect you. Do you honestly think I would go to the trouble of getting you the equipment and helping you reach the ship just to send drones after you? Do you think I would place more value on silencing you than on killing the Formics?"

"Maybe you were killing two birds with one stone," said Victor.

"Wow," said Lem. "Just wow. You know, I had heard of cases of severe paranoia, but I've never actually seen one in person. Fascinating."

"You forget I'm holding a gun," said Victor.

"Who cut off our communication?" said Imala.

Lem hesitated before answering. "I did. And I had very good reasons, though I doubt you'll agree with me."

Lem explained them. He was right. They didn't agree.

"Can I shoot him in the kneecaps now?" Victor asked.

"You take the right kneecap, I'll take the left," said Imala.

Lem held his hands up. "I did everything I could to

save you. You may not agree with my decisions, but I did what I thought was right for you. We can still help each other in this. I want to stop the Formics as much as you do. I'm taking steps independent of my father to further protect Earth. We're setting up a shield of ships to stop any additional reinforcements. Benyawe and her team have developed a weapon to help in this effort. I can take you to the warehouse and show it to you. I want the team to see you anyway. Maybe they'll stop hating me once they know you're alive."

"Why would they hate you?" asked Victor. "Other than the obvious reasons of you being a lying snake and a selfish slug, I mean."

"Cutting your communication was my decision alone. Benyawe and the other engineers had nothing to do with it. They all despise me because of it."

Victor gave a face of mock surprise. "Someone despises you? I can't imagine why."

"You've asked your questions," said Lem. "Now I ask mine."

"Why should we tell you anything?" said Victor.

"Because I'm your benefactor. Because I made your expedition possible. And since the Formic ship is still hovering in space, you obviously failed to disable it. I want to know why, what happened, and what the next steps are. I know you were inside the ship, Victor. What did you see?"

Victor looked to Imala as if to ask how they should proceed.

"Victor took several hours of vids," said Imala. "He explored much of the interior of the ship and he has an idea on how to disable it. How to *really* disable it this time."

"Our first attempt didn't work because of the drone attack," said Victor. "I lost the explosive before I could plant it. But I doubt the explosive would have been sufficient anyway. We need to kill every Formic aboard and *then* seize the ship for ourselves."

"Wonderful," said Lem. "I agree. How do we do that?"

"There is no *we* here," said Victor. "We go our way and you go yours. Taking down the ship is our business now. Protecting Earth can be yours."

"You'll need resources," said Lem. "People, equipment. No one will give you the freedom that I will."

"We've heard this sales pitch before," said Victor. "And we nearly died because we listened to it. Do you honestly think either of us would ever work with you again?"

"Where will you go?" said Lem. "The military? They will cut you out of the equation. They'll take your vids and they'll brush you aside. In their minds, you're nobodies. You don't know infiltration, you don't know demolition, you're not soldiers, you're not qualified to even think about this kind of thing, much less execute an op. You're an auditor and a free miner with criminal records. Period. They'll commend you for your bravery and intel, then they'll show you the door. That is, assuming they don't call the police on you. Then they'll do their own thing based on what they see in the vids. Their own plan, their own approach. And guess what? It will fail. Why? Because they're the military, led by careerist generals who are more interested in elevating themselves and preserving their dynasties than in taking risks and breaking convention."

"There are good people in the military," said Imala.

"Of course there are," said Lem. "Ninety-nine percent of soldiers and officers are the salt of the Earth, heroes in every sense. I salute them. Too bad those ninety-nine percent won't be the ones making the decisions about your intel. You want evidence? Look at every military op that has been conducted since this war began. Fail, fail, fail. All because of incompetent leadership."

"And you think your leadership is better?" asked Victor.

"I'm not volunteering to lead anything," said Lem. "This would be your op. You pick the staff, you pick the equipment. You manage it. I simply supply the resources."

"Then you pull the plug when it's not going your way," said Victor.

"Wrong," said Lem. "I would give all oversight to Benyawe. I trust her judgment now more than my own. I learned that the hard way."

"There are other avenues besides you and the military," said Victor. "We could go public with this. We could release the vid on to the nets."

Lem laughed. "What would that accomplish? Giving the world a glimpse inside the ship doesn't cause it to suddenly explode. You still have to strike it. You still need a team to conduct an op."

"We would get a team," said Imala. "People would rally behind this. People with skills and talents and ideas. They'd volunteer."

"Yes, and in practical terms what you're describing is a logistical nightmare," said Lem. "How do you manage the deluge of volunteers from all over the world? How do you manage their ideas? Their resources? How do you determine if you even *want* their help? They could be nutcases. Or worse. Most of them won't have any of the skills you need or be qualified to help. Who's going to tell them that? You?"

"There are ways to filter people and find who we need," said Imala.

"True," said Lem. "But who's going to set up those

systems? You? Do you even know how to do that? That takes time and man hours. And anyway you're not looking for individuals. You're looking for a team. Soldiers. Experienced professionals. Men and women with very specific combat expertise. How do you form a cohesive team when you have people coming from different cultures, languages, opinions? Many of these people will be enemies. You can't just throw them together and hope for the best. Assuming you even get them to be cooperative, they would need time to train as a team. And who's going to command them? Who makes that call? You two? It's not an easy choice to make. When soldiers don't have a preexisting command structure, they're at each other's throats in minutes."

"You make it sound like humans have never worked together before," said Imala.

"Have you forgotten what happened the last time you uploaded something onto the nets?" said Lem. "You warned the world of an invasion, and did they come together, did they unite under a flag, did they make rational decisions and value the opinions of others and work as one? No. They yelled at each other and floundered around like imbeciles and left us with no global defense. They practically rolled out the red carpet for the Formics. And when the Formics blew them to hell, did Earth get its act together? Did we suddenly wake up and say, Gee we should probably unite on this, folks. No, we did a little more floundering and a little more imbecilic posturing, and now we have no fleet in space to protect us and a fractured global leadership."

Victor and Imala glanced at each other and said nothing.

"And why does Earth fail to learn its lesson?" Lem said. "Why do we persist in this divided idiocy? Because the world is full of prideful bastards, that's why.

Everyone believes they're smarter than everyone else, more capable than everyone else, more justified than everyone else. Humility went extinct a long time ago."

"Sounds like you're describing yourself," said Imala.

"You're right," said Lem. "That's exactly what I'm describing. And the world is more like me than either of you. Earth isn't a free-miner family, Victor. It might have been all harmony and roses on your ship, but it's the opposite on Earth."

"We had our disagreements," said Victor.

"Of course you did," said Lem. "Every family does. But when it was decision time, the family moved forward as one. Even if half or more disagreed with the direction, everyone went along with the plan to maintain the integrity of the group. You won't have that luxury with Earth. Nobody cares about the group."

"You don't think much of people, do you?" said Imala.

"I managed companies before I came to Juke," said Lem. "I know how people think. The kind of global come-together you're talking about is a pipe dream. It would fall on its face in a week. It's not sustainable, particularly without any system of government. The minute volunteers disagree with your approach, they'll either quit or splinter off. They have no incentive to stick with you. Then everyone will try to do their own thing, and we'll accomplish nothing. We'll be right back where we started. Nowhere."

"So it's your way or failure," said Victor. "Is that what you're saying?"

"I am offering you what no one else will," said Lem. "Go public with this, and I can guarantee you you'll be cut out of it, faster even than the military will do. The military will consult with you at least, initially anyway, because they'll recognize the significance of what you've accomplished. Not the public. And certainly not your financiers. They'll protect their investment. They'll use their own people or people they consider more qualified than you. You'll be kicked aside. No one on Earth will feel confident putting the planet's future or their money into the hands of wanted criminals, both under the age of twenty-five. Sorry. That's a fact."

"But *you* will," said Victor. "But *you* we can trust. Excuse me if I seem a little skeptical."

"You have every right to be," said Lem. "But if what I've said hasn't convinced you, this will: If you go public with this and ask for Earth's help, all of your equipment and people would need to be launched into orbit. Do you have any idea how much time that would require to prep and execute, how much money that would take? By the time you've gathered funding and a team and organized a launch, Earth could be a charcoal briquette. I'm already out here. I'm a hop away from the Formic ship. My resources—which are vast—are here, in space. I am ready to move right now."

"Engineers and equipment aren't enough," said Victor. "We need soldiers as well. You said so yourself. Those you don't have."

"True," said Lem. "But I know how to get them."

"So you say," said Victor. "Why should we believe you?"

"You shouldn't believe me. I've given you every reason not to believe me. But that doesn't change the fact that I am the best chance you've got. You may despise me, but I can help you like no one else can. I will give you freedom to operate like no one else can. I would equip you like no one else can."

"Yes, and then you'd cut us loose the moment we're no longer convenient," said Victor.

"No. That won't happen."

"It did before," said Victor.

"I thought I was doing you a favor. You may not

believe that, but it's true. And up until that moment I had done everything in my power to stop the drones. I have witnesses who can testify to that fact."

"You can pay people to say anything, Lem. You certainly have the money for it. Testimony means nothing."

Lem laughed and tossed up his hands. "Fine. You win, Victor. I'm Mr. Evil. I'm Beelzebub himself. The Lord of Darkness. That's me. Is that what you want me to say? Is that why you broke into my apartment? To gloat?"

Victor said nothing.

"Why are we even having this conversation?" said Lem. "Nothing I say is going to convince you otherwise. You want to walk out of here and put everything you've learned into the hands of incompetent idiots? Be my guest. You want to condemn the human race to extinction, by all means, don't let me stop you. But if you want to end this and send these bugs back to whatever rock they crawled out of, let me help you. I care about people, Victor. You can scoff and roll your eyes all day if you'd like, but it's true. If it wasn't, I wouldn't have gone to all the trouble I did to find your mother."

The words were like a blow to Victor's chest. He suddenly felt unsteady on his feet.

"She's alive, Victor. And if you put down that gun, I can show you exactly where she is."

CHAPTER 12

Rena

On a salvage ship in the outer rim of the Asteroid Belt, Rena Delgado sat alone at the helm, typing a report at a terminal. It was three hours into sleep shift, and the lights in the helm were dark save for the glow of the screen and the small spotlight above her. The report was a detailed description of all the parts the ship had recovered in its most recent salvage jobs. Navigational equipment, heating systems, wiring, furniture, everything they had stripped from the derelict ships they had come upon. Most of the descriptions were simple and brief. Year, make, model, condition, and any noticeable defects that would influence its price.

But every so often, Rena and her crew would strip something really complex. A drive system, for example. Or an oxygen generator. Something that had a lot of moving parts and a potentially large resale value. These had to be described in great detail, with an account given of all its constituent parts and functions.

And since no one knew ship parts as well as Rena, and since no one could inspect them so thoroughly or determine their value so accurately, the chore of writing the salvage report naturally fell to her.

Rena didn't mind the work. The writing was tedious, yes, but it kept her mind busy.

Plus, whenever she would begin to describe a new part they had found, a memory of Segundo would spark in her mind. He had repaired and replaced so many parts on El Cavador that he had practically rebuilt the ship from the inside out.

Rena remembered every repair. How could she not? Segundo would come back to their room at the end of each work shift and detail everything that had happened to him. People he had talked to. Gossip he had heard. Repairs he had made. It had become a ritual between them. And Rena would listen as she worked, preparing the navigational maps for the next work shift. Then, when Segundo had finished, she would do the same, re-counting everything of interest that had happened at the helm.

She had thought nothing of those moments at the time. They were so normal, so wholly unremarkable. And yet Rena would give anything to experience any one of them again.

But no, it did her mind no good to wish for what she could not have.

She pushed the memories aside and looked down at her handwritten notes. She was only three-quarters of the way through the report, she realized. It would be hours before she finished.

She debated going to bed, but if she did, she wouldn't be able to continue until the following evening. The crew would need this terminal throughout the day. There was another terminal in the cargo hold where the survivors from El Cavador stayed, but Rena knew she wouldn't get anything done there. Trying to concentrate among eighteen women and thirty-seven children would be an exercise in futility. No one ever gave her a moment's peace. If there was any issue whatsoever, they all felt the need to bring it to her attention.

"The toilet in the restroom is clogged again, Rena."

"The baby has a rash on its legs, Rena."

"The twins need more blankets, Rena."

"There's a pipe dripping in the corner, Rena, and the droplets are floating everywhere."

Look at this, Rena. Solve this, Rena. Listen to me complain again, Rena.

Even some of the children came to her now, unloading their problems to her instead of going directly to their mothers.

"Felipe pushed me and I scraped my elbow."

"Marcella called me poop head, Rena. That's a bad word."

"Jose Luis took my crackers, Rena, and he won't give them back."

Rena would kindly direct them to their mothers, but this did little to deter them. They still came flying back later with some other complaint—crying sometimes, angry, frightened. There had even been one moment when Rena had overheard one of the mothers, Alicia, say to her youngest child Bixxi, "You better stop crying right now, young lady, or I am going to go get Rena."

What was *that* supposed to mean, Rena had wondered. Was she the enforcer of discipline now, the designated spanker?

No, she had realized. She had become the father. They had lost all of their men to the Formics, and now, without any of the women and children consciously making the decision, they had chosen Rena to fill that void.

There were times when she wanted to scream at them all. I am not in charge. Do not come to me with your problems. Solve them yourselves or go to the captain. I don't really care.

But that wasn't true exactly. She did care. The children, wild and obnoxious as they were, were just children after all—children who had each suffered a great loss. It broke Rena's heart to think of it. She had known each of their fathers; she had seen them interact with each and every child—playing together, laughing together, flying around the cargo bay together.

They were moments that could never be repeated. And for the younger children, they were moments that would soon be forgotten. It struck Rena as the greatest injustice of the universe. These little minds, who so desperately needed to remember their fathers, would almost certainly forget them with time.

She finished the report three hours later and sent it immediately via laserline to the nearest trade station on the asteroid Themis.

In the past few weeks, the interference had slowly dissipated, and communication across distances was gradually coming back online. Themis wasn't that far away, and Rena was confident the salvage traders there would spark to something on her list.

Rena watched the screen, waiting for the alert that would tell her the transmission had been received. She must have fallen asleep at some point, because the next thing she knew the screen chimed, and she jerked awake.

There was a message from Themis.

Transmission received. Have FWDed to salvage
     buyers.
Note: News feeds back online. Info on war.
Subscriptions are 100 C a week.

The words of the second line stopped Rena cold. There was a massive laserline receiver on Themis, and apparently they were getting feeds relayed to them from Earth again.

She wrote back immediately.

Can you do a search in the news feeds? I am looking for information on my son. Victor Delgado. He
flew from the K Belt to Luna in a quickship to warn
Earth of approaching Formics. Ship of origin was
El Cavador. Any information is appreciated.

It was an hour before she received a reply.

100 credits to search the feeds.

She almost smacked the screen. They wanted to charge
her to do a simple search? A task that would take them
only a few minutes? A child could do it. She could get a
subscription for a week and do the search herself for
that price. Didn't they read her message? Victor had
gone to warn Earth. Didn't that mean anything to them?

No, of course it didn't. They were on Themis. A rock
of money-grubbers, if ever there was one.

She pushed herself away from the terminal and flew
immediately to Arjuna's cabin.

It was several hours before the end of sleep shift, but
she knocked on the door anyway. When no one answered, she knocked again. She heard movement inside,
and a moment later the door opened. Sabad, one of
Arjuna's wives, squinted at the light. Rena sighed inside. Of Arjuna's three wives, Sabad was the only one
with whom Rena did not get along. The girl was young,
barely over twenty, and she had not yet borne Arjuna
any children.

Before Rena and the others from El Cavador had
come aboard, Arjuna's three wives had each enjoyed
their own room. But everyone had to sleep somewhere,
and sacrifices had been made when the ship's crew had
doubled in size. Now all of Arjuna's wives shared the

same room, and Sabad seemed to hold Rena personally responsible for the inconvenience.

"Do you have any idea what time it is?" Sabad said, hovering in the door frame, giving Rena a look that would wilt flowers.

"I need to speak to Arjuna," said Rena.

"It can wait until morning, whatever it is."

"No. It can't. We just received a laserline from Themis. They're getting news feeds from Earth again."

"Good for them. You can tell my husband in the morning."

He's not just *your* husband, Rena wanted to say. He's Ubax's husband and Kaaha's husband, too, two of the other Somali women on board. You should use the plural possessive pronoun, Sabad, and say "our."

But Rena was not one to be petty—not out loud at least—so she simply said, "I apologize for the interruption, Sabad, but I think Arjuna would want to know this immediately."

"Do you claim to know the mind of my husband better than I do?"

"Of course not."

"Then go back to your little hive of spoiled children and leave us alone."

She began to close the door, but Rena stopped it with her hand. Normally Rena was mild-mannered and slow to rile, but Sabad was pushing the wrong buttons. The children from El Cavador were anything but spoiled. Those who were old enough to work did more on the ship in an hour than Sabad did in a day. Rena was just about to say as much when Arjuna appeared in the doorway. He was shirtless, and his black skin was almost invisible in the darkness. "What is it, Rena?" His voice was deep and froggy from sleep.

She told him about the laserline from Themis.

Arjuna considered a moment, then pulled himself out

into the corridor and turned back to Sabad. "Go back to bed, Sabad. I will be there in a moment."

Sabad folded her arms. "Whatever you have to say to her, I can hear it, too."

"I said go back to bed, woman."

There was a bite in his tone, and Sabad relented. She gave Rena a final withering look then slammed the door in her face.

"She doesn't like me very much," said Rena.

"No. She doesn't. She thinks you're competition."

"Competition for what?"

"My affection."

Rena felt her cheeks flush.

Arjuna laughed softly. "Do not look embarrassed, Lady of El Cavador. I am not proposing marriage. I am telling you how a young woman's mind works. She has given me no children. She worries I will tire of her and turn to another."

"You *do* turn to another. Frequently. You have two other wives. I never know who I'm going to find in your room when I knock."

Arjuna shrugged. "It is hard to keep a schedule. I let the wives decide. There are many nights when none of them come to me. I can't say I blame them. It was much easier before you came. Each of the wives had her own room. I went to them. Now they share a room. The gods only know what they talk about."

Rena felt embarrassed. She had only thought of the inconvenience she and the family had been to the wives. She hadn't given much consideration to what it might mean to Arjuna. "I'm sorry," she said. "I didn't mean for us to cause marital strife."

Arjuna brushed the words away. "You have turned this ship into a moneymaker. That's what matters. This could be our biggest haul yet. All because of you."

It was true. A week ago they had come upon a derelict

Juke vessel that appeared to be picked clean by vultures—which were aggressive salvagers who were little more than pirates. Arjuna was ready to dismiss the ship, but Rena had encouraged him to investigate it nonetheless. "Vultures often ignore the smaller parts in their rush to gut the ship," Rena had said. "Half the time they don't know what they're looking for. It won't hurt to look a little closer."

It hadn't hurt. They had found the drive system mostly intact, and the oxygen generator had needed only minor repairs. Those two parts alone should earn them more than all of their other salvages combined.

"We can't afford a subscription," said Arjuna. "One hundred credits a week is ridiculous. No salvage ship can afford that. We barely make enough to eat."

"They don't expect us to pay a hundred a week. They expect us to talk down the price."

"To how much?"

"Half that. Maybe as low as forty."

"Which we still can't afford. And Earth is a long way away. What good would the news do us here?"

"It's Earth," said Rena. "It's our home."

"Is it? When was the last time you were on Earth? Twenty years ago?"

"Unless the Formics are defeated, we are cut off, Arjuna. No supply lines will get through. We will die out here."

"I am aware of this. But our tracking the news feeds won't prevent that from happening. We are powerless to help, Rena. The Formics will win or lose regardless of us." He crossed his arms and studied her a moment. "Are you sure this is not about Victor? I know you want closure, Rena. I understand that."

"Not closure. That suggests he didn't make it to Luna. I'm certain he did."

"You say that, but I see the doubt in your eyes." He

sighed softly. "He tried to cross the system in a quick-ship, Rena. This is impossible. There is no chance your son is still alive."

"Don't talk to me about chances. You do not know my son."

He held up his hands. "I have offended you. That was not my intent."

Rena ran a hand through her hair, calming herself. "This is not just about Victor. There are other advantages here. With a subscription we would have a continuous link to Themis's receiver. We'd be in the network. We'd get news from distant places in the Belt. We could better track vultures."

"These are all wonderful benefits, Rena. But we can't afford it. We are a salvage ship."

"What if we weren't?"

Her question confused him. "What are you saying?"

"What if we made this a mining ship?"

He laughed. "The Gagak is no mining ship. We're barely a salvage ship."

"What difference does that make? El Cavador was in no better condition when we started."

His smile faded. "You're serious about this."

"If we're mining rock, we'll make far more money. The thought hadn't occurred to me until now, but it makes complete sense. We can help each other. The women and I want our own ship. The faster we bring in revenue, the faster we can make that possible."

"Consider what you're saying, Rena. We don't have the equipment. We would need smelters, diggers, quick-ships. We don't have any of that."

"So we get it. Piece by piece. We're salvagers. We find what we need, or we trade for it. We've got some of that stuff in our haul right now. Not much, but enough to get started."

He shook his head. "We don't have a credit rating,

Rena. Even if we could dig, Luna would never take anything we send them."

"*You* don't have a credit rating, but El Cavador does. I propose a partnership. Your ship and your crew; plus my crew, our expertise, and our credit rating. We split the profits. It's not as far-fetched as it sounds."

He looked uncomfortable. "No. I am sorry. A partnership is out of the question."

"You can't do this without us, Arjuna. We know the business. We know the tech. We have the credentials. It's only fair that you make us full partners."

"I agree. That is only fair. But I cannot partner with you, Rena. It's not possible."

"Why not?"

He hesitated. "Because . . . you are women."

His words surprised her so much that it took a moment for their full meaning to sink in. Of course, she thought. He was Somali, a patriarchal society. He would lose face with his crew if he partnered with women. They would think him weak, soft, unmanly. He would lose command, maybe even his wives. A stronger man would step in and claim them, and Rena and the others would be pushed aside.

"You must understand," he said. "It is nothing against you personally. This is simply who we are. You have your culture, and we have ours. I cannot ignore that for convenience."

"No, you can't. The partnership wouldn't last. We would be ostracized. And so would you."

"There is one possible solution," he said, "but I do not think you will like it."

She looked at him and waited.

"What you are proposing is a merger of tribes, Rena. This happens all the time in my country. It is done through a marriage."

She blinked. "Marriage?"

"If I marry all nineteen of you, then you would be one with our tribe. My crew would agree to a business partnership. You would not be equal in station to my current wives, however. They are of my tribe by birth. You are not. You would be considered my concubines."

Rena smiled, and it took everything she possessed not to start laughing. "Arjuna, I am flattered that you would so willingly take us on as your concubines, but we cannot marry you."

"Then this conversation is at a close. I cannot enter a partnership with women who are not my wives. There would be mutiny."

Rena considered this then said, "Why don't we say that our husbands are away? We have never recovered their bodies. And in our tribe, women can speak for the family in their husbands' absence. Ours would be a merger of tribes that recognizes our husbands in absentia."

He shook his head. "My crew knows that your husbands have died, Rena. You have discussed their deaths with some of them. It doesn't matter that we have not seen their bodies. We have seen your grieving faces, and that is worse."

"What about the boys? Franco is twelve. That's Bella's son. He is the oldest male. We could say he is the leader of our tribe and this merger is his wish."

Arjuna shook his head. "He is not a man grown. He cannot speak for the tribe."

"Then what about Victor? My son. He *is* a man grown. If I can prove that he's alive, he would be the head of our tribe, would he not? He would speak for us. He could approve this merger."

Arjuna frowned. "Why do I feel like I've just been painted into a corner? Do you lay all of your snares so delicately, Lady of El Cavador?"

"You can't keep calling me that," said Rena. "I'm not the only lady from that ship."

"No, but you are the most regal of your tribe. The most worthy of that title."

"I didn't lay a snare. It just worked out that way."

"That's what's every fox would say."

She smiled. "In my tribe, to call a woman a fox is to call her beautiful."

"You are certainly that, Lady, but in my tribe a fox has a different meaning altogether."

"So are we in agreement?"

He gestured toward the helm. "Come. Let us see if the chief of your tribe still lives."

CHAPTER 13

India

Mazer was running on a treadmill in a government safe house in New Delhi when the call finally came. He looked at his beeping wrist pad, saw that it was Wit, and stepped off the treadmill to answer it.

"Where are you?" asked Wit.

"Exercise room. Trying to keep from dying of boredom. Please tell me we can leave this building and be useful again."

It was their tenth day in India. After a rocky entrance into the country—during which the Indian Air Force had threatened to shoot them down and fired a volley of warning shots—Wit had gotten on the radio and secured them a military escort to New Delhi. A decontamination crew had met them at the airport, and once Mazer, Wit, and Shenzu were clear of their biosuits, the military had taken them directly to the safe house, where they had remained under house arrest without any contact with the outside world.

"Shower and meet me and Shenzu in the lobby in ten minutes," said Wit. "A car will take us to Gadhavi's labs. He believes he has the answer."

The goo guns they had brought from China had been

confiscated the moment Mazer had landed in New Delhi. Dr. Gadhavi and his team had supposedly been hard at work on a counteragent ever since.

Mazer jogged back to his room and hit the shower. He met Wit and Shenzu in the lobby a few minutes later. A car and two junior officers of the Indian army were waiting outside. The officers sat in the front and drove them north of the city to a large government compound surrounded by military checkpoints. The driver weaved through the campus until he parked at the curb of a white office building. A decorated officer of the Indian military in his mid-fifties met them at the curb. He smiled wide when Wit stepped from the vehicle. The two men embraced and then Wit turned to the others.

"Captain Rackham, Captain Shenzu, I present a dear friend of mine, Major Khudabadi Ketkar of the Indian Para Commandos. His men trained with the MOPs before the invasion."

Ketkar smiled good-naturedly and shook everyone's hands. "What Captain O'Toole means is that his MOPs ran circles around our PCs. Like a cat playing with a blind, three-legged mouse. He even had the gall to kill me once during a mock battle. In my own office. I'm still assembling the shattered pieces of my pride." He laughed, winked at Wit, then gestured to the main entrance. "But come. They are waiting for us."

He led them inside to a security checkpoint, where a woman gave them each a visitor's badge. A large brass seal hung on the wall behind her. It featured a Bengal tiger standing on an outcropping of rock above a cluster of lotus flowers. It bore the words: NATIONAL BIO-DEFENSE AGENCY. There was more written at the bottom in Devanagari script, but Mazer had no idea what it said.

Ketkar escorted them deeper into the building, passing through a wide atrium. There was an air of opulence to the place—not flagrantly so, but it was certainly not the bland utilitarian décor Mazer had come to expect from government agencies. Marble floors. Palm trees. A fountain. It felt more like a luxurious hotel. They went through another door and then they were outside again, this time in a beautifully landscaped plaza in the center of the building. Benches, flowers, pathways, small fruit trees. Ketkar stopped and faced them. "Before we go down, I wanted to take a moment to apologize on behalf of my government for keeping you confined to the safe house since your arrival. I've been ordered to tell you that we did so solely for your own protection, but you're all too smart to believe that. This is a delicate political situation, gentlemen, as you can imagine, and my superiors are taking extreme precautions. No one was quite certain what to do with you, so they kept you locked down while they argued the matter."

"What's to argue?" asked Shenzu. "We came here for help."

"Yes, but you didn't come here on behalf of the Chinese government. This was not a sanctioned mission. You came here as three rogue soldiers. That made a few members of our National Security Council uneasy. Our relations with China are tense as it is. Many feared how China would respond if we helped you."

"If the counteragent works," said Shenzu, "China will take it gladly."

"Yes," said Ketkar, "but we're not convinced that giving the counteragent to the Chinese military is the best course of action."

Shenzu couldn't hide his surprise. "What are you saying? You will let China burn? You will stand by while millions more die."

"You misunderstand me, Captain. India wants to help. And will help. But handing over the counteragent to your military will not necessarily produce the best results. Your army is exhausted and spread too thin. You've lost your best field commanders, and you have pockets of survivors regrouping into units without any clear command structure. You're fragmented and disorganized, Captain. We're not certain China can get the job done."

"You don't mince words," said Shenzu.

"This is war, Captain, not a dinner party. India cannot allow the Formics to reach our borders. We must do everything in our power to stop them now, in China. Dropping off barrels of the counteragent at the Chinese border won't cut it."

"What are you proposing?" asked Wit. "Troops?"

"Essentially," said Ketkar. "The president wants to broker a deal with the Chinese in which we offer the counteragent if they agree to allow Indian PCs into China to help administer it. That's why I'm involved in all of this."

"The PCs are certainly capable," said Wit.

"Yes, but the Chinese have been vehemently resistant to outside troops," said Mazer. "Especially from India and Russia. It's not like India is an ally. Are you sure China will agree to this?"

"They don't have a choice," said Ketkar. "They're lost without the counteragent. The entire southeast coast has fallen, from Hong Kong to Shanghai. Their economy is in ashes."

"Even so," said Mazer. "What if China refuses? India can't hold the counteragent hostage. China would go public. They'd say you have the solution but aren't sharing it. They'd say you were letting their people die. They'd paint you as heartless bastards. The world would despise you overnight. China would then put so much international pressure on you, you would be forced to give it to them anyway."

"It won't come to that," said Ketkar. "Captain Shenzu here will see to it that China approves."

Shenzu laughed. "Whoever told you I have a position of influence is sadly misinformed, Major. I am no one. A lowly captain. Nothing I say to the CMC or Politburo holds any weight whatsoever. I doubt I could even get a message through the people who filter their communications."

"You underestimate yourself," said Ketkar. "And it's not the CMC or Politburo you'd be addressing. It's the people of China and the rest of the world."

"What did you have in mind?" asked Mazer. "A press conference?"

"A demonstration of the counteragent," said Ketkar. "We'd have every major news outlet covering it live via holo. Shenzu and Dr. Gadhavi will be the stars of the show. Gadhavi conducts the demonstration. He would make it theatrical."

"And what am I to do?" said Shenzu. "Clap and look Chinese? If so, we're in luck. I excel at both."

"Your part's more involved than that," said Ketkar. "Following the demonstration you would then make a few heartfelt comments to the press."

"Again," said Shenzu. "I'm nobody. Why would the press care what I have to say?"

"Because you are the liaison officer of the great General Sima, the brilliant Chinese commander who destroyed a Formic lander. You will say that Sima ordered you to bring a sample of the gas to Dr. Gadhavi in the event that something happened to the Chinese science team."

"You want me to lie on camera?"

"General Sima is an international hero," said Ketkar. "And now that he's deceased, many in China see him as a martyr. A symbol. Sending you here is precisely the type of move a brilliant commander like him would make."

"So Sima gets credit for yet another victory he had nothing to do with," said Shenzu.

"Are we certain Sima is dead?" said Mazer. "I don't mean to be indelicate, but it would be embarrassing if we did this only to have Sima appear on the nets debunking the whole operation."

"He's dead," said Ketkar. "His body was recovered in Lianzhou five days ago. There was such admiration for the man, the Chinese made a concerted effort to find him and handle his remains respectfully."

Shenzu said, "So I speak to the press and tell a flagrant lie about my former commanding officer. What good will that do?"

"You'll say more than that," said Ketkar. "You'll praise General Sima for his foresight, yes. But you will also call the development of the counteragent a shining example of two nations unifying under a single cause to defeat a common enemy. The whole world should emulate this pattern. We must all stand united."

"You're making this a political speech," said Shenzu. "I am not a politician. Nor can I speak on behalf of my government."

"You won't be speaking on their behalf," said Ketkar. "You'll be speaking on your own behalf. As a liaison officer, as a husband, as a father to your children."

Shenzu regarded him skeptically. "What does my family have to do with this?"

"Everything," said Ketkar. "Their safety motivates everything you do, Captain. We know you better than you might think. We know, for example, that you are one of the Anonymous Twelve."

Shenzu didn't move or respond.

After an awkward silence, Mazer looked at the others and said, "Am I the only one here who doesn't know what that means?"

Ketkar said, "The Anonymous Twelve is the name the Chinese military has given to the unknown Chinese military personnel who gave you MOPs the nuke you needed to destroy the lander. They are, in that sense, traitors to their country. Captain Shenzu here was critical in orchestrating that entire effort."

Mazer turned to Shenzu. "Is that true?"

Shenzu took a deep breath before answering. "What I did, I did for China, its people, and my loved ones. Action had to be taken."

"You helped get us the nuke, and then you arrested us?" said Mazer.

"I arrested you under Sima's orders," said Shenzu. "Well, actually he had given the arrest orders to another officer, but I intervened and requested that he give them to me instead. I wanted to ensure you weren't harmed in the process."

Mazer turned to Wit. "Did you know this?"

"No," said Wit, "but I suspected."

Shenzu faced Ketkar. "So you intend to blackmail me, Major? Is that it? If I don't say what you want me to say and perform for the cameras, you will reveal my crime to my government and keep me from my family forever?"

"We don't have to blackmail you," said Ketkar. "We don't even have to ask you to do this. You will do it because you know it's the right thing to do. This is more than just two countries putting aside their differences for the greater good, Captain. This is the beginning of a new Earth, a new way of operating, one that can only lead to greater peace among all nations. This is what we should have done before the Formics arrived."

Ketkar put a hand on Shenzu's shoulder. "Now is the

time, Captain. General Sima has started a movement. You can give it life. Your words could be the first intelligent approach to this disaster that anyone has heard."

"You seem to have a very specific idea of what I should say. Is there a speech written?"

"Someone wrote one, yes. It was excellent. I told him to burn it. This has to come from you. It has to be genuine."

Shenzu was quiet a moment. "Show me the counteragent. Then we'll talk."

Ketkar smiled and beckoned them to follow. "This way."

He led them to a small structure in the center of the plaza that turned out to be a set of elevators. They climbed in, and Ketkar slid back a concealed panel and entered a code. The elevator descended.

When it stopped, they stepped out into a bright, immaculate corridor. Through the windows to their right and left, Mazer saw technicians and scientists in blue biohazard suits working with various machines, scanners, and diagnostic equipment. Ketkar kept moving, leading them deeper into the complex down a series of corridors. Finally they stepped into an observation room with a vaulted ceiling. The wall to Mazer's left was solid glass. The room beyond it was mostly empty save for a metal table to one side atop of which sat various plastic boxes and liquid containers.

A short Indian man in his late sixties was standing in the observation room at a computer terminal. The sleeves of his blue oxford shirt were rolled up past his elbows. Gloves made of reflective sequined fabric covered his hands and forearms. His face brightened when he saw them. "Captain O'Toole. We meet again."

"Dr. Gadhavi. A pleasure, as always."

Gadhavi approached, and Wit introduced Mazer and Shenzu.

Gadhavi bowed. "Welcome to India, gentlemen. I am sorry we are meeting under these circumstances. Please, won't you stand here behind this line? I'm told everyone's ready and we can begin."

It was only then that Mazer noticed the small cameras on the wall behind them. Other spectators would be watching apparently.

Gadhavi walked to the center of the room in front of the glass wall where a red circle was painted on the floor. As soon as he stepped in it, holoprojectors above him turned on and bathed him in a holofield. He put his back to the glass and faced them, directing his words at the cameras. "The Formic gas is a highly toxic, cell-wall-degrading enzyme solution. In principle, it's not unlike, say, phytopathogenic fungi here on Earth, which degrade plant biomass at an alarming rate. The difference of course is its toxicity. The Formics' gas is a thousand times worse than our nastiest fungi. It eats through lignocellulose, for example, which is often resistant to enzymatic degradation, as if it were cotton candy. And we've all seen what it can do to humans. It breaks down cell walls and initiates a proteolytic process that's not unlike what our digestive system does to a bite of steak. It short, it turns biomass into gooey pulp. That's the bad news."

He turned around and faced the glass wall.

In the holofield, his sequined gloves twinkled in the light.

He raised his arms to the side, and two long robotic arms in the other room lowered from their recessed hiding place in the ceiling. Gadhavi walked in place, turned his head slightly to the right, and the robotic arms moved along a track in the ceiling in the direction Gadhavi indicated. The arms came to a stop at the table, and Gadhavi spread his fingers apart. The ends of the robotic arms split and separated, forming matching digits.

Using the bot arms as an extension of his own, Gadhavi lifted two sealed, liter-sized jugs off the table, carried them to the center of the empty room, and set them a distance apart on the floor.

Then he turned and faced the cameras.

"Those two containers beyond the glass wall each hold six hundred milliliters of the Formic solution, or 'goo' as the soldiers call it. The protein looks like this."

A giant model of a globular protein appeared in the holofield beside him.

"As you can see, it has a very complex tertiary and quaternary structure in which the polypeptides fold around each other to essentially form a sphere. This shape is maintained by hydrogen bonds and ionic forces. Altering its shape through heat, a change in pH, or nonreversible inhibition renders the enzyme denatured, or useless. The molecular structure may be alien and unlike anything we've ever seen, but the laws of chemistry are universal. We may not have mastered interstellar flight, but we do know how to shake up a molecule. That's the good news."

He flicked his hand, and the protein disappeared. Then he turned and faced the glass wall again. He lifted his arms, maneuvered the robotic arms back to the table, and picked up a glass jar of orange liquid with a screwed top.

"This, ladies and gentlemen, is our counteragent, an enzyme inhibitor, preheated to sixty degrees Celsius. When it's fired at the goo, the heat causes some of the Formic enzymes to vibrate so violently that the delicate bonds that maintain their molecular structure are broken. The inhibitors take care of the rest, rendering the entire enzyme solution useless. But that's not even the fun part. Once the molecule changes its shape, we can do whatever we want with it, including turning it against the Formics."

Gadhavi moved his hands. Inside the other room, the robot arms came to life and unscrewed the lid from the jar. When they were finished, the bot arms set the jar back on the table and lifted a shotgun from a gun case. A sprayer mechanism with its own barrel adjacent to the shotgun barrel was mounted on the underside of the weapon. The bot arms picked up the jar of orange counteragent again and screwed it into the bottom of the sprayer.

Gadhavi said, "We have two objectives in China as far as the gas is concerned. One, clearing the air of what's already been sprayed, and two, destroying the goo guns and other caches. This weapon is designed to do both. For the gas in the air, it can spray a mist."

Inside the room, the lid popped off one of the two jugs of goo on the floor. Gas poured upward, a swirling fog of grayish green vapor.

Gadhavi got into a firing position.

In the other room, the gun unleashed a thick stream of orange mist into the cloud. When the two solutions met, the fog became a fireball that flashed bright and then snuffed out a heartbeat later, like a lit match tossed into a pan of gunpowder. The now empty jug skittered across the floor and bounced off the opposite wall.

"The other jug is like a goo tank," said Gadhavi. "We made it with a substance of similar durability. The shotgun round has an armor-piercing slug that punctures the goo tank and releases pellets of our counteragent into the goo. Since both solutions are concentrated, the reaction is even more volatile."

The robot arm cocked the shotgun, aimed, and fired. The jug took the round dead center and shot across the floor, spinning. One second passed. Then another. Nothing happened. Then the jug detonated like a bomb, and tiny fragments of shrapnel pinged against the glass.

Gadhavi turned around and faced them. "Since it's

orange, spicy, and cooks Formics, we're calling the counteragent 'Delhi Duck Sauce.' " He smiled at his own joke.

"How do we know the goo has been neutralized?" Wit asked. "You've demonstrated that you can create a violent reaction, but you haven't proven that the air is clear. How do we know there aren't lethal traces of it still in there?"

Gadhavi's smile broadened. "Captain O'Toole. You never disappoint. Always with the tough questions. But you're right. Pyrotechnics will not solve our problem if the counteragent doesn't completely neutralize the goo. I couldn't have asked for a better setup to the final portion of our demonstration."

Gadhavi faced the glass again and made a few hand gestures in the holofield. In the demonstration room, a door slid open, and a chimpanzee stepped out into the room.

"The demonstration room has not been ventilated since I released the gas," said Gadhavi. "The air has not been filtered in any manner. The test subject is breathing the same air that was exposed to highly lethal doses of the gas only moments ago."

Long handrails lowered a foot from the ceiling. The chimp jumped up and grabbed them and began swinging around the room.

"Even with increased breaths and when moving to all corners of the room, the test subject remains perfectly healthy. No melting of the skin, no cell degradation. I could release a dozen more animals or people in the room with the same result. And should you require it, I can analyze the air and prove the gas is neutralized."

For a moment, Mazer and the others were too stunned to speak.

"How quickly can you mass produce this?" asked Wit.

"The formula isn't terribly complex," said Gadhavi. "If we could commandeer a few chemical facilities with the right capabilities, we could make a few thousand barrels in a week. If China were to join in the effort, we would make four times that many."

"What about the weapons and shotgun rounds?" said Shenzu. "How long would it take to mass-produce those?"

"The assault weapon is an industrial paint sprayer bolted to a shotgun," said Gadhavi. "There's also a heating mechanism attached to the sprayer to keep the duck sauce hot. That requires a heavy battery. Our prototype is fairly crude. The gun isn't balanced well. We're not weapons designers. We only made that one for the demonstration. Same with the shotgun slugs. Mass-producing those would take time, I suspect."

"We don't have time," said Wit. "We need to mobilize soldiers now. If a team of scientists unfamiliar with weaponry can retrofit a shotgun, soldiers should be able to do so in their sleep. Who cares if the gun is balanced or not? It works. That's all that matters."

"Even if soldiers do it themselves," said Ketkar, "we still need to supply them with detailed instructions."

"We will," said Wit. "MOPs made a site on the nets for sharing combat tactics with the Chinese military: stoptheformics.net. We upload the instructions there and wherever else we think the military may be looking. In the meantime, we contact every manufacturer in the world who makes a similar paint sprayer and we kick their production lines into overdrive."

"We'll need more than foot soldiers," said Shenzu. "We'll cover more ground if we retrofit military aircrafts with crop-dusting sprayers."

"That would take time," said Mazer. "You'd have to gut the aircraft to make room for the tanks, then build and modify the sprayers for every class of aircraft. Plus you'd need to train pilots. We could mobilize faster if we enlist aerial firefighters and seasoned crop dusters. Their planes are ready to go, and they have the needed skill. I consider myself a decent pilot, but liquid falls differently than cargo or bombs. It's easy to overshoot or drop too early. I'd much rather have a crop duster at the stick."

"And fire crews," said Wit. "The chemical reaction is so volatile, we should have two to three fire crews shadowing every assault team. In fact, China should immediately begin training a quarter of its army on fire control, particularly in urban areas. If we burn cities to the ground, we haven't done the Chinese any favors."

Mazer nodded. "Strike teams will need flame-resistant suits over their biosuits. Something that can withstand intense flash fires. We'll find plenty of those in heavy manufacturing and firefighter units. Maybe we ask firehouses and the private sector all over the world to donate what suits they have."

Ketkar stepped forward. "Yes, there is much to consider. And China would be wise to involve all of you in the strategic development of the operation. But unless China agrees to troop assistance, unless we have fresh boots on the ground, we won't make a dent in the Formics. Captain Shenzu, are you willing to face the cameras?"

"I should give the speech in Chinese," said Shenzu. "If it's coming from the heart, I should speak in Chinese."

Twenty-four hours later, Major Ketkar stood at a rostrum before a crowd of three hundred reporters, humbly thanking them all for coming. They had gathered inside a vast empty hangar at a weapons test site northeast of New Delhi. Behind Ketkar was a massive glass terrarium as big as a small home. The terrarium had been Ketkar's idea. He had ordered its construction early in the week and had filled the bottom of it with earth. Shrubs and small trees had been planted to simulate the terrain in China, and a projected image on the back wall showed a beautiful rice field in a green mountain valley.

"What would you have done if I had said no?" Shenzu had asked when he saw the setup.

"We knew you wouldn't," Ketkar had said. "You love your country."

Every seat in the hangar was taken. Most of the reporters were correspondents stationed in India and working for the major networks. Others had flown in for the event from Europe, Africa, and the Middle East. Thousands more were watching the event live throughout the world. Holoprojectors and traditional 2-D cameras were set up all around the stage. A few special seats had been reserved down front for the Chinese ambassador to India and his senior staff.

An Indian Para Commando in a fire-resistant yellow biosuit was inside the terrarium holding the modified paint-sprayer shotgun. Gadhavi had wanted to use the robotic arms again, for safety, but Ketkar had flatly refused. "Soldiers will be doing this in the field. I want the press to see China being saved by a PC. Besides, you look like an idiot in those socks and gloves. Late-night comedians would have a field day with that. We need the world to applaud us, not mock us."

From his place at the rostrum, Ketkar introduced the PC and briefly gave an account of his impeccable service record and training. The subtle message was clear: PCs are excellent soldiers and would be an asset to the war.

Ketkar then turned the rostrum over to Dr. Gadhavi who walked on stage wearing a white lab coat over his oxford shirt and slacks.

"But I never wear a lab coat," he had told Ketkar before the presentation. "That's so cliché."

"You'll wear it and you'll smile about it," Ketkar had told him through gritted teeth.

They had rehearsed the presentation several times beforehand. Gadhavi really worked the crowd. They laughed at his two jokes, and listened intently as he went through the chemistry of it all. Ketkar had worried that this part was too dry and needed some more cutting, but Gadhavi had pushed back, and Ketkar had acquiesced. It had been the right decision. The crowd was hanging on every word.

Then it was showtime.

Inside the terrarium, a Formic emerged from behind a large shrub. A goo gun was strapped to its back, the wand in its hand. The special effects company had done its best to make the creature look fearsome and lifelike, and Ketkar had to admit they did an impressive job. It hung from a wire rig positioned in the ceiling and moved out like a marionette. A murmur from the audience. A few people gasped.

When the PC aimed the weapon, it was absolute silence. When he fired at the goo tank, and the Formic and goo pack exploded in a fireball of absolute devastation that sent Formic parts flying in every direction, the room erupted with applause and cheers. Some people were out of their seats. One woman near the front was actually crying.

For a moment Ketkar wondered if the demonstration alone was enough. Even the Chinese ambassador was cheering. But no, this was theater, the energy of the crowd. Beijing would be a different story. Shenzu was the pièce de résistance.

Gadhavi waved and exited to another round of applause. Then Shenzu walked on stage. The crowd quieted. Another murmur went through them. A Chinese officer had not been on the agenda. Shenzu walked past the rostrum and faced them center stage. He waited for total silence, then gave the speech from memory in Chinese. English subtitles appeared on the front of the stage beneath him, visible to everyone. When he mentioned Sima's name, there was a murmur among the audience. Sima? *The* General Sima?

"He told me about his children and grandchildren," said Shenzu. "He said he would do anything to protect them. He asked me about my own children. Six-year-old Shidhu and two-year-old Mingshu. My duty to them is greater than all others, he said."

He gestured back to the PC in the terrarium. "I thank my brother in the Para Commandos and the good Dr. Gadhavi, who have worked so hard to honor General Sima's final request and to take steps to keep all of our children safe."

My brother.

Ketkar smiled. He had read the speech several times, but that part always hit home in his heart. A Chinese calling an Indian his brother. And not a politician posing for photos at some summit. A soldier. A common man. It was the entirety of the message summed up in two simple words. Shenzu need not mention any proposal for troops. That was for others to handle. His job was to pave the road for others to follow.

And they would follow, Ketkar knew. The last part of the speech left no question in his mind.

"Let us come together," Shenzu said. "All of us, not just China and India"—as if such a thing had already happened, as if their alliance was already sealed—"but all nations. We will need everyone's help, everyone's hand, everyone's might. China is where the war began, but a united Earth is where the war will end."

They cheered him. They rose to their feet. The Chinese ambassador came to the lip of the stage and shook his hand.

Ketkar cued the house lights. There would be no

Q&A session. End with a bang, when the mood was high. Shenzu was escorted off by aides. So sorry, Captain Shenzu has other duties. Then the doors were opened, and the reporters released.

The microblogs lit up immediately. The vid had played live all over the world, and everyone took to the nets. Women were asking if the PC was single. Someone found photos of Shenzu's adorable children, and those spread like wildfire. Sima's photo was passed around as well. Someone put his head on the body of the PC in the yellow jumpsuit with the caption: WANT SOME DUCK SAUCE WITH THAT, BUG FACE?

But the posts from the citizens of China were the ones that got the most bounces and reposts. Vids of women crying, giving heartfelt thanks. Their deceased sons and husbands in the military will not have died in vain. Children cheered. Celebrities echoed the cry for unification. And on and on in a deluge of unstoppable support—all of it linked with the net tag: EARTHUNITED.

Ketkar returned to his temporary office in the hangar and waited. It was only a matter of time now. He looked again at the maps. He would accompany Mazer, Wit, Shenzu, and a team of PCs to the doughnut tower where a large cache of goo was stored. Destroying it would be their first mission in China. A sort of ceremonial kickoff event with plenty of pyrotechnics.

He would likely lose Mazer, Wit, and Shenzu after that. The Chinese would insist that they help with the operation's development. Ketkar would almost insist upon it. He had greater faith in their strategic thinking than his own or anyone else's in either military. That would put the three of them in a war room somewhere instead of in the thick of the fighting, but the operation already had its share of martyrs. What it needed now was minds.

Messages from his superiors flooded his in-box. They

all praised him for the press conference. The subtext was obvious: Remember me when you're promoted, Ketkar. I am your true friend. Let us rise together.

Ketkar deleted them after reading the subject line. They were from parasites and careerists.

It wasn't until later that he received the message he had been waiting for, an encrypted one that would self-delete after he had read it. It was the only message that mattered, the one that would cement his future.

There were only two words: Well done.

And to Ketkar's great surprise, Ukko Jukes had included a smiley face emoticon.

CHAPTER 14

Dragon's Den

Bingwen and the MOPs were standing on a dusty two-lane road ten klicks southeast of Dragon's Den when the truck arrived to pick them up. All around them was death and rot. The road they were on cut through the center of a valley filled with rice fields, and the Formic gas had killed everything here a long time ago. Paddy frogs lay belly-up in the muck, their skin sun scorched and dry as a raisin. A bloated water buffalo lay half submerged in the mud, decomposing amid a cloud of flies. The rice crop lay withered and black atop the standing water, the surface of which glistened with a toxic oily film. The sight of it all made Bingwen grateful for his radiation suit, which kept out the gag-inducing smell of decay.

The truck parked directly in front of them, and the Chinese soldier behind the wheel hopped down, moved to the back of the truck, and lowered the gate for them to board. He wore a biosuit, and when he turned back, Bingwen saw that he was only a boy. Fourteen at the most, not even old enough to drive. The suit was probably the smallest size available, but like Bingwen's it hung limp on the soldier's narrow shoulders like a rubber blanket.

Were boys lying about their ages now to enlist? Bingwen wondered. The influx of Indian commandos was alleviating the burden on the Chinese military, but maybe it wasn't enough. Maybe China still needed anyone willing to join the fight.

Bingwen doubted the military would take him, however. He was small for an eight-year-old, and even the most lenient of recruiters wouldn't believe him a day over ten.

A young Chinese lieutenant got out of the cab on the passenger side, and Bingwen knew at once that there would be trouble. The lieutenant was tall and thin with a hard, tight line for a mouth and suspicious eyes that darted between all of the MOPs in an instant. A sidearm was holstered at the waist of his biosuit, and his hand rested on it as he approached. He spotted Bingwen and crinkled his nose.

"I was told to bring in soldiers, not boys." His English was good, but his accent was heavy.

"He's part of our unit," said Deen.

"A boy among a group of men. One can't help but wonder what you used him for."

Bingwen didn't understand the lieutenant's meaning, but it was clearly offensive. Deen smiled in that way he did sometimes when he wanted to throttle someone.

"What's your name, Lieutenant?" Deen asked pleasantly.

The lieutenant put his hands on his hips. "Li."

"Well, Lieutenant Li, we're MOPs. We've spent the last two weeks blowing up transports and skimmers and about three hundred Formics, give or take, without any word from our commanding officer. So when he calls us out of the blue and tells us to meet him at Dragon's Den, we obviously stop what we're doing and come. He's even going to send a truck to pick us up. Great, says I. But then you show up, and something tells me you didn't read your orders very closely because you're being difficult."

"I was told to pick up MOPs, not children."

"Bingwen is a MOP. A little shorter than most maybe, but he's been an integral part of our success."

Li scoffed. "You gave a weapon to a child?"

"He may not carry a gun, Li, but he knows the land, he knows the language, and he knows a few ways to kill Formics. He's got tactics in that little head of his that none of us had considered. His takedown idea for the transports has resulted in about . . ." He looked at the others. "How many would you say? Ten, twelve destroyed transports?" He turned back at Li. "Can you say that, Lieutenant? Can you say you've been responsible for destroying a dozen transports?"

Li glanced down at Bingwen, and there was only disdain in his eyes.

When he lifted his gaze back to Deen, he said, "I'm to take you to a secret military facility. It's no place for a child."

"Agreed," said Deen. "But Dragon's Den is a big place, we're told. There are camps of civilians there as well. There's shelter and food for those who need it. Surely Bingwen has earned that much."

"The camps are beyond capacity."

Deen sighed. "Lieutenant, get on your radio. Call Dragon's Den. Ask for Captain Wit O'Toole. He's probably swapping war stories with a few of your generals right now. I'm sure they won't mind the interruption. Ask them if it's all right if Bingwen comes. I'm willing to bet all the tea left in China that you were supposed to bring him anyway."

Lieutenant Li scowled.

"Or, if you prefer to be difficult," said Deen, "kindly point us in the direction of Dragon's Den, and we'll walk there ourselves. When you arrive, you can explain to your commanding officer why you failed such a simple assignment."

The lieutenant's grip tightened around his handgun, and for an instant Bingwen thought everything would end badly. But then Lieutenant Li came to his senses and removed his hand from his holster.

"Very well. The boy may come. But all of you must relinquish your weapons."

Really? thought Bingwen. Are you that desperate to assert your authority? You make a mistake and rather than accepting it and moving on, you try to manipulate us some other way? How did this guy become a lieutenant?

But Deen wasn't having it. He started walking toward the back of the truck. "If we get attacked by a Formic death squad, Lieutenant, I doubt you want our weapons up in the cab with you."

And with that the MOPs loaded up into the truck fully armed without another word. Bingwen sat between Cocktail and ZZ, and when Deen sat across from him he gave Bingwen a wink.

They drove across blackened countryside and through mud so thick that twice the MOPs had to get out and push. Much of the land had been scoured—or stripped clean by the massive Formic harvesters that collected all the biomass the Formic gas had killed. In those areas, there was nothing left behind except for long strips of naked earth.

But there were also places where the Formic gas had done its work, but no harvester had come. These were the grisliest sights. Corpses, human and animal, vegetation black and dissolving, all of it slowly melting into the mud. Bingwen turned away as he always did.

Mother had died that way. Father, too.

He stared at the tips of his boots and tried to take his mind elsewhere.

The truck finally slowed and pulled into a massive hangar in the side of a mountain. The giant sliding doors closed behind them with a clang, sealing them inside. Bingwen and the others took off their helmets and breathed in fresh air.

The hangar was being used as a garage, Bingwen saw. Dozens of mechanics were hard at work repairing and outfitting all class of vehicles and aircraft: adding armor, installing guns, ripping parts from junked vehicles and welding them onto others. The air smelled of grease and rubber and burned wiring.

Bingwen stood with the others to climb down from the truck, when Mazer appeared at the tailgate. He saw Bingwen and smiled. "Hey, troublemaker. Long time, no see."

Bingwen couldn't help himself. He leaped from the back of the truck into Mazer's arms.

Mazer laughed and lowered him to the ground. "Whoa-ho-ho, you've gained about a thousand pounds, Bing. What are they feeding you? Boulders?"

"How was India?" asked Bingwen. "Why didn't you radio us?"

"Boring. And they wouldn't let us call anyone. Did you see the doughnut tower explode?"

"About a dozen times on the nets. Deen was trying to make the sound the ringchime on his wrist pad. Did you see the vids we uploaded at the site?"

Mazer gave Deen a disapproving look. "I did. And I wonder what possessed Deen to allow an eight-year-old near a firefight."

"You're one to talk," said Deen. "You took Bing to the lander. And anyway, he wasn't near the firefight in that vid. He was tucked away elsewhere. We kept him out of danger. Mostly." He shrugged. "And maybe you've forgotten how obstinate this kid can be. He's more stubborn than Wit."

"I heard that."

They turned. Wit approached them from behind.

The MOPs all greeted him with smiles, embraces, and slaps on the back.

ZZ said, "Done with your vacation, Captain?"

"Yeah," said Cocktail. "While you were getting foot massages and grapes fed to you in India, the rest of us were fighting a war."

"If I had a sucker, I'd give you one, Cocktail," said Wit. He smiled warmly. "I'm glad to see you all safe."

They hadn't suffered a single casualty since Wit and Mazer had left them. They all knew it was nothing short of a miracle.

"It's Bingwen," said Bungy. "He's our good luck charm."

Lieutenant Li cleared his throat. "Pardon me, gentlemen, but we are on a schedule." He gestured to the boy who had driven the truck. "Private Hun here will escort your boy to the civilian barracks. The rest of you will come with me."

Bingwen's high at seeing Mazer took a nosedive. It wasn't fair. How long had they been standing here? Two minutes? Three? He had barely said hello.

Mazer took a knee in front of Bingwen, and the two of them embraced.

"Can I visit you?" said Bingwen.

"Absolutely not," said Lieutenant Li.

Mazer gave Li a withering look. "He was asking me, hotshot. Go splash some cold water in your face."

He turned back to Bingwen. "It's a restricted area, Bing. I'm not allowed to leave either."

"What are you doing in there?"

"Looking at maps and arguing with people. Believe me, you're not missing anything."

"Sounds important."

"It's called Operation Duck Sauce."

"That's classified," said Li. "He shouldn't know that." Mazer and Bingwen ignored him.

"Do you think we'll win?" asked Bingwen.

"I think we have a decent chance. Now that everyone is helping. But we're a long way from winning."

"Getting the Indians involved, that was smart."

"I can't take the credit for that. But yes, smart. They're good soldiers. Companies are helping as well. They're shipping supplies. We're getting equipment all the way from the U.S. and South America. It's quite the operation."

"What will the MOPs be doing?"

"Helping to manage everything, leading strike teams from here. China has lost a lot of its commanders. They need people they can trust to lead the various units."

"You should be leading the whole army."

Mazer laughed. "Hardly. But I'm learning how that's done. Captain O'Toole is as good with a million soldiers as he is with three or four."

Lieutenant Li cleared his throat again. The MOPs were waiting.

Bingwen said, "So we'll be near each other and yet a world apart."

"You'll be out of the fighting, Bing. That's what's important. This is a safe place."

"So this is good-bye?"

Mazer put a hand behind Bingwen's head. "It will never be good-bye between us, Bing." He pulled Bingwen's face close until their foreheads and noses touched. Then he pulled away. "In Maori culture, that's a *hongi*, a traditional greeting. It means we are both *tangata whenua* now, people of the land, brothers, sharing in the breath of life."

Bingwen nodded. "Brothers."

He threw his arms around Mazer's neck and they embraced a final time. Then Mazer stood and tousled Bingwen's hair.

"Stay safe, troublemaker."

They parted and Bingwen began to turn away but then he remembered something. "Oh, and Mazer."

Mazer turned back.

Bingwen tapped his forehead with a finger. "One in the head, good and dead."

Mazer smiled. It had been something Captain O'Toole had said to the men repeatedly, and it had grown into a sort of salutation whenever one of them went off to scout ahead or leave on patrol. It meant: If you see a Formic, don't hesitate. Put a bullet in its brain.

"We're a bad influence on you, Bing."

"Terrible. I'm probably scarred for life."

Bingwen followed Private Hun toward a metal staircase that led downward to the refugee camps. As they descended Bingwen asked in Chinese, "How old are you?"

"Eighteen," Hun said.

"How old are you really?" asked Bingwen.

Hun looked sheepish and lowered his voice. "Fifteen."

"You enlisted here?"

Hun nodded. "My village is gone. My mother, grandmother, little sister, they all . . ." He shook his head, not wanting to speak of it. Then he found his voice again. "I didn't have to do any training. I just told them I drove farming equipment, and they gave me a uniform."

"You think they'd give me an assignment?"

Hun scoffed. "You? How old are you? Seven?"

"Eight."

"Laundry maybe. Or latrines. But as a civilian. Not a soldier."

Bingwen shrugged. "Doesn't make much difference, I suppose."

Hun seemed affronted. "Of course it does. As a soldier you can fight."

"Did they give you a weapon?"

"Well, no. But if it comes to a fight, I'll take one, you can be sure of that."

They continued downward until they reached the bottom level, where Bingwen began to hear the cry of infants, the chatter and shuffle and movement of hundreds of people living in a small space.

"You're to go to Mama Goshi," said Hun. "She's the keeper of Claw. And believe me, she's not going to be happy to see you."

"Claw?"

"There are four barracks in Dragon's Den, each named for a part of the dragon. Claw, Fire, Fang, Wings. You're in Claw."

"Why won't Mama Goshi want to see me?"

"Because you have a stomach and you're a kid, which means you'll eat food and not prove very useful. A drain."

"I'm not completely useless," said Bingwen.

Hun smiled as if he thought Bingwen naïve.

They arrived at a warehouse-sized room that was now a camp. Hundreds of cots were packed together; hammocks hung between columns; bedrolls lined the walls and everywhere else, save for narrow aisles between the rows of living spaces. Women, children, the elderly, all practically on top of each other.

"Welcome to Claw," said Hun. "You might want to put that helmet back on. It smells like piss and sweat and antiseptic in here."

And worse things besides, thought Bingwen. He passed a washing station where women scrubbed sheets and clothing in large plastic buckets, then hung them dripping wet on lines above drainage grates in the floor. He passed a group of old men huddled around a holopad that looked almost as old as they were, the news reporter on screen flickering and fading as the signal came and went. He passed others who stared back at him, their faces blank and despondent. Mothers nursed infants. Old men coughed. Children ran and played, oblivious to their plight. Injured people with bandages lay in cots at a nurses' station. A shriveled old woman in the corner clutching a bundle of blankets rocked back and forth softly singing a lullaby. If there was an infant in her bundle, Bingwen didn't see one.

Bingwen tried smiling as he made eye contact, but no one returned the gesture.

Hun led him to the back corner where several sheets hung from the ceiling to form a small room. Mama Goshi was inside cutting open a box. When Hun introduced Bingwen, Mama Goshi grunted with exasperation and said, "And what am I to do with a boy? Especially one in a rubber suit meant for someone twice his size. What ails you, boy? You keeping a virus in there just for yourself?"

She was wrinkled and weathered and slightly humpbacked, wearing a pink flowered dress long faded from the sun and a pair of mismatched slippers.

Bingwen bowed. "No, Nai Nai. I'm healthy."

Mama Goshi nodded, pleased. "You were taught to respect your elders, at least. By your parents, I suspect. Both of them dead."

It didn't sound like a question, but Bingwen nodded nonetheless.

"Well, off with the spacesuit. No one obviously cares that I don't have room or food for another mouth, even one as small as yours, but I see I don't get a say in the matter." She waved a dismissive hand at Hun. "Get out of my face before I change my mind."

Hun hurried away without another word while Bingwen stepped out of his radiation suit. Mama Goshi put her hands on her hips and appraised him. "Skinny and scrawny and probably good for nothing. Can you clean toilets?"

"Yes, Nai Nai."

The old woman waved a hand again. "Enough with the formalities. I'm Mama Goshi here. Keep calling me 'Nai Nai' and people will think you're my real grandson, which you aren't and never will be."

"No, Mama Goshi."

She nodded. "Fast learner. Good. What's your name?"

He bowed again. "Bingwen."

"Well, Bingwen, when I say I don't have food for you, I mean it." She pointed to a small pile of boxes. "You see these? They contain today's food. Bottles of protein vitamin drink. That's our diet. It tastes like grass and grit, but it keeps us alive. Now, there are nine hundred and seventy-eight people in Claw. And I'm supposed to feed them all with this."

It wasn't enough. It wasn't enough to feed half that many.

"So if you think you're out of the woods down here," said Mama Goshi, "you're mistaken. This is only a different kind of hell."

"I can work," said Bingwen.

"You will. Until your fingers bleed, if I have my say. In the meantime, go find a place to sleep over there." She gestured to a row of cots where children were gathered.

He bowed. "Yes, Mama Goshi."

She turned away from him and began to speak with someone else who had approached. Bingwen got the message: He was dismissed. He scooped up his radiation suit and went to the cots.

A circle of boys sat on the floor playing rock dice. Behind them a girl about nine years old was kneeling by a cot, dabbing a sick boy's forehead with a damp cloth. She saw Bingwen, stood, and glowered at him.

"I'm Bingwen. Mama Goshi sent me here to find a place to sleep."

"There's no room," said the girl. "Not even for a stick like you. Beat it."

"Is there an adult I can talk to?" asked Bingwen, looking around.

The girl narrowed her eyes.

"This here is orphan alley, Stick. Kids without guardians. We're the table scraps. You want to go cry to an adult, you'll have to go somewhere else."

The young boy on the cot clutched his stomach and moaned.

"What's wrong with him?" asked Bingwen.

"What do you care?" said the girl.

"Has he seen one of the nurses?" Bingwen asked. He gestured toward the nurses' station he had seen near the entrance.

"Oh I get it," said the girl. "You want us to cart him off to the nurses so you can get his cot. Well forget it. He and I share. This cot is *ours*."

"I don't want your cot. I'm happy to sleep on the floor. I just meant he looks like he needs help. Are there any doctors down here?"

The girl relaxed somewhat. "There are two, for all four thousand of us. We're on the list to see one in two days. Maybe." She looked back at the boy, concerned. "He's getting worse. I tried to take him to Mama Goshi, but he can't even walk anymore."

Bingwen could see the resemblance now. They were

siblings. A younger brother. "I have a device that's like a doctor," said Bingwen. "It's called a Med-Assist. It can tell people what's wrong with them and explain how to fix it." He put down his suit and pulled the Med-Assist from the knapsack draped across his back. The boys playing dice were suddenly curious. The holopad had belonged to Mazer Rackham and was designed for military field use. Before it had lost its charge on the mountain, Bingwen had used it to save Mazer's life.

"We can help each other," said Bingwen. "You let me sleep here, and I'll help you with your brother."

The girl looked skeptical. "A magical device, huh?"

"Show me where I can charge it," said Bingwen, "and I'll show you how it works."

Several of the younger boys jumped up, volunteering, but the girl pushed one to the ground and threatened to do the same to the others. "I'm taking him. You dirt clods stay with Niro." She turned to Bingwen. "If you're lying about this device, Stick, I'll put a boot up your crack."

"You don't wear boots, Pipo," teased one of the boys.

"Shut up," said Pipo, "or *you'll* need a doctor."

"Ooh," said the boys. "The tigress is loose. The tigress is loose."

Pipo ignored them. She motioned Bingwen to follow her, and she led him to a charging station out in the main tunnel. A line of people were waiting with various items: lanterns, wrist pads, space heaters. Bingwen and Pipo got in behind them.

"If you *are* lying about this device," she said. "I mean it. I'll cut you in your sleep."

She was all bluster and no bite, Bingwen saw. He wondered if she had always been that way or if the Formics had done this to her. Probably the latter, just as the Formics had changed him, bringing his survival instinct front and center and burying the person he used to be under a mountain of grief.

What had she endured? he wondered. Had she seen her parents die? Had she found their corpses as Bingwen had? Or had she been spared that? Maybe she and her brother Niro were merely separated from their parents. Maybe they clung to the hope of reuniting somehow.

"So where are you from?" asked Bingwen.

"What do you care?"

"I'm from Dawanzhen. Or a village near there anyway. My family farmed rice."

"Yeah, you and everyone else. So what."

"How long have you been here?"

"This isn't an interview, Stick. Stop asking questions."

"Sorry. I haven't seen someone my age in a while. I guess I'm kind of hungry for conversation."

"Well the rest of us are hungry for food. So unless you've got some in that pack of yours, keep your questions to yourself."

"Get used to questions. That's how the device makes a diagnosis and determines what to test. It asks a lot of questions."

Her scowl softened. "Like what?"

"Like how long has your brother been hurting?"

She looked worried again. "Since last night. It started as a stomachache, but now he can't bear it. I stole some pain pills from the med closet, but I wasn't sure how much to give him. Bug said if I gave Niro too much, his heart might stop." She opened the palm of her hand to show him four white tablets. "What do you think?"

"I think we need to hurry and charge this."

Pipo saw that he was serious, grabbed his wrist, and pulled him to the front of the line. She pushed the girl aside who was using the charger and gave it to Bingwen, who immediately started gathering juice into the device. People in line objected, some cursed. A woman threatened to intervene, but Pipo gave her a look that would melt stone and told her that they were charging this for

Mama Goshi who needed it immediately and if the woman didn't like it she could go take it up with Mama Goshi herself. Then the Med-Assist was ready, and Pipo and Bingwen were running off.

Back at the cots, the children gathered around when Bingwen booted up the device and placed it over Niro's stomach.

"This isn't going to hurt him, is it?" asked Pipo.

"No," said Bingwen. "Just have him lie still." He tapped through the commands, typed in the symptoms, and listened to the instructions.

"What language is that?" said one of the boys.

"English, bonehead," said Pipo. "What does it say, Bingwen?"

"It says I need to prick his finger and check his blood."

For a moment he thought Pipo would object, but then she gripped her brother's hand and nodded for Bingwen to continue. Bingwen swabbed Niro's fingertip, retracted the disposable needle prick, and stuck the boy's finger. Niro cried out and Bingwen placed a drop of blood on the scanner. "He has an infection," Bingwen said once the results came in. "And now it's telling me to press on his stomach."

"No!" said Niro.

"You said you weren't going to hurt him," said Pipo. "So far that's all you've done."

"This is how the device works," said Bingwen. "I do some tests. The more results it has, the more accurate the diagnosis. This is exactly what a doctor would do."

Pipo hesitated again. Niro clung to her. The other boys looked uneasy. A few adults had gathered to see what the commotion was about.

"I can't advance unless I do this," said Bingwen.

Pipo bit her bottom lip a moment then held Niro tighter. "Do it quickly," she said.

Bingwen set the device aside. "What hurts worse, Niro, when I press down on your belly or when I release?" He didn't need to wait for an answer. Niro cried out when Bingwen released the pressure. Bingwen checked the appropriate box and placed the device over the stomach. "Now hold still. It's going to take a series of images. This part won't hurt at all."

Tears had welled up in the little boy's eyes, and Pipo looked on the verge of crying as well. Several adults had heard Niro cry out, and a crowd was slowly gathering around the bed. When the results came in, the device said it was 97.5 percent confident of the diagnosis.

"His appendix is about to burst," said Bingwen.

Pipo's eyes widened. "Burst? What does that mean?"

"It means we need to find a surgeon immediately. They need to remove it."

Pipo sprinted to retrieve Mama Goshi, and the old woman arrived a moment later, puffing and irritated at being disturbed. She scowled and gestured at the gathered crowd. "What's all this?"

"Niro's stomach is going to burst," said one of the boys.

"His appendix," said Bingwen. He showed Mama Goshi the device. He could tell from her expression that she couldn't read English or understand the scans she was looking at. But she did seem to understand Niro's moaning and the worry on the faces of the gathered adults. Mama Goshi unclipped her communicator from her hip and called the doctor. She tried explaining the issue, but she couldn't answer the doctor's questions or properly pronounce the terms Bingwen keep feeding her. Finally she gave up and thrust the communicator into Bingwen's hands. "*You* tell her."

Bingwen read to the doctor the full diagnosis: acute pain localized to the right iliac fossa; elevated white blood count; rebound tenderness and guarding in the right lower quadrant of the abdomen; he shared the numbers for hemoglobin, hematocritin, blood sugar; he described the results of the ultrasound and CT scans, which had identified an inflamed appendix with pus, fibrin, and congested blood vessels on the surface. Bingwen didn't know many of the English words and thus what their Chinese equivalent would be, so he simply pronounced them in English and hoped the doctor understood.

When he finished, the doctor said, "How old are you?"

"Eight. But I don't understand most of what I'm telling you. All I know for certain is that Niro needs surgery immediately. Can you come?"

"Yes. I'll send someone to get him right away. You did good."

Two soldiers arrived minutes later with a gurney and took Niro away. Pipo insisted on going with him, but the soldiers wouldn't allow it. When they were gone, the crowd dispersed. Bingwen could see the adults whispering to each other, passing the news.

Pipo stared at the exit where Niro had gone, and Bingwen tried to reassure her. "The doctor sounded kind. When I told her it was appendicitis, she didn't seem nervous. I'm guessing she's done that surgery many times before."

Pipo turned to him, and for an instant he saw the girl she had been before the war, small and afraid and delicate.

Mama Goshi asked to see the Med-Assist device again. "Where did you get this?"

"From a soldier," Bingwen told her. He didn't want to tell her it was Mazer's and that Mazer was somewhere in the facility. He worried she might try to return it to him.

She gave it back to him and said, "Come with me."

Bingwen followed her to the nurses' station where a boy lay on a cot.

"He says his ears and jaw hurt," said Mama Goshi. "Can your doctor pad tell us why?"

Bingwen looked at the boy, and the two nurses seated around his cot regarded Bingwen curiously. They were not real nurses, Bingwen saw. They were mothers and grandmothers from farming villages, simple people, doing as best as they knew how, which medically wasn't much.

Bingwen set up the device and followed the instructions. Soon the device asked that he attach an otoscope head to the camera lens. It showed him a picture of one, and he asked the nurses if there was such a thing in the medical supplies. One of them left and returned with a few options. Bingwen attached one as best as he could and continued. The boy had a severe inner ear infection, and the Med-Assist recommended the appropriate dose of antibiotics and pain medicine.

Mama Goshi had him scan other people next. A woman had a ruptured disc in her neck. A man had a sinus infection. A crying baby had acid reflux. A pregnant woman wanted to know the sex of her unborn child. Some of the people he could help; others he couldn't. Sometimes they had ailments the device couldn't identify. FURTHER LAB WORK REQUIRED, it would say. Or ADDITIONAL TESTS NEEDED. Or PLEASE SEE A DOCTOR FOR FURTHER ASSISTANCE. Other times it prescribed medicine that the facility simply didn't have.

Word of the failures didn't spread nearly as quickly as the successes, however, and soon people from Fang, Fire, and Wings were coming for a diagnosis, forming a line that stretched down the tunnel.

Bingwen pulled Mama Goshi aside. "What you're having me do is rather dangerous," he said. "I'm not a doctor. The device is for emergencies in the field, when a real doctor is inaccessible. It's a last-resort option. It can be wrong. These people need a real doctor."

"We don't have enough," said Mama Goshi.

"Then we need to get some," said Bingwen. "Can you take me outside the facility?"

"Why?"

"The Med-Assist can't get a sat connection this far underground, and I know someone who can help."

She announced to those waiting in line that they were taking a break. Then she took him up a service elevator to the garage. Bingwen had retrieved his radiation suit, and he slipped it on once they reached the main door. Two soldiers guarding the exit stopped them when they approached.

"He needs a moment outside," Mama Goshi told them. The men looked at each other, shrugged, and let Bingwen out.

"Knock twice to be let back in," said one of them.

"And don't let the Formics eat you," said the other.

They closed the door behind him. It was night out. Bingwen walked a short distance away until he got a strong signal. He checked the time. New Zealand was four hours ahead. It was the middle of the night there, closer to dawn. She had told him to call at any hour, however.

She answered on the third ring, her voice groggy. "This is Kim."

"It's Bingwen," he said. "The boy. From China. I'm sorry to wake you."

She was instantly alert. "Bingwen. I've been so worried. Are you safe? Where are you?"

He hardly knew her. He had never even seen her face. She had helped him perform the surgery on Mazer, and he had learned afterward that she and Mazer had been . . . what? Not husband and wife yet, but whatever came before that. A couple? And yet despite this brief tenuous connection she and Bingwen had shared, he felt as if he *did* know her, that she was someone special to him. A friend, yes, and maybe even more than that. Not a mother, no. But *like* a mother. A half-mother. A woman who knew him and valued him and worried over him. He would never say as much to her, of course, and he had never even thought such a thing prior to this moment. But it felt so wonderful to be fretted over, thought about, remembered, that he found himself smiling.

"I'm safe," he said. He told her everything then, all of it spilling out of him. About the base, the conditions, Mama Goshi and Pipo and Niro and Hun, the fourteen-year-old driver. He told her about the cocky Lieutenant Li and the sick people in Claw and Fire and the other barracks. He wasn't sure why he was divulging every detail, but it felt like such a release to talk to someone. Mazer was fine, by the way, he told her. He had healed. He was healthy. He could run and move. It was as if he had never been hurt.

She broke down at that point. At first Bingwen didn't realize she was crying. There was only silence on her end, and for a moment he thought he had lost the connection.

"Dr. Arnsbrach?" he said.

"I'm here," she said, her voice shaky.

He felt like an idiot then. Mazer was her first concern. He had lost the connection with her shortly after Mazer's surgery when the device's battery had depleted, and Kim had not yet heard how Mazer had recovered. She had been sick with worry all this time, and Bingwen had just yammered on and on about trivial things when it was Mazer she wanted to know about.

When she collected herself, she apologized and blamed her emotions on the lack of sleep and told him more than once that under no circumstances was he to tell Mazer that she had cried. "Promise me, Bingwen."

He promised.

She asked him where Mazer was now.

"He's here at this underground facility. He's helping to lead the soldiers from here. It's some big operation. I don't think they're sending him out to fight. I think he'll stay here where it's safe."

The line went quiet again.

"Are you still there?" he asked.

She sniffed. "Yes, I'm just . . . relieved."

Bingwen was suddenly angry. "He should have called you and told you all this himself."

"It's complicated, Bingwen."

"No, it isn't. It's good manners."

She laughed. "Oh Bingwen. I hope you and I can meet in person someday."

He remembered why he had called. "I need your help. We need doctors. There are thousands of people here and hardly any medical staff. I know you can't send doctors. This is a war zone. The skies aren't safe. But would you or any doctors you know be willing to see patients via the nets? Through holos? You can't treat them obviously. At best you could partially examine them and diagnose them. People here could conduct whatever tests you needed, assuming we have the equipment for it. We'd be your hands. None of us have any medical training, so we wouldn't conduct any procedures or surgeries if they were needed. We would leave that to the real doctors here. That would be their focus. Instead of spending time examining patients, they could dedicate all their time to performing procedures only they can do. So we identify the emergencies, they address them. More people could be seen that way, and we could hopefully avoid what almost happened with Niro."

When she spoke again, the worry in her voice was gone, replaced with steel-hard confidence. "Bingwen, I'm going to my office right now. There are several non-profits that do this sort of thing. I'll get our people on it immediately."

"What's a nonprofit?"

"A charity. A group of people who help for free. In this case, doctors. There are some charities in the U.S., Europe, South America, two in Africa. Give me a few hours to contact them. We can probably find several who speak Chinese. In the meantime, we need equipment for the transmissions and numbers for the up-links."

"I've seen some holo equipment here on site," said Bingwen. "I'll work on that."

"Should I speak to someone in charge?" asked Kim. "A commanding officer? Get the military's help?"

"I don't even know who that is. I'll ask around. If we can't find out who to ask, I say we do it without permission and ask for forgiveness later."

He could hear the smile in her voice. "Bucking authority for the good of the people? I think Mazer is starting to rub off on you, Bingwen."

Bingwen beamed. It was the greatest compliment anyone had ever given him.

CHAPTER 15

Reunion

FROM: WUHUoutpost784@wuhuindustries.net
TO: lem.jukes@jukelimited.net
Re: El Cavador

Rena Delgado and others from El Cavador are no longer here. They left almost two months ago aboard a salvage ship named Gagak. Captained by a Somali named Arjuna. Sorry. No additional information.

The message was projected on the wall-screen in Lem Juke's office, and Victor read it a second time as a mix of emotions welled up inside him. Mother? On a salvage ship? Victor couldn't imagine it. Why would she get on a salvage ship? And with a Somali, no less.

"If she got on a ship, I'm sure she had a good reason," said Imala. She and Lem were standing behind him. They had all seen the message.

Victor turned to face her. "You don't know Somalis, Imala. They're vultures. Pirates. They strip derelict ships to the bone. Sometimes with the crews still inside them. They don't care. They rape, kill, and *then* they'll rob you."

"That can't be who these Somalis are," said Imala. "It says she left on a salvage ship. If she had been abducted, the message would have said so. I take this to mean she went voluntarily."

"Imala's right," said Lem. "If this Gagak were a crew of vultures, they never would have reached the outpost. The WU-HU defenses would have pulverized them before they got within ten klicks of the place."

Victor glowered. "What do you know about it?"

"Plenty. WU-HU is a competitor. We know their operations inside and out. Those outposts are fortresses. They're engineered to fend off pirates. And speaking of which, not all Somalis *are* pirates. There are crow crews as well. They live by salvage law. They hate vultures as much as anyone, maybe even more so because vultures give Somalis such a bad rep."

"It doesn't make sense," said Victor. "Why would they leave? They would have been safer at an outpost."

"Apparently your mother didn't think so," said Imala. "If she left, she had reasons. She had women and children with her. Maybe these Somalis offered them passage somewhere."

"Yes, but where? My mother and aunts have nowhere to go."

"We have the name of the ship," said Lem. "We'll find it and contact it directly."

"They're a salvage ship," said Victor. "They're not going to have an account with Luna. They won't likely be in the network. We may not be able to reach them until they dock somewhere. That could be months from now. And if they do their trade off the market, as most salvage crews do, they won't register when they dock. Which means we may never find them."

"Leave that to me," said Lem.

By late the following day, Lem had located them. He approached Victor in the warehouse and handed him the coordinates on a portable datascreen. "They're near an asteroid called Themis in the outer rim of the Belt."

Victor flipped up his welding visor and stared at the datascreen. "But . . . how did you find them?"

"Black magic. You'll also be happy to know they're on the network. And since we know they're near Themis, we know their relay route. There are probably a dozen to twenty stations between them and us, so at best it will take several hours to get a response, and that's assuming all the switchboards are operational and the laserline gets through clean. But hey, it doesn't hurt to try."

Victor looked down at the datascreen and then back up at Lem, feeling sheepish. "I can't afford to send a message through that many relays. I have some money that my family gave me, but it's probably not enough."

"I'll cover the expense," said Lem. "Whatever it is, and for however long you talk. I owe you that much."

"Thank you."

They found an empty office in the warehouse filled mostly with boxes of junk and broken equipment. Lem cleared the desk with his arm, knocking most of the items onto the floor and kicking up a cloud of dust. Then he set down the terminal and made a sweeping gesture with his hand. "It's not a luxury suite, but it's private at least. And maybe the only quiet place in the warehouse. I won't tell anyone where you are. I set up a laserline account in your name. It's there onscreen. Take your time."

Lem began to leave.

"Why do this?" asked Victor. "Why help me?"

Lem paused at the door. "I'm not a monster, Victor. I know I may appear that way to you after everything I've done, but I'm trying to make things right here. Besides, I have a mother, too, you know."

"Here on Luna?"

"No. Home. In Finland."

"Are you close?"

Lem laughed sadly. "I haven't spoken to her since I was five years old. She abandoned me and my father. She's a despicable person. I can't stand the thought of her. But I see what you feel for your mother, and I envy that."

He walked out and closed the door behind him.

Victor shook out the contents of a crate, turned it over to use it as a seat, sat down in front of the terminal, and began to type.

Just outside the women's restroom on the Gagak, Rena Delgado rubbed her eyes with her thumb and index finger and tried to stay calm. Julexi and Sabad had ambushed her in the corridor as Rena had left the restroom, and now she was getting an earful.

"We're not engineers, Rena," said Julexi. "We can fix things here and there, but we can't turn this ship into a digger. It's ludicrous."

The restroom was at the end of the corridor, so Rena had a wall behind her. She couldn't retreat that way. Julexi and Sabad had her boxed in.

The two women made an unlikely pair. Julexi had lost her husband Pitoso on El Cavador, and she had argued and questioned every one of Rena's proposals and decisions ever since. Sabad, Arjuna's youngest wife, despised everyone from El Cavador. How these women had formed an alliance, Rena could only guess. What was the saying? The enemy of my enemy is my friend?

"Your stay here was intended to be temporary, Rena," said Sabad. "Arjuna, in his kindness, took you in for a time because he pitied you. It was not an invitation to alter our entire operations. What gives you the right to come onto *our* ship and tell us we're doing everything wrong? Do you think yourself so much better than us?"

Arjuna took us in because he needed laborers, Rena wanted to say. Which is what we've been doing since we got here—working our fingers to the bone, which is more than I can say for you, Sabad, whose only occupation seems to be whining, backbiting, and flirting with the other men on your husband's ship.

But aloud Rena said, "No one is implying that your operations are flawed, Sabad."

"Then what are you implying? That our work is beneath you? That the salvage trade is for a lower class? Is that what we are to you, Lady of El Cavador? A lower class? Because we are Somali?"

Rena sighed inside. Why did Arjuna persist in calling her Lady of El Cavador? Didn't he see that it angered Sabad?

Of course he saw, thought Rena. That was probably the reason why he was doing it. To annoy her, a way of publicly poking her with a stick. Everyone saw how Sabad would move around the ship half naked, lingering in the engine rooms where the men would ogle at her healthy breasts. It wasn't uncommon for the Somali women to go bare chested, but Sabad put hers on parade, twisting her hips as she moved through the room, so her breasts would sway back and forth in zero gravity like an invitation. Arjuna had told her to cover herself on more than one occasion, but Sabad had merely found ways to avoid him.

Is that what you're doing, Arjuna? Rena wondered. Annoying your wife through me?

"There is no caste system on this ship," said Rena. "There are two tribes. Ours and yours. We are equals."

"We are not equals," said Sabad. "This is *our* ship. You are guests here."

"We have formed a partnership," said Rena. "Making the Gagak a mining ship is Arjuna's wish as well."

"It is a false partnership," said Sabad. "You cannot form an alliance without a male leader among you."

"Our male leader is on Luna," Rena said—although in truth she wasn't sure if that was accurate. Once the ship had logged in to the network, Rena had trolled through the news feeds until she had found Victor's name. It hadn't been difficult. When the invasion began, several news outlets had recalled the video a young free miner named Victor Delgado had uploaded onto the nets and that everyone had dismissed as phony. Rena had done some additional digging and learned that Victor had been arrested by the Lunar Trade Department for various ridiculous charges involving his flight into Luna. He had escaped custody, however, and that's where the trail ended. Maybe he was on Luna, maybe he wasn't. Maybe he had gone to Earth. Maybe he had tried to return to the K Belt. Maybe he was trying to find El Cavador. She wished she knew.

But for the moment, what she did know was enough: He was alive. He had made it to Luna. He had done the impossible.

It struck her as ironic that he had made such a sacrifice only to have the world reject him. All that way, all that suffering, and what does Earth do? How do they thank him? By throwing him into prison. It was a wonder more families hadn't fled the insanity of Earth and taken up the mining trade.

"If your son is on Luna, why doesn't he talk to us?" said Sabad. "How do we know this alliance is his wish? Are we to take your word on it?"

"Our Council of women met and voted on the matter," said Rena. "Victor is our chief in absentia. The Council makes decisions in his absence."

"First off," said Julexi. "Victor is not our chief. I don't

care if he's the oldest male or not. That doesn't make him our leader in our culture. Second, the Council's vote is meaningless. We're not a true council. We haven't been a true council since the Incident."

She meant the destruction of El Cavador and the death of all the men. That's the name Julexi had given it. The Incident. Rena found the word offensive. It sounded so insignificant. Uncle Jorge having too much to drink at a birthday party. That was an incident. Victor as an infant peeing into the air during his baptism and unleashing droplets of urine throughout the cargo bay. That was an incident. But the death of half of their crew, the shattering of their livelihood, the orphaning of their children, the widowing of the wives, the ripping in half of their families, was not an incident. It was far more than that.

"Our true Council included our husbands, Rena," said Julexi. "Sensible men. And if they were here, they would laugh this idea of yours to scorn. It never would have been put to a vote. The group you call the Council now is a grieving pack of terrified widows who will jump at the chance at any return to normalcy. What's that, you say? A mining ship? Just like El Cavador? Why yes, let's do that! Even though they have no idea how to actually pull it off."

"Our women are making intelligent, informed decisions, Julexi. We discussed the challenges in detail. We debated the issue five times. Everyone's voice was heard, including yours. This was not an emotional decision. It was a financial one. We are much more likely to achieve the independence we want if we make this move. I honestly think it's in our best interest as women and in the best interest of our children."

Julexi threw her hand up in exasperation. "That's what you always say. It's in the best interest of *our* children." She pointed in the direction of the cargo hold.

"None of those little ones are your children, Rena. Not one. They're ours. So I don't see why you think you have the right to speak on their behalf."

Rena forced herself to smile and keep her voice calm. "Forgive me, Julexi. I misspoke. I say 'our' because that's what I've always said, ever since Victor was born. But you have kindly reminded me that my inability to have more children after Victor removes my right to use that possessive pronoun once Victor is gone. I assure you, hereafter, I will say 'your.' "

Julexi folded her arms. "Now you're being snide."

"No, Julexi, I am apologizing. Whether you accept it or not, is your decision. As for the Council, nothing would make me happier than to have Pitoso and Segundo and the others back among us. But that's not going to happen. As much as we want it to, it's not. That leaves us with two options. We can be paralyzed by our husbands' absence and make no decisions whatsoever and float through the rest of our existence. Or we can adapt to this and still function as a family, and take control of where we're going. I prefer the latter option. And I strongly suspect that our husbands would prefer that, too."

Julexi burst into tears.

Rena had to bite her tongue. This is what Julexi always did when her arguments fell apart. The moment she realized that logic was against her, she resorted to her one defense mechanism. Tears.

She knew, of course, that this would silence any argument. All she had to do was open the floodgates and suddenly anyone who had held a contradictory position now found themselves taking Julexi into their arms and whispering words of comfort.

Rena had fallen for it the first few times Julexi had done it, especially shortly after losing the men. When any one of them would cry, Rena would swoop in and embrace them and hold them close. She felt like crying herself, and mourning together was one way to cope.

But Julexi had turned it into an art—probably without even realizing she was doing it. Her tears weren't fake, after all. As far as she was concerned, they were as real and warranted as all others. To suggest otherwise would be an offense.

"I'm sorry this is difficult for you, Julexi," said Rena. "And I'm sorry, Sabad, if you disagree with the decision Arjuna has made. I suggest you take it up with him. Now, if you'll excuse me."

She wedged her way between them and launched up the corridor.

But over the course of the day, as she worked in the helm with the navigators, Rena couldn't help but wonder if Julexi was right. Could they *really* do this? Repairing a broken heat coupler was one thing, installing a mining drill onto a salvage ship was quite another. None of the women had ever attempted such a thing. Segundo and Victor over the years had done all that.

Could Rena? Was she honestly capable of installing a lug processor, for example? Could she calibrate a digging stabilizer? And was the Gagak even structurally sound enough to house the needed equipment? What if it wasn't? When would they find that out? On their first official dig as the ship ruptures and breaks apart from the vibrations?

Oh Segundo, she thought. Am I doing the right thing? Is this truly what's best? Am I helping or hurting? You could probably look at this ship and know in an instant if such a thing was possible. I am lost without you, *mi amor.* Lost. Sometimes I feel confident about what we're doing, but most times I want to simply fly away and be alone. How I wish you were here, *mi vida.* Helping me, guiding me, holding me.

She imagined what it would be like if Segundo *were*

here. He and Arjuna would likely be close friends. They were of a similar temperament. She could see the two of them laughing together. And at the end of the day Segundo and Rena would go back to their cabin—and yes, they would have their own cabin!—and the two of them would laugh at how foolish Sabad was being, and Segundo would sashay around the room and shake his chest the way Sabad did, and Rena would laugh and slap him playfully on the arm and tell him he was being mean.

"Rena?"

Rena looked up from the holoscreen she had been staring at.

Edimar, her niece, was floating beside her. Fifteen years old now, and looking more like Lola, her mother, every day. Edimar had been a close friend to Victor. She had been the one to first spot the Formic ship approaching the system using the ship's motion-detection telescope known as the Eye.

Edimar had always been a little girl in Rena's mind, isolated up there in the Eye of El Cavador, watching for collision threats and keeping them all safe.

But she was hardly a little girl now. The last year had seen a growth spurt. She was nearly a woman grown—tall, full chested, slender in the arms and legs. Not old enough to marry, of course, but old enough to give boys heart palpitations. It had happened once on the Gagak. One of the Somali boys her age had whistled at her, and Rena had quickly gone to Arjuna to put an end to it.

Rena smiled. "Mar, I'm sorry. I didn't you see there."

"Can I speak to you for a moment?"

"Of course."

They left the helm and went to the bay window at the bow of the ship. The immensity of space was before them. It was not a real window, of course—merely a projection from the cameras outside. But it looked real, and it must have reminded Edimar of the Eye, because Rena always found her here, floating at the window, staring outward, as if looking for something lost. Perhaps her sister Alejandra, Rena thought. Or her father Toron.

Edimar said, "I need you to ask Arjuna something for me."

"Okay."

"I know I can technically go to him myself. He's said as much. Anyone on board can approach him. But I'd rather you do it."

"All right."

"Now that we're on network, I want to get on the Parallax system."

Rena furrowed her brow. "Should I know what that is?"

"It's a group of telescopes orbiting the system. Juke set them up years ago. With them, scientists can look way out into deep space."

"Why have I never heard of this?"

"Because they're for academics, researchers. We had no use for that kind of data on El Cavador. We were focused on finding nearby asteroids, not on looking into deep space. And besides, we weren't on the network. It wasn't available to us anyway."

"Why do you want to get on Parallax?"

"When I saw the Formic ship coming into system, it was only a few weeks away at that point. But if I had had a stronger scope, and if I had known precisely where to look, I might have seen it long before then."

"What are you saying?" asked Rena. "You think the Parallax satellites may have seen the Formic ship before we did?"

"I think it's possible, yes. But I won't know unless I look at the database from the past two to three years or so."

"But if the Parallax scopes had seen the Formic ship, wouldn't they have warned everyone?"

"Remember, these scopes are computers. They only do what we program them to do. Nobody has their eye to a lens, analyzing every little odd thing the scope sees. That would take too long. And it would be an enormous waste of time anyway. Most of the objects out there are harmless. All astronomers are worried about are collision threats. So they programmed the scopes to flag only those light-reflection objects that pose a threat to Earth. Everything else gets ignored. Essentially, if it's not on a trajectory with Earth, if it's not following normal parabolic patterns, nobody cares."

"Okay. Makes sense."

"It makes sense, yes, but there's a gaping hole in that practice. It doesn't account for anomalies. Like when an object decelerates or when it changes from one trajectory to another. The scopes should flag those type of objects, too, but they don't."

"Why not?"

"Because no one thought it was possible. Objects that behave that way are clearly extraterrestrial. And astronomers gave up on looking for extraterrestrial life way back in the twentieth century. Research in that field became unfashionable. Academics would have been laughed to scorn if they had suggested the scopes look for such things."

"Well they're kicking themselves now," said Rena.

"My point is, it's very possible that the scopes saw the Formic ship earlier without flagging it for analysis. And if something doesn't get flagged, it might as well not exist. It goes unseen and unnoticed in the archives."

"Yes, but wouldn't astronomers be sifting through that data now?"

"You would think," said Edimar. "But no one is. I went on the system and checked."

"Wait. You've already been on the system?"

"As a guest," said Edimar. "I did what any college kid can do. You can log on and see what the current objects for analysis are. But that's it. You can't access the archives. And that's where the answers are."

"So you need deeper access. Is there a fee involved?"

"Well, yes, but I'm not proposing we pay it. We couldn't afford it, and they wouldn't approve us anyway. We're not a university."

"Then how do you get access?"

"I set up a bogus username and I piggyback on a university's current account. It wouldn't be difficult. And it's not like anyone polices the system. Why would they? It's research, not a bank."

"But it is illegal."

"Technically. And that's why I need Arjuna to approve this before I do it. There are people on this ship looking for any reason to make us leave. And I don't want to be the person to give them a reason."

Rena smiled. Edimar, so young and yet so wise.

She took Edimar's hands. "You're growing up too fast, Mar. Your father would be proud of you. I know I am."

"So you'll talk to Arjuna?"

"I'll talk to him. And he'll say yes."

Edimar looked out the window a moment. When she turned back, Rena saw that there were tears in the girl's eyes. "This will never be home, Aunt Rena. No matter what we do to this ship, no matter how much we modify it or equip it, it will be never be home."

Rena felt as if her heart would break in two. She gently squeezed Edimar's hands. "You're not wrong, Mar. Home was El Cavador. Home was Segundo and your father and Alejandra and everything the way it was. And no matter what we do here, no matter what changes we make, we can never have that home again." She reached out and put a hand on Edimar's cheek. "But that doesn't mean we can't be happy, Mar. It may not be the happiness we had before, it may feel like a lesser version of it for a time, we may not even feel it some days at all. But we have to believe more will come. We have to hope. You've suffered more than most, Mar, and I wish I could fix that. But I can't. All I can do is be with you and your mother and the others and try to make something new. Maybe not a home. Maybe that won't come until later. But I believe it will come, Mar. With your brains in this operation, how could it not?"

Edimar smiled, and the two of them embraced.

A voice shouted from down the corridor. "Ms. Rena."

Rena turned and looked. One of the crewmen from the helm, Magashi, was calling to her. "You better come to the helm quick, Lady."

"What's wrong?"

"You have a message," said Magashi. "Arjuna said to bring you at once."

"From the traders?"

"No, no, Lady. From your son."

FROM: helm%comms@gagak481.net
TO: vico.delgado@jukelimited.net
Re: Found at last

Dearest Vico,

My son. I have read your letter five times now. Every time I do, I cry. You would have been proud of me: I have held back tears for a long time now. I have tried to be strong. But to know that your fingers actually typed the words I was reading, to know that you're alive and safe, I became a slobbery mess. It's only a matter of time before the crew here starts calling me "nose faucet" or something worse. Somalis love nicknames.

Edimar was with me when your letter came. She sends her love. You wouldn't recognize her if you saw her, she's grown so much.

All of the women and children are here as well. I have read them your letter. If I were to include all the messages they asked me to pass along on their behalf, this would take forever to type. Suffice it to say, you're loved and missed.

In fact, this might be a good time to inform you that you're the chief of our tribe. It's a long story, but essentially we need you to approve our partnering with Arjuna and his crew to turn the Gagak into a mining vessel. I've convinced myself that being the wife and mother of two brilliant mechanics qualifies me to lead this effort. So far no one has put me in a padded room. Should I self-commit?

In your letter you ask about Mono. It breaks my heart to tell you that he snuck back on to El Cavador before the WU-HU ship had decoupled. I'm so sorry, son. He was on El Cavador when it was lost.

I wish I could be there with you to give you this news. It seems so cold and impersonal to do it this way. I know he was like a brother to you. I hope you find some comfort in knowing that you were always in his thoughts. From the moment you left, you were always the subject of conversation if Mono was around. Vico this and Vico that. His love for you was as pure as any little boy's can be. Remember him, son. And let his love for you make you stronger.

I'm sorry you learned about your father from Lem Jukes. That angered me more than you know. When I see you next, I will tell you all and we can grieve together. In the meantime, to answer your question, I am fine. Losing your father was like losing myself, but I am holding tight to memories and finding peace wherever I can.

You mentioned that you plan to attack the Formic ship with a team of soldiers. Don't. I know it's cruel and selfish of me to ask such a thing, but I'm going to be cruel and selfish. The thought of losing you so soon after finding you is almost unbearable.

Build whatever they need. Design whatever the mission requires. Give them every scrap of brilliance that brain of yours can produce. But don't give them you.

You need to experience life, Vico. There is so much you haven't lived. Fall in love. Be loved by someone in return. Have children, as many as your future wife can give you. Love them. Grow old with them. That is a joy you have not yet experienced, and it is the greatest joy of this life.

Maybe it's this Imala girl. I like her spunk. You don't mention her age, but if she's working and out of college, she's got a few years on you. So what. I was four years older than your father, as you know. And he wouldn't have had it any other way.

Stay alive, son. That's all I ask.

From the moment you've left, I've kept you close, and that's where you will always be.

All my love,
Mom

CHAPTER 16

Holopad

Bingwen set up the doctors' clinic in an alcove on the lower level of Dragon's Den. Kim had come through with so many doctors willing to help staff the clinic via holo that Bingwen could have opened a small hospital if he had had that many holopads to work with. But, as it happened, he had only been able to scrounge up six—begging donations from those who owned one and raiding the supply closets when the soldiers weren't looking. But six holopads amounted to six doctors, and that was more than the people had enjoyed before.

"Tell me where it hurts, Ni Ni," Bingwen asked the old woman in Chinese.

The woman was stooped and frail, with gnarled hands as wrinkled as raisins. They were seated at a small table, atop of which lay a holopad. Above it, hovering in the air, was the head of a doctor from Fresno, California.

The connection was strong. Bingwen had set up several repeaters from the equipment upstairs, and the resolution of the doctor's face was so clear, it was almost as if he were there.

There were five identical setups elsewhere in the alcove. Each with a patient, holopad, doctor's assistant, and doctor. A line of fifteen people waiting to be seen extended out of the alcove and into the main tunnel.

The old woman said, "It would be easier to list off where it doesn't hurt, little one. Every part of me that bends aches like fire. Knuckles, hips, knees, toes. I've got more arthritis than a geriatric ward." She laughed and showed that half her teeth were missing.

Bingwen gave her a warm smile. Then he leaned his face into the holofield and translated what she had said.

The doctor from Fresno was one Bingwen had never worked with before, a young general practitioner who looked Chinese and had a Chinese name but who couldn't speak Chinese to save his life.

"Is she allergic to any medication?"

"No," said Bingwen. "I already asked her that. In the past she's mostly taken antiinflammatory drugs along with a pain med called glordical. Are you familiar with that one?"

"Yes, but I doubt you have that on base."

"We don't. Last time I checked we had six pain meds." He rattled off the names to the doctor and waited.

The doctor prescribed her one and gave Bingwen very specific instructions about the dosage. Then he made Bingwen repeat it all back to him.

It always went this way when Bingwen worked with a new doctor. They always spoke to him as if he were a toddler, as if children were incapable of anything. Usually, when they first saw Bingwen, they would assume there had been some mistake and they would insist on speaking to an adult. And Bingwen would have to go and get one of the adults who worked as doctors' assistants to come over and reassure the doctor that yes, Bingwen is in fact a doctor's assistant and yes he is in fact quite capable. The doctors never believed the adults, but they had no choice but to work with whatever assistant they were given.

So they would sigh and shrug and shake their heads in exasperation, and then they would charge ahead and hope for the best. After a few patients, they would realize that Bingwen wasn't as incompetent as they had assumed, and things would proceed much faster.

A few of the doctors who worked with Bingwen had even started asking for him by name. They had quickly learned that no one spoke English as well as he did, and that made all the difference in the world. Visits were faster, diagnoses were more accurate, and patients got the best care when the language wasn't a stumbling block.

But translation wasn't the only area in which Bingwen excelled. As a doctor's assistant, he was the doctors' eyes and hands on this side of the world, and he had quickly learned his duties over the last seven days. He could take blood, administer shots, check vitals, conduct bone scans. He knew when a blood-pressure reading was high and when a liver-enzyme reading was low. He knew what lungs with pneumonia sounded like and what an infected eardrum looked like. He had become so good in fact that oftentimes the other doctors at the other stations would ask for him to step in and help the doctor's assistant with something beyond mere translation.

So he wasn't surprised when Pipo tapped him on the shoulder and told him he was needed over at Station Four.

Bingwen finished with the old woman and explained where she needed to go to pick up her prescription from the medical officer. Then he left his screen and hurried over to Station Four. To his surprise, there wasn't a patient waiting. Nor a doctor's assistant. Both chairs were empty. But the holopad was there, with an empty holofield above it. That either meant no one was there or the person on the other end didn't want to be seen.

Bingwen climbed up into a chair and put his face into the field.

Kim's head was there on screen.

Bingwen smiled. "Is this a personal call? There's no patient here."

Her expression was serious. "Bingwen, I think you'll hear me better with the audio bud in your ear."

He understood immediately. He put the earpiece in, picked up the holopad and left the alcove. He found a side tunnel nearby that led to an empty storage closet. Bingwen slipped inside and locked the door behind him.

"Alone and private," he said.

Kim relaxed. "There are some people on the line with me, calling in from Luna. They want to talk to you."

"Me? Why?"

"I'll let them explain. Will you speak with them?"

"Put them on."

Two other heads appeared in the holofield. One was a woman—early twenties, sharp features, dark complexion, black hair. The other was a man, a few years younger. He was ethnic as well, but different. South American maybe.

"Hello, Bingwen," said the woman. "My name is Imala Bootstamp. This is my friend Victor Delgado."

The names meant nothing to him. "How can I help you, Ms. Bootstamp?"

"I need to speak with Captain Wit O'Toole and Captain Mazer Rackham. I'm told you're at the same facility where they are."

Bingwen felt uneasy. He wasn't sure if he should reveal anything to this woman.

"I'm making you uncomfortable, Bingwen," said Imala. "I don't mean to. I know you want to protect Captain O'Toole and Captain Rackham. I don't mean them any harm. I need their help."

"Are you reporters?"

Imala smiled. "Hardly. We're working with a team of engineers on Luna to infiltrate and destroy the Formic ship."

"Infiltrate? You mean get inside? Don't the Formics vaporize every ship that approaches it?"

"Every ship but ours," said Imala. "We've reached it, Bingwen. We've already been inside it. And while we were there we found a weakness. We think we know how to destroy it. Only, we're not soldiers. We need a capable, organized strike team to partner with us. We were hoping the MOPs would at least hear us out."

"Why contact them through me?" said Bingwen. "Why not go through the military?"

"We heard about the doctors' program you set up. That put us in contact with Dr. Arnsbrach. When she told us of your connection with Mazer Rackham, we knew we had our answer."

"Also, you asked the military already and they said no," said Bingwen.

"Correct."

"Why not contact Wit through his superiors at Strategos? Or Mazer's superiors in New Zealand?"

"We tried that as well," said Imala. "Neither have had any contact with Captain O'Toole or Captain Rackham since right before they left India. The Chinese at Dragon's Den are restricting any outside communication."

"I don't know how to help you," said Bingwen. "Wit and Mazer are in a restricted area. I can't reach them."

Imala seemed crestfallen. "I see."

"But if you prove to me that this is legitimate, if you can show me that you have in fact penetrated the ship's defenses, I'll do everything I can to connect you with the MOPs."

"How will you reach them?" asked Imala.

"Let me worry about that," said Bingwen. "Kindly show me proof, and I'll do what's necessary."

Imala nodded. She looked down at something on her console on her end. "We're sending you a clip, Bingwen. It shows you the inside of the Formic ship's cargo bay and the wreckage from human ships collected there. Along the wall, you'll see Formics pulling carts. Do you see it?"

The vid had started playing in the holofield to Bingwen's right. He stared at it. "Yes. I see it. Who took this vid?"

"I did," said Victor.

"And you can get a team of soldiers back in there?" asked Bingwen.

"I will or I'll die trying."

The was good enough for Bingwen. "Send me your uplinks. I'll take a holopad to Wit and Mazer and connect them to you directly. Give me a few hours." He disconnected the call, put the holopad into his knapsack, then went and found Pipo.

"I need to get inside the restricted area and see the MOPs," he said.

"That's impossible," said Pipo. "There are guards, hololocked doors. You'd never get in."

"I have to try. But I need your help. Can you pretend to be my sister?"

She raised an eyebrow. "Your sister? Why?"

"I need someone to argue with me and validate my story. It'll be more believable that way."

"You're asking me to argue with you?"

"And hit me as hard as you can."

Pipo smiled. "I like this idea."

He told her what he had in mind and they made their way to the commissary where the officers ate. The trick was to pick the right target. It needed to be an officer of high rank, someone who had access to the entire facility and who could access MOPs without first going to a superior. A colonel or higher, Bingwen figured. And he needed to be an unsympathetic soldier, a real rulebook zealot.

Bingwen knew he couldn't break into the restricted area. There was too much tech, too much security. But he also knew he didn't need to. As long as adults thought they were in control and making the decision, you could get them to do whatever you wanted.

He and Pipo hid in the tunnel outside the commissary until Bingwen saw the perfect candidate: a callous-looking colonel who snapped at a junior officer for not immediately forfeiting his place in line for someone of superior rank. The junior officer bowed and begged pardon, but the colonel kicked the man out.

"You want to talk to *that* guy?" asked Pipo. "He's a buffalo butt."

"Exactly," said Bingwen. He reached into his knapsack and pulled out a map of an abandoned military base where he and the MOPs had once camped. It wasn't the perfect prop for the job, but it would have to do.

He and Pipo waited until the colonel finished his meal and made his way back to his vehicle parked out in the tunnel. Then Bingwen ran up to him with the map in his hand and bowed low.

"Please, sir, please take this. One of the Anglo men must have dropped it."

The colonel looked ready to give Bingwen a kick then stopped. "Anglo men?"

"In the restricted area," said Bingwen. "Please. Could you return it? I'm sure the man will want it back."

The colonel snatched it from Bingwen's hand and examined it. Deen had scribbled a few notes on the map, identifying a few of the buildings in English as Bingwen translated the Chinese characters.

"You say this came from one of the Anglo men?" the colonel said. "That's impossible. They don't come over here."

Bingwen looked uncomfortable. "No, sir. They're not supposed to. But . . . he . . . I mean, the man . . . sometimes at night . . ."

The colonel narrowed his eyes, suspicious. "What man?" He grabbed Bingwen by the shoulder. "Answer me."

Pipo ran up on cue and bowed low. "Sir, forgive my brother. He is a fool. I will take that map. It belongs to our sister."

Bingwen glared at her. "Go away, Pipo. I'm giving it back."

"It's not yours to give, Bingwen. It belongs to Ju-long."

"Who is Ju-long?" said the colonel.

"Our older sister," said Pipo. "She prizes that map, sir. Ignore my brother."

"Did one of the Anglo men give this to your sister?"

"We do not want trouble, sir," said Pipo. "Forgive the intrusion. You are a busy man. We will not bother you any further." She extended her hand for the map.

The colonel clung to it. "I asked you a question."

"You're making it worse," Bingwen said to Pipo. "Go away." He looked back at the colonel. "It is not Ju-long's fault, sir. She is beautiful to look upon. She did not ask for the visitor."

"Visitor, eh?" said the colonel. "When? When did he see her?"

"Don't say another word, Bingwen," said Pipo.

"Please do not fault Ju-long," Bingwen said to the colonel. "She is eighteen. He promised to marry her after the war, take all of us out of China."

"Shut up," said Pipo.

"I do not believe the man, sir," said Bingwen. "He only

says what Ju-long wants to hear. He gives her gifts to be alone with her. Like this map."

Pipo clenched her fists. "I said shut up, Bingwen."

"You must give him back the map," said Bingwen. "Then he will think Ju-long is not interested. He will not come anymore."

Pipo hit him. A swat on the arm, the face, the back, the head, anywhere her flying hands could reach him.

The colonel pulled them apart and pushed Pipo away, who had started crying.

"You'll ruin it!" she screamed to Bingwen. "You'll ruin everything!" She turned and ran away.

The colonel grabbed Bingwen by the collar. "What does this man look like?"

Bingwen cowered slightly, afraid. "All Anglos look alike to me, sir. I would know him on sight, but I don't know how to describe him. A soldier, strong, short hair. When he comes next, I'll make note of his features."

The colonel considered a moment then opened the passenger door. "Get in."

Bingwen's eyes widened. "But . . . where are we going?"

"I said get in." The colonel grabbed him by the scruff of the neck and forced him inside.

They drove through two security checkpoints and down several side tunnels. None of the guards stopped them.

The colonel parked and led Bingwen through a series of secure doors, holding tightly to Bingwen's collar as if he feared Bingwen would run away. They barged into a large briefing room where Mazer and the MOPs and a half dozen senior Chinese officers were gathered around a holotable filled with schematics and maps and images. The room fell silent. Everyone turned to Bingwen and the colonel.

"Point to him!" said the colonel. "Point to the man!"

Bingwen looked at all of their faces. He met Mazer's eyes and gave him the subtlest of nods, hoping Mazer would understand.

"Well?" said the colonel. "Who was it?"

A Chinese soldier without any rank on his jumpsuit stepped forward. "Colonel Chua. To what do we owe this unexpected visit?"

The colonel grabbed the back of Bingwen's collar again. "Major Shenzu sir, you will pardon the interruption, but you have a security breach that must be resolved. One of these Anglos has been sneaking into the civilian barracks and cavorting with a woman."

Shenzu frowned. "That is a serious accusation, Colonel. I'm assuming you have proof of this?"

The colonel pushed Bingwen forward. "Point to him, boy."

Bingwen walked up to Mazer, took the holopad from his knapsack, and gave it to him. "This is yours, Captain Rackham. I stole it from your pack before you went off to destroy the lander. It was wrong of me. I am sorry."

Mazer took the device and examined it. "Yes. I was wondering what had happened to this. You shouldn't have taken this, Bingwen."

Bingwen hung his head, ashamed. "I know. I beg your pardon."

Colonel Chua came forward, confused, furious. "What is the meaning of this? Is this the man or not? Speak, boy. Did this man come to your sister?"

Bingwen turned to him and bowed. "Forgive me, sir. I do not have a sister. I deceived you so that you would bring me here and allow me to return this stolen property. These men are honorable. They would never do what I suggested. I am yours to punish as you deem appropriate." He held out his hands.

The colonel looked ready to hit him.

"Colonel," said Mazer. "Perhaps you will allow me to

punish the boy. His behavior is inexcusable, and since I'm the reason why he's here, I feel as if I am responsible. These lies he has told threaten the alliance that MOPs and China share. And he should have known what a foolish thing it was to say." He looked angrily at Bingwen, and Bingwen knew it wasn't an act.

"There was a little girl who lied as well," said the colonel. "What of her? Who will punish her?"

Mazer bowed. "You are just and thorough, Colonel. Please, allow us to remove this burden from you. We will find the girl as well. You have far more weighty and important matters to address than the petty pranks of ungrateful children."

The colonel nodded. "Ungrateful indeed." He shook a finger at Bingwen. "Is this how you thank us? We give you shelter, food, medicine, and you mock us."

Bingwen almost laughed. The man was talking as if he had rescued Bingwen from the clutches of a Formic. Yet Bingwen had a sneaking suspicion that were it up to the colonel, all the refugees would be turned away.

"Please, Colonel," said Mazer. "I'd hate for you to be bothered any further. I assure you the boy's punishment will be swift and severe."

The colonel nodded, content. Then he scowled once more at Bingwen and left.

Mazer took Bingwen by the arm, "Major Shenzu, please excuse us for a moment."

He roughly led Bingwen out of the room. As soon as the door was closed behind them, he released Bingwen and said, "Follow me."

His tone was sharp. He was not happy. He led Bingwen down a hall, through a series of doors and into a large empty cafeteria.

"I'm going to assume you have a very good reason for the stunt you just pulled," said Mazer. "A very, *very* good reason. Because telling a lie like that was an enormously stupid thing to do, Bing. I hope you know that."

"It had to be a bad lie or the colonel wouldn't have brought me here. It was the best one I could come up with in the time that I had. I couldn't have reached you otherwise. I'm sorry."

Mazer sighed, sat down on the floor, and leaned against the wall. The holopad was still in his hand. "Why bring me this? What's on it?"

"Uplinks to a team on Luna who have infiltrated the Formic ship and who know how to destroy it. They want to team up with you and the MOPs. You're supposed to call them."

Mazer stared at him. "How did you get this information?"

"From Dr. Arnsbrach," said Bingwen. "Well, she connected me to them anyway."

Mazer looked surprised. "You spoke to Kim?"

"She helped me set up the holo hospital."

"Holo hospital?"

"Long story," said Bingwen. "Do you really want to hear about that now?"

"Later," said Mazer. He started typing on his wrist pad.

"What are you doing?"

"I'm asking Wit to join us. He needs to hear this as well."

Wit arrived a moment later, and Bingwen told them everything he knew. When he was done, Wit said, "Victor Delgado. That's the name of the kid who uploaded the vid and tried to warn Earth." He turned to Bingwen. "And the vid you saw of the interior, it looked real?"

"Looked legit to me," said Bingwen.

Wit thought for a moment then said, "We take this to Shenzu and make the call together. We need a hard line to make the connection anyway. We can't do it in here.

We'll put it on the big table and see what they have to say."

"The Chinese won't like this," said Mazer. "We're helping command their army. They'll think we're abandoning them."

"We won't abandon the op. We'll suggest they bring in Major Ketkar from India to help run things here. There are other Chinese officers who have been shadowing us who show promise. Shenzu can do plenty. The op is practically on autopilot anyway."

"Are we winning?" asked Bingwen.

"I wouldn't say that," said Wit. "Not even close. But we're certainly doing better than we were. The counteragent is working. It's devastating the death squads. We've retaken a few of the coastal cities. No one can go back there yet—not for a long time to come. Maybe years. But it gives us a little hope."

Wit turned to Mazer. "You're right to worry about the operation. But this is the mothership we're talking about. Their supply line, their home base. If there's a chance we can destroy that, that flips this war on its head."

"Agreed," said Mazer.

Wit turned to Bingwen. "You did good, Bingwen. But next time be more careful with your lies."

CHAPTER 17

Cocoons

Lem Jukes stood at the wall screen in his office looking at several dozen mug shots of some of the most lethal men in the world. The photos were projected there in front of him, filling the wall, each accompanied by a window of data: name, languages spoken, skill set, combat experience, references, contact information. Some were in groups. Others were solo hires. It was quite the mixed bag. African mercenaries, special forces units, corporate security outfits. They were all hard men—many of whom, Lem suspected, were no more honorable than the thuggish guns-for-hire coming out of Eastern Europe.

"I don't like the looks of these guys," said Despoina. She was barefoot and sitting in one of Lem's frayed office chairs, hugging her knees to her chest. "They look like criminals, like the kind of guys you'd see on those true crime specials. You know, the guys who break bones for mob bosses." She dropped her voice and adopted a gangster accent. "Hey, bossy, you want I should rip off Guido's fingers here? I'm thinkin' he might of squeaked to the popo."

Lem regarded her. "What does that even mean? That sounds vulgar."

"Popo? It's slang in the U.S. for the police. You know, the fuzz, the badges, the doughnut patrol. Don't they have slang for the police in Finland?"

Lem shook his head and looked back at the screen. "The youth of America."

Despoina gestured to the screen. "All I'm saying is they look like a pack of bruisers. Not a single one of them is smiling."

"They're killers, Des. They're hired by governments to silently snap people's necks in the dead of night. These photos are how they market themselves. They're supposed to look tough. People who hire these kinds of people want tough. Would you hire a strike team that looked like they came from IT?"

"Hey, I know guys in IT who work out and who could pin you in under two seconds flat."

"A maimed bunny rabbit could pin me in under two seconds. I'm a lover, not a fighter."

"I'll say," she said.

He looked at her and saw that she was winking at him. Not in a seductive way, but in a mockingly seductive way. Des couldn't wink her left eye without giving it serious concentration, and it looked ridiculous whenever she tried, as if it took all of her willpower to close that eye without closing the other. It had become a joke between them.

"You shouldn't even be here," said Lem. "You're my father's secretary. People will get ideas."

She slithered out of the chair and sidled up next to him. "Oh really? What kind of ideas?" Two of her fingers walked up his arm to his shoulder.

He gently took her hands. "I'm serious."

Her smile faded. "I'm here on official business, Lem.

Your father wanted you to review some files. They had to be couriered over. I volunteered."

"You shouldn't have."

She pulled her hands away and folded her arms. "Okay, now you're being rude."

He took a breath and gently took her hands again. "Des, I like you. We have a nice time together. But you don't know my father. If he were to suspect that there was any sort of relationship between us, it would not go well for you."

"Why? What would he do?"

"Honestly, I don't know, but he wouldn't like it. He thinks women are a distraction."

She smiled. "Good distraction or bad distraction?"

He sighed. "Can we talk seriously here for a moment? This is important."

Her face fell again. "I'm trying to help, Lem. I thought you wanted my help."

"I do, yes, but—"

"It was me who found out about that doctors' clinic at Dragon's Den. You were ready to give up on the MOPs. I found that lead for you."

"Yes. You helped. That was a good idea."

"You thought it was a dumb idea when I first presented it. You said so."

"It still hasn't panned out. We haven't heard from the kid. And you have to admit, putting the fate of the world in the hands of a ten-year-old is a dumb idea. What if he doesn't get through to the MOPs?"

"First of all, he's not ten. He's eight. And secondly, I could say the same about you, putting the fate of the world in the hands of a roguishly handsome, brilliant billionaire seems like a dumb idea, too."

He slid his hand around her waist. "Where's the painfully shy girl I saw in my father's office a few weeks ago?"

She came in close. "All grown up."

He kissed her. It was a dumb thing to do. He had already decided not to see her again. Father was right on that point: She was a distraction, particularly now, when he was so focused on the mission at hand. He had planned in his mind how to break it to her gently—and now here he was, pulling her body tight against his, kissing her mouth, the line of her jaw, the top of her neck—

The door opened. A woman's voice. "Oh."

Lem broke away. Imala was standing in the doorway. "Sorry. I didn't know I would be interrupting."

Lem took a step to his right, brushed the front of his shirt. His face felt hot. "You didn't, you're not. Ms. Crutchfield here was merely bringing me some information."

Imala was grinning. "That looked like quite the exchange of information."

Lem ran a hand through his hair. "Is there something you wanted, Ms. Bootstamp?"

"Captain Wit O'Toole of the Mobile Operations Police is on the line. He wants to talk."

"Good. I'll join you in a moment."

Imala left and shut the door.

"I'm sorry," said Des. "You're right. I shouldn't have come. That was dumb."

Lem adjusted the cuffs on his shirt and ran a hand through his hair again. He didn't look at her. "Everyone's going to be watching the office door now. Don't come out when I do. Slip away a minute or so later when everyone's focused on the holo."

She nodded. "Right. And I won't come again."

No, thought Lem, you won't. You won't come near me at all. This is over. But aloud he said, "Tell my father I'll review the files."

"He only wants to help however he can, Lem. I don't

think he's as maniacal and sinister as you think he is. At least, I haven't seen that side of him."

"Try living with him for thirty years."

She took his hand. "You want the MOPs, Lem. Do whatever you can to make it happen. These thugs here on the wall aren't a backup plan. They can't deliver like MOPs can."

He laughed. "What makes you an expert?"

"I'm not. Everybody who follows the news knows what the MOPs are. They blew up the lander. They brokered the alliance with India. They've taken down almost as many transports as the entire Chinese military. They're very good at what they do."

"They've always been my first choice."

"They're your only choice. They're white knights. These guys"—she gestured to the wall—"freelancers. They work for whoever has the fattest purse. No ethics, no scruples, they're in it for the money and the thrill of the kill. You need people who can think like Victor and remain faithful like Imala. That's MOPs."

"So you're my counselor now?"

"No. I don't presume to be anything, except a friend who wants to see you succeed."

He pulled his hand away and moved for the door.

"And Lem . . ."

He turned back.

"I know nothing will ever happen between us. I know that. I'm not naïve enough to think otherwise. All I ask is that when you tire of me, whenever that is, you're nice about it."

After a silence, he nodded once and said, "I better go."

Then he walked out.

Mazer was standing in the back of the war room beside Bingwen, apart from the MOPs, who were gathered around the holotable, waiting. Wit had connected with Luna, but Imala had run off to fetch someone. Now the holofield above the table was active but empty.

Shenzu had politely asked the Chinese officers to leave the room before Wit had made the call, and to Mazer's surprise they had obeyed without hesitation—even those who outranked Shenzu. They simply bowed and walked out. The military had promoted Shenzu to major when they had all returned to China, but they might as well have made him a general for all the deferential treatment he was given.

"You don't have to stand back here with me," said Bingwen. "I'm good in the shadows by myself."

"I can see the holofield from here," said Mazer. "And you're much better company."

The truth was, Mazer didn't feel comfortable standing with the MOPs. He was not one of them, after all. He never had been. They had always treated him like one of their own, of course—they had teased him as brutally as they had teased each other—which was a form of acceptance among such men. But he was not a MOP. He had failed their test, and these men hadn't. He could fight alongside them, operate as one of them, but he could never consider himself one with their unit. Which was fine with Mazer. He held no grudges. He had not been ready when they had tested him. And in fact, failing that exam, getting rejected by Wit so long ago, was the best training anyone had ever given him.

He squatted down and faced Bingwen. "How's your arm? I didn't hurt it when I pulled you out of the room earlier, did I?"

Bingwen rotated his shoulder. "No. You were easy on me. I knew you were acting."

"I wasn't completely acting. I *was* mad. But I knew there had to be a good reason for you to pull a stunt like that. Who's the girl who helped you?"

"Her name's Pipo."

"She's not your girlfriend, is she?"

"I'm eight, Mazer. I'm not supposed to have girl-friends until I'm in my late teens or early twenties."

Mazer laughed. "You've got it all mapped out, haven't you?"

"You should call Kim."

The words came out of nowhere and stopped Mazer cold.

Bingwen frowned. "She worries about you. If she's a friend, it would be nice to call her. I think she would like that."

"You've talked to her a lot?"

"Every day for the past week. She's the best doctor we have in the clinic. By far. Why are you smiling?"

"Because you know what makes a good doctor. I don't think I knew that when I was eight years old. I probably would have based that judgment on who gave the fewest shots."

"It's how they treat people," said Bingwen. "Some doctors are kind, but others are . . . I don't know the word in English. Not mean, but—"

"Brusque?"

"I don't know that word."

"Impatient? Callous? Cold?"

"Cold? That means something other than tempera-ture?"

"It means they don't seem nice."

"Right. They don't seem nice. They're scientific about treating people."

"You don't know the multiple definitions of cold, but you know the word 'scientific'?"

Bingwen shrugged. "Some words stick, some words don't."

"So Kim is one of the nice ones?" said Mazer.

"The nicer of the nice ones."

"Nic*est*," corrected Mazer. "Nicer is for two. Nicest is the superlative."

"I don't know what 'su-per-lative' means. Stop using words I don't know."

Mazer nodded. "Give me a list of all the words you don't know, and I'll be sure not to use them."

"You're one to talk," said Bingwen. "Your Chinese is awful."

"I thought I did okay."

"You talk Chinese as well as Mongo did."

"Who was Mongo?"

"Our family water buffalo."

"Your English is better than my Chinese. I'll give you that."

"So you will call Kim?"

Mazer took a breath. "It's complicated, Bing. When you get older life gets more complicated."

"I think she loves you. Like how my mother loved my father. She didn't say that to me. But she does."

She did. Mazer knew she did. She had told him so. Just once. But it was enough. He thought of that moment often. They had gone to the salt marshes of Manukau Harbor. She had wanted to see the thousands of migratory godwits who had gathered there to feed. He and Kim had stood in one of the many wooden towers built along the shore for birdwatchers. Mazer had brought her a pair of military binoculars.

"They'll fly over eleven thousand kilometers without taking a single break," Kim had said.

"Sounds like the military," Mazer had said.

"From here to northern China and then on to Alaska and back. The longest single flight of any species."

A salty breeze was blowing in from the water, lifting her hair away from the nape of her neck. The air smelled of brine and mud and eelgrass. The song of thousands of chittering godwits was not as loud as

Mazer had thought it would be. And he marveled at how they moved on the water, lifting together as a single unit, undulating in the air like a giant wave as they shifted, circled back, landed, and took to the air again, like a single organism with a thousand different sets of eyes.

"They're monogamous, you know?" Kim had said. "All that flying, all that distance; tens of thousands of them crammed into a small space like this, all of them looking exactly alike. And yet somehow they snuggle up next to their mate at day's end. Somehow they find each other."

"In Maori culture, the birds are the messengers of the gods," Mazer had said. "Legend has it that the first of our people came here in a fleet of *waka,* or canoes, following the flight of the godwits. They were the guides the gods had given us. There's a song about it that the children sing."

"Do you know it?"

"Most of it."

"Let's hear it."

He laughed. "What, you want me to sing it? Now?"

"We're alone. I won't laugh, I swear. I think it's fascinating. You don't talk about this kind of stuff. Your culture, I mean. I want to know about it."

"It's a children's song, Kim. It's in Maori."

"I'll never ask you to sing anything ever again. I promise."

He had felt silly, but there was such pleading in her eyes that he had acquiesced and sung it. He had even done the hand motions: the paddling canoes and the flapping and swooping of the godwits. She had watched his every move, the corners of her mouth curling up into a smile. When he finished, her eyes were misted with tears and she had told him that she loved him. The words had come out of her almost in a whisper.

He had not expected it. But to hear her say it was like lightning in his chest.

He didn't know how to respond. Did he love her as well? And if he did, what were the consequences of him saying so?

The silence between them had lingered.

She wiped at her eyes, slightly embarrassed. "I don't expect you to say anything, Mazer. I know you're not ready to say those words. But when you are, if that moment ever comes, say them to me in Maori."

Two weeks later he had left for China.

Bingwen was watching him. "You're thinking of her right now, aren't you?"

"I'm glad you got to speak with her, Bingwen. That makes me very happy. She's a very special person to me, and so are you. When my friends become friends, I'm happy."

Bingwen had smiled and was about to say something when a voice from the holotable filled the room.

"Greetings, gentlemen. My name is Lem Jukes. Thank you for returning our holo."

The man's head and torso appeared above the holotable. He gestured to his right and motioned others to join him in the holofield. "Victor, Imala, join me in here please. Gentlemen, I'd like you to meet Imala Bootstamp and Victor Delgado, the team that has infiltrated the Formic ship and who will lead this effort." Lem looked at something slightly to the left. "Thank you for setting up cameras on your end. We see you have everyone gathered."

Wit went through the introductions, leaving Mazer and Bingwen for the end.

"Thank you for connecting us, Bingwen," said Imala.

There was a time delay that took some getting used to. Wit and Lem kept talking over each other, realizing too late that they were doing it, and then they would stop and restart again. But soon they got into a rhythm. And once the Luna team began their presentation, things went much faster.

Lem showed them several vids from inside the Formic ship that featured the cargo bay, sleep chamber, garden, launch tubes, narrow passageways, and helm. Victor then described how he and Imala had reached the ship, and Lem went into detail about what resources he could offer in terms of weapons, suits, whatever the team needed.

"We're a large group," said Wit. "We obviously can't fit in the shuttle Victor and Imala used. How do you propose getting us to the ship?"

"Using the same principle," said Lem. "We put you in a ship, disguise it to look like flotsam drifting harmlessly through space, and you float right up to the hull of the mothership. However, since there are so many of you, we obviously can't put you all in a single shuttle. Even if we packed you in like sardines, the shuttle would be too big and too conspicuous. The Formics would notice it, even if you were moving slowly and weren't on a collision course."

"Loading all of us into a single ship is a bad idea anyway," said Cocktail. "If something were to happen to the shuttle, the entire strike team would be lost. That's putting all of your eggs in a single basket."

"Agreed," said Lem. "It's safer to split you up. In fact, we propose putting each of you in your own individual vessel."

A schematic appeared in the holofield. It was a small tube-shaped ship with the outline of a prostrate man inside of it—not unlike a coffin or a sleep chamber. "We call them 'cocoons,'" said Lem. "Our engineers are building them now. As you can see, there's only enough room for a single passenger. And it's a tight squeeze. You won't be able to move much at all, but that's for your own safety. The smaller the cocoon, the less likely it will be tagged as a collision threat. We'll attach small electrodes to your muscles to keep them active as you drift."

"How many of these cocoons are you building?" asked Wit.

"Twelve," said Lem. "Victor will go in one, plus eleven from your party. But we recommend that all of you come to Luna. You'll need to train for a couple days to get used to maneuvering in a zero-G environment, and not everyone excels at that. We recommend that those who do well in zero-G constitute the strike team."

ZZ said, "If twelve identical pieces of wreckage float toward the ship, won't the Formics notice that?"

"They won't be identical," said Lem.

Random pieces of scrap metal began attaching themselves to the exterior of the cocoon in the holofield.

"Each cocoon will be uniquely disguised to look like wreckage. We'll use the same approach Victor and Imala did. Paint, scorch marks, torn metal, broken conduit, whatever we can scrounge up. Some of you will be flat. Some of you will be bent forward slightly. We're randomizing the shape, too. If you're lucky, you'll get a flat one."

Lem reached forward with his hands and rotated the schematic, giving them a better view of the small propulsion systems at the rear and sides of the vessel. "To further save on room, we're not including any flight controls or avionics. Instead, the cocoons will be remotely controlled. All you'll have to do is climb inside, and our drone pilots will do the rest."

"Even with those adjustments," said Deen. "Twelve pieces of flotsam doesn't seem very inconspicuous. It worked for Victor and Imala because they were one piece of scrap. Twelve is a lot more than one."

"Consider the size of the thing," said Mazer. "It's

enormous. The cocoons could come from all sides and angles. And we could stagger their arrival over the period of a day or more so everyone isn't getting there at the same moment. In fact, depending on how we design the op and the individual objectives, arriving at different times is best anyway. The first wave infiltrates the ship. A second wave secures and holds the passageways. A third wave takes the cargo bay. Et cetera."

"That's the idea," said Lem. "And our shipbuilding crews intend to help in another way as well. Your twelve cocoons won't be the only pieces of wreckage approaching the ship. For the Formics to ignore you, you must blend in with the environment. But you can't be invisible if you're the only things *in* the environment. So we're making at least three hundred other remote-controlled projectiles to create a sea of wreckage around the Formic ship that we completely control. These mini floaters will be smaller than the cocoons in most instances, but collectively they'll create a haze of wreckage for you to drift through."

"Beyond that," said Victor, "the mini floaters will also allow us to test the sensitivity of the Formics' collision-avoidance system. In other words, if the Formics start firing at anything that twitches, regardless of how slow it's moving, we'll know we need to reevaluate our approach."

"When will these cocoons be ready?" asked Wit. "And for that matter, how quickly can you build three hundred remote-controlled projectiles?"

"We have an entire production line dedicated to this effort," said Lem. "It's the largest such facility of its kind in the world. I have a warehouse full of people who are working around the clock. My father is putting the weight and resources of his company behind this. Juke Limited is committed to ending this war. We've built a shield of ships between Earth and the Formic mothership. Now we're ready to end this once and for all. That is, if you'll join us."

"You've told us how you'll get us there," said Wit. "What happens next? Arriving is only the beginning. You said you had discovered a vulnerability?"

"That is the carrot we'll leave dangling," said Lem. "Agree to work with us, and we'll show you how to cripple the ship and kill everyone on board. Otherwise, we'll take this strategy to another strike force. There are others we can approach, but our strong preference is to work with you."

"We need to debate this among ourselves," said Wit. "But if we agree, how would we get to Luna, and how quickly could we make this happen?"

"Give me a verbal commitment, and I will send an aircraft to retrieve you and carry you to one of our launch sites in Finland."

"How will you retrieve us?" said Wit. "We're in the middle of a war zone. The skies aren't safe."

"Let us coordinate that. China is being more agreeable to opening its air space, and Juke has aircraft throughout Southeast Asia. The logistics we can work out. Our priority now is cementing the strike team. We will await your answer."

The Luna team said their farewells, and Wit disconnected the call.

"Well?" asked Wit. "What does everyone think?"

The room was quiet a moment then ZZ said, "I'm not crazy about those cocoons. No movement. No flight controls. I'm not claustrophobic, but I think I would be after a few hours. And what do we do if our suit malfunctions? Or if the remote controls fail? Float off into oblivion? Asphyxiate? We can't exactly call for help. We'll be far away from each other. The moment we rush to another's aid, our cover is blown and the Formics start shooting."

"We wouldn't be able to defend ourselves either," said Cocktail. "I don't like that. We'd be floating targets. And not just for a brief amount of time either. It will take us days to float to the ship if we're drifting at a negligible speed. And it's not the boredom that bothers me. It's knowing that I could be vaporized at any moment. That would drive me insane. I think the concept is brilliant, but if the Formics were wise to us it would be like shooting fish in a barrel, and we'd be the fish."

"I agree," said Lobo. "The cocoons are loco. But they're also an idea that might, actually, God willing, work. I'm not too keen on the idea of climbing inside one either, but I feel better knowing they're being built by Juke. This is the most advanced ship manufacturer in the world we're talking about. If anyone can do this, they can."

"I'm with Lobo," said Mazer. "Lem Jukes strikes me as a little too arrogant for his own good, but there's no denying the fact that the man has resources. No government on Earth makes as big a commitment to space tech and engineering as Juke Limited. Better suits. Better life-support systems. And their shipbuilders live and breathe this world. They understand the conditions, they know the physics. If they say they can build a cocoon that will look like a hunk of harmless junk, I believe them. I agree with Cocktail and ZZ that the cocoons have their drawbacks, but there's no golden solution here. Any approach is going to be high risk.

"But even if they didn't have any of that to offer—the ships, the suits, none of it—even if they didn't have so much as a belt buckle to give us in terms of equipment, we still need these people. They have Victor. The guy not only got inside the ship, but he also got to the heart of it and back out again. Without detection. The intel he has changes everything. Until an hour ago, that ship was a giant question mark. With Victor we have something to work with. We wouldn't be going in blind. We could actually plan an infiltration with some degree of confidence. And when they say they know how to destroy it, I believe them. Whatever vulnerability they've discovered, whatever they have up their sleeve, they seem pretty confident about it. I say go."

"Shenzu?" said Wit. "What say you? If we do this we'd be abandoning our post here."

Shenzu dismissed that with a wave of his hand. "The past week has been a master's class for our field commanders. They have learned much from watching all of you. And China will be open to other outside commanders as well. That tide has turned. Ketkar from India will come. Others from Europe and the U.S. will come as well. Strategists we can rally in abundance. I will see to that. For whatever reason, my voice has some weight now. This isn't a concern. The rarity in this war is a strike team that's cohesive enough, trained enough, and single-minded enough to pull this off. That's us."

"Us?"

"Of course," said Shenzu. "Don't think for a second that I'm not coming with you."

CHAPTER 18

Soldier Boy

When Bingwen heard that he'd be joining the MOPs and Chinese officers for dinner, he expected the food to be better than a sludgy protein drink. Canned vegetables perhaps. Or maybe crackers with an MRE, if he was lucky. So when the server in the cafeteria line handed him a plate loaded with steaming beef strips, fluffy white rice, and fresh sautéed vegetables, Bingwen stared at it, stunned. "Is this all for me?"

Mazer was ahead of him in line and picked up a bowl of pudding from the dessert racks. "You don't have to eat all of it if you don't want to."

"Are you kidding?" said Bingwen. "Of course I'm eating it. This is more than I ever got at home. Can I have one of the puddings, too?"

"Help yourself. It's à la carte."

"What does that mean?"

"It means you can pick and choose whatever you want."

"In that case, I'm taking two."

Bingwen grabbed a bowl of chocolate pudding and a slice of peach pie and put them both on his tray.

Mazer tugged at Bingwen's sleeve. "All right, hippopotamus. Better come with me before your eyes make promises your stomach can't keep." He led Bingwen to a small table in the dining hall away from the MOPs and Chinese officers scattered elsewhere around the room.

"Do you eat this well every day?" said Bingwen. "Or is this a special occasion?"

"Why?" said Mazer. "What do they normally feed you?"

Bingwen mimed the ingredients as he described them. "Scoop a shovelful of dirt into a blender. Add sugar and water. Toss in some spinach leaves and a teaspoon of bile. Blend to a nice disgusting paste."

"It can't be that bad."

"It is. Sometimes when they cut our rations, I almost don't mind."

"Your rations? I didn't know the food situation was that bad. Now I feel guilty for eating this."

"You shouldn't. You're guests of China. You're commanding armies. You need your strength. We're rice farmers. We've been half starved since we were born."

"Was it really that bad in your village?"

Bingwen shrugged. "Sometimes. Not usually. We'd get fruit and meat every once in a while. The best is when one of the water buffalos got too old. Then we'd feast like kings. Have you ever had a buffalo burger?"

"I've had buffalo wings," said Mazer. "But those aren't the same thing."

"Buffalos don't have wings," said Bingwen.

"It's what we call tiny, spicy chicken wings."

"Then why don't you call them chicken wings?"

"Don't let logic spoil all the fun in life," said Mazer. He stabbed some of his beef and ate it. "I'm curious. What do you think of the proposal from the team on Luna?"

"What do I think of you climbing inside an iron coffin and floating through space like a sitting duck? I think you're several kilos short of a bushel."

"You wouldn't do it? If you were a soldier, I mean."

"I'd do it in a heartbeat," said Bingwen. "I'd be the first one to climb inside. I want to blow that ship to a billion little pieces. That doesn't make the op any less crazy."

Mazer nodded, as if that was answer enough. After a moment, he said, "I've talked to Shenzu about you, about where you came from, about what you and I have been through. I told him what you did for me. How you saved my life. He was very impressed."

"I'm a very impressive young man. That's why I got two desserts. I've earned them."

"I'm serious, Bing. I told Shenzu that they should give you special attention."

"I like keeping a low profile," said Bingwen.

"Too late for that. Shenzu looked you up in the government database."

"I'm in a database?"

"Of kids who have taken the placement exams."

"I haven't taken the exam yet. I'm not old enough. I've only taken practice tests."

"They keep a record of those as well. Shenzu says you did exceptionally well on all of them."

Bingwen shrugged. "I'm good at taking tests."

"You're good at a lot of things. Shenzu has recommended that you be sent to a special school."

Bingwen stopped chewing. "A school? Where?"

"Somewhere in northern China. I don't know where exactly. Shenzu didn't reveal much. I got the sense that it's somewhat secretive. All I know is that it's a military school for a small, select group of children. Gifted children. They would provide you with everything. Room, board. You would never go hungry again."

"A military school? They want to make me a soldier?"

"You already are a soldier, Bingwen. They want to make you a *better* soldier. But this has to be your decision. You have to do this because you want to, because you think you have something to offer, not because Shenzu said so or because I'm the one telling you about it. This is your call."

"When would I go? Once the war's over?"

"A transport leaves for the north in the morning. You would be on it."

"Tomorrow?"

"It's safer in the north, Bing. I know it feels safer here underground, but we're still in the middle of it. I'd sleep better at night knowing you were far away from here. Even if you don't want to go to the school, say that you will. Lie. Let them carry you out of here. Then run like a rabbit when you get there."

A school. The idea was so unexpected, so out of nowhere, that at first Bingwen didn't know how to respond. A school. Tomorrow. It was happening too fast. And yet isn't this what he had always wanted? Wasn't this the reason why he used to get up hours before dawn every day and sneak into the library, just so he could study more than everyone else, just so he could have more time with the computer, just so he could improve his chances of getting out of the village someday?

And wasn't this what Mother had wanted? That he escape? That he make something of himself? Bingwen knew that Father had wanted that for him as well, even though Father had never said so aloud. But Father didn't have to say it; it was there in his eyes every time something went wrong with the crop or the equipment—a look that said, Be better than this, Bing. Do more than this. Don't stay in this mud hole. Don't subject your children to this life, as I have done. It was a look that said more than a hundred thousand words ever could. It had motivated Bingwen to study as much as he had. He didn't want Father to have to show that face again. Instead, Bingwen wanted Father to wear another expression. A look of pride. A look that said, That's my son. I made that kid. I did something right, after all.

"I'll go," said Bingwen. "On the transport and to the school. No lying required."

"You sure?"

"On one condition."

Mazer smiled. "You're making conditions now?"

"There's a girl my age and her younger brother back in my camp. Pipo and Niro. They get to come as well. Not to the school. I can't control that, but on the transport. They get carried out of here and taken somewhere safe up north. An orphanage where they'll be cared for, maybe. Or to a family who will take them in. Someone kind."

"I'll talk to Shenzu."

Bingwen nodded. "And one more condition."

Mazer sat back and folded his arms. "You're in a bargaining mood, aren't you?"

"I'm giving my life to the military. That has to be worth something. And I might as well get what I can now. Once I'm a full-fledged soldier, I'm in their control. I won't have much negotiating power."

"More true than you know. What else do you want?"

"I want you to come with me."

There was a long silence. "You know I can't do that, Bingwen."

"You could be a teacher at this school. A trainer. Who knows more about being a soldier than you do?"

"I have a job to do, Bing. I have to end this."

"I know," said Bingwen. "I know you do. But I had to at least ask." He poked at his pudding with his spoon, then he looked back up at Mazer. "At least tell me you wish you *could* come."

Mazer smiled. "I would be a pretty good teacher, wouldn't I?"

"Oh you'd be terrible. You're too serious. You're always scowling. Like a crotchety old man. You'd scare all the students. We'd call you Professor Mazer Geezer. But I think I could tolerate having you around."

"I'm stronger than you, remember?" said Mazer. "I can dump that pudding on your head."

Bingwen put a giant spoonful in his mouth and smiled. "Considering how good this is, I don't think I'd mind."

That night they put Bingwen in an empty dorm room in the restricted area that had two sets of bunk beds and a bathroom with a shower. A small brown jumpsuit was waiting for him when he arrived, folded neatly on one of the bottom bunks. It sported a patch of the Chinese flag over the left breast. Bingwen felt the material. It was soft and stretchy and brand-new.

He showered and then slipped into the jumpsuit. Surprisingly it fit. Why the military had clothes for someone his size he could only guess.

He was still awake much later when a pair of Chinese officers arrived, escorting Pipo and Niro. Bingwen thanked the officers for their trouble, then welcomed Pipo and Niro inside. Each of them was carrying a jumpsuit like his, still wrapped in plastic. They had no luggage or other belongings.

"We get to sleep on a bed?" said Niro. "Our *own* bed?" He climbed up onto one of the bottom bunks and lay on his back. "Come feel this, Pipo. It shapes to my body."

Pipo looked around the room suspiciously. "Where are they taking us, Bingwen?"

"Captain Shenzu says there's a camp near Wuhan. And not a camp like we have here, where everyone is hungry and fighting for a place to sleep. This camp is for government employees and their families. It's special.

There are international aid organizations there with food and supplies and clothes. Shenzu says you and Niro will have a place there."

"Are you coming with us?" asked Niro.

"No. I'm going somewhere else. To a school. I'm not sure where exactly. But I'll be with you until we reach Wuhan."

"Where's Wuhan?" said Pipo. "We don't know anyone in Wuhan."

"It's several hundred kilometers north of here," said Bingwen. "Far from any fighting. In Hubei province."

She sounded angry. "Why would we go there? Our village is here."

"You can't go back to your village," Bingwen said gently. "It's gone."

She screamed in his face. "Don't say that! Don't you ever say that!"

She ran to the other bottom bunk and threw herself onto it, burying her face in the pillow and crying. Bingwen didn't know what to say. Niro went to her and lay down beside her, draping an arm around her back. Bingwen wanted to leave and give them some privacy, but Shenzu had ordered him to stay in his quarters for the evening. And anyway where would he go?

After a moment he went into the bathroom and lay down on the mat beside the shower.

He must have fallen asleep because when he opened his eyes again the lights were out and a blanket was draped across him. A soft melody drifted in from the dorm room—Pipo singing a lullaby. Bingwen sat up and listened in the dark. Pipo couldn't remember all of the words, so she hummed the parts she didn't know. Her voice gradually softened until finally all was quiet. A moment later the bathroom door creaked open and Pipo poked her head in.

"You're awake," she said.

"Thanks for the blanket," said Bingwen.

"That was Niro's doing. I just put him to sleep." She gestured to the toilet. "I need to pee. Do you mind?"

Bingwen got up, left the bathroom, and climbed up into one of the top bunks.

When Pipo was finished, she came out and stood in the bathroom doorway for a moment, as if she couldn't decide where to go. Then she climbed up onto Bingwen's bunk and sat at the other end of the bed. Neither of them spoke for a moment until Pipo said, "Do you know what happened to your parents? I mean . . . are you sure that they're gone?"

"I'm sure," said Bingwen.

She nodded.

Another long pause.

"Did you have any brothers or sisters?" she asked.

"I'm an only child," said Bingwen.

"I had three older brothers. Longwei, Qingshan, and Yusheng. They worked in the factory with our parents. Everyone worked there. Niro and I were in the schoolhouse. I don't remember who saw the smoke first, but we all went out to see. The Formics were everywhere, spraying their smoke. In the fields, at the houses, the factory was full of it. Whoever it touched fell to the ground and didn't get up. Niro ran toward the factory, screaming for Mother. I almost didn't catch him. He fought and kicked and hit me. I had to drag him away. We hid in a drainage pipe under a bridge. I kept waiting for someone to call out our names, to come looking for us, my brothers or my father. But no one ever did. After two days we left the pipe and smelled real smoke. The factory was on fire. One of the survivors had burned it to stop the death smell. But the fire only made it worse. We watched it burn. Everyone we knew was inside it. The smoke was burning our eyes. Niro threw up, and I thought maybe we would die, so we ran away. We didn't know where we were going. We were both so thirsty. Soon we found other people walking, and we joined them." She shrugged. "Then we came here."

Bingwen didn't know what to say. "I'm sorry."

She shrugged again. "Sometimes I think maybe Mother wasn't in the factory. I tell myself maybe she had gone home for something. Maybe she felt ill that day. And then I think Father would have gone home, too, because if Mother was sick, he would not want her to be alone. That's Father's way. And then I think about Longwei and Qingshan and Yusheng, and about how they were always running off and getting into trouble, and maybe they skipped work that day, too. And then I think, if I had just gone home, if I had taken Niro home instead of running away, we would have found everyone there waiting for us."

She shook her head and was quiet a moment. "I'm sorry that you're sure about your parents, Bingwen. But at least you're sure. At least you know."

She was too young to have to think this way, Bingwen thought. They were all too young.

"You don't have to go north, Pipo. No one's going to force you. I only wanted to get you and Niro to a safer place. If you want to stay in Claw, just say the word."

"We'll go," said Pipo. "I only wish all of my family was going with us."

She climbed down from the top bunk and crawled up into the bed next to Niro.

Bingwen lay back on his mattress and stared up at the ceiling. He had never slept on a bed before—back home he had enjoyed a thin foam mattress on the floor and nothing more. This was like a hundred of those stacked on top of each other. Yet soft as it was, it wasn't until much later, long after he heard Pipo breathing slow to the rhythm of sleep, that Bingwen was able to relax his mind enough to drift off as well.

In his dreams, the factory burned and the skeletons danced and the flames rose up and licked the sun.

After breakfast, Bingwen led Niro and Pipo to the elevator where Mazer had said to meet them. To Bingwen's surprise all of the MOPs had come to see him off.

"Nice uniform," said Deen. "I suspect we'll see some stars on that in the near future."

"Years from now," said ZZ. "When he turns ten."

They all laughed.

Cocktail took a knee, tousled Bingwen's hair, and said, "When Captain O'Toole finally comes to his senses and realizes he's too old to be leading us, we'll give you a call, Bing."

"I'm too old already," said Wit. "You can have the job now if you want it, Bing. Although I think you're too smart to take it."

"School first," said Bingwen. "Then I'll come back and whip your butt into shape, Cocktail."

Everyone laughed and patted him on the back and wished him well. When Bingwen stepped into the elevator with Shenzu and Pipo and Niro beside him, Bingwen realized he was actually excited. It wasn't until the doors were closing that he realized he hadn't said a word to Mazer. He met Mazer's eyes at the last moment, and then the doors were shut and the elevator was ascending at a high speed. He wanted to tell Shenzu to stop the thing, to go back, to give him another moment, but it was too late.

"The transport will take you to Chenzhou," said Captain Shenzu. "From there you'll catch a train there to Wuhan. That's where the three of you will part ways. All of your documentation is on this." He handed Bingwen a wrist pad. It wasn't small enough for a child, but it was smaller than the typical adult size. Bingwen snapped it on his wrist and tightened the strap as far as it would go.

"You won't be traveling alone," said Shenzu. "An officer is headed that way. He'll escort you."

The elevator stopped, and they stepped out into a small room with tight-fitting biosuits hanging on hooks along the walls. A closed airlock door was in front of them. Shenzu grabbed three child-sized biosuits and passed them out. "Slip these on over your jumpsuits. You'll only need to wear these until you get to Chenzhou."

Bingwen stepped into his suit and sealed up the front. "Why do you have our size, by the way? I thought this was a military facility."

"It was designed to protect senior Party members and their families," said Shenzu, "including their young children." Shenzu sealed his own suit tight then checked each of theirs. Then he crossed the room and opened the airlock. Bright sunlight poured in, and Bingwen raised an arm to shield his eyes. A small landing pad was before them, cut into the side of the mountain, several hundred feet up. A Formic transport was parked there. When the children saw it they recoiled.

"It's all right," said Shenzu. "This one is ours. We stole it and figured out how to fly it. It will take you to Chenzhou."

Three members of the crew were outside in their biosuits conducting preflight checks.

"Can I sit up front with the pilot?" asked Niro.

Pipo tugged on his hand and shushed him. "Don't ask questions. We sit where we're told."

Shenzu opened the door and helped them inside. Human seats with safety harnesses had been bolted to the floor. Someone in a biosuit was already buckled into the jump seat opposite Bingwen. It wasn't until Bingwen had snapped his own harness and the door was closed that he got a good look at the man in front of him. It took Bingwen a second to place the face. With a sickening feeling in his stomach he realized it was Lieutenant Li, the officer who had come in the truck to take the MOPs to Dragon's Den, the lieutenant who had wanted to leave Bingwen behind out of spite, the idiot who had insisted they leave their weapons in the cab of the truck.

A mudbrain.

Great, thought Bingwen. This should be a pleasant flight.

He smiled and extended a gloved hand. "Hi. I'm Bingwen. I don't think we officially met before. Thank you for giving us a lift that day."

The lieutenant looked at the hand as if it were gangrenous. "Fifty demerits," he said, tapping a note onto his wrist pad.

"Excuse me?" said Bingwen.

"For improperly addressing a senior officer. You are in the Chinese military now, boy. That means you follow protocol. You don't thrust your hand at someone unless it's holding a knife and you plan to use it. I am your senior officer. You will therefore always address me as 'sir' and 'Lieutenant Li.'"

"Yes, sir."

"Did you not hear what I said?" snapped Li. "Are you deaf as well as ignorant? I said you will address me as 'sir' *and* 'Lieutenant Li.'"

"Yes sir, Lieutenant Li, sir. My apologies. I didn't know the protocol."

"Fifty demerits," said Li, making another note on his wrist pad. "You do not run your mouth whenever you choose, boy. This is not the schoolyard. You will speak when asked a direct question or when given permission." He shook his head. "They told me you were intelligent. I see already that they were mistaken. You are not fit for the school they're sending you to. You have the aptitude of a cow. Isn't that right, boy?"

"That is correct, Lieutenant Li, sir."

Bingwen had to practically spit the words out they sounded so unnatural and awkward to his ears. Is this what he had signed up for? Was this what awaited him in the military once he graduated? Toads like this guy?

The flight crew had climbed into the cockpit. They continued their preflight check and then lifted off. Bingwen's stomach roiled as they dropped from the mountain and headed north.

"May I ask a question, Lieutenant Li, sir?" asked Bingwen.

Li rolled his eyes. "The correct inquiry is, 'Permission to pose a question, Lieutenant Li, sir.'"

"Permission to pose a question, Lieutenant Li, sir."

"What?"

"Will you be escorting us all the way to Wuhan, Lieutenant Li, sir?" asked Bingwen. "Or will we get a different escort at Chenzhou?"

The corner of Li's mouth curled up into a grin. "I am more than your escort, boy. I am not getting off at Chenzhou or Wuhan. I'm going with you all the way. I am your new teacher."

CHAPTER 19

Despoina

Lem walked out of his office and shouted loud enough for everyone in the warehouse to hear him. "Can I have everyone's attention please!" The workers all stopped what they were doing. Welding visors were raised, saws were cut off and silenced. Twelve cocoons occupied the floor space. Their main body and propulsion system had been built in the Juke production facility, but once they were finished there, Lem had brought them here to be camouflaged. Benyawe had suggested it.

"Let the team here contribute," she had said. "Let Victor and Imala show them how it's done. It will boost morale. We all go home and watch the vids of what's happening in China, and it eats us up. We feel helpless. The shatter boxes are well into production. The ships in the shield have been outfitted. We're not doing much right now. Put us to work, and you'll win some much needed popularity points."

She had been right. The mood in the warehouse in the past few days had improved dramatically. People were smiling, joking. Instead of giving Lem the cold shoulder, they were greeting him and including him in conversations. Two people had even thanked him.

"I just heard from Captain Wit O'Toole of the Mobile Operations Team," said Lem. "We have our strike team. We are a go, people."

They cheered. They embraced. They applauded.

No, they weren't just applauding. They were applauding *him*. He smiled, raised a hand, pumped a fist. They cheered louder. It was glorious.

He couldn't bask in it, though. He raised a hand for silence. They quieted. "This is good news, yes. But we've still got work to do. Let's keep at it. The faster we finish these cocoons, the faster we can kick the Formics' asses."

Oh how they cheered at that, as he knew they would.

He gave another wave, retreated back into his office, and closed the door.

He wanted to tell someone. He shouldn't call Des. He needed to begin to distance himself from her. She was getting too attached.

She answered her personal wrist pad on the fifth chime, and her face appeared on his wall screen. "Why are you calling me here?" she said quietly.

"Are you at your desk?"

"I stepped away to answer. I thought we agreed for you not to contact me at the office."

He shrugged. "We checked your wrist pad. It's not being tapped. I couldn't wait to tell you."

"Tell me what?"

He told her. She was giddy. "I knew it. I knew you could do this."

"We haven't done anything yet. Chances of this thing succeeding are still one in a thousand."

"Not with you leading it."

"I won't be leading it. Victor is."

"You're outfitting him. You're the general, he's the

field commander. How are you getting them out of China?"

"The Chinese military is helping. They've confiscated a few Formic transports and retrofitted them for human flight. They'll fly them out of the country in twelve hours. Then they'll catch a shuttle to Luna in Kokkola."

"Where's that?"

"Finland."

"I'm proud of you."

Someone had turned on music out in the warehouse. It sounded like a party was heating up.

"Will I see you tonight?" she asked.

He shouldn't see her. Sooner or later they'd be discovered. It had been nice to have a little company, but there was no need to string her along. That would be cruel.

He must have still been high on adrenaline and endorphins because he said, "There's an Italian restaurant in the East Side called La Bella Luna. Meet me there three hours from now."

"But that's a public place."

"Come hungry," he said. "Their house lasagna may be the best thing I've ever eaten."

He disconnected and went out into the warehouse. He didn't know the song, but he didn't care. He took Dr. Benyawe by the hand, spun her once, and then led her onto the floor with the others. He had never tried dancing in Luna's low gravity, but apparently Benyawe had. Lem could barely keep up with her.

"Not much for dancing?" asked Imala.

Victor looked up from the terminal screen in the dusty storage room he had been using as an office. "I'm rewatching the vids from inside the ship. When the Formics cut open that pilot."

Imala made a face and came in and sat on a box. "Why look at that again?"

Victor turned back to the screen. "I don't understand it, Imala. They eviscerate him and then dig around inside him as if looking for something."

"Maybe they're not looking for anything. Maybe they're reaching in to make sure his heart has stopped beating."

"Maybe."

"You can't find meaning in this, Vico. There might not *be* meaning, not that a human mind can understand anyway."

"What's inside the human abdominal cavity?"

"You're not giving up on this, are you?"

"Come on. You went to college. What's inside a man in this region?" He drew a circle in the air above his stomach.

"I don't know. Your large and small intestines mostly."

"What else?"

"Higher up you've got your stomach, liver, duodenum—"

"What's a duodenum?"

"I don't remember exactly. I only remember the name because it sounds funny."

"What else?"

"Gallbladder, diaphragm, kidneys, pancreas. Does it matter? If they were looking for one of those things, they would have pulled it out."

"Good point. The fact that they came out empty-handed suggests they were looking for an organ that wasn't there." He considered a moment. "And really, they can't possibly know our anatomy anyway. Not this quickly. The only anatomy they truly know is their own."

"You're saying they were looking for one of *their* organs? That doesn't make any sense."

"Sure it does," said Victor. "Maybe they have a critical organ that serves some vital purpose for them, and they want to see if we have it too."

"Such as?"

Victor shrugged. "Could be anything. Maybe it's the organ that lets them communicate mind to mind."

"We don't know for certain that they do that."

"They communicate somehow, Imala. And it's certainly not by talking."

"Has this ever happened before? Has anyone else ever witnessed the Formics do this? Eviscerate people and dig around inside them, I mean."

"Why?"

"How many Formics would you have to cut open to see if they have kidneys like ours?"

He understood her meaning. If the Formics were looking for an organ, they would only have to look inside one person to see if they found it.

Imala pulled her box close to the terminal, and they searched the nets together. They quickly found dozens of gruesome images of eviscerated people all over China.

"These images were posted at different dates," said Victor. "Some at the start of the war, some as early as this morning."

"That throws your theory out the window," said Imala. "If they were looking for an organ, they would have stopped eviscerating people a long time ago because they would have known early on that we didn't have it."

"Unless the different Formics scattered around China aren't talking to each other and they don't know what the other Formics have or have not discovered."

Imala stood. "That's what I'm telling you, Vico. This is a pointless circle of speculation. We can't possibly know what's in their heads."

Victor leaned back in his chair. "But if we could

understand them, Imala, if we could get in their heads, maybe we wouldn't have to fight."

"I don't think it matters, Vico. They don't seem like the negotiating type."

Victor didn't have a response to that.

Imala leaned against the wall. "Are you ready for this? The MOPs? The cocoons? The ship?"

Victor took a breath and leaned forward in his chair. "If something happens to me, there's a message here on this terminal I want you to send to my mother in the Belt. It's all programmed in. This one here. Just double tap it, and away it goes."

"You can write her a different letter and send it yourself when this is over."

"I mean it, Imala. Promise me you'll do that. That's all I ask."

"Nothing's going to happen to you, Vico. That's my promise to you. I won't *let* anything happen to you."

"That's a promise you can't keep, Imala."

She laughed. "You don't know me very well, do you, Vico?"

"Is this really a good time to be popping the champagne glasses?" said Ramdakan. "You haven't even started the assault yet."

They were sitting in Lem's office. The music and dancing in the warehouse had stopped, and everyone had returned to work.

Lem had thrown up an image of the city of Imbrium on the four walls, giving the impression that he and Ramdakan were sitting in the middle of a small park in the heart of the city. Ramdakan kept dabbing at his head with a cloth and sipping from the lidded goblet Lem had given him.

"Festivities boost morale, Norja," said Lem. "You

should try it sometime. People might actually enjoy working for you."

Norja looked horrified. "Why would I want people to *enjoy* working for me?" He said the word like it was poison. "That makes them complacent and lazy."

Lem took a sip of his fruit drink. "Why I am not surprised to hear you espouse that philosophy. Then again, you are my father's chief financial adviser. You must be doing something right."

"Which leads me to why I'm here."

"You didn't come for the dancing?" Lem asked.

Ramdakan ignored that. "The Chinese have confiscated and retrofitted Formic transports. This is a serious problem."

"Actually it's an enormous convenience. That's how we're getting the MOPs out of China. But I suspect you already knew that part, too. Tell me, who on my staff is your source of information? I'd so like to know so I can pinch their ears off."

Ramdakan spread his hands and smirked. "Please, Lem. You made the announcement to a room full of Juke employees. You think that intel isn't going to get back to me?"

"I like how you call it 'intel.' Feels military. That's the business I'm in now these days, you know. Military operations. Oh, wait, your little mole already told you that, too, didn't he? Gosh. Snitches spoil all the fun."

"Will you stop being juvenile for a moment?"

Lem leaned back and put his hands behind his head. "No, Norja. I won't. This is who I am. You don't think I have a shot at achieving anything in this company, I'm the scorn of everyone on the Board, why should I bother performing for you? I'm Lem Jukes, remember? The son of Ukko Jukes, forever stuck in the shadow of his father. Isn't that what you said, Norja? Something to that effect?"

"This isn't about you, Lem. This is about the company."

Lem leaned forward. "Let me tell you exactly why you're here, Norja. Cut me off, if I'm wrong here. You're all in a tiff because you've just learned that China has Formic transports in their possession. This appalls you for two reasons. One, you didn't already know this fact, which means your lines of intel out of China have crumbled. And two, your panties are really in a wad because one of our primary competitors, WU-HU, is based out of China and they will almost certainly get their hands on that Formic tech, which they will promptly reverse engineer and use to their great economic advantage."

"Yes, but—"

Lem held up a finger. "I changed my mind. Don't cut me off. I'm just getting started. Where was I? Ah, yes, reverse engineering.

"So now here you are, Norja Ramdakan, Esquire, conscientious member of the Board, come to my office to impress upon me the importance of preserving some of the Formic tech inside the mothership. The secrets to interstellar travel are there, after all. New drive systems, self-sustaining life-support systems, alien alloys, advanced navigation, a ship that can travel at a significant fraction of lightspeed. The laundry list of goodies up for grabs is long indeed. And each little widget is its own fortune waiting to happen.

"With a prize like that in the hands of Juke Limited, nothing and no one could stop us. We would be the most powerful and profitable corporate entity for centuries to come. We would open the stars to humankind, forever preserve our species by spreading throughout the universe. How am I doing so far?"

Ramdakan cleared his throat. "Yes, well, you clearly understand what's at stake. But—"

"But the question on your mind is: How do we preserve something we're about to destroy?"

"It's a valid question," said Ramdakan.

"It most certainly is, and the answer is, you can't. You can preserve some tech, sure, but you can't preserve it all. This is a war, Norja. When the smoke clears, we can pick up the pieces and see what we've got. But we're not going to put the bottom line before the fate of Earth. My father and I agree on that much."

"Precautions can be made, Lem. You can take steps now to ensure that the most tech is preserved."

"I am taking such steps. Victor Delgado and I have discussed this. He knows we need to preserve as much tech as possible. He understands the value of that ship."

"He's not a Juke employee."

"Your point?"

"The legal team worries that his lawyers might evoke salvage law and claim that he is entitled to a percentage of anything taken from the ship."

"Ah, the lawyers. Yes. We can't forget them. Those wonderful, endearing lawyers. And I suppose the same could be said for other members of my strike team. Mazer Rackham, the MOPs . . ."

"They would have to sign release forms that absolve them of any rights of ownership."

Lem laughed and shook his head. "Welcome to the team, boys. Please sign these forms that will make us rich and not you."

Ramdakan looked irritated. "You act like you're not a member of the team here, Lem. I remind you, this is a Juke Limited operation. You may have spearheaded the whole effort, but you've done so as an employee of this company using employee resources." He pointed to the door. "Those coffins out there are the property of this company, not you."

"They're cocoons," said Lem. "Calling them coffins is

bad luck. I'm going to have to ask you to throw salt over your right shoulder a few times. Or is it your left shoulder? I can never remember."

Ramdakan grit his teeth. "I'm glad you find this all amusing, Lem, but remember who is calling the shots here."

"Let me guess, it's not me."

"The Board. And frankly we're not thrilled with the idea of Victor Delgado or Imala Bootstamp having any part in this operation whatsoever."

"Is that so?"

"Who's liable if something happens to them, Lem? The company? There's a ride through judicial hell. That's the last thing we need."

Lem was suddenly angry. "Wrong, Norja. The last thing we need are Formics spraying us in the face with their little wands and melting the flesh off our bones. Which is precisely what *will* happen if we don't destroy that ship, which we are going to do *with* Victor and Imala. So unless you have another item of business, I'll excuse you to get back to the nice side of Luna."

"You don't want me as an enemy, Lem."

"No, I want you as an absent friend. Are we done here?"

"If you won't budge on Victor, I'm told not to push the matter. But you must at least have a Juke engineer with the strike team. Someone who can assess the tech there before the attack."

"There are only twelve cocoons, Norja. If I give up one, I lose a MOP."

"Then postpone and make more."

"We're not postponing."

"Then make room for an engineer."

"Fine. I'll ask Dr. Benyawe."

Ramdakan laughed. "Benyawe? She's what, in her sixties?"

"You never ask a woman her age, Norja. Don't you know that's bad manners?"

"You can't be serious."

"She's the best engineer on staff, and I trust her more than I trust myself. I don't know why I didn't think of her before. She could be a great help to Victor."

"She's not physically capable."

"We won't be tossing around bundles of hay, Norja. She will observe and record and document and consult. And she stays surprisingly fit. She could run you into the ground, I suspect."

"The Board won't like this."

"That tears me up inside, Norja. Really it does. Hopefully I can make it up to the Board by dropping the most valuable tech the world has ever seen into the company's lap." He stood. "Now if you'll excuse me, I have preparations to make."

He crossed to the door and opened it. Norja reluctantly got to his feet. Lem escorted him out of the building to make sure he was gone. It wasn't until Lem had returned to the warehouse that he saw the vid crew. Two cameramen, with big lights on their shoulders were filming a worker, who was being interviewed by Unna, the Danish reporter with short pink hair who had interviewed Lem in his apartment. She wore a tight blue jumpsuit this time, with just as much skin exposed.

Simona, with her holopad in hand, was standing off to the side by the vid crew. She saw Lem and quickly hurried over. "Now before you go nuclear, hear me out."

"Why is this woman and her cameras in my warehouse?" He maneuvered past Simona. "Hey, you with the cameras, I didn't say you could film in here. Shut that off!"

The cameramen startled, swiveling toward him, blinding him with their lights.

Unna, the reporter, smiled and kept her cool. "Mr. Jukes, just the man we want to talk to."

Lem shielded the light from his eyes. "Unna, tell your boys here to kill the cameras."

"We're here on invitation from Juke Limited, Mr. Jukes."

"Kill the cameras or I will smash them into tiny pieces."

Unna's smile disappeared. She turned to the cameramen and dragged a finger across her throat. The cameramen killed the lights and switched off the cameras.

Lem held out his hand. "Now give me the data cards."

The cameramen hesitated.

Simona said, "Can I talk to you in private, Lem?"

A crowd had gathered.

"Give me the data cards, or I will hit you with a lawsuit so hard your head will spin."

The cameramen looked to Unna, who nodded. They removed the data cards from their cameras and handed them over. Lem dropped them into his pocket and turned around. "Simona, let's chat."

They didn't go to his office. Lem worried he might end up shouting so loudly, they would hear him in the warehouse. So they crossed to the far side of the facility to a big utility room where all the HVAC equipment was housed.

"What a lovely meeting place," said Simona.

He folded his arms. "I'm waiting."

She dropped her shoulders and exhaled. "This was PR's idea. A bit of history could be in the making here. They wanted to capture it."

"And do what with it?"

She tossed a hand up. "Whatever they do with this

kind of thing. Press releases, corporate training vids, company documentary. We have vaults of footage like this, Lem. We do this for every major project we undertake. This is standard practice."

"We're not doing this to promote ourselves, Simona. This is not some product we're offering in a catalog. This is about stopping human suffering. If we turn on the cameras, we look like insincere opportunists."

"I said as much to PR. I told them you wouldn't like it. They told me to come anyway."

"I want them out."

"Fine."

"Fine?"

Simona shrugged. "I'm not going to argue with you. I agree with you."

"That's a first."

"Wonders never cease."

There was something different about her, Lem realized. "You cut your hair," he said. "It used to be much longer."

"Yes well I needed a change."

"I like it. It's nice."

Her cheeks flushed. She tucked a strand of hair behind her ear. "Yes well, there's something else you need to know, Lem. And I don't know how else to say this."

"I'm listening."

"I keep track of your father's schedule, as you know, and various communications he receives. Sometimes I see things I'm not supposed to see."

"Like what?"

She tapped her holopad and gave it to him.

It was an e-mail from Despoina to Father. It was a summary of the conversation Despoina and Lem had had the other evening. She had typed up all the details he had shared with her about the upcoming mission. Most of it was insignificant information, but there were a few juicy bits in there about what Victor intended to do inside the ship.

Lem didn't read the whole thing. There was no need. He handed the holopad back to her. His mouth felt dry. He didn't look at her. "Thank you for showing me that."

"Lem . . . I'm sorry."

"Don't be.

"Do you want to talk about it?"

"Absolutely not."

She nodded. "Well . . . I'll go remove the vid crew before they start shooting again." She paused a moment as if she meant to say more, then she thought better of it and left.

He stood there alone, staring at a giant heat inductor. How could he have been so foolish? He had wrangled Des in to get information from Father when all along Father was playing the same game. Only Father had played it better. Father had known Lem would try such a thing. And so he had set the trap and let Lem walk right in.

Of course Lem would go for the shyest and most vulnerable in the office. She would be easy prey. And so Father had hired a . . . what? A prostitute? Is that what Des was? A woman of the night? An actress who hadn't achieved the success she had hoped for and thus had settled for acting jobs of a different variety?

It was so obvious now. The way she had played coy that first day in the office, baiting him, making him think he was winning her over with his charm.

How much of her story was true, he wondered. Any of it? Maybe she really was from San Diego. That would be safest. She could speak about it with confidence. Street names and such. Claiming to be from somewhere she didn't know would be risky.

He had slept with her. And he had actually believed that it was special. Not every time, of course; there was a getting-to-know-you phase. But now, to think that all her awkwardness, all her insecurities, every moment, every glance she gave him, every laugh, every smile, it had all been a fabrication. It made him want to throw up. She was a breathing lie. The most vile and false of people. She had played him again and again and again.

Why had he told her anything? Why had he been so asinine? Of course she was fishing for information. Of course she was taking notes. Oh sure, she had thrown him an occasional bone or two, to keep up the façade of giving him information—all of which were obviously lies.

This explained her quick reversal of personalities, he realized. One day she's shy, the next day she's suddenly coming out of her shell. He had assumed that this was the product of the sudden attention he was giving her. He had made her feel special. Of course she would be more confident. But no, she was merely moving from Act One into Act Two.

This is low, Father. Even for you.

He checked the time. He was to meet her for dinner soon. That was obviously out of the question at this point. He could never been seen with her again. It made him sick to think that he had almost appeared in public with her. How stupid. They would almost certainly be photographed. And then the world would be frantic to know who she was. It would only take a quick search on the nets to find her true identity. He didn't want to think what other pictures there might be of her out there.

He could see the headlines once her true identity was revealed. He could picture them in his mind.

Was that your final play, Father? To humiliate me in front of the world?

Of all the life lessons Father had ever given him, this one stung the worst. It was so menacing and disgusting, so dark in its design, that Lem had to steady himself against the wall. Is this how little you think of me, Father? Is this what I am to you?

You did it to yourself, Lem, he could hear Father say. I didn't make you flirt with my assistant. I didn't make you give up information. You did that all yourself.

The saddest part of it all? He would have told Father all of those details himself if Father had only asked.

He took a moment to compose himself, to gather his thoughts. He began making phone calls. There were people he knew of, all of them paid under the table by Ramdakan. Police, Lunar Trade Department, shuttle pilots. Lem had never dealt with them before, but he knew Ramdakan called on them often.

Lem's instructions were clear. They would go to her home in the night. They would arrest her. It wouldn't be hard to plant evidence. Drugs would be easiest, Lem figured, but he left that to the officers' discretion. They were the pros here. She was to be put on the first shuttle to Earth, her Luna visa revoked for life. They were not to hurt her—Lem wouldn't stoop to her level—but they were to be swift. If she cried a few tears, if the experience shook her up, well perhaps she would think twice about continuing in this line of work. He transferred money from his untraceable accounts to the places they indicated. The whole business took less than ten minutes.

Her arrest would need to be a surprise. If he didn't show up at the restaurant, she would get suspicious. He sent her a text begging her forgiveness and asked to meet for breakfast instead. He gave her the name of a diner near her apartment. She wrote back and told him not to work too hard. He needed his rest.

He almost ripped his wrist pad off and threw it to the floor.

He wanted her to know she had not beaten him in the end. He wrote her a scathing message, naming her what she was really was. Then he programmed his wrist pad to send it in two days, after she had returned to Earth.

When he was done, he found himself on the verge of tears. He had liked her. That's what cut deeper than anything. He had warmed to her. Over time, meal after meal, moment after moment, he had genuinely come to like her.

There was not a word to describe what he felt for Father now. Hate was far too kind.

CHAPTER 20

Train

By the time the Formic transport had flown over the Jiuyi mountain range and into Hunan province, Bingwen had seen more Formic aircraft in the sky than he cared to count. Some flew in groups of twos or threes, flying so close together that their wings were almost touching. Others flew in clusters of a dozen or more, all packed tight and moving as one—like a single-minded hive of bees.

There were no windows on the transport, but someone had installed a large terminal screen in the main cabin. There were six active screens on it, all linked to the sensors and cameras outside.

"There," said Niro, pointing at a cluster of clouds on screen. "Four more of them, moving in and out of the clouds. Do you see them?" He was beside Bingwen in the jump seat, his safety harness loose around his tiny frame.

Lieutenant Li was sitting opposite them, head back, eyes closed. "Stop fidgeting and be quiet. The Formics think we're one of them. They're not going to bother us."

"How can you be sure?" asked Niro.

Li opened his eyes and regarded the boy. "Because if

we leave them alone, they'll leave us alone. They ignore nonaggressive aircraft. It's a fact we learned far too late. And also, the military wouldn't put me in this ship if there was any real risk."

"Why not?" asked Pipo.

"Because I'm an important person. I'm to be a teacher at a special school. The military wants me safe. They're taking every precaution to get me to my destination."

"Maybe Bingwen is the important person," said Pipo. "Maybe the military wants *him* safe. Maybe you're one of the precautions they've put in place to protect *him*."

It was not a smart thing to say, Bingwen knew. He tried to get her attention. Don't be a hothead, Pipo. Stay quiet.

Li regarded Pipo as if she were something stuck to the bottom of his shoe. "What's your name, girl?"

"Pipo."

"And where are your parents, Pipo?"

Pipo's confidence fell. "I . . . I don't know."

"That's too bad. Because if you did know, I would be sure to send them a note telling them what a disrespectful child they have. How dare you speak to your elders that way? Have you no honor?"

Pipo looked at the floor.

"I suspect your parents are dead if they haven't claimed you by now, but that is probably a mercy. At least they will never see what you have become."

Pipo raised her face, her expression one of shock. Then her whole body collapsed against her harness, and she sobbed into her hands.

"Yes, yes," said Li. "Cry your tears. Perhaps you will speak with greater caution in the future." He leaned back again and closed his eyes.

Bingwen reached far across the space between them and put a hand on Pipo's back. She grabbed it like a lifeline thrown to her. Bingwen wanted to say something, but words would only incite Li and make it worse.

An hour later the pilot announced their approach into Chenzhou. Bingwen watched the terminal screens as they flew over the city and headed toward the railway station. There were tens of thousands of people crowded at the rail station's entrance, a mob so large that it spilled into the streets and stretched for several blocks south.

"Why are there so many people?" asked Niro.

"They all want to get north," said Lieutenant Li. "When we land, stay close to me and move fast."

The transport came down on a landing pad inside a fenced-off area adjacent to the station. Crowds of people lined the fence, and they screamed and pushed against each other to get away from the transport.

"They think we're Formics," said Bingwen.

Li slid open the door and stepped out. "It's all right," he shouted. "We are human. Stay calm."

The relief on the people's faces made Bingwen want to cry. Mothers with infants, children, the elderly. Some in fine clothing, others in rags. Many carried bags. They had thought they were about to die.

Li motioned Bingwen and the others to come. "Hurry now." He led them up the sidewalk toward the station. Bingwen held tight to Pipo's and Niro's hands.

People at the fence cried out as they passed.

"Let us in."

"Open the fence."

"My daughter is sick," shouted a man, holding up a toddler.

"We'll pay you."

Children extended their arms, palms up, begging.

Bingwen felt helpless.

A pair of soldiers stood guard at a side entrance to the station. They saluted as Li approached. One of them opened the door. Inside was an employee locker room.

When the door was closed behind them, Li removed his biosuit and gave them each a heavy plastic bag.

"Stuff your biosuit in the bag. Keep that bag with you at all times. Do not set it down for any reason. Otherwise, it will be stolen. Wear only your brown jumpsuits on the train until you hear the alarm. Then get into your suit as quickly as possible."

"What does the alarm sound like?" Pipo asked.

"An alarm," said Li. "Now move."

Bingwen quickly shed his suit and stuffed it in his bag. When they were all done, Niro hugged his bag tight against his chest, his eyes wide with fear.

Pipo put an arm around him. "Everything will be fine, Niro. Bingwen will take care of us. We're getting on a fast magnet train. You've always wanted to ride one, right?"

Niro nodded.

"Well now's your chance," said Pipo.

"Stay right behind me," said Li.

He led them through a set of double doors and into one of the main terminals. To Bingwen's right a dozen high-speed passenger trains were stationed at concrete platforms, all of their doors open, loading passengers. Beyond the trains and the vaulted ceiling of the terminal were the magnet tracks and the distant safety of the north.

To Bingwen's left was chaos. Thousands of people were crammed together at the main entrance. A hundred armed soldiers were trying to keep order. Some held dogs on short leashes. Others shouted commands: Stay in line! No pushing! One at a time!

Barriers had been set up that funneled people to a long row of tables, where soldiers were sitting with holopads. One by one the civilians came forward and put their face into the holofield. A window of data would appear with the person's ID, address, photo, medical history. The soldiers flicked through the data quickly. If the civilian passed inspection, the soldier waved them through and ordered them to proceed to one of the platforms where the trains were waiting. There were more lines at the trains, and soldiers rechecked people and gave them a door assignment.

A man at one of the tables was told he couldn't pass. The soldier pointed to the exit and told the man to leave. The man became hostile, yelling, waving his arms. Two soldiers appeared and took him roughly away toward an exit. The man kicked and struggled and shouted curses. A third soldier stepped in and struck the man in the head with the butt of his rifle. Bingwen heard the crack over the din. The man went silent and limp. The soldiers dragged him through a set of doors that led outside and dumped him on the concrete.

"This way," said Li. "Stay close."

Bingwen didn't have to be told twice. He clung to Niro's and Pipo's hands and stayed right at Lieutenant Li's heels. They weaved their way through the crowd near the trains. Lieutenant Li shouted for the people to make a path. The command in his voice demanded obedience. The people hustled to the side.

When they reached the fifth train, Li pushed his way to the front of the line, where soldiers were loading people.

Li saluted a captain and gestured to Pipo and Niro. "These two, sir. Orders from Dragon's Den." He extended his wrist pad. The captain extended his own wrist pad, bumped Li's, and read the information that was transferred. Then the captain snapped his fingers at a female soldier to his right. "Two orphans. Car twelve."

The female soldier came forward and took Pipo and Niro by the hand. "This way please."

And then she was leading Pipo and Niro away, taking them up the platform where the crowds weren't allowed to go, up to a car near the front of the train. Pipo and

Niro both looked back at Bingwen, confused, afraid, helpless.

What was happening? Bingwen wondered. Weren't he and Li getting on this train as well?

No. A heartbeat later Li pulled Bingwen away, leading him toward the far side of the terminal.

They were abandoning Pipo and Niro, he realized. They were going their separate ways without any good-byes or explanation. Bingwen wanted to resist, argue, question, object. He looked back at the train. The crowd waiting to board had already filled in the gap. Pipo and Niro were gone from sight.

For an instant, Bingwen considered yanking his hand free and running back to the train. But what good would that do? The soldiers would only grab him, and Li would be furious.

Ahead was another set of doors with a pair of soldiers standing guard. The guards let them through. Now they were in a second terminal, identical to the one they had just left—only this one was empty. No crowds. No trains. No soldiers. Li didn't slow his pace.

He glanced down at Bingwen and smiled. "You're angry with me. Your little face is a mask, but I know you're angry."

Bingwen said nothing.

"I didn't give you a chance to say good-bye. You think I abandoned them."

Bingwen kept his head bowed, submissive. "You did what you thought was best, Lieutenant Li, sir."

"And you disagree?"

"You are my commanding officer. It is not my place to disagree."

Li laughed. "You learn quickly, boy. But come now, I give you permission to speak freely. Out with it. No punishment will come to you regardless of what you say."

Bingwen knew that was a lie. Li may not give him demerits, but he would resent Bingwen if Bingwen spoke his mind. No, silence was better.

After a moment, Li released Bingwen's hand. "I've made you too cautious, I see. Very well. I order you to speak, boy. A soldier who doesn't think for himself is of no use to his army."

Bingwen chose his words carefully. "You did not want to make a scene. A long farewell could lead to tears, objections. A swift separation was best. People were waiting to board. Emotions were high. To warn us ahead of time would have complicated their departure."

Li nodded, content. "A good officer must do what is prudent, boy. Never what is convenient. I did not give you warning because in war, warnings rarely come. Will the Formics warn us of an attack? Will they send us a holo before they swoop in and gas us? Never."

We're not Formics, Bingwen wanted to say. We're humans. We can still be decent. We can still be kind. But aloud he said nothing.

"Let this be a lesson to you, boy. To coddle the weak is to weaken them further. Will you hold your soldiers' hands in battle? Will you kiss their booboos and tell them there are no such thing as monsters? Because there *are* monsters now, Bingwen. Real monsters. Monsters who will come in the night and cut your stomach wide open and play with your insides. You do your soldiers a great disservice by treating them like delicate glass bowls. Those children are young, yes, but a lesson in pain will strengthen their resolve. Fear is the medicine they need. That is how you keep soldiers sharp and alive. To be kind, to be gentle, is to lie. That lowers their guard. To be their friend is the most destructive thing a commander can do."

Bingwen almost stopped walking then. If this was the military, if this was how they expected him to treat people, he wanted no part of it.

He glanced to his left; the exit was twenty meters away. If he ran now, if he squeezed through that turnstile and made for the doors, he might get outside and disappear in the crowds before Li could grab him.

But then Bingwen remembered the faces beyond the fence. Their fear, their desperation. They knew the Formics were moving north.

No, Bingwen couldn't run. Not yet. Li was his ticket out of the fighting zone. If he wanted to ditch later he could. For now his only choice was to follow and obey and hope that Niro and Pipo would forgive him.

Li led them to the end of a platform, where they descended a short ladder to the ground and headed north into the train yard. They followed one of the magnet tracks. Bingwen could hear it humming with current, and he wondered what would happen if he stepped onto its wide metal surface.

Every twenty meters or so, there was a spacer in the tracks made of thick black rubber, where they crossed, moving west through the train yard. Soon they came to a short side track where a row of maintenance cars was waiting. Soldiers stood guard, and they checked Li's credentials. Then the chief officer tapped his wrist pad, and one of the maintenance cars floated forward on the track. It was a small, roofless two-passenger car, with a bed in the back for tools and supplies.

"Get in," said Li.

Bingwen climbed aboard, and Li did likewise, tapping his wrist pad with the front console. The car shot forward on the track, smooth as glass, moving of its own accord. It changed tracks at a few switches and then cut west across the northern part of Chenzhou, putting the train yard behind them.

There was evidence that Chenzhou had been a thriving city recently. But now the roads were empty and the factories were still and silent. Tall, concrete apartment complexes appeared vacant and abandoned.

"There was a volunteer evacuation three weeks ago," said Li. "Most people left then. Those who stayed behind had nowhere to go in the north, or maybe they had never been anywhere else and were afraid to leave. Either way, it's mandatory now. That's who you saw at the station. The stragglers. The foolish. Let that be a lesson as well. When an order is given, you better obey it."

"Permission to pose a question, Lieutenant Li, sir?"

"Ask."

"Will the trains keep running until everyone is safe?"

"Some will get out. Most won't. The trains will stop soon. We can't afford to let them become contaminated. The people left behind will have to make do." He smiled at Bingwen. "So you see, I saved your friends' lives. I'm not as cruel as you think."

You put them on a train as you were ordered to do, thought Bingwen. You did the minimum required of you. You were cruel when you could have been kind.

Aloud he said, "Thank you, Lieutenant Li, sir."

The track turned north, and Chenzhou was suddenly behind them. Bingwen began to wonder where they were going. Surely they weren't taking a maintenance car all the way north.

After a few hundred meters, the trees and vegetation began to thicken into dense forest. Bingwen inhaled deep. The wind in his face was cool and clean. It carried the smells of greenery and earth and a coming rain. Bingwen had almost forgotten the world could smell this way—free of the stench of death and smoke and rotted vegetation. It made him think of the fields of home, of the way the cool mud would squeeze between his toes as he worked alongside Father in the paddies. It made him think of Mother, of how she would scold him one moment and then take him into her arms and laugh with him the next. It made him think of Hopper and Grandfather and running through the fields in the morning before sunrise so he could get more study time on the computers.

All of that was in this smell, the smell of China, of freedom, of home.

Ahead was a checkpoint. The car stopped at the gate. A soldier looked over Li's credentials and waved them through. Half a kilometer later they reached the military depot. The train was so long that Bingwen couldn't see where it ended. Soldiers were everywhere on the two platforms on either side, loading equipment and supplies. Pallets of food, blankets, medicine—enough to fill a city.

Li parked the maintenance car on a side track and then led Bingwen up onto one of the platforms. They weaved their way among workers, heading toward the front of the train. Li paused at a pallet of food and opened a box, coming away with two MREs.

By the time they reached the end of the platform and boarded the train, Bingwen had worked up a sweat. They found an empty passenger car near the front and sat facing each other.

Li tossed Bingwen an MRE. "Eat."

Bingwen peeled back the wrapper and bit into the wafer. It tasted like pork and cheese.

"Permission to pose a question, Lieutenant Li, sir?"

Li rolled his eyes. "I'm beginning to regret teaching you that. It's annoying." He bit into his wafer. "What?"

"Why do the Formics leave our nonaggressive aircrafts alone?"

"You don't have a theory?"

"Yes, but it's based on little information."

"Let's hear it anyway."

"Back at my village, we would sometimes get these

gnats. They'd buzz around in small swarms over the paddies, hovering in place and not really bothering us. Normally we would ignore them. But if you weren't paying attention and walked into their swarm, they'd get in your face and bite you."

"So the Formics are gnats."

"No," said Bingwen, "*we're* the gnats. I think the Formics leave the nonaggressive aircraft alone because they don't consider us a threat until we start biting. As soon as we get in their face, they realize we're there and brush us aside. Otherwise, we're insignificant to them."

"So humans are gnats. Doesn't sound like you hold much confidence in the human race."

"It's how the Formics *perceive* us. We think of them as an enemy. An equal. But maybe they see us as something far, far inferior, something barely worth their notice."

"Maybe," said Li.

"And if that's true," said Bingwen, "it makes me wonder what their true purpose is. A rice farmer doesn't come down to his paddies to swat at gnats. He comes to tend rice."

"What's your point?"

"My point is I don't think the Formics came here solely to kill us."

"They've killed twenty million people, Bingwen."

"Oh they're killing us. There's no question of that. And they're doing it effectively and intentionally. But that's not the primary reason *why* they're here. If it were, we would be their only target. They would always come after us. But initially they didn't. They killed all living things. Grass, trees, crops. All life. We need to ask ourselves why."

"I'll ask you: Why?"

Bingwen shrugged. "Some people might say that they're here to destroy the planet, that this is what they do as a species. They move through the universe killing all life. Maybe they're afraid intelligent beings will evolve enough to be a threat to them. So they kill everything to protect themselves against possible future attacks."

"Kill your enemy before he becomes your enemy."

"Yes."

"Is that what *you* think?"

"It's possible. Maybe even likely. But I don't think it's the only explanation. I think it far more likely that Formics are farmers."

Li raised an eyebrow. "Farmers?"

"Or whatever comes *before* farmers. Once, in my village, we had a few hectares of forest where we wanted to plant other crops besides rice. So we burned down the forest and cleared the land. It took awhile for the soil to heal, but once it did, it was rich and ready for planting. I think the Formics are doing the same, stripping the land to prepare it for crops. You can't just throw seed on the ground among what's already growing there and hope for the best. You have to remove everything that's currently seizing nutrients and start completely over."

"It's called 'terraforming,' " said Li.

"What's that?"

"What you're describing. It means they're preparing the ground for plant life that fits their own protein structure. We've known this is what they're doing for some time now."

"Why don't I hear people talking about this?"

"You're eight years old. Adults don't have these conversations with children. And anyway most people are idiots. They don't care about the why. They only care about what threatens them."

"I care about the why," said Bingwen.

"Which is why you're on this train. The military needs people who ask why."

They finished their meal, and the train pulled away

an hour later, loaded with food and supplies. Other soldiers joined them in the passenger car, all of them heavily armed.

Later, in the middle of the night, the train suddenly stopped, throwing the passenger car into chaos. Equipment fell from storage compartments. Men tumbled from seats. Bingwen jerked awake.

Li checked his wrist pad. "Something's wrong."

He got up and moved toward the front of the train. Bingwen fell in behind him. When they reached the driver's cab, they found the engineer shaken.

"What's wrong?" asked Li. "Why have we stopped?"

"Bandits," said the engineer, pointing out the front window. "They've set up a barricade. I had to stop or we would have crashed."

Bingwen went to the front window. The headlights of the train shined out into the darkness, illuminating thirty men ahead of them on the right side of the track. Most of them were armed with rifles, machetes, or farm tools. A large man sat on a horse at the front of the mob, a rifle resting in the crook of his arm. Thirty meters farther down the track, a huge bonfire made of felled trees burned in the center of the track, surrounded by heavy iron beams, old farming equipment, and large metal drums, all obstructing the way.

Li grabbed the radio from the front console and switched it to external speaker. When he spoke, his voice boomed outside the train. "These tracks are the property of the People's Republic of China. To obstruct them is treason."

The man on horseback must have had a projection device because his response was just as loud. "You are no longer in China. We have claimed our independence. The village of Chuanzhen and its lands are ours now. Your government forced us to grow cash crops instead of the crops we need to live on. Now we have no food.

And since trade in this region has collapsed, how are we to survive? How can we feed our children? No one will accept our money because the whole financial system has shut down here. We have no choice but to charge you a tax for crossing our lands. We know you have food and supplies on board. Share what you have with us and we'll clear the track and let you go."

"I am not the commanding officer on this train," said Lieutenant Li. "I cannot speak on his behalf. Let me consult with him and return with his answer."

"You have three minutes," said the man on the horse.

Li switched off the radio, unholstered his pistol, and gave it to the engineer. "Stay by this door," he said, gesturing to the side entrance. "If anyone tries to come inside, shoot them."

The engineer took the gun, holding it daintily. He was not military.

Li left the cab and moved back deeper into the train. Bingwen followed. In the third car they found fifty soldiers loading their weapons, checking their gear, putting on body armor.

"There are about thirty of them," Li told the soldiers. "All of them are traitors. Some are armed with machetes and old hunting rifles. I doubt many of them can shoot straight, but take out the rifles first just in case. There may be more in the trees on either side of the train. Look for heat signatures. I suggest getting off near the back and then coming up on either side using the trees for cover. Once it starts, they'll break and scatter. Be quick and clean."

They were going to kill the villagers, Bingwen realized. They were going to mow them down where they stood. It wasn't right. Most of the people looked half starved. They were simply trying to survive. His village probably would have done the same.

Bingwen dared not speak up and object, however.

That would be disrespectful. He would infuriate Li, which would make Li all the more insistent that they proceed with his plan. Nor could Bingwen run outside and warn the people. Li would arrest him as a traitor—or worse shoot him with the others. And besides, giving the people a warning would only put their rifleman on alert and lead to casualties on both sides.

No, there was only one course of action to prevent bloodshed.

Bingwen turned on his heels and walked back to the front of the train. He moved past the engineer without a word, opened the side door, and went outside. The night air was cold and smelled of bonfire smoke. A narrow ledge curved around the front of the train. It was more than wide enough for Bingwen. He sidled to the front and shouted to get their attention.

"Friends and respected elders. I am Bingwen. I am from a rice village south of here near Dawanzhen. I know you. I am one of you." He pointed to the man on the horse. "You are my uncle Longwei, my mother's brother, bold and strong and mindful of his family." He pointed to an old man with a rifle. "You are my grandfather, wise and kind and protective of his grandchildren. All of you are doing what *they* would do, to help their families, their village survive. Only they're dead, killed by the Formics."

The people were silent, watching him. The horse whinnied. The bonfire crackled. The tree leaves rustled softly in the wind.

"I saw them die. My friend Hopper and my cousin Meilin were two of the first, buried in a mudslide when the Formic lander set down by my village. Theirs was a quick death. They were lucky. Most in my village were killed by the gases. Children like me. Infants wrapped in their dead mothers' arms. My mother, my father." His voice cracked, the emotion welling up inside him, but he swallowed, controlled himself and moved on. "The Formics killed them all and left them to rot in the fields. You have not experienced such things this far north. You are hungry, yes, but you have been spared the worst of this war. If the Formics are not stopped, they will come here soon. And no amount of food, taken from us or grown in your own fields, can save you."

He gestured to the train behind him. "On this train we have soldiers who are trying to figure out how to kill the Formics before they come to this village. I don't know if they'll be ready in time to save your people. But they might—if you let them pass."

He scanned the crowd, letting his eyes meet theirs. "Or you could fight them, try to steal everything. Maybe you win, and kill the soldiers. You would eat for a few days, yes, but then who will defend you when the Formics come? Or maybe they win, and you die. What will your families do then?"

The door on the driver's cab opened, and Lieutenant Li stepped out onto the ledge, his hands raised, showing he was unarmed. "The boy says it true. We can share what we have. We have food for a week's journey on the train. What if we divide it with you? We'll journey on half rations. You'll have food for a few more days. We won't have Chinese killing Chinese."

Bingwen looked at him. Had Li had a change of heart? Had he seen the wisdom of what Bingwen was proposing?

"Send four of your men onto the train," said Li, "and we'll give them boxes of food to carry."

"How do we know this isn't a trick?" said the man on the horse. "You could hold my four men hostage, demand that we remove the obstruction. I need some assurance."

"I will send out four of our men," said Li. "They will be unarmed. You can keep them hostage while your men recover the food. I assure you no harm will come to your men."

The man on the horse considered for a long moment, then he turned to the mob and ordered three men to come forward. The men shouldered their rifles and approached the train. The man on the horse dismounted and joined them. Lieutenant Li opened the door for Bingwen to come inside. Four unarmed Chinese soldiers were in the driver's cab when Bingwen reentered. They wore no armor or gear. Li held open the door for them, and the four men exited the train. They then approached the mob, hands raised. A few in the mob held their rifles ready, just in case.

The horse rider, their leader, came up the ladder first, followed by his three men. When they were all in the driver's cab, the horse man said, "I am Shihong. This is my son, Renshu. And these are my fellow free citizens, Youngzhen and Xiaodan."

The men each bowed in turn. They were simple, humble people, Bingwen saw—farmers, with little to no education, most likely. Their clothes were warm but threadbare. They looked more like peasants than bandits.

"I am Lieutenant Li of the People's Liberation Army. Won't you come this way please?" He motioned to the hallway leading from the cab into the train.

Shihong, their leader, glanced out the front window and hesitated. Outside the four soldier hostages stood in the train's headlights with their hands behind their heads, defenseless. Shihong then turned to Bingwen and studied him, his eyes boring into Bingwen's. Whatever he saw there, it gave him his answer. He turned to Li and nodded. "Lead on."

Li escorted them into the train. They passed through several passenger cars until they reached a cargo hold where dozens of pallets of supplies were stored, all lashed to the walls of the train. Bingwen exhaled. He had feared some trap.

Shihong eyed the pallets, and a look of relief came over him. His eyes misted. He placed a hand on one of the food boxes and smiled. "What will you give us?" he asked, turning back to Lieutenant Li.

"Exactly what you deserve," said Li.

Then he raised a pistol and shot Shihong in the chest. Bingwen jerked, startled.

Three more quick shots. The heads of the three other men jerked back, each leaving a spray of red mist in the air. They crumpled. Shihong stumbled back against the pallet of food. He blinked, looked at the red stain blossoming on his chest, then fell.

Three soldiers stepped out from behind pallets in the cargo hold, each of them holding a rifle. Bingwen could hear more gunfire outside. Quick, automatic bursts.

"Get them out before they bleed over everything," said Li.

The three Chinese soldiers set their rifles aside. One of them slid open the side door, and a burst of cold air filled the cargo hold. The gunfire was louder now. Bingwen could see nothing but forest outside, but there were flashes of light from the gunfire ahead. The three soldiers dragged the dead men to the door and dumped them outside onto the gravel. It took two of them working together to move Shihong.

Lieutenant Li tapped something into his wrist pad. "Very clever of you, Bingwen. Distracting them like that, winning their trust. That made this much easier."

Bingwen stared down at the pool of blood by the pallet. It was thick and black in the semidarkness.

All was quiet outside now. The four soldier hostages appeared at the door and climbed inside, each carrying a small pistol. More soldiers followed them in, wearing body armor and carrying heavy rifles.

Li faced Bingwen. "You hate me. But governments cannot tolerate banditry. Ever. We can't negotiate with bandits because it never ends. More people turn to banditry because it pays. Still, we did their village a service. Now they have thirty fewer mouths to feed. We may have just saved the lives of the rest of the villagers."

Bingwen's eyes were vacant, his arms slack at his side. He stared at the blood.

"And maybe we didn't," said Li. "But I saved the rations my soldiers need. I fed *you*. I kept *you* alive. Was I wrong?"

"There is no right and wrong," said Bingwen. "You decided. You acted. You won. Now we clear the track and get the train moving again."

Li nodded and holstered his weapon. "I see that you understand war."

What I understand is you, thought Bingwen. Power without honor, order without civilization.

He was not going to run away, he decided. He would go to this school. He would become a soldier. But he would not become the monster of war they hoped to make him. He would not become Lieutenant Li. He would become what the world needed. A Mazer Rackham. Decisive, yet kind. Lethal, yet gentle. Otherwise, the Lis of the world would run the military, and it would make no difference if we won or lost this war.

CHAPTER 21

Strike Team

When the MOPs' shuttle arrived on Luna, they all came down the exit tube with such giant, clumsy, bumbling steps, bouncing off the walls and each other, laughing like a bunch of schoolchildren, that Victor was certain the whole operation was doomed to failure.

"These are our super soldiers?" he whispered to Lem. The two of them were standing in the terminal, waiting to greet the arrivals.

"They're not used to Luna's gravity," said Lem. "Everyone's like this their first time. They'll adapt."

Two MOPs collided at the end of the tube and fell into the terminal on top of each other. This seemed like an invitation to the others to add to the dog pile, and soon there was a mountain of flailing arms and legs in puffy spacesuits, amid laughter and curses and a good deal of shoving.

"This isn't instilling in me much confidence," Victor said to Lem.

Three more soldiers appeared in the tube, bringing up the rear. They moved with greater caution, taking measured steps. Victor recognized their faces through their visors: Wit O'Toole, Mazer Rackham, and Shenzu. By the time they reached the terminal, the other MOPs were on their feet and steadying each other.

Wit shook hands with Lem and Victor. "So much for making a good first impression."

"You made your first impression long ago, Captain O'Toole," said Lem. "Welcome to Luna."

There were introductions all around. Victor had already learned their names and faces from their dossiers, but he made a show of learning them now.

"Space born, eh?" said Cocktail. "We must look like a pack of uncoordinated imbeciles to you."

"You'll get the hang of it," said Victor. "Right now your mind is accustomed to your body moving in a certain way. The gravity here throws that out of alignment. Once we get in zero-G, you'll find it much easier."

They loaded into a large skimmer and left the gate, heading back toward the warehouse.

"There are a few legal matters we must attend to before leaving Luna," said Lem. "I apologize in advance. Our corporate attorneys want to ensure that we don't get sued in the event of an injury or your demise. You'll need to sign a few things."

"'Your demise,'" repeated Bungy. "I love lawyer-speak. 'Your demise.' It's so polite. In reality it means an alien gutted you and melted your face with toxic goo, but 'demise' is so much more delicate."

"What's the difference between a porcupine and two lawyers in a sports car?" asked ZZ. After a silence he said, "The porcupine has the pricks on the outside."

The men chuckled. Victor didn't get it. Apparently prick had multiple meanings.

"What's the difference between a catfish and a lawyer?" asked Cocktail. "One is a bottom-dwelling, garbage-eating scavenger. The other is a fish."

The men laughed. They were not at all what Victor had expected. He had envisioned gruff men with steely

eyes and serious dispositions, lethal killers ready to snap
a neck at a moment's notice. But these men were like his
uncles and his father: easygoing, relaxed, a family. To
Victor's surprise, this didn't unsettle him. If anything it
put his mind at ease. He had worried that soldiers would
scoff at his direction and dismiss him as so many others
had done. But these men, like the men of home, seemed
like the type who would listen to any idea, regardless of
where it came from.

"What happens after we appease the lawyers?" asked
Wit.

The men fell silent. It was down to business now. All
eyes were on Lem.

"We'll leave Luna for a cargo freighter called the
Valas," said Lem. "It's positioned out in space just beyond Luna's gravity well. It's one of the largest vessels
this company has ever built and it will serve as our base
of operations. All of our equipment and support team
are already there. We'll stay on the Valas for a few days
as you learn to move in zero-G. Victor will be your
teacher. You'll have very specific duties once you're inside the Formic ship, and you'll train for those as well."

"What duties?" said Wit. "We've chased your dangling carrot, Lem. We're here. Now tell us how we're
going to destroy the ship."

"By being plumbers, Captain O'Toole."

"I beg your pardon."

Lem laughed. "Plumbers, Captain. You know,
wrenches, elbow grease, exorbitantly high hourly rates.
You need not show your butt crack when you bend
over, however. Victor will explain everything shortly."

They docked at the warehouse. Ramdakan was waiting inside with a team of lawyers. Tables had been set
up. Documents were presented and signed. It was all
very quick and orderly, but it dampened the mood considerably. The MOPs never questioned anyone. They

read their documents and signed. When it was done, Ramdakan thanked them, wished them luck, gathered his crew, and left.

"It's ironic," said Deen. "Usually lawyers pounce on you *after* you've destroyed something."

Lem then introduced the MOPs to the various warehouse workers who had come out to meet them and wish them well. The MOPs were kind and gracious. They went around the room thanking everyone for their hard work and contributions. The more Victor watched them, the more convinced he became that Lem had chosen well. They were obviously fine soldiers—their accomplishments in the field were evidence of that. Yet they were also decent human beings, which was just as important, if not more so.

Simona took vids of everything with her holopad.

"Are you recording that for PR or for you?" Lem asked her.

"For you," she said. "You'll want to show your grandkids someday."

Ukko Jukes arrived minutes later, surprising everyone. He went around the room, shaking hands like a politician up for reelection. Victor could tell Lem was annoyed, though Lem was doing his best not to show it. Simona continued with the vid recording.

Victor wanted to approach Ukko and put a boot between his legs. Hello, Mr. Jukes. This is for nearly killing Imala with the drones. Kapow! But he kept quiet and stayed in the back of the room as far from Ukko as possible.

When Ukko was done making the rounds, he spoke loud enough for all to hear. "When I learned that my son was planning this mission, I've never felt prouder as a parent." He paused as if overcome with emotion.

Victor rolled his eyes. Was anyone believing this for an instant? He looked around the room. Everyone was attentive except for Lem, who was picking a piece of invisible lint off his jacket.

"I'm proud that Juke Limited could help in some way," said Ukko. "If there is anything you men need, just say so, and I will see to it personally." He smiled warmly. Then he extended his hands to the side. "I know all of us come from different countries and cultures, but let us link hands for a moment. All of us. Don't be shy. That's it. Everyone take the hand of the person to your right and left. You too, son. You're the leader here. We need you most of all. That's it. Now I want each of you to look around this circle. Look at the faces before you. This is what Earth can be. All of us joined together in purpose, working as one against a common enemy. This is true strength. The talents and skills of all. United."

Ukko scanned the crowd, meeting their eyes. "Now, let us take a moment of silence. And in that silence, pray to whatever god you have. Pray that those who are about to embark on this dangerous effort will return to us whole and sound. Pray for our brothers and sisters in China, and for the soldiers there, too, and their families and loved ones. And most of all, pray that Earth will be ours again, a stronger Earth, a better Earth, an Earth that will never shake again at such evil."

Ukko bowed his head. Everyone in the circle did the same except for Lem, who stared straight ahead at his father, saying his own silent prayer, perhaps.

After a full minute, Ukko lifted his head and thanked them again. Then as quickly as he had come, he waved and departed.

Lem took control of the scene again, and ten minutes later he, Victor, and all the MOPs were loaded into the shuttle and lifting away from Luna.

They docked with the Valas, and everyone undid their harnesses and floated through the hatch. Imala and Dr. Benyawe were there to greet them, having come up earlier. More introductions were made; then they all moved to the helm where the holotable had been prepped. Lem instructed everyone to anchor their feet to the hooks in the floor around the table, and then he turned the time over to Victor.

The Formic ship appeared in the holofield. Victor used his stylus to rotate it 360 degrees so that everyone could see it from all angles. "This ship is still largely a mystery." He pointed to the crown of tubular rods encircling the point of the teardrop. "This apparatus here, for example. We have no idea what this is. Many suspect that it's field-generation equipment, and I tend to agree with them. But how the Formic shields work is still a giant unknown. They block tiny space particles as the ship moves through deep space, and they deflect any projectile fired at the ship. Yet I was able to approach and enter the ship without any resistance. Why? Does the shield require an enormous amount of energy to maintain and thus is only turned on when the Formics are in flight or when they detect a threat? We don't know. All we do know is that this type of tech is priceless." He zoomed in on the field generators. "Humans don't know how to do this. Yet field generation is critical if ever we want to attempt interstellar flight."

He zoomed in to the rear of the ship. "And this is the propulsion system. It's powerful enough to move a ship of this mass up to a significant fraction of the speed of light. We're nowhere close to tech like that."

He zoomed back out. "And what about Formic communications? How does one ship speak to another? We have no idea. I didn't find anything in the ship to answer that question, but the answer must be there somewhere. And whatever it is, it has the potential to revolutionize our own communication infrastructure, both out here in space and down on Earth. I could go on. My point is, there are likely hundreds, if not thousands of innovations inside this ship far beyond anything we've developed or ever could develop. It is a treasure trove of tech that could open new doors and possibilities for all of us. I'm not exaggerating when I say this ship could change the world."

"So this is about seizing tech?" said Shenzu. "I thought we were fighting a war here."

"We are," said Victor. "But this is also about making Earth stronger. We can't simply blow the ship to smithereens."

"Why not?" said Shenzu. "That would certainly swing the war in our favor. Who cares if we get a shield generator? I'm more worried about ending this."

"But that's exactly Victor's point," said Mazer. "Destroying the ship would not be the end. Winning this war may not be the end. This ship came from somewhere. There are more Formics out there. And the reason why they have beat us so far is because their tech is so superior. But if we can learn their tech and reverse engineer it, we can better protect ourselves from future attacks. We would level the playing field. This isn't about creating a tech boom on Earth, it's about winning this war and any future war. It's about strengthening ourselves militarily. If we blow that ship up, we'll have destroyed our best chance at defeating the Formics next time."

"Mazer's right," said Wit. "And even if the Formics never bother us again, there's a chance something else will come along. Something worse. We should always learn everything we can from the enemy and use that to better defend ourselves."

"So we don't blow it up," said Shenzu. "Agreed. But what *is* the plan? We still have a war to end."

"We kill all the Formics on board," said Mazer. "Then we cripple the ship so it can't go anywhere."

"Mazer's right," said Victor. "We don't want the ship running back to wherever it came from and rallying reinforcements. Our primary mission is to make sure it has flown its final flight."

"How?" said Wit.

Victor tapped the ship with his stylus and two dozen cannons appeared on the surface. "The ship has two main defenses. The first is the cannons. Each of them is stored in a recessed hole that closes at the top when not in use. When the ship is threatened, the cannons emerge, unfold, and fire at whatever is approaching the ship. When they're done, they fold back inside, and the aperture over the hole seals shut again. The good news is, many of the cannons were destroyed by Ukko Jukes's drones. So much of the work has already been done. The other good news is, taking out the others will be easy."

He moved to the side and called up another model in the holofield—this one of a large closed aperture. "We know precisely where all of these cannons are located. To take them out of commission, all we need to do is weld the aperture shut so it can't open."

He picked up a sheet of steel that was attached to the side of the table. It was roughly two meters long and one half meter wide. "Each of your cocoons has been designed to carry eight sheets of steel this size. That's more than you'll need, but you'll be carrying extras in case something happens to any one of you en route. To disable the cannons, you and a partner will weld three sheets of steel atop each cannon aperture."

Three sheets of steel appeared atop the closed aperture in the holofield. They were positioned a short distance away from each other near the center and formed a triangular shape. "As you can see, each sheet of steel lies across at least two blades of the aperture, locking it closed. This triangular shape is the strongest. You and your partner will be assigned two cannons. This is your welding tool." He held up the small, handheld device. "You'll lock down each sheet of steel with magnets, then you'll wipe the welder along the edge of the steel. It will melt easily. Apply light pressure and you'll push the melted steel onto the Formic surface. It will feel like spreading icing on a cake. And that's it. Locked with the steel, the apertures can't open. Cannons are inoperative."

"Easy enough," said Cocktail.

"The next part isn't so easy," said Victor. He moved back to the holo of the ship and tapped it with his stylus. The hull vanished, revealing the network of pipes beneath the surface. They numbered in the hundreds, with all of them running parallel to each other from front to back.

"This looks like the skeleton of the ship," said Victor. "Like framing rods. But these lines are actually pipes. They channel plasmoid, which we'll simply call plasma, throughout the piping system. Now, I don't think the plasma is always in the pipes, like water, because it would cease to be plasma. It's probably held in reserve somewhere and released into the pipe system when needed. How they contain it, I have no idea. They have shield generators on the ship's exterior, so if I had to guess, they likely use the same type of shielding, or a variation of it, to store up the plasma. Where, I don't know. What I do know is that when the ship is threatened, plasma enters the pipes and travels to T-shaped nozzles positioned every few meters throughout the piping system."

He tapped with the stylus again, and hundreds of dots appeared along the pipes. Then he zoomed forward to one of the dots, revealing it to be a nozzle.

"Each of these nozzles is connected to an aperture on the surface of the ship. These are small apertures, no bigger than a dinner plate. When attacked, the Formics open the apertures and the nozzles somehow laserize the plasma. It's not a true laserization, because it's not pure energy. That's just the term I'm using because the plasma comes out in a very narrow stream, rather like lasers, though by no means as close to parallel."

A brief animation played, showing one of the nozzles emit a narrow, destructive stream.

"Our job," said Victor, "is to access the pipes from inside the ship. Once we're done disabling the cannons, we'll gather here at this destroyed cannon. This is where I entered the ship. The hole inside is already cut and ready. There's a shaft there that leads directly to the cargo bay. It's a tight squeeze, but we'll likely go undetected." He zoomed forward into the ship, coming to rest in the cargo bay. "The pipes are behind the inner wall, which is composed of dense metal plates. We'll first cut away a large section of plates and expose the pipes underneath. I'd suggest we remove at least forty square meters of plates."

Victor drew a square on the inner wall.

"That's huge," said Deen. "That's almost half the size of an American football field."

"For us that's big, yes," said Victor. "But remember, this is a big ship." He zoomed back out to see the ship as a whole. Forty square meters suddenly looked demonstrably smaller.

"Removing these plates will be tricky," said Victor. "We have to do so without damaging the pipes underneath. The right equipment will help. You'll be cutting with lasers set to a specific depth. And you'll also have scanners that will let you see the pipes beneath the plates so you can cut between pipes whenever possible. This will be the most time consuming and dangerous part of the operation. Not only because we can't damage the pipes, but also because Formic repair teams will come to fix the plates as soon as we start removing them."

"How many Formics are in a team?" asked Wit.

"The group I saw had four. But that doesn't mean there won't be more."

"So we'll need a cutting team and a defense team," said Mazer. "Where will the Formics be coming from?"

Victor pointed. "Possibly from this large shaft here. But there are dozens of shafts that feed into the cargo bay. Repair crews could come from any one of them. Or from several at once. We have no way of knowing."

"Not a good position to be in," said Mazer. "The cutting team will be very exposed. There's some ship wreckage floating inside the cargo bay that could provide some cover, but the cutting crew will still be susceptible to enemy fire. The Formics, on the other hand, will have plenty of cover at the shaft entrances."

"What do you suggest?" asked Wit.

"We booby-trap the shafts," said Mazer. "It needs to be silent so as not to alert others on the ship. Do you think we could replicate what you did on the goo tower?"

"You mean electrify the shafts?" said Wit.

"Maybe just the last five meters of the shaft," said Mazer. "Maybe we create a mesh netting, like a bag that's open on both ends, and we lay it flat against the inner wall. The Formics come up, they poke their heads out. And we zap them."

"If we had a few weeks to build the nets," said Lem. "But we're at the eleventh hour here."

Benyawe stepped forward to the holofield and started flipping through files. "We may not need weeks. Juke already has nets like this made of thin metal mesh for securing loads on cargo vessels."

A catalog entry of the mesh netting appeared in the field.

"We could have it flown here from Luna," said Benyawe. "The team tapes it down along the inner wall of the shaft, being sure not to obstruct the track in the floor, and we're set. Question is, how to electrify it."

"That would be easy," said Victor. "Couple drive batteries would do it. And a few hundred meters of cable. We set the batteries in the cargo bay rigged to a manual switch."

"There are dozens of shafts," said Lem. "You're talking about a ton of equipment we don't have room for. The cocoons are designed to hold a person, his weapon, his tools, the steel, and that's it. How do we get all of these nets and cables and batteries to the ship?"

"The cocoons are covered in space junk to camouflage them," said Victor. "We remove some of that junk and replace it with batteries and spools of cable. We scuff them up and paint them so they still look like debris. If we need more space, we could attach some of the equipment to some of the small pieces of drift debris. The drone pilots then fly those pieces near to where we enter the ship. Then we recover the equipment and we're set. Or—and this is the least attractive option—we could remove one person from the mission and fill one of the cocoons with the equipment we'll need."

"I'd rather not lose a person," said Wit. "If we can make it work with the cocoons' exteriors and the drift debris, we should."

"We'll make it happen," said Benyawe. "We have members of our engineering team on hand for needs like this. We can get the supplies and start making the modifications to the cocoons immediately. Our drone pilots will use the debris drones to carry anything else that doesn't fit straight to the cannon. Those will arrive before you do. All you'll have to do is recover them."

"Good," said Wit. He turned to Victor. "Walk us through the rest of it. We've cut away a huge section of wall plates and exposed the pipes. Now what?"

"Now we rotate all of the exposed nozzles inward so they point toward the middle of the ship. Once that's done, everyone exits the ship and gathers at this point here."

Victor drew a circle on the hull, a distance from the cargo bay.

"Meanwhile, two people are outside the ship here, directly above the spot where the nozzles have been rotated. Armed with paint guns, they'll paint a giant square on the ship's exterior in phosphorescent paint that matches where the plates have been removed inside the cargo bay. Once the crew inside is clear, the paint sprayers will paint a giant 'X' in the square. Like so."

He demonstrated with his stylus.

"Then the paint sprayers will attach these glow rods near the paint to make it glow and move here to join the others outside the ship a safe distance away."

A small spacecraft appeared in the top left corner of the holofield.

"A pilot will then fly a small fighter directly *above* the rotated nozzles, aiming for the 'X.' The Formics will see the fighter approach, decide it's a threat, and order one of the cannons to extend. This will obviously fail as we will have already disabled them. The Formics will then fire the gamma plasma, opening the nozzles where the 'X' is located. Those nozzles will be rotated inward, however, so the gamma plasma will blast through the ship and blow a hole out the other side. The radiation from that blast will dissipate throughout the ship and kill most of the Formics inside."

"So we trick them into using their own weapon against themselves," said Deen. "I like that."

"Whoever flies that fighter needs to fly as straight as an arrow toward the 'X,'" said Wit. "The Formics will likely open up other nozzles we haven't rotated. Beams of gamma plasma will encircle the fighter from all sides. He'll essentially be flying inside a tunnel of plasma. If he deviates in any way, he'll fly into the line of fire and be obliterated."

"The pilot's not a *he*," said Imala. "It's a she. I'm doing it."

Everyone looked at her.

Victor was so surprised it took him a moment to find words. "Imala . . . we agreed that one of the MOPs would do this."

"It should be me," said Mazer. "I have the most flight experience."

"Not in space you don't," said Imala. "I'm the most qualified pilot here."

"I flew an antigrav ship on Earth," said Mazer. "I'm familiar with flying with minimal gravity."

"Minimal gravity is a world away from zero gravity," said Imala. "You're used to maintaining an orientation. This fighter has boosters on all sides to maintain a straight course. You've never flown that way. None of you have. It has to be me."

Several people turned to Wit, deferring to him.

"If Imala says she can do it, I believe her," said Wit. "What about radiation, Victor? If she's flying through a tunnel of gamma plasma, won't she die of radiation poisoning?"

It took a second for Victor to gather his thoughts. He was staring at Imala, who was looking back at him, arms folded defiantly, daring him to question her. "We've . . . added several layers of shielding to the fighter," said Victor. "That should protect her. Also she'll be wearing a radiation suit like the rest of us."

"Why not use a drone?" said Mazer. "Wouldn't that be safer?"

"We considered that," said Victor, "but the radiation from the gamma plasma would interfere with the drone pilot's connection to the spacecraft. A human pilot inside the vessel is more reliable."

"Sooner or later she's going to fly into the Formic ship," said Mazer.

"She'll be decelerating the whole time," said Victor. "And we don't think the Formics will fire the gamma plasma for very long. Once the crew at the helm realizes what's happening, they'll shut off the gamma plasma. At that point the vacuum of space will work to our advantage. Any remaining radiation will be sucked out into space. We wait an hour or so to ensure it's clear, then we go in, mop up, and seize the helm."

Victor made a gesture with his stylus, and the holofield disappeared. "That's it. The ship will be ours."

Everyone waited for Wit to respond. He looked around the room. "All right, people. Let's shoot holes in this. What are we forgetting?"

There were several questions. Someone asked about the suits they would wear. Benyawe answered, pulling up the holofield again and showing them the radiation suits her team had designed.

"How long will we be in these suits?" asked ZZ.

"The cocoon flight to the ship will take three days," said Benyawe. "That's a long time to remain motionless, but you need to drift that slowly. We dare not risk you moving any faster. The suit will stimulate your muscles, and you can access food and water at any time through straws in your suit."

"How do we go to the bathroom?" asked Bungy.

Benyawe pointed to the apparatuses on the suit and explained.

"Looks painful," said Deen.

"Like all things in space," said Victor. "It takes some getting used to."

They talked for another hour, hashing out the details; then Mazer, Shenzu, and the MOPs followed Victor into the cargo bay. Victor had them line up along one wall while holding the handrail. He showed them how to launch, point their bodies, and rotate midflight to land feetfirst on the opposite wall. It was a simple move he was sure they would grasp easily, but when he invited them to try, they were awkward and tentative. "I feel like I'm going to fall," said Deen, clinging to the handrail. "I know there's no gravity, but my brain doesn't want to release the idea of an up and down. It wants to maintain the orientation we had when we came in here."

After several attempts, they gradually began to master the mechanics of the movements; although none of them ever felt particularly comfortable doing so. "Flying in the corridor is easier," said ZZ. "There's an up and down out there, and the space is confined. When we come into a big room like this, I feel this existential panic."

"It's not easy to rewire the brain," said Wit. "And that's essentially what we're doing here."

It struck Victor as strange that anyone would struggle with such an easy movement. It was second nature to him. He had been flying and launching since before he was walking.

"What's the trick, space born?" asked Deen. "You make this look easy."

Victor shrugged. "No trick. I root myself like each of you. I just do it without a gravity-conditioned mind."

"If we weren't trained paratroopers, we'd be doing much worse," said Cocktail. "We've got landing and rolling down. It's the leaping and positioning of the body that's difficult."

They practiced for several hours, making gradual improvements. Victor began to wonder if they would have been better off enlisting miners, who were clearly more accustomed to maneuvering in zero-G. But no, once they got the practice weapons out, it became obvious that the MOPs' soldiering skills were far more critical here. Their individual movements might be imperfect, but they thought as a group, functioned as a team, often without even speaking to one another.

Next Victor brought out the practice pipes that Ben-yawe and her team had built. They were similar in design to the pipes and nozzles of the Formic ship. Victor and two of the MOPs set them up on the far wall, and they practiced flying to them and rotating the nozzles.

They ran the drill over and over again. They practiced cutting thick sheets of metal with the laser cutters. They flew up and down the tight corridors of the Valas. They set up targets in the corridors and practiced hitting those on the move. They split into two teams and battled against each other. They played again with all of them against Wit. Or all of them against a group of three. Shenzu and Mazer held their own against the others. Victor was no soldier, and despite his superior maneuverability, he was almost always the first person tagged.

When they stopped hours later, they were all soaked in sweat.

That night no one had trouble sleeping. The Valas continued its slow approach to the Formic ship, and the next day they did all the same drills again, only now while wearing their bulky radiation suits. They were far less graceful in those, but they quickly adapted to the slight decrease in mobility. Benyawe joined them in their exercises. No one objected to her being part of their group, especially when they saw how easily she flew or how deftly she handled the tools and nozzles.

At day's end, everyone agreed they were as ready as they were going to be. The MOPs drew straws to see who would go. Wit was a given, as was Victor, Benyawe, and Shenzu. That left eight spaces. The others were all equal in their abilities, so they couldn't choose based on skill. In the end it was Bungy, ZZ, Cocktail, Deen, Bol-shakov, Lobo, Caruso, and Mazer.

They slept eight hours. By then the Valas was in position and the cocoons were ready, loaded with the batteries and cable. The team ate, dressed in their suits, and climbed into their cocoons. Imala was there to see them off. The technicians from the engineering team sealed them in one by one. Victor was the last to climb inside his cocoon. His helmet was in his hands. Imala floated before him, one foot anchored to the decking.

"Fly straight," Victor said.

"I will." She brushed a hair out of her face and looked at him, concerned. "Stay close to Mazer and Wit. And don't do anything stupid."

"This whole plan is stupid."

"No. It isn't, Vico. It's a good plan. Just come back safe, okay?"

He nodded. "In my family, we would always say, '*Si somos uno, nada nos puede dañar.*'"

"Which means?"

"If we're one, nothing can hurt us."

"Let's hope you're right, space born."

They embraced. It was a clumsy move with him in his radiation suit. After a moment she stepped back. Victor snapped on his helmet and wiggled down into the cocoon. He connected his suit to the muscle stimulators and gave the technicians a thumbs-up. They closed the lid and all went dark. Victor turned on his HUD and watched as Imala and the technicians left the bay and sealed the hatch behind them. In front of him, the giant bay doors slowly opened, revealing the immensity of space and a tiny red dot glinting far in the distance. Then the propulsion system on his cocoon gave a hiss, and he was away.

CHAPTER 22

Nozzles

Mazer touched down so gently on the surface of the Formic ship that he hardly felt the impact at all. The magnets on the cocoon initiated, and a message on his HUD told him that he was sufficiently anchored to get out. He turned the release lever by his head, and the lid above his face came free. The view before him took his breath away. The vastness of space was like a black abyss dotted with a billion pinpricks of light.

The cocoon was standing on end, anchored at his feet, he realized. He would have to climb up out the top, away from the surface of the ship, and then swing his body downward as he initiated his boot magnets.

It wasn't supposed to work that way. The cocoon was supposed to be flat against the hull, so that Mazer was on his back and could crawl out easily. I'm here for two seconds, and already everything's going wrong, he thought.

He didn't want to move. The cocoon—dangerous as it was—felt safer than the nothingness before him. He swiveled his head to the side and saw the red surface of the ship stretching out before him like a vast metal plain. He looked in the other direction, and saw more of the ship that way. It was bigger than he had imagined it, and he suddenly wondered if a hole forty meters square would be big enough to cripple the thing.

He was alone, he realized. He saw no other cocoons. There were pieces of debris out in space, but they were all so small and so far away that he didn't know if they were part of the mission or not. They had planned to stagger their arrival, but Mazer was to be one of the last to arrive, not one of the first. Was he the only one who had made it? Had the others been vaporized by the collision avoidance system?

He gripped the edge of the hole and pulled himself up, suddenly afraid that he would rock the cocoon and break the magnet's hold on the ship. Every muscle in his body tensed as he freed his feet and slowly swung downward. When his feet made contact and his boot magnets initiated, he realized he had been holding his breath.

He bent down, opened the cocoon's compartment near his feet, and pulled out his shoulder pack filled with tools. He strapped it to his back and checked his HUD. They had agreed to radio silence until they were all inside the ship. It was probably an unnecessary precaution—Victor and Imala had used radio to no ill effect—but Wit wasn't taking any chances. In the meantime Mazer could sync his HUD with the latest updates from Valas, which was tracking everyone's position and progress. With the sync, Mazer would be able to see which cannons had been disabled, if any.

When the sync came through he learned that he was the last to arrive. The person before him had arrived three hours earlier. Cocktail was supposed to be his partner in disabling two of the cannons, but the team hadn't waited for Mazer. They had disabled the cannons without him and were now moving toward the cargo bay.

Mazer brought up the map of the ship's surface in relation to his own position and saw that he had a long walk ahead of him. The cannon where he would enter the ship was several hundred meters away.

He began walking, taking soft, tentative steps across the hull, being careful to firmly plant one boot magnet before lifting another. It would be just his luck to step too quickly, lose his grip, and slip away. Death by walking.

After a few minutes he was into a rhythm. His legs were getting quite the workout, though. The magnets were strong, and each step took some effort. He was sweating profusely and breathing heavily when he saw the first cocoon in the distance lying flat, far off to his right. A minute later he saw another one to his left. When he started passing pieces of the drift debris, he knew he was getting close. He stopped and checked one of the pieces, but of course whatever equipment it was carrying had already been retrieved and carried inside.

Mazer pushed on and finally reached the damaged cannon. He crawled down into the hole and made his way into the ship. There were two bubbles over the hole, forming a makeshift airlock. When Mazer was inside the ship and the hole was sealed behind him, he turned on his radio. For a moment he heard nothing, then Wit's voice crackled in. "Make sure that wiring is secure."

Mazer said. "It's Mazer. Checking in."

"About time," said Wit. "We're in the bay setting the nets. So far so good."

"Heading your way."

He moved up the shaft. They had watched Victor's vid several times, and it was odd to experience it now in person. He passed the glow bugs, which seemed particularly agitated after so much traffic. He kept his eyes open for cart pushers but saw none.

They were done setting the nets by the time he arrived. A series of wires crisscrossed the space to a large bank of batteries anchored to the far wall, where Victor was making final adjustments.

"Oh sure," said Deen. "Mazer shows up when half the work is done. Slick move, kiwi."

Mazer smiled but said nothing. The team was gathering at the wall where they would expose the pipes. Benyawe was marking off the area with spray paint.

Mazer had been assigned to stand watch. He picked a spot high up on the wall opposite the shafts and anchored his feet. He scanned the shafts back and forth looking for any signs of movement. The plates came away faster than Mazer had expected. The lasers cut quickly and accurately, and it was easy to simply push the cut pieces away in zero-G.

They were three-fourths of the way finished when Mazer saw the first Formics. "Victor, I've got movement in shaft thirteen." The team had spray painted numbers above each shaft. Mazer zoomed in with his visor and put his rifle to his shoulder. "It's one of the large carts. Filled with wall plating. Repair crew."

Victor's voice came over the radio. He was positioned at the batteries and switches. "How many?"

"Can't tell. The shaft is dark. I can only make out vague shapes. At least five. Maybe more."

Mazer checked his HUD. The cutting crew had stopped and taken cover.

"Are they on the netting?" Wit asked.

"Not yet," said Mazer. "They're probing it."

They knew something was different. They weren't animals, baited into a simple trap. They're too intelligent to fall for this, thought Mazer. They're as smart as us. If not smarter.

One of the Formics stepped tentatively onto the mesh, approaching the end of the shaft. Then another one came forward. Then a third.

"Not yet," said Mazer.

A fourth. A fifth. Was that all of them?

They pulled the cart forward. It was close to the lip of the shaft.

"Now," said Mazer.

Victor triggered the juice, and the Formics were seized by the electricity. Mazer launched across the space toward them. He had attached his laser cutter to the barrel of his assault rifle. He sliced through the first two Formics before he had landed, cutting them in half. A stream of blood oozed from the top halves as they slipped away from the bottom half.

Mazer came to rest to the right of the shaft. He twisted, bent forward, and cut through the others. It was gruesome work. One moment they're shaking, seized by the electricity. The next moment they're in pieces seeping droplets of blood into the air.

"Cut the power," said Mazer.

"It's cut. You're clear."

Mazer swung down into the shaft and shined his light into the darkness to see if he had missed any. The shaft was empty.

"Clear," he said.

"We need to move quickly," said Victor. "If they *can* speak mind to mind, they might have gotten off a message."

The crew returned to cutting, moving fast.

Mazer grabbed the pieces of sliced Formics and tossed them toward the floating debris in the cargo bay in case any others came down this same shaft. Then he shot back to his position on the opposite wall. The front of his suit and his right hand were slick with blood. He tried wiping his hand on the wall to get rid of it, but it didn't help. He put his rifle back to his shoulder and scanned back and forth, watching for movement. The shafts remained still and dark. The cutting team cut away large squares of wall. Others were already busy rotating the nozzles of the exposed pipes. Mazer had worried that the nozzles would prove stubborn or the pipes would pinch, but Benyawe led the effort and was giving careful instruction that seemed to be working.

A Formic launched from shaft twenty-five, heading straight for the cutting crew. Mazer hadn't even seen it approach the shaft entrance. Caruso, who was also on watch and perched far to Mazer's left, saw the Formic first and sliced it in the air with his laser cutter before Mazer had time to react. Four sections of the Formic separated and continued their flight to the opposite wall. The severed bloody pieces smacked into the pipes, leaking fluid.

A Formic shot from shaft fifteen. Two more from shaft thirty.

"Victor, turn on the power!" said Mazer. "All shafts."

Victor acknowledged and cranked up the juice as Mazer and Caruso sliced the Formics soaring across the space. Formic body parts spun and bled and ricocheted off the walls.

"Double-time, people," said Wit. "This place is going to be crawling with bugs any minute. Bungy, ZZ, get outside and start painting our giant square for Imala. Mazer, Caruso, check the shafts. We may have lost our element of surprise."

Caruso nodded. "I'll take the shafts on the left. Mazer, you take the ones on the right."

Mazer acknowledged and launched, his rifle up, the light on the barrel illuminating the shaft directly in front of him. A dozen sets of eyes in the darkness stared back at him, glinting in the beam of his light. One of them launched directly at him, arms outstretched, maw open. It was right when Mazer was going to rotate his body so he could land gracefully beside the shaft entrance. He fired instead. The laser went through the Formic's face, down its back, and out the other side. Mazer only had time to raise a protective arm before he collided with the corpse. They bounced off each other clumsily, with Mazer spinning away, out of control.

"Formics!" said Caruso. "Shafts twenty-one through twenty-four. I count fifty, maybe more. Shaft twenty-five, too."

Mazer struck something hard. A floating piece of debris. He was disoriented. He tried to right himself. Something hard collided with him, clinging to him, striking him in many places at once. A Formic. They crashed into another piece of debris. Mazer was in an awkward position. On his stomach. He didn't know up from down. Something struck his helmet. He flipped around to see the Formic had a piece of debris in its hand. A sharp sliver of wreckage, jagged at one edge. It would puncture and cut through Mazer's suit.

Mazer fumbled for his rifle. He had wrapped the strap around his arm so he wouldn't drop it, but the strap had twisted, and now there wasn't enough slack to swing the rifle forward. He yanked, pulled. The Formic raised the sharp weapon up to deliver a blow.

And its head exploded in a burst of automatic fire.

But not from Mazer's rifle. He looked to his left. Cocktail was holding his rifle up. "Grenades. In the shafts. Move, move!"

Mazer got his feet under him. All around him grenades were being pitched into the shafts like baseballs. They exploded inside. Formics were launching outward from the shafts. Lasers shot across the space, slicing them in two. The mesh nets were holding most of them back, but every Formic in the ship would know they were here now. Mazer unsnapped the concussion grenade from his belt then pushed off the debris. He didn't move as quickly as he would have liked—the debris wasn't anchored. He floated slowly. The shaft in front of him had a handful of Formics tentatively approaching the mesh netting. Mazer threw in the grenade. Its magnet base snapped to the shaft wall. A Formic was inches away from it. It turned its head to look at it just as the grenade detonated.

Mazer reached the wall. Shafts were all around him. A few Formics were stuck on the mesh netting convulsing. Mazer sliced them. The shaft to his right had Formics crawling forward. He reached in and fired his automatic, bullets pinging around the shaft. He chased them with a grenade for good measure. Victor had been wrong about the Formic count. There were more than a hundred on board. Much more.

Several from the cutting crew had left their post to join the fight. Mazer looked back at the pipes. Most of the wall plates were cleared but there were still a lot of nozzles to rotate. They weren't going to make it. They couldn't hold this many Formics coming from this many directions for much longer. They didn't have enough people.

Wit shouted over the radio. "Mazer, you and Cocktail clear the exit shaft. When we're done with the nozzles, we need a clear path out of here."

Of course. If there were Formics in the shaft with the glow bugs, the MOPs would have no way out.

Wit continued shouting orders. He made new assignments to take on the shafts and ordered others who had joined the fight to get back to the pipes and turn the nozzles. "We have to turn them all. If we miss just one, it will vaporize Imala."

Cocktail was suddenly beside Mazer. "We need to hold that shaft. Any ideas?"

"We need one of the wall plates," said Mazer. "Help me."

They flew to retrieve one of the discarded wall plates. There were more grenade explosions and automatic fire all around them.

"Here," said Mazer. "Let's use this one."

"What for?" said Cocktail.

"We're going to make a shield. Help me fly it to the shaft entrance."

They each got on one side of it and, on the count of three, launched with it toward the glow bug shaft. When they arrived, Mazer shined his light in the shaft and saw three Formics scurrying forward. He annihilated them with three quick bursts.

He turned back to Cocktail. "They're coming up the shaft. We've got to clear a path and hold them back. We need to cut this wall plate down so that it's the shape of the shaft, only smaller. Then we'll get behind it, and ram our way down the shaft."

Cocktail nodded. They slid the wall plate over the shaft and started cutting. Large chunks fell away.

"Snap your magnet grips to it," said Mazer. "We'll use those as handles."

They had hand discs in their tool bags. Mazer removed one and placed it on the wall. Then he gripped the magnet and held the wall plate like a shield.

Something collided with the shield. Formics inside the shaft, trying to get out. A second collision. A third.

Mazer unsnapped a grenade. Cocktail nodded. On three, they moved the shield away for an instant to allow Mazer to drop the grenade in the shaft where three Formics were inches away. Mazer and Cocktail snapped the shield back into place, and the grenade detonated on the other side.

Cocktail made two more cuts on his side, and the shield slid forward into the shaft like a wall.

"Cut a hole for your rifle and sight," said Mazer.

Mazer cut one for himself, and a second hole for

his light, which he quickly secured with some metal tape.

"Ready?" asked Mazer.

Cocktail nodded.

They braced their feet against opposite walls and pushed their way up the shaft. The dead Formics clustered at the wall, obstructing their view.

"Rotate the top forward," said Mazer. "Let the corpses pass."

They rotated the shield so it was horizontal. Mazer grabbed the Formics and pulled them to his side to clear the path. The bodies were wet and limp and bleeding. Others were blown into parts. An arm, a torso, a head. Mazer pushed back the instinct to vomit and moved quickly. When it was clear, he and Cocktail snapped the shield back into place and pushed on.

They didn't get far before they encountered more Formics. Mazer shot through the rifle slit. It was hard to miss. The Formics crumpled, bled, died. The glow bugs were in a frenzy, buzzing all around them, their luminescence filling the shaft. The shield had knocked their nests away. They shot back and forth across the shaft, bouncing off the wall.

Mazer and Cocktail pushed on. They could hear the radio chatter from inside the cargo bay. It didn't sound good. Shouts, explosions, quick orders. ZZ was down. Bolshakov, too. Both of them dead. The news washed over Mazer like a wave. There was nothing he could do but clear a path for the others.

Slowly, tediously, they charged up the shaft. Objects started pinging off the shield. Projectiles. Thin small metal needles about half the size of a pencil, fired from a Formic weapon.

"They're armed," said Cocktail.

He and Mazer fired, and those with the needle shooters fell.

"I can't see well," said Cocktail. "Too much obstruction."

Mazer checked the shaft ahead of them. It was clear. "Let's rotate and clear the path."

As soon as they rotated the shield, the glow bugs poured inside like water, shooting back down the shaft toward the cargo bay. Cocktail and Mazer furiously pulled at the dead Formics to get them out of the way.

A glint of light ahead of them in the shaft caught Mazer's eye. He turned in time to see a Formic holding a jar weapon. The light inside was swirling and ready to fire.

"LOWER THE SHIELD!" he shouted.

Too late. A thick glob of mucus slammed into Cocktail's chest, pulsing with light. Cocktail looked down at it, shook violently, and exploded.

Mazer was slammed against the inside of the shaft, stunned, disoriented. A red mist filled the air around him. Blood had splattered across his visor, obstructing his view. Ahead of him, through the haze, he saw a swirling disc of light.

Mazer steadied his arm, squeezed the trigger, and emptied his clip.

CHAPTER 23

Casualties

Lem stood at the helm of the Valas and watched the vids in the holofield with a sinking feeling. The strike team was getting hammered. It was chaos in the cargo bay. ZZ and Bolshakov had flatlined. Cocktail's biometrics had gone completely silent. The remaining helmetcams were projected all in front of him, but the movements were so erratic and fuzzy, it was difficult to tell what was happening.

A technician approached him. "I'm sorry to disturb you, Mr. Jukes, but we're getting strange reports from Earth."

"What type of reports?"

"The Formics, sir. They're all returning to the landers."

Lem followed the technician back to his console.

The tech had a vid on screen. "This is from surveillance cams in the city of Chenzhou." The tech pressed play. A Formic death squad was spraying a crowd of hundreds of people outside a rail station. Gas billowed forth from the Formics' wands, enveloping those trying to escape. Men and women gasped and fell. The Formics advanced in a wide line, meeting no resistance. A time code in the bottom of the feed was counting off the seconds.

"What am I supposed to see?" said Lem.

"Right here, sir."

The Formics suddenly stopped spraying, turned around in unison, and ran.

"Where are they going?" asked Lem.

"To their transport, sir. They then climb inside and fly southeast."

"So?"

"So every Formic on Earth is doing this. They're all returning to the landers. I have dozens of vids coming in every minute, all showing the same behavior." Twenty vids began playing on the tech's terminals. Formics in skimmers, foot soldiers, harvesters, transports. As Lem watched, the Formics all abandoned their attack, or turned their harvester, or changed direction midair.

"How do you know they're returning to the landers?" asked Lem.

The vids all disappeared, replaced with two new ones. Each showed one of the remaining Formic landers still entrenched in southeast China. The giant circular structures were half buried in the earth, each larger than the world's biggest athletic stadium. The center of the lander had opened at the top, like the middle of a doughnut, and now every class of Formic ship was flying inside and docking—like a hive sucking in all its bees.

"What are they doing?" asked Lem. "Are they retreating and hunkering down? Why withdraw?"

"I don't know, sir."

"Go back to the first vid you showed me. From Chenzhou. Play that again."

The tech brought that vid forward and hit play. They watched again as the Formics stopped spraying, turned, and ran back to their transport.

"Go back," said Lem, "back to the moment when they stopped spraying."

The tech obeyed and rewound again.

"What time did that happen? Note the time code. Down to the second."

The tech clicked back frame by frame. "About 4:32 p.m. and 53 seconds."

"Now do the same to one of the other feeds you've received," said Lem. "I want to know the precise instant when the Formics made for the landers. The exact time."

"Yes, sir."

He watched as the technician worked, choosing one of the other vids at random. There wasn't a time code on this one, but the data was stored in the file. After the tech had bookmarked the instant on the vid, he dug into the file and found the answer. "4:32 p.m. and 53 seconds."

"The same exact moment," said Lem. "It's as if they were all told to return to the landers at precisely the same time. How is that possible? None of them is wearing any communication devices. Did the military intercept any message? A transmission of sorts? A sound in the air? Any communication whatsoever?"

"Not from the Formics, sir. Not that's been reported. No one ever has."

Lem didn't like this. Victor had theorized that the Formics communicated mind to mind, but Lem had dismissed the idea. It was completely unscientific.

And yet he couldn't deny that Formics always seemed to move as one, as if they *were* communicating.

"Check the other vids," said Lem. "Make sure the time is the same."

But even as the technician went back to work, Lem knew what the answer would be. They had all received a message at the exact same instant.

The notion frightened him. When Victor had said that the Formics communicated mind to mind Lem had assumed he meant two Formics beside each other, in the same room perhaps, sending a message across the short distance between them. Even that had seemed preposterous, but this, this was something else, something wholly inexplicable. The Formics were scattered all across southern China, hundreds of kilometers apart—on the ground, in the air, in valleys, in mountains. And yet the voice they had heard, the voice of authority that had given them a command—and which they had all obeyed without hesitation—was a voice strong enough to reach them all. Instantly.

Lem felt the hair on the back of his neck stand on end. It was as if he had suddenly peeled back a layer of the Formics and discovered something far more sinister underneath. That voice belonged to someone. And Lem got the sense that it was more dangerous and more powerful than anything he had seen so far.

Another one of the technicians leaned back and got his attention. "Mr. Jukes. You better come see this."

Lem joined him at his console.

"Not all of the transports are returning to the landers, sir. Some of them are lifting up into the atmosphere."

"Show me."

Two video feeds appeared on the terminal screen in front of the tech. They were both taken from people's personal cameras. In each, the transports shot up into the clouds.

"You're sure these aren't heading toward the landers?"

"I'm sure, sir. I tracked them. They're moving away from the landers, out over the South China Sea, gaining altitude." More blips appeared on his screen. Three. Four. A dozen. Twenty.

"What's happening?" said Lem.

The technician was busy for a moment before answering. "These are all transports, sir. They're all heading into space."

"Contact Captain Chubs on the Makarhu," said Lem. "That's one of the Juke ships maintaining the shield above Earth. Tell him he's got a few dozen transports heading his way. I want their shatter boxes ready and loaded. Those transports are heading back to the Formic ship. Tell him that under no circumstances is he to let a single one through."

"Yes, sir."

Lem hurried back to the first technician.

"I've checked a few more vids, sir, and you were right. The Formics all respond at the same time."

"Forget that. You have a new job. I want you to pull up the feeds coming from the strike team inside the Formic ship. I want you to tell me exactly the moment when the crew first made contact with a Formic inside. The moment our men were discovered."

The tech rewound feeds and searched and worked.

"Don't give me *our* time," said Lem. "I want to know what time it was in China. The time zone you mentioned before."

The technician took a moment more. "It's tough to say when that exact moment was, sir. Is it when we first shocked the Formics, when the others attacked later—"

"When we shocked the first one."

"That would be 4:32 p.m. and 48 seconds, China time."

"Five seconds before all the Formics on Earth received their message. That can't be a coincidence."

"What are you thinking, sir? You think the Formics on the ship called the others back to help?"

"What else could it mean?"

"Five seconds isn't enough time, sir. That's barely enough time to form a response, let alone send and receive a transmission to Earth. There should be a time delay."

Lem wasn't going to argue the point. Part of him didn't think it was possible either. But there it was.

"I'm going to my fighter," Lem said. "Send me updates on the strike team. I want to know the instant they disable that ship."

He flew out of the helm and to the back of the ship to the locker rooms. He put on his suit and helmet and flew to the airlock. His fighter was anchored to the hull of the ship outside. He waited for the airlock to give him the all clear, then he opened the hatch. The tube led straight to his cockpit. He flew in, buckled up, and decoupled. His fighter drifted away. He moved slowly toward the rear of the Valas. Then, he put the Valas between him and the Formic ship so the Formics couldn't see his movements, then he punched it and rocketed toward the shield. He had sixteen shatter boxes loaded into his sling. He hadn't trained as much as the other pilots. There hadn't been time. But he had flown all of Benyawe's simulations, and she had dubbed him a decent shot.

He hoped she had been right. If the shield fell, if a fleet of transports reached the Formic ship, all was lost. Wit and Mazer and the others wouldn't last an hour.

Imala sat in her fighter several hundred kilometers away from the Formic ship, watching the helmet feeds and feeling completely helpless. She wanted desperately to rush to Victor's aid, to do something, anything, but she couldn't. If she moved, the Formics would fire too soon. She would trigger the pipes and nozzles and unleash the plasma prematurely, while everyone was still inside. She would kill the entire strike team.

She dared not say anything over the radio either. Talking to them would only distract them from the job at hand. All she could do was sit and wait for her cue: for them to tell her that they were out, that she was a go.

But what if that message never came? What if they were overrun in the shafts? What if they were trapped inside?

"Fly back to the Valas," Victor had said. "If we fail, get safe."

She had nodded at the time, but she had never intended to obey. If they rotated the nozzles, she was going to charge, even if they failed to get out, even if the mission was essentially over. She could still do her part. She could still cripple the ship.

Her console beeped. It had detected the "X" painted on the surface. She pulled up the image and zoomed it. There it was, glowing as promised. Bungy had come through. The "X" was sloppy, but it was enough for the computers to detect and target. ZZ was supposed to have helped paint, but he had been hit in the shaft right at the exit.

Imala closed her eyes and shook her head. Three dead. And so far only Bungy was out.

She gripped the flight stick. Her hands were trembling. Victor wasn't half the solider ZZ had been. Not even close. And if ZZ hadn't made it . . .

No. She couldn't think that way. She had to act on facts. And the only fact that mattered right now was that the "X" was painted. The nozzles were turned. All of them. She was going. Whether the crew got out or not she was going.

Victor launched up the shaft, breathing hard. He collided with Benyawe, who collided with whoever was ahead of her. They had been moving this way for almost a hundred meters now, advancing up the shaft in a stop-go-stop-go manner. They were all positioned in a line, but you could only advance when the person ahead of you advanced. And the space—which was narrow and tight to begin with—was now cluttered with Formic corpses.

Victor waited for the line to advance. Shenzu was behind him, with Deen bringing up the rear, firing a steady stream of ammo and lasers back down the shaft toward the cargo bay. Dozens of Formics were clamoring up the shaft after them, crawling on top of each other, scrabbling forward, coming up the shaft like water rising in a well.

"Move!" Deen kept yelling. Or, "More clips! More clips!"

Ammo clips kept being passed down the chain to Deen, who shot at and sliced the Formics to ribbons as he shuffled backward up the shaft. This didn't slow the Formics in the least, however. The advancing mob consumed the dead ones and pushed them back, surging forward, never slowing.

"Move!" said Deen. "Launch!"

Benyawe had a clear path. She launched, and Victor launched right behind her, colliding with her before she had reached the person ahead. That sent her into one of the walls and stopped her.

"Keep moving!" said Deen. "Don't stop!"

More flashes of gunfire. More launching. More orders screamed. Victor's heart was hammering in his chest. They weren't going to make it. Deen would be overrun any moment. The Formics were less than ten meters away.

Victor felt a rush of air. The hole ahead. Wit had reached the hole and pulled it. The air in the shaft was being sucked out into the vacuum of space.

There was ten meters of empty space between Victor and Shenzu behind him, who had stopped to help Deen fight back the onslaught.

Suddenly a wall slid down into place just below Victor's feet, sealing off the shaft and leaving Shenzu and Deen on the other side with the Formics.

"What happened?" said Benyawe.

"The shafts," said Victor, "they're gas isolated. They must automatically seal when they detect a leak. There's nothing you can do. Keep going. I'll cut them free."

She launched away.

Victor bent down the shaft and immediately started cutting with his laser. It seemed painfully slow. He wasn't going to reach them in time. The Formics would overrun them, and when he opened it, he would only unleash the Formics onto himself.

After a long painful minute, the hole was cut. Shenzu immediately burst through, colliding hard into Victor and sending him ricocheting up the shaft. Another rush of air as the vacuum sucked up the shaft from below.

"Where's Deen?" Victor shouted.

A moment later Deen's head appeared through the hole, he was still firing his laser below him. Victor couldn't see; Shenzu was blocking his way.

"He's hit," said Shenzu. "Three in his legs."

Deen tried to push off with his legs, but it was no good. His legs were useless. Victor saw the projectiles protruding from Deen's thigh, like narrow black darts.

"Take him," said Shenzu. "I'll bring up the rear."

He passed Deen up, who winced and moaned.

"We need to get these out now," said Victor. "We're in the vacuum of space. Your suit is punctured."

"You can't pull them out," said Deen. "I'll bleed to death. You've got to patch the holes with the darts still in."

Shenzu was firing down in to the hole, but not with the same urgency that Deen had before. The Formics left in the shaft were asphyxiating.

"Do it," Deen said to Victor. "Put the seal casts on now. I'll die if you don't."

Two of the darts had embedded close together into the meat of his right thigh. The other one was protruding from his left calf muscle. Deen was wincing from the pain and gritting his teeth.

His suit had detected the punctures and inflated rings around the damaged area to seal off the escape of air, but this was only a temporary fix. Victor would have to move quickly. He unzipped his tool bag and pulled out his med kit. Shenzu did the same. They each had a seal-ant cast. One cast was big enough to cover both of the darts on this leg. A second cast would go over his calf.

"I need to cut the darts first," said Victor, pulling out his laser. "You've got three inches protruding. When I put on the cast, it will squeeze the area tight and press the dart deeper into your leg. I need to cut as close to your leg as possible."

"Don't talk. Just do," said Deen.

"This is going to hurt."

Victor gently pressed the suit down around the first dart as far as he could. Deen winced and went rigid but said nothing. Being careful not to damage the suit, Victor made the first cut, then the second, then the last.

Deen tried to laugh. "I'll make sure you get your field medic certification when this is over, space born."

Victor delicately slid the first cast over Deen's boot and up his leg to his thigh, pausing at the darts. The cast was essentially an elastic sleeve until it was turned on, at which point, it squeezed the area tight as a glove and sealed everything at the edges.

"Do it," said Deen.

Victor slid the cast up over the two darts and punched the button. The cast shrunk and Deen screamed through gritted teeth. When the cast stopped, Deen's breathing was labored, and his face was red and perspiring. "Do the other one. Faster this time. I'm losing my patience."

Victor did. Deen swore and banged a fist against the inside of the shaft.

When it was done, he exhaled and said, "Whew! We should charge admission to this place. This is more fun than an amusement park."

They got moving again. Victor clawed his way forward, pulling Deen behind him, who had no use of his legs. Benyawe was long gone, so the path was clear and they moved quickly. Shenzu brought up the rear.

They found Mazer waiting inside the shaft just beyond the exit hole. There was so much blood on Mazer's suit that for an instant Victor thought the man was dead. Then Mazer moved and waved them to proceed up the hole, offering to be the last man out. The shield Mazer had made and pushed up the shaft was ahead of him, bloody and tossed to the side. Mazer had apparently set up a defensive position here to keep the Formics from taking the shaft from the other direction. Now a gas-isolation wall sealed off the shaft ten meters ahead.

No words were said. The blood obviously wasn't Mazer's.

Moments later they all were outside. The rest of the team was already at the rendezvous point on the surface a distance away.

"Hold still," Victor said to Deen.

The spool of wire was still on Victor's belt, left over from wiring the batteries. He quickly wrapped several meters around Deen's chest and then tied it off to his own shoulder bag. "I'll pull you behind me. The wire will hold, but we can lock wrists if that will make you feel more secure."

"A hospital bed on solid ground would make me feel

secure," said Deen, "but a good grip and strong wire will suffice for now."

They got moving across the surface, with Deen floating behind Victor like a kite, clinging to his hand. Minutes later they saw the others, clustered together in the middle of a giant aperture. It was the top of one of the launch tubes the Formics had used to launch reinforcements down to Earth. The gamma plasma couldn't reach them here.

As soon as Victor and the others were inside the circle, Wit said, "Okay, Imala. You're on. Light up and fly straight."

Imala's voice crackled back over the radio. "Roger that."

She was trying to sound confident, but Victor could detect a hint of fear in her voice. He had installed several large blinking lights to make the ship as conspicuous as possible once Imala started. Victor looked up, zoomed in with his visor, and saw in the distance the tiniest twinkle of light.

Imala tapped the boosters and rotated the ship slightly to get it into position. This would be the most difficult part of the process. The computer had a lock on the "X," and the guidance system would do most of the work. All she had to do was make sure the ship was in alignment from the get-go and slow down as soon as she was able. It was a simple job, really. Anyone could have done it. She might be the most qualified space pilot of the bunch, but it didn't have to be her at the stick. Victor had known that, of course. And yet he hadn't argued the point when she had insisted it be her. Maybe he had seen the determination in her face and he had known better than to press the issue. Or maybe he simply had understood that she needed to do this, that she had to contribute somehow.

She'd like to think it was the latter reason: that he understood her.

The shapes on her screen aligned and turned green, signaling she was set.

She tapped the boosters and accelerated. Heavy metal plates covered the ship completely, acting as a radiation shield, but the cameras outside fed straight to her HUD. The lights blinked and ran back and forth across the front of the ship like a home decorated for the holidays. A neon sign that read SHOOT ME wouldn't have been more obvious.

Five minutes passed. Then ten. The ship was still a tiny dot in the distance. It would be better if the Formics fired sooner than later. The closer she got to the ship, the narrower the tunnel she would be flying into.

The ship grew in size. They should have fired by now. Were the Formics inside all dead, she wondered? Had Victor and the others killed the Formics who monitored the ship's defenses?

Suddenly she was bathed in light. A square of it all around her, like diving into a cube. It felt as if the tips of the spacecraft were inches from it. She fired retros and kept the ship steady, slowing down but still moving at a decent speed. The radiation reading outside was well into the red.

The Formics would shut it off any moment now, she knew. They would realize they were killing themselves, and they would turn off the gamma plasma.

Only they didn't. It continued.

Imala was suddenly seized with panic. If they didn't shut it off, she would die. She would fly right into the ship. If she wasn't crushed on impact she would ricochet into the line of fire. Or, if she slowed to a negligible speed, she would drift into the plasma.

Had it not worked? Maybe the rotated nozzles hadn't fired inward. Maybe the act of rotating them had simply made them inoperable. Maybe the ship wasn't damaged at all and this was all for naught.

She tried calling Victor over the radio, but of course that was impossible with all the radiation. She yelled at the cube of light. Yelled for it to stop.

But it didn't.

"Why haven't they killed the plasma?" asked Wit. "They should have shut it off by now."

They were gathered around his holopad above the launch tube. On screen it looked as if the Formic ship was being skewered. Beams of plasma shot forth from one side, encircling Imala, while the rotated nozzles fired a column of plasma out the other side, blowing a hole clean through.

Only now it wouldn't stop.

"What's happening inside the ship?" asked Mazer.

Benyawe had left sensors in the cargo bay and shaft. She checked her wrist pad. "Radiation levels are skyrocketing. They're much, much higher than we thought they would be. A hundred times higher."

"What about the Formics inside?" asked Mazer.

"Dying or dead," said Benyawe.

"And the flight crew?" said Wit. "The ones who are supposed to turn off the plasma?"

Victor opened his holopad and checked the cam feed he had left in the helm. Formic corpses floated in the space. "They're dead as well."

"So there's no one to shut off the pipes?" said Shenzu.

"What happens if we don't shut them off?" asked Mazer. "Other than we lose Imala?"

"Gamma radiation superheats if it's on too long," said Victor. "Everything will burn up and melt. The whole ship will become radioactive."

"So we lose all the tech," said Deen.

"And we all die," said Benyawe.

There was a brief silence, then Wit said, "Victor, do you know how to shut it off? If I go to the helm could you walk me through it?"

"You can't go in there," said Victor. "The ship is superheated. You'll die of radiation poisoning. Even in your suit. The levels are way too high."

"Could I make it to the helm and shut off the pipes before I die?"

Victor stared at him. "But—"

"Answer the question. The longer we stand out here, the hotter the ship becomes and the less chance I have. Would I survive long enough to get it done?"

"Um, yes. Maybe. I can't be certain. It depends on how quickly you reach the helm. I wouldn't go through the cannon hole. We're much closer here. You could cut a hole where we're standing and fly down the launch tube. You'd be very close to the helm."

"Send the directions to my HUD."

"But I can't walk you through the steps once you get there. The radiation might interfere with the transmission. I should tell you now just in case." He rotated his holopad. "This is the helm. You see this large wheel. Rotate it as far as it will go counterclockwise."

"That's it?"

"That's it. No computers. No buttons. Just a big wheel."

"I'll do it," said Mazer.

"You're too small," said Wit. "The radiation will kill you faster. I'm the biggest and have the best chance of getting there. Mazer, you're in command."

Mazer looked surprised. "But . . . I'm not one of your men."

"You're as much a MOP as I am. You always have

been." He walked away from the group to the center of the aperture. He took out his laser cutter and started cutting a hole wide enough for someone to crawl through.

"Turning off the gamma plasma won't be enough," said Victor. "You also need to ventilate the ship."

"How?" said Wit.

"By opening all these launch tubes," said Victor. "They go all the way around the ship."

"That sounds like a lot of work. Do I have time for that?"

"There's a single wheel. Rotate that clockwise and all the tubes will open."

"Another wheel?" said Wit. "I thought these Formics were innovative."

"Fancy tech, simple controls."

"Show me where the wheel is."

Victor pulled up images of the ship's interior from his vid. "You'll see a console like this at the base of the tube. The wheel is here." He circled it with his finger and sent to Wit's HUD.

"Anything else?"

"Yes, all of us need to come inside this launch tube as well. We'll seal the bottom hatch once you go. That way, when you ventilate the ship, we won't be outside and bombarded with all the radiation."

"What about the top of the launch tube? Can I close this one, yet keep the other ones open? You need to be sealed in tight, both at the bottom and the top."

Victor showed him the image again. "Each individual console has an override wheel. At the base of this launch tube here. Turn it to close this tube only."

"Turn three wheels. This is easier than I thought."

He finished cutting and pushed the cut manhole down into the launch tube.

Victor got down beside him. "It should be me, Wit. I know the way. I've watched them turn the wheel."

"This is not open for discussion," said Wit. "Now follow me into the tube and seal it shut behind me." He pulled himself down into the manhole, got his feet anchored inside and launched downward toward the bottom of the tube.

One by one they followed him in.

Lem fired the shatter boxes, and they catapulted away from his fighter, spinning through space like a thrown bola. War was all around him. Juke mining ships of the shield were battling a swarm of Formic transports in near-Earth orbit. The Formics outnumbered them two to one, and the transports were just as nimble in space as they had been on Earth. Lem couldn't tell who was winning. Everything was happening too quickly.

There had been an order at the beginning—a coordinated effort to take the Formics together. But that had gone out the window the moment the shooting started. Now it was every man for himself.

Lem's spinning shatter boxes zeroed in on their target and snapped to opposing sides of the transport. An instant later, the tidal forces were ripping the transport to shreds, breaking down molecular bonds and turning every molecule into its constituent atoms. One second it was a transport. Two seconds later, dust.

To Lem's right, a mining vessel was sliced in half with a laser. The ship's lights flickered and extinguished. Screams were heard over the radio. Equipment and bodies were sucked out of the two severed pieces. Lem's fighter arced right, dodging a laser and avoiding the same fate. A transport had zeroed in on him. He released another set of shatter boxes at his pursuer, but the shot was wide and the shatter boxes spun off into space.

Lem dove. The transport tailing him dove after him. Lem spun, twisted; the transport responded, mirroring his moves. A laser narrowly missed him on the right. He fired a third pair of shatter boxes, but these missed as well. Another dive and spin and twist. Still he wasn't free. He banked right and narrowly avoided colliding with a different transport. He fired behind him and obliterated that one, but the original pursuer held its course.

Lem accelerated and spun left. He couldn't keep this up. He would soon vomit or pass out. The G-forces were overwhelming. His equilibrium was shot. His harness held him tight, but his body was being flung back and forth against the straps like a ragdoll.

He spun again, fired again, missed again.

He had gotten off a few lucky shots. That was it. He was out of his league here. He was not a combat pilot. Why had he thought he could do this? What was he trying to prove?

Ahead of him a mining ship broke apart as two transports cut into it at once. Lem spun away to get clear of the line of fire.

He was going to die, he realized. The only reason he had lasted this long was because he was such a small target.

A laser to his left missed him by inches. He dove again, spun away.

No one would grieve his loss, he realized. There would be headlines and sad admirers and a few blips on the nets about how he had died heroically, but no one would really care. Not deeply. Not in any meaningful way. They would shake their heads, call it a shame, and move on.

Those who actually knew him might even call it a relief.

Father would care, he thought. Father would grieve. Despite whatever it was they had between them, Lem was still his son.

And Simona. She would be upset as well, almost like a friend might, despite how he had treated her.

He thought of Des. Not the real Des. But the person he had thought she was. The fake Des. Young and bright-eyed and full of affection. That version of her would have grieved.

But of course the real Des would only laugh at such news. What a fool, she would say. How easily played.

He wondered where she was now. In another man's arms? Another man's bed? No, not a man. A customer.

The transport giving chase disappeared from his holofield, turned to dust.

A familiar voice sounded over the radio. "You have me to thank for that, Lem," said Chubs. "I take personal checks or money transfers."

Lem smiled. "How many times have you saved my neck now, Chubs?"

"More than I can count. But I hope you're keeping a tally."

Chubs. The man who had been his cocaptain for their two-year trip to the Kuiper Belt. Not a friend, necessarily. But certainly a welcome sight now.

Ten minutes later it was over. Nine of the mining ships were lost. The others were intact and celebrating over the radio, thrilled to be alive. It was then that Lem realized the Valas had been trying to contact him. He responded to their pinging. "This is Lem. Go ahead."

"Mr. Jukes. The landers. They're taking off."

After ten seconds in the ship Wit's nose was bleeding. He felt like he was being cooked in a microwave. Every instinct told him to fly back to the safety of the launch tube and seal himself in tight with the others. The heat wasn't just burning him, it was sucking him dry, draining the life out of him like a vacuum. He had never felt so weak or sick in his life. He gripped the wheel at the base of the launch tube and turned. All of the launch tubes except for the one where the others were waiting opened with a whoosh. He could feel the air around him being sucked out of the tubes; like standing against a heavy gale. Had his feet not been anchored to the floor as Victor had suggested, he might have been sucked out as well.

The air depletion went on for almost a minute. Formic corpses flew by him, along with various small items that hadn't been tied down—all of it whisked out of the tubes and into space. Wit could feel the heat in the room dropping, as if the furnace had been turned down from high to medium heat. When it was over he stood there a moment gathering himself. There was more for him to do, he knew. He had another task. He had remembered what it was a moment ago, but it had slipped away.

Crackling static in the earpiece. "Captain O'Toole."

That was his name. Someone was calling him. The team from the tube. He turned and faced them. They were at the glass watching him, their faces concerned. Then he remembered.

"I'm all right. It's . . . not bad. Like a . . . really hot sauna. The radio gets through . . . that's good. I'm . . . going to need it."

"Let me come in and help you," said Victor.

"No. I've already been exposed. There's still radiation . . . in here. Just talk me to the helm. I've got the map . . . but my mind can't . . . focus."

"He's too disoriented," someone said. "He'll never make it."

"Shut up and let Victor talk," another voice said.

"Move around to the other side of the console," said Victor. "You'll see a passageway on your left."

Wit tried moving. His feet wouldn't come. "My . . . feet."

"Your boot magnets are initiated," said Victor. "I'll decrease their strength from here. Get ready to launch."

Wit pulled again, and this time one foot came free. He pushed off with the other and flew to the wall, making his way around the console.

His nose was bleeding worse now. There was nothing he could do to stop it. His hand couldn't reach inside his visor.

"Where's Imala?" someone asked.

"Getting close," said Victor. "She's going as slow as she can. We need to hurry."

"I'll get there," said Wit. "It's not far."

His insides were burning, like someone had built a fire in his gut. His eyes were burning, too. He wanted desperately to rub them.

Wit found the passageway. Victor told him which direction to go. Wit obeyed.

He and Father were tossing the football. The big one, the one they used in the NFL. It hurt every time Wit caught it. Like catching a big inflated stone.

Father was drawing the run on the palm of his hand, explaining a buttonhook. "You run out downfield. Then after twenty yards, about where that tree is, you turn back to the line of scrimmage and I hit you with the pass." Wit nodded. He was eight years old and big for his age.

The ball hit him in the face, square in the nose, blood was everywhere, all over his shirt. Momma would be furious. It was a school shirt. He wouldn't cry, though. Not with Father watching. The tears were there in his eyes, ready to jump out, but he wouldn't let them come. "Don't lean your head back, son. Lean it forward. Let it drip into the grass." Mother came out with the dishrag. Wit could taste the blood in his mouth. "This is why they wear helmets," Father had said, wiping gently at Wit's nose. "Does it feel broken?"

"No, sir."

"You sure?"

"Yes, sir. I just hit it hard is all."

"You caught it with your face is what you did."

"You should use one of those foam balls, David. He's too small for the real thing."

"No I'm not, Momma. I just caught it wrong. It was my fault. Please, Daddy. Let's do it again."

Father chuckled. "Your nose is still bleeding son."

Your nose is still bleeding.

Your nose is still bleeding.

Your nose is still bleeding.

"Captain! Can you hear me?"

Wit jerked awake. He was in a corridor. Floating. Alone. A dead Formic floated to his right.

"Captain. Wit. It's Victor. Can you hear me?"

"Yes . . . I'm here."

"You're not responding. You missed the turn. You have to go back."

"Go back. Yes. I'm sorry."

Wit reached out to the nearest wall. Lifting his arm took more energy than he thought he had. He turned his body. He was so hot. So very hot. He had lost control of his bowels, he realized. Thank God for his suit.

"Sir, you need to hurry."

"Yes . . . I'm moving."

He pulled himself forward, using a pipe as a hand-hold. One hand over each other. It surprised him that he still had hands. It felt as if they had burned off. It felt as if everything had burned off, as if he were floating through flames.

As if . . .

He was sitting too close to the fire. He would melt the bottom of his sneakers if he wasn't careful. The smoke was thick and kept blowing in his face. Lana Taymore was beside him—lithe and freckled and wearing flip-flops. Her legs were longer than his, it seemed.

He had told his parents he was sleeping over at Harry Westover's house. That's what all the guys had told their parents: there was a sleepover at Harry Westover's house.

Some people were drinking. Wit had no idea how they had gotten the beer. Curt Woback was playing a guitar on the other side of the fire, murdering a folk song. Someone else was trying to sing along, but she didn't know all the words.

Smoke billowed into Wit's eyes again, and he fanned it away.

"Smoke follows lovers," someone said. "Smoke follows lovers."

They meant him and Lana, Wit realized. Which was stupid. She was a junior. She didn't know he existed.

"You're so immature," Lana said. She tapped Wit on the arm. "Come on. Let's leave the children. Help me get some firewood."

He got to his feet.

"Uh oh," Curt said. "They're off to the bushes. Watch yourself, O'Toole. She's got smoke fever."

They started chanting. "Smoke fever. Smoke fever. Smoke fever."

Wit followed Lana into the woods, his cheeks flushed. He hadn't brought a flashlight. He couldn't see a thing. Thin branches snagged at his face. He tripped on a stick. He bent down and picked it up. His eyes were slowly adjusting. There were other sticks nearby. He picked those up too and added them to his arms.

Lana was ahead of him. She wasn't picking up anything. "Hurry up, slowpoke."

He followed her. There was a path. He could barely make it out in the dark. They reached a pond. She walked out onto the wooden pier. He looked around. The trees were dark on all sides. He was still holding the sticks. He joined her at the end of the pier. She pulled her T-shirt off over her head in one fluid movement. She was wearing a black lacy bra underneath.

She looked at him funny. "What? You don't know how to swim?"

"Captain. You're not responding, sir."

Victor's voice again.

"I'm here," said Wit. "I'm awake."

"You've arrived, sir. You're at the helm."

Wit looked around. It was true. The helm was there before him. The hatch was open. There were the controls. There were the dead Formics. He pushed his way inside. The wheel was to his left. He reached it. Somehow he lifted his hands to it, gripped it.

"You can do this," said Victor. "Counterclockwise. As far as it will go."

It took a moment for Wit to remember what that meant. A clock. He knew what a clock was. The hands moved one way. "Counter" meant the other way. Counterclockwise. He pulled the wheel but it wouldn't budge. He tried again but nothing happened. Maybe when he was stronger he could have done this. But not now. He was too hot, too weak and empty. He felt so drained even breathing was difficult.

He hawked up another glob of blood and spat it out. It floated there in his helmet.

"It's . . . not moving."

"It will, Captain. It will. Try again."

He tried again. Nothing happened. He wanted to sleep. That's what he needed now more than anything, to sleep, to close his eyes and rest. Sucking in air was so difficult now. He didn't have the strength for that, let alone the strength to turn a wheel.

"You can do this, Captain."

"No . . . I can't."

His voice didn't sound like his own. It sounded like an old man. A dying old man—raspy and phlegmy, with rattling in the lungs.

"Try again," Victor said.

I am trying, Wit wanted to scream. I'm giving it all I have. There just isn't anything left anymore.

He pushed and turned. He changed his grip and tried again. It felt as if his gloves were filled with shards of glass. The tiniest amount of pressure on his fingers and palms sent lightning bolts of pain up his arm.

And still the wheel didn't move.

"I . . . can't. Nothing . . . left in me."

"Give me the holopad," a voice said. "Captain, it's Deen. Can you hear me?"

Deen. He knew that name. A friend's name. There were memories attached to that name swirling around in the soup of his mind. He tried reaching for one, but it ran through his fingers like water. Deen. A name he knew. He tried to say it aloud, to give it meaning, to define it more in his head. But when he opened his lips, no words came out, only the softest exhalation of breath.

Then the world faded. Blackness crept in from all sides. For a moment he thought he was dead. But no, he could still feel the heat, he could still hear his own wheezy, labored breaths. His eyes had stopped working. That was all. There was a word for this condition, this blackness. A simple word. He knew it. It was right there in front of him. He blinked and squinted and blinked again—an action that took enormous effort—but he still saw only darkness.

"His blood pressure is dropping fast," said a voice.

"Captain, it's Deen. We're going to sing you a cadence. That's what moves a soldier. Isn't that what you always said, sir? The beat moves the feet. The feet moves the man. The man moves the world."

Yes, thought Wit. He had said that. Many times. A marching cadence. Yes, that's what he needed.

"It's a cadence you taught us, sir. One you learned in the SEALs."

The SEALs, thought Wit. I am a SEAL. Before I became a MOP I trained as a SEAL. The memory made him smile.

Deen began, leading the group, shouting each line alone in the singsongy rhythm of the cadence. The others echoed him, shouting as one.

"Heyyyyyy there, Army!"

"Heyyyyyy there, Army!"

"Backpacking Army!"

"Backpacking Army!"

"Pick up your packs and follow me!"

"Pick up your packs and follow me!"

"We are the Sons of UDT!"

"We are the Sons of UDT!"

Wit smiled and gripped the wheel. He had sung those words a thousand times during Hell Week, the most rigorous, painful, five and a half days of his SEAL training. He had thought he would die at the time. He had never experienced such physical exertion, such pain, such relentless battering to his body. But the song, the song had steeled him. The song, sung by brothers, had carried him through. It had carried them all through. For twenty-four months of backbreaking training, it had carried them through.

The Sons of UDT. That's what the SEALs were. The Underwater Demolition Team was the precursor special commando unit to the SEALs. The UDT had been the crazy ones, the pioneers of combat swimming, from World War II through Vietnam. The cadence was a message to every other branch of the military. Come. Run alongside us, fight with us, whatever you can do, we can do as well. Sea, land, air. We are the sons of the UDT.

Deen didn't stop. He knew every verse. Sing, Deen, Wit wanted to say. Sing for me.

"Heyyyyy there, Marine Corps!"

"Heyyyyy there, Marine Corps!"

"Bullet-sponge Marine Corps!"

"Bullet-sponge Marine Corps!"

"Pick up your steps and run with me!"

"Pick up your steps and run with me!"

"We are the Sons of UDT!"

"We are the Sons of UDT!"

It was not about physical strength, Wit reminded himself. It was 90 percent mental, 10 percent physical. That's what the SEAL instructors were looking for: men and women who could disregard the pleadings of the body. Pain was nothing, sleep was nothing. What was freezing water to a SEAL mind? What was chafed skin, wrecked muscles, bleeding sores? The body *chooses* to be sore. The body *chooses* to be exhausted. But the SEAL mind rejects it. The SEAL mind commands the body, not the other way around.

The wheel was nothing. The radiation was nothing. The blood in his nose and throat and gums and bowels was nothing. The heat was nothing. The Formics were nothing. They were bugs to be squished, bugs to be stepped upon.

He tried turning it again. It wouldn't obey. The beat of the cadence was like the beat of a drum. He hawked up another globule of blood, spat to the corner of his helmet, and tried turning it again. His arm was going to rip out of its socket. Fine. Take my arm. I have another. And here take my leg, I have another one of those, too. And here take my torso, take it all. But you can't have my mind. I am a son of the UDT. I am a son of David and Jeanine O'Toole. I am a son of Earth. And you, you bug-eyed bastards, cannot have my mind.

He pulled, he twisted, he grit his bleeding teeth.

Something broke inside him, something snapped or came loose. A muscle perhaps, or a ligament, or bone. Wit ignored it. He pulled, straining, screaming, burning in the darkness.

The wheel turned. An inch at first. But then more. Two inches. Three. Six. Twelve.

"Heyyyyyy there, Navy!"

"Heyyyyyy there, Navy!"

"World's finest Navy!"

"World's finest Navy!"

"Set a course and follow me!"

"Set a course and follow me!"

"We are the sons of UDT!"

"We are the sons of UDT!"

CHAPTER 24

Landers

The gamma plasma disappeared. The tunnel of light was gone. Imala responded immediately and spun away, getting clear. She had been in a slow drift for over an hour and it had become harder and harder to stay within the tunnel. Four more kilometers, and she would have collided with the ship. That was far, far too close.

She punched the rockets and took off, accelerating away as fast as she could, the G-forces slamming her against her seat.

"I'm clear," she said over the radio. "I don't know if you can hear me, Vico, but I'm clear."

Inside the sealed launch tube, Victor and the others stared at Wit's biometrics on the holopad. All of the numbers had dropped to zero. The heart monitor was a flat line. The flashing message that had beeped and warned of an impending fatality had gone silent. Deen and the others had stopped singing. There was no need to continue anymore.

Imala's voice crackled over the radio. She was clear.

She was alive. She was laughing. She didn't yet know what had happened.

Before anyone could speak, another transmission came. "Acknowledge. Acknowledge. Repeat. If you can hear me, Victor, acknowledge."

It was Lem. Victor wiped his holopad clear and popped up the holo antennas in the four corners. Lem's head appeared before them.

"Lem. It's Victor. We read you."

"Where the hell have you been? I've been hailing you for ten minutes."

"You weren't getting through. It was the radiation. We've taken the ship."

"Yes, well the Formics know that and now they're coming to take it back. Both landers have launched from Earth. Every Formic on the planet climbed back inside the landers, and now they're coming for you. All of them."

The landers? Victor looked at the faces of the others. No one said a word.

"Our shatter boxes are useless," said Lem. "They won't initiate unless they're exactly opposite each other, and the cables aren't long enough to get on opposing sides of the lander obviously. Our lasers aren't doing much better. We're leaving scratches and scorch marks and that's it. The landers' shields must be down, but we don't have the firepower to take advantage."

"Are you still in the Valas?" asked Victor.

"I'm in my fighter," said Lem. "I'm with ships of the shield. We're tracking with the landers, coming your way, but we can't stop them. Nothing can stop them."

"We can't let them reattach to the ship," said Mazer. "If that happens, they'll retake it. It's over."

"They'll retake it," said Deen, "but they can't go anywhere. We scuttled it."

"They'll repair it," said Mazer. "They'll kill us, fix the ship, and get right back to taking Earth."

"What about a nuke from Earth?" said Victor. "If their shields are down—"

"Won't work," sad Lem. "None of us are armed with nukes. If we had a military fleet already out here, it would be a different story, but we don't. We've got a few mining ships with a few useless weapons. I'm sorry. Maybe we can reach you first and get you out in time."

"I'm not leaving," said Mazer. "We took this ship and we're holding it."

"How?" asked Shenzu.

"We destroy the landers before they reattach," said Mazer. "This ship is a weapon. We use it against them. We've done it once. Let's do it again."

They all looked at Victor.

"Is that possible?" asked Shenzu.

Victor thought a moment. "Maybe. If we can leave the launch tube and get back inside the ship. Benyawe, what are the radiation levels?"

"They've plummeted ever since Wit cut the gamma plasma. And they're dropping further by the second. It's nearly ventilated. In a few minutes, we could probably go back inside."

"Probably?" said Shenzu. "I'd like something a little more definitive than 'probably.' "

"If Benyawe says we'll be fine, we'll be fine," said Victor. "And I'm with Mazer. We should hold the ship and destroy the landers, if we can."

"What are we suggesting here?" said Shenzu. "Fire gamma plasma at the ship? We can't do that. If we open the gamma plasma again, we'll send radiation back into the ship through the rotated nozzles. We'd kill ourselves."

"So we rotate the nozzles back again," said Victor.

"Flip them back around?" said Deen.

"I know how to roll the ship," said Victor. "The apertures in that area are still open. No one has closed them. If we turn the gamma plasma back on, those same nozzles will fire and no others. I'll go to the helm and rotate us so we're pointing those nozzles at the landers when they arrive. Then I turn the wheel and we blast it."

"You'll only hit one of them," said Mazer. "You won't hit both. Can you rotate the ship fast enough after you hit the first one to slice through the second one?"

"Probably not," said Victor. "The other lander would simply change course and avoid it."

"So we need another way to take out the second lander," said Shenzu.

"A way they don't anticipate," said Benyawe.

"We don't have any other weapons," said Deen.

"Yes," said Mazer. "We do. We have the launch tubes. Each is like the barrel of a gun. Victor, you knew how to seal off the tubes and open them. Do you also know how to launch something in them as well?"

"I watched the Formics do it," said Victor. "I studied the mechanism. Yes. We can launch something."

"What exactly?" said Deen. "Last time I checked we didn't have a giant bullet in our ammo packs."

"The ship debris from the cargo bay," said Mazer. "We load a bunch of scrap into the tubes and we fire it like shrapnel."

"Won't that just bounce off the lander?" said Deen.

"The launch tubes are extremely powerful," said Victor. "And I know how to increase the tension in the springs. It would fire like a cannon. It would rip through anything."

"Theoretically," said Deen.

"There's no guarantee of anything, if that's what you mean," said Victor. "But I think it could work."

"How do we move ship debris from the cargo bay to the tubes?" asked Shenzu.

"The same way the Formics move anything big," said Mazer. "We use the big carts. Victor showed us the passageway. From here to the cargo bay isn't far, but it's going to take tremendous effort. We're in a zero-G environment, but we still have to deal with mass and friction. Moving a hundred pound slab takes just as much force. And stopping it is even harder because there's no friendly friction with the ground to slow it down. Plus, because downness is not available, we'll have to wrangle objects in every direction. It's going to take a lot of fine motor control to move anything. Inertia applies as much as ever. Start something moving in a direction and it will continue pretty much forever unless you exert enough force to stop it. We're going to have to work together."

"There are eight of us," said Deen. "How are we supposed to do all of this before the landers arrive?"

"Victor goes to the helm," said Mazer. "The rest of us go to the cargo bay and start turning nozzles. When the nozzles are ready, we load as much wreckage into the big carts as we can carry and hurry back here. Then we load the tubes and we're in business."

"I'll need a pair of eyes," said Victor. "Someone will have to go back outside and lie flat against the hull. They'll have to help me aim and tell me when to fire. I don't know how to use the Formics' targeting system."

"I can do that," said Deen. "I won't be much use in the cargo bay with these legs. I have to be helpful somehow. Victor could carry me outside and anchor me down before he goes to the helm."

"I can do that," Victor agreed. He turned to Lem in the holopad. "We're going to need some time, Lem. Can you stall the landers?"

"That's like asking a bunch of dragonflies to stop a passenger jet," said Lem.

"There are other ships," said Victor. "Call them all. Every ship in your father's fleet in near-Earth orbit. Every ship on Luna. Get the Valas involved. Get them all involved."

"I'll do what I can," said Lem. "But hurry. We won't be able to hold them for long. If at all." He disconnected.

"Benyawe," said Victor. "What are the radiation levels now?"

"Low enough," she said. "We're good to go."

"Then let's move," said Mazer.

They flew down to the bottom of the tube where there was a small airlock. Mazer opened it and led the group through. Victor and Deen stayed behind and watched Mazer lead the others into the passageway that led to the cargo bay. When they had disappeared, Victor said, "Are you sure you're up for this?"

Deen smiled. "Hey, I got the cake job. I lie around and give you orders. That's like being on holiday. Plus I get a front-row seat to all the fireworks."

Victor flew him back up to the top. They removed the manhole Wit had cut and climbed back outside. They found a spot on the surface of the ship halfway between the launch tube and rotated nozzles. Victor lowered Deen to the hull and laid him gently on his back, anchoring him in place with disc magnets that he secured to Deen's belt.

When he was done, Victor pulled on the magnets, testing their strength. "There. You're not going anywhere."

Deen was hugging his rifle to his chest. "How am I supposed to direct you in rotating the ship?"

Victor pulled out his holopad and turned on the field. A model of the Formic ship appeared in the air. Victor made four quick moves with his stylus, and three axes appeared, skewering the ship. "Here's the ship," he said, pointing. "X axis, y axis, z axis. Here's where the nozzles are." He tapped the ship in the holo and illuminated the area. "This holo feeds to my HUD. Spin the ship with your hands to align it with whatever is coming. I'll do my best to mimic your movements. I'll also be watching through your helmetcam, but I'll need verbal cues from you as well. You need to tell me when I'm tracking with the target. I can't remain stationary and wait for them to fly over the line of fire. I need to be rotating and keeping the target in the line of fire when I pull the trigger. I can't miss that way."

"Tell you when you're tracking," said Deen. "Got it. Anything else?"

"If I miss, shoot down the landers with your rifle."

Deen smiled. "I'm good. But I'm not that good."

Victor extended his hand. "Good luck."

Deen shook his hand. "Luck's got nothing to do with it, space born. When it's time to kill, it's all in the skill. Shoot straight, brother. And let's all go home."

Victor left him there and returned to the manhole. He flew down the launch tube and crawled under the base of the tube. He found the mechanism that increased the force of the launch and began fiddling with it to set it to maximum power.

"Vico. It's Imala, can you hear me?"

Her voice was like a blanket of calm in his ear. "I'm here, Imala."

"I've got us on a private line," she said. "I've been listening. I'm sorry about Wit and the others. What can I do?"

"You can get clear, Imala. Head back to Luna. I'd feel much better if I knew you were safe." He was using the wrenches he had brought for the nozzles. They're weren't the best tools for the job, but they were all he had.

"I can help stop the landers," said Imala.

"You don't have any weapons, Imala. We covered your collision-avoidance lasers with shielding plates. You're nothing but a flashing hunk of metal at this point."

"You say that to all the girls."

"I'm serious, Imala. Please. At least one of us needs to get out, to tell everyone what happened here."

"Don't talk like that. Like you're giving up."

"I'm not giving up, Imala. But I'm also keenly aware of what we're up against here. If we don't make it, this war needs to go on. People need to learn from our mistakes. You can help them."

There was silence on the line for a long moment. "All right," she said. "I'll go back."

"Will you? Or are you only saying what I want to hear?"

She didn't answer directly. "Stay safe, Vico. If you need anything, I'm here on the line."

He finished with the launch tube. Then he moved to an adjacent tube and did the same. When he was done, he spray painted a giant "X" on the hatch of each tube so that Mazer would know which ones had been set. Then he gathered his tools and flew to the helm.

The lights from his helmet swept the helm when he arrived. He saw the Formics first, floating in the space, their four arms limp at their sides. He pushed one out of his way and there was Wit, still at the wheel. Victor launched to him and turned him over. Wit's face was red, blistered, and covered in blood. Victor gave Wit's hand a squeeze. "*Vaya a Dios, y al cielo más allá de éste.*" It's what his family always said when someone passed on. Go to God, and to the heaven far above this one.

He released Wit's hand and gripped the wheel. He blinked out a command and brought up the model of the ship with the three axes, the one in Deen's hand. Next came Deen's helmetcam feed. He pushed that over into the corner of his field of vision and waited.

———

Mazer turned a few nozzles in the cargo bay, but it quickly became apparent that everyone was much faster at the task than he was. They had done it before; he hadn't. They moved with confidence; he moved with caution. He was only getting in their way.

He left Benyawe in charge of the effort and launched back across the bay to the shaft they had just exited, the one that led back to the launch tubes. They had found several large carts along the way, and they had pushed them all here for loading. The question now was: How would they move the pieces of wreckage floating in the middle of the bay to the shaft? There was nothing to anchor their feet to in the middle of the room. They couldn't launch to the wreckage, and expect to launch back. Everything was a free-floating object. They wouldn't have any leverage.

The solution was right there in front of him, he realized. Victor had unspooled several hundred meters of wiring across the bay, connecting all of the mesh nets to the batteries. It looked like a haphazard spider's web, but it was exactly what Mazer needed. He launched again and began cutting and collecting the wire. By the time the team had finished with the nozzles, he had twisted and semi-braided the wiring into three long, thick ropes. One of the ropes was tied around his chest and thighs like a harness.

As Benyawe and the others joined him at the shaft entrance, Mazer called to Victor. "Nozzles are rotated. We're gathering the wreckage now."

"Hurry," said Victor. "Lem doesn't think he can hold them much longer."

Mazer faced the others. "All right. Listen up. We make three teams of two. Each team has a fisherman and a hook. The fisherman anchors his boots here at the shaft entrance and holds one end of the rope. The hook ties the other end around his chest and thighs like so." He raised his arms so they could see how he had tied the harness. "Then the hook leaps out and seizes a piece of wreckage. The fisherman reels them both back in, and the team works together to get the wreckage into the cart. If the piece proves too big for the cart, cut it down if the cuts can be made quickly. Otherwise ditch it and grab something else. Target pieces that are smaller than the cart but that have some mass to them. Engines, drive systems. We're making cannon shot here. The denser the better. We keep fishing and loading until these carts are full. Shenzu, you're with me."

They all moved quickly, pairing off and making their harnesses.

Shenzu seized his end of the rope, set his boot magnets to maximum, and signaled to Mazer that he was ready. Mazer launched toward the wreckage and landed on a hunk of fuselage. It spun and twisted from the force of his impact, but Mazer held on. Shenzu quickly pulled in the slack on the rope, and the fuselage steadied. Mazer snapped his hand magnets to it and called back to Shenzu that he was ready. Shenzu pulled him in, and the two of them loaded the fuselage into one of the carts.

After fifteen minutes they had filled five carts. The wreckage was bulky and oddly shaped, so they only fit two to three pieces per cart, but Mazer figured it was enough to arm two launch tubes.

"Everybody take a cart," said Mazer. "If you're wearing a harness, consider wrapping the rope around the cart and pulling it like a horse. You'll be able to see where you're going. We form a line and we move double-time. Shenzu you and Benyawe share a cart."

"Because I'm old and feeble?" said Benyawe.

"Because we have five carts and six people," said Mazer. "Because you've turned more nozzles than anyone and because we need you rested." He had noticed her movements were becoming sluggish. He couldn't have her slowing down the line.

"Now let's move!"

They moved. Mazer led them out, pulling his cart behind him like a beast of burden. The load was weightless, but the wheels on the cart were old and rusting and slow to turn, and moving that much mass proved more exhausting than Mazer had thought. Inertia took over once they got going, but he was sweating profusely before they had gone ten meters. They quickly picked up their pace however, hurrying toward the launch tubes. The others followed, lagging slightly behind but hustling nonetheless.

They were still a short distance from the launch tubes, when Victor came over the radio. "Here they come!"

Victor had seen the landers on the nets. He knew they were large. He had seen how everything around them seemed small and insignificant in comparison—the aircraft that had attacked them, the jungles or mud slides that had surrounded them, the villages and cities near them. The landers had dwarfed them all. But in each of those images, the landers had been mostly submerged into the ground. Now he was seeing them in their entirety. Massive. Unstoppable. Mountains of mechanical engineering. A swarm of mining ships were firing at the landers, and Victor was relieved to see that the ships were in fact inflicting damage. Not much, but the landers' surfaces were riddled with cuts and gouges and scorch marks. The landers might be big, but they weren't indestructible.

They were coming in a line, Victor saw, one right behind the other. If he was going to destroy them both, he would have to do it quickly. There wouldn't be much time between shots. He needed to destroy one with the gamma plasma and then chase the second one with the plasma beams back into the line of fire of the launch tubes. If the second one didn't retreat from the gamma plasma, great. Victor would destroy it the same way as the first. But Victor didn't suspect that would be the case. "Mazer, what's your status?"

"We just reached the launch tubes with the carts."

"I marked the tubes with paint," said Victor.

"I see them," said Mazer. "We're moving there now. We'll need a few minutes to load the wreckage."

"You've got about four minutes. Maybe five. Then they'll be on top of us."

"We'll load what we can," said Mazer. "Hopefully it will be enough."

Victor blinked a command to connect directly to Deen. "Talk to me, Deen."

"You're going to get one shot at this," said Deen. "They're big, yes. And that means they're easy to hit. But it also means they're resilient. Put the beams right through it, dead center. I say we wait until they're as close as possible, directly above the nozzles so you can't miss."

"Lem," said Victor. "Pull back your ships. Get the miners out."

"Roger," said Lem. "Good luck."

Victor saw the holo model of the ship rotate. His hands were already on the levers and switches he would need. He had watched the vids a dozen times, learning from the Formics at the helm, studying how they handled the controls and moved the ship. He mimicked them now, moving the levers and rotating the ship.

Deen continued to make slight adjustments, and Victor continued to follow him. The minutes passed quickly, and the first lander had grown so large in the window that it seemed like a collision was inevitable.

"More to the left," Deen said. "You're rotating too

quickly . . . Down four degrees . . . Left another degree . . .
That's it. Keep it coming. Almost. There you go. Now
you're tracking. Hold that rotation. You've got him."

"Mazer, are you loaded?" Victor said.

"One of the tubes is loaded," said Mazer. "That's all
we had time for."

"That's going to have to do," said Victor.

"The underbelly is coming up," said Deen. "You're
still tracking. Hold that rotation. Ten more seconds.
Steady. Three. Two. One. FIRE!"

Victor spun the wheel clockwise as hard and fast as
he could. On Deen's helmetcam he saw the beams of
gamma plasma explode outward, puncturing through
the lander as if it were tissue paper. The lander continued moving forward, breaking apart.

"Now rotate back!" said Deen. "Come back, cut
through it, slice it in half."

Victor's hand flew back to the levers. He stopped the
rotation and rolled the ship back the way it had come,
cutting through the lander like a saw as the lander continued its trajectory. There was cheering and shouting
in his earpiece. From the mining ships, from Imala, from
the team in the launch tubes.

The second lander was already retreating. Victor tried
rotating faster, but the mothership wouldn't respond fast
enough. He wasn't going to hit the other lander with the
gamma plasma. "Get ready, Mazer."

"I'm at the console," said Mazer. "How do I fire?"

Victor pulled up Mazer's helmetcam so he could see
what Mazer was seeing. "Move your right hand to the
right," said Victor, "three levers over. There. That's it.
When Deen gives the signal, push that forward. Deen,
you're our eyes. Tell us when."

"You need to move the ship, Victor," said Deen.

The model of the ship rotated in Victor's HUD. He
tried to mimic it.

"Faster," said Deen.

"I'm rotating as fast as I can," said Victor.

"It's opening!" said Deen. "It's opening!"

It was true. The bottom of the remaining lander was folding backward like two parting lips. A swarm of Formic transports and skimmers poured out, like a hive of angry wasps. Fifty. A hundred. All moving like a single mass, spiraling downward toward the mothership.

"Stay on the lander!" said Victor. "That's our target!"

Deen gathered himself. "Ten degrees to the right. Two degrees down. Three degrees. Four. That's it. Closer. Closer. Keep it coming. Keep it coming. Okay, now you're tracking. You've got it, you've got it. Now, Mazer! FIRE!"

Mazer pushed the lever forward, and the contents of the launch tube exploded upward like a cannon. The wreckage moved so quickly, that Victor didn't see it on his screen. All he saw was the top of the lander exploding, like the exit wound of a headshot. Large chunks of the lander's hull spun away, leaving a gaping hole in the roof of it.

There were more cheers over the radio, but Victor ignored them. "We need to finish it with the gamma plasma, Deen. It's wounded, but it's not out. Guide me. Let's go!"

Deen gave him the directions, helping him rotate. Victor sliced through the second lander once, twice, cutting it to pieces.

"They're on the hull!" said Deen. "They're landing."

Victor turned the gamma plasma wheel hard counterclockwise, shutting it off. Then he looked at Deen's helmetcam, and saw with horror that several transports had landed on the hull, surrounding Deen. Formics poured out of them, wearing pressure suits. Deen was already firing. His laser sliced through a whole row of them, cutting them in half. Their bodies burst apart like overripe fruit.

But the Formics were armed as well. And they had him from all sides. The darts came all at once. Deen didn't even make a sound.

Lem spoke over the emergency frequency and addressed every mining ship that was there. They were nearly thirty in number. Corporates and free miners alike. Many of them were the surviving ships from the shield, but there were others there as well. He had called to them in desperation. When the landers had launched and escaped the atmosphere, Lem had sent out an emergency message to every ship within the sound of his voice. Ships docked at Luna. Ships in a holding pattern above Imbrium, waiting for permission to land. Come, he had said. For the good of Earth, for the good of the human race, come.

They had abandoned what they were doing and answered his call. Not all of them. But most had. Italians, Africans, Argentineans, Dutch. He had ordered them to slow the landers, and they had obeyed. Now here they were, outnumbered three or four to one.

"This is Lem Jukes. This war ends right here and right now. I will give five million credits in cash to the mining ship that takes out the most skimmers and transports. Repeat, five million credits in cash. Ships of the shield, only use shatter boxes if you're sure of your target. I don't want any friendly-fire casualties. And take out the transports landing on the mothership. Do not let them retake that ship."

The miners rushed forward, whether out of a love for Earth or five million credits, Lem couldn't say. But it didn't matter. If the team held the ship, he'd get a thousand times that much for whatever tech they recovered inside.

Lem dove at a transport and sliced it in half. He spun

away and sliced through another one. Then a third. They were all packed so tightly together, it was hard to miss.

A mining ship to his left was cut to ribbons, attacked by four transports at once. The transports didn't stop, even when it was obvious the mining ship was lost. They crashed into it like kamikaze fighters, using themselves as missiles and tearing the ship to shrapnel. It wasn't until Lem had flown past and checked his holofield that he realized he knew the ship well. It was the Makarhu, the ship he had captained to the Kuiper Belt. Chubs and the crew were gone.

A short distance away, well out of the fighting, Imala watched the battle unfold and again felt completely helpless. I should be among them, she told herself. They need all the help they can get.

If she could only ditch the radiation shields that covered her weapons. If she could shed them somehow, she might be useful. But no, that was impossible. She had watched Victor weld the plates on, she had seen how meticulously and carefully he had ensured she was properly shielded.

Two skimmers broke away from the fighting and moved unhindered toward the other side of the Formic ship. None of the mining ships gave chase. In the confusion of the battle, none of them seemed to notice.

Where are you going? Imala wondered. She grabbed the stick and accelerated, taking off after them. They were making for the hole in the back of the ship, she realized, the hole the gamma plasma had made. They were trying to get inside the ship that way.

"Victor, can you read?"

"Imala, please tell me you're safe on Luna."

"There are two skimmers heading for the hole in the

ship. If they land, if they get through, they will make for the helm. You need to get out of there."

"I'm not leaving, Imala. We're holding this ship."

"Then call the others to come help you."

"They've got their hands full, Imala. The Formics are pouring down the launch tubes."

She came around the other side of the ship just in time to see the two skimmers fly into the hole. "They're inside, Victor. They're in. I'm going after them."

"Negative, Imala. You are not equipped. You have no way to stop them, nowhere for you to go. You can't land in here."

She ignored him. The hole was the same size as the tunnel of gamma plasma she had flown through. She could do this. And she did have a weapon, she realized— she did have a way to stop them. Her fighter. Herself. She could ram them from behind, she could push them into something, crush them.

She angled her approach to come at the hole head on. She saw the skimmers now, far inside the ship. They had stopped to a slow drift, and Formics in pressure suits were leaping from them and clinging to the inside of the mothership, grabbing at anything they could. Two of them scurried into the ship, disappearing from view. Then two more. It was too late to stop them, but she could stop the others.

"Imala, listen to me," said Victor. "Don't do this. You can't stop in the tunnel."

But she could stop. She *would* stop. But not before she did her part, not before she did what she could to save him.

She entered the hole. The interior of the ship rushed past her. Her console was beeping. "Warning! Warning! Collision imminent."

It all happened in an instant. She collided with the first skimmer and sent it careening into the wall. Her impact foam inflated, slamming her back against her seat and encasing her in a tight inflatable cloud. The skimmer bounced back and hit her. By then she had rotated. She struck something protruding from inside the ship—she never saw what—and started spinning end over end down the tunnel. She smashed into the second skimmer and crushed it. The Formics were thrown, shattered, ripped apart. She saw it all happen in her HUD in a blurred, spinning flash of violence, and then she struck something else, and all went black.

They were pouring down the launch tubes in a flood of bodies. Hundreds of them, rushing downward in a fury. Already there were twenty or more inside the ship, firing their weapons. Caruso was down, a dozen darts in his chest and back and throat. Bungy and Lobo had found cover with Benyawe and were mowing down Formics from their position, slicing through them as quickly as they could.

But it wasn't fast enough, Mazer realized. The Formics would overrun them any minute. "Lobo, we need to seal the tubes shut and launch them. Bungy, hold your position with Benyawe. Lobo, you take the tubes on the right. I'll take the tubes on the left. Do you know which lever to push?"

"Affirmative."

"Don't worry about orientation. There is no orientation in space. Launch back and forth between walls. Upside down, right side up. It doesn't matter. Keep your movements random. Change your approach every time. Don't give them a pattern to follow. Don't let them predict where you'll be."

"I got it."

"Bungy," said Mazer. "Give us as much cover as you can."

"Will do."

"Ready," said Mazer. "Launch!" He pushed off with his feet. Landed on the wall nearby and launched again. In three quick leaps he was at the console. He spun the big wheel, closing all the tubes at the top and bottom and trapping hundreds of Formics inside. Then he pressed the lever to launch the tube nearest him. The mechanism shot upward, catapulting the Formics up against the ceiling and into each other in a bone-crushing mass of suits and limbs and broken bodies.

Mazer didn't stick around to relish the moment. He was already leaping away, moving to the next tube, repeating the process. Darts pinged on the wall where he had been only a moment before. He fired his laser as he twisted through the air, taking out a cluster of three Formics who were giving him chase. He reached the second tube. A large crowd of Formics was gathered at the base of the tube, scratching at the locked hatch in a desperate attempt to climb inside. Mazer pushed down the lever, launched the tube, and sent them to their deaths instead.

Imala blinked her eyes open and thought she might be sick. She felt dizzy and disoriented and sore. The world was warbling like a tapped tuning fork. Her whole body was one giant bruise. She initiated her helmet lights and gave the order to deflate the foam. It unstiffened and she pushed it away from her face.

"Imala, can you hear me?"

Victor's voice. "Vico. Hi. Don't let me forget where I parked."

"Are you hurt?"

"Not at all. Just sitting here sipping lemonade with my feet up."

"Let me rephrase. Where are you hurt?"

"Pretty much everywhere. But I don't think anything's

broken. Your precious shields took most of the impact. And my new best friend, Mr. Impact Foam."

"Stay there. I'll come for you when this is over."

"Wrong. You've got at least four Formics coming to your position. I'm on my way."

"No, Imala. You don't have enough oxygen to leave your ship."

"I've got at least fifteen minutes of emergency reserves in my suit."

"You may not reach me in fifteen minutes."

She blinked the command to open the cockpit canopy. To her surprise, it obeyed. The top had caved in slightly, and she had worried it was too damaged to operate. She undid her harness and disconnected her suit from the ship.

"Warning! Warning! You have disconnected life support."

"Override warning," she said. "Silence system. Display oxygen remaining."

The numbers appeared on her HUD. She wasn't sure if it was fifteen minutes' worth. She needed to calm her breathing and make it last as long as it could. She pulled herself out of the cockpit and crawled up the side of her ship. The gamma plasma had seared through everything on the mothership as evenly as a knife through butter. Imala didn't want to touch the edges in case they were radioactive or sharp enough to cut her suit. She hopped into a corridor beside her and landed on the far wall. She couldn't tell which was the floor and which was the ceiling. "Vico, send me the map of the ship. Show me where you are in relation to my position."

"I don't know where you are exactly, Imala. And my map isn't comprehensive. I didn't explore every corner of the ship."

"Send me what you have. Can you see my helmet-cam?"

"Yes, but it doesn't mean much. The shafts and corridors all look the same."

"But if I keep moving in the direction I'm going, I'll get closer to you, right?"

"Go back to your ship, Imala. Reattach your oxygen. Please. I've already lost too many people close to me. I can't lose you, too."

That almost stopped her. The pleading in his voice and everything behind it—it almost turned her around. What could she do anyway? She didn't have a weapon.

"Do you have a weapon, Vico? Did Wit bring a gun to the helm?"

"I have my laser cutter, Imala. And I've barred the hatch. I'm fine."

A laser cutter could make a formidable weapon, true. She had one herself, now that she thought about it. An emergency one in the pocket of her suit, for cutting away her harness or cutting away the cockpit canopy in the event of a crash. She unzipped the pouch and pulled it out. It was such a little thing.

She launched up the corridor. A barred door wouldn't stop the Formics. They would find a way in. And when they did, they'd pull Victor apart. If she could find one of the big shafts from the vid, or maybe the main corridor that scooted the garden, if she could find any of those, she could get to the helm.

She checked her oxygen. The numbers had gone down significantly. I'm coming, Vico. I'm coming.

Victor listened to the celebrations. The surviving miners were cheering over the radio, singing and shouting in a multitude of languages. They had wiped out the last of the Formic transports and skimmers—including the ones that had landed on the hull of the ship. Lem and a few others had strafed those from above, slicing them in two.

None of the Formic ships had fled or retreated in the end. Instead, they had turned and launched themselves at their enemies. Only twelve human ships had been lost, which was nothing short of a miracle considering how many Formic ships there had been in the swarm.

The Formics were distracted, Victor realized. That's why the miners had won. The Formics were so focused on retaking their ship, so determined to win back what they had lost, that they had been blind to anything else.

Victor removed his laser cutter from his tool bag and severed the rod that held the gamma plasma wheel to the console. The wheel drifted away, leaving a metal stump behind. If Imala was right, if Formics *were* coming, he would make sure the helm was useless when they arrived. He cut off switches, sliced off levers, slashed every surface of the controls. Lem would go ballistic when he saw the damage—all that alien tech destroyed! But it wasn't destroyed completely. Not really. With a little time, a smart team of engineers could piece it back together and figure out how it all ticks. For now, however, Victor would do what he knew needed to be done: Remove the Formics' last hope and chance. End it once and for all.

When he was done, he looked at the cutter in his hand and smiled. Funny that it would come to this, in the end. It wouldn't be a nuke or another WMD, but a tool every decent mechanic carried in his bag.

A heavy object slammed against the hatch. It was not human. No one was calling him on the radio. It hit the hatch again. A third time. The bar he had put in place wouldn't hold. Not for very long. Maybe if he had carried with him a few other tools, he could have secured it better. Father would be disappointed. A good mechanic is never without his—

The hatch door exploded inward, flew across the room, and struck him, knocking him back against the far wall. The pain was instantaneous. His upper arm was broken. Maybe his collarbone as well. His vision was blurred. His visor was cracked. The laser cutter was gone from his hand. He initiated his boot magnets, and they snapped to a wall behind him.

The Formic scurried into the room. It was wearing a pressure suit and carrying a jar weapon. It went straight to the console, ignoring Victor. It saw the damage. Its eyes moved back and forth across the bank of controls, taking it in. It stood there a long moment as if unable to comprehend what it was seeing. Then its head turned, and it saw him. It raised its weapon. Light spun within the jar. Victor was cradling his arm. He deactivated his boot magnets and leaped to the side just as a glob of mucus slammed into the wall where he had been positioned. Victor careened into another wall, landing on his shoulder. Searing pain shot through him, like breaking his arm all over again. The membrane on the wall exploded. Victor recoiled into the corner. He was behind a bank of levers and switches, not concealed at all, really. He looked to his left and right for a weapon, but there wasn't one.

The Formic approached and regarded him. Victor waited for it to raise the weapon again. It had a clear shot. Victor had nowhere to go. Five seconds passed. Ten. But still the jar didn't move. The Formic cocked its head to the side. Its eyes seemed to grow in their intensity.

It's trying to speak to me, Victor realized. It's sending me a message. Victor listened but heard nothing, felt nothing, sensed nothing. Then the Formic's face relaxed. A small black device was suddenly in its hand. Victor had seen that device before, the first time he was in the cargo bay. It was the tool they had used to eviscerate the pilot.

The Formic reached out with the device.

There was a flash, and the creature's hand holding the device was no longer connected to its body. The hand drifted away, spinning slowly. Another flash and a line appeared at the Formic's midsection. A line that had not been there a moment before. Slowly, the top half of the Formic slid away from the bottom half, and the life in the creature's eyes faded.

Victor turned and saw Imala at the hatch entrance with her laser cutter. She flew to him and attached her own suit to his. "I'm borrowing some of your oxygen. Tell me where you're hurt."

"I thought you said there were four of them."

"There were. Mazer killed two and is chasing down the last one. We're safe. Where are you hurt?"

"My arm and collarbone. Maybe ribs, too. Hurts to breathe."

She tapped the medical screen on the side of his suit. "No external bleeding. No holes in your suit. Visor's cracked, but it's not leaking. Don't move. I'll tell your suit to give you something for the pain."

"No offense, but do you know what you're doing?"

"It's a mild sedative, Vico. The system knows your size and weight. It won't let me give you too much."

He felt a small prick in his arm, and in moments much of the pain subsided. His muscles relaxed. His breathing normalized. (He had been taking short, quick breaths to keep his chest from expanding.) He turned to her and studied her face a moment. "You crashed your ship, Imala. That was stupid."

"Or you could say, 'Thanks for saving my life, Imala. You're the most amazing human being in the world and my hero.'"

He smiled. "I was getting to that."

CHAPTER 25

International Fleet

A Juke mining vessel carried Mazer and the other survivors back to the Valas for the return flight to Luna. The mining ship docked above the freighter's cargo bay and extended a tube down to the airlock. The medic team and several of the engineering techs were all waiting at the hatch inside. Victor came through the airlock first, and the medics whisked him away to the sickbay, with Imala close behind. Mazer came through the airlock next, pulling behind him the body bag that held Wit O'Toole. A pair of techs took it with the greatest reverence. There were also bags for ZZ, Deen, Bolshakov, and Caruso. Collecting Cocktail's remains had been a messier business, but Bungy and Lobo had found some, and there was a smaller bag for him.

The engineering techs then escorted Mazer and the others to the decon showers. Mazer was instructed to stand in a box while still wearing his radiation suit and to scrub himself clean with chemicals. If the technicians were bothered by the blood on his suit they gave no sign. Mazer then sucked up the chemicals and shed the suit for disposal. He was given clean clothes and then directed into a room barely bigger than a closet. There were storage cabinets on the wall, and a small holotable.

"What am I doing in here?" Mazer asked the tech.

"You have a holo from Earth, sir." The man left and closed the door behind him.

A holofield appeared above the table. Mazer put his head into the field and waited. A man's head appeared. Midfifties, clean shaven, square jaw, buzzed head. Definitely military. Probably eastern European.

"Captain Rackham, my name is Lieutenant Colonel Yulian Robinov of the Russian Ministry of Defense. I currently act as chair of Strategos, the international military body that operates under the direction of the United Nations and dictates orders to MOPs. Captain O'Toole reported directly to me."

Reported. Past tense. So he knew what had happened.

"My condolences, sir. Captain O'Toole was the finest commander I have ever had the privilege to serve under."

"He was the finest soldier I have ever known. Period," said Robinov. "His loss is a great tragedy. But I assure you his sacrifice today will be remembered." He paused then continued. "What I am about to tell you now, Captain Rackham, is highly classified. In seventy-two hours, the entire world will know, but until that time I ask that you exercise discretion and not reveal this information to anyone. Are we clear?"

"Yes, sir."

"In three days time, the New Zealand Special Air Service to which you belong will no longer exist. Nor will the Russian military, or the American military, or any national military for that matter. The leaders of the world are forming an International Fleet, a single global military force that will defend the human race against any future Formic attack. We have been divided throughout the course of this war, Captain, and that division was nearly our undoing. If we remain divided, the Formics will wipe us out of existence. It's time to unite our strengths and resources. I'm sure I need not give the full speech to you."

"No, sir."

"Every active serviceman like yourself will have the option of finishing his years of committed military service with the International Fleet or enlisting with the IF for a new term of service. Our hope is that this announcement will inspire millions of new soldiers to join our cause. The key word here is inspire.

"The Mobile Operations Police will be used as the model for the International Fleet. We'll call MOPs a microcosm of what we hope to achieve on a global scale. If the victory today is reported as a MOPs victory, therefore, we will give Earth clear evidence that an international military is not only possible, but also has already achieved great victories. With less than a dozen MOPs, we brought the Formic army to its knees. Imagine the global security we can provide with a whole army of likeminded soldiers."

Mazer nodded. "So you'll make heroes of Captain O'Toole and the other casualties, and bill this as a MOPs operation in order to build support for and acceptance of the fleet."

"It's propaganda. We recognize that. But it's necessary. This mission must be a MOPs mission. Lem Jukes served his purpose and will be given credit for such, but the soldiers were MOPs."

"Except for me and Shenzu."

"You two break the myth. Shenzu is an asset since he already helped facilitate an alliance between India and China. He embodies the International Fleet, in that sense. Plus the Chinese adore him. When he enlists, millions will do the same."

"Then there's me," said Mazer. "The unknown out-sider, the soldier to whom Captain O'Toole gave command. If people know I was involved or led any aspect of this op, suddenly this isn't a MOPs mission since I'm not technically a MOP."

"You see our dilemma."

"It's easily solved, sir. I'll never reveal my involvement in the operation. Mazer Rackham was never here. I don't play the game you'd want me to play anyway. I don't smile for cameras and speak to audiences. There are others far better suited to that."

"I see you are exactly the soldier Captain O'Toole said you are."

"I am the soldier I am largely *because* of him, sir."

Robinov seemed to relax. "Can I assume then that you will enlist in the International Fleet, Captain?"

"If the paperwork is ready, sir, I'll fill it out right now."

Victor was sitting up in bed in a clinic on Luna with his arm and shoulder in an inflatable cast. Several news feeds on the wall-screen showed the live celebrations all over the world. China, the Americas, Europe, Africa. Parades, fireworks, raining confetti, people waving tiny flags to the camera.

"Looks like we're missing the party."

Victor turned. Lem stood at the doorway. "The war's over," said Victor. "That's cause to celebrate."

Lem came and stood by the bed. "Doctor says your surgery went well. Both breaks were clean and easily repaired. You'll make a full recovery." He gestured at the room. "This is a company clinic, so you obviously won't be charged for your care. Anything you want, just say the word, and the nurses will get it. Swiss chocolate. French pastries. Bavarian goat cheese. Go crazy."

"How long do I have to stay here?"

"That's up to you. The doctor is willing to discharge you this evening. Do you have a place to stay?"

"Not exactly."

"We'll put you in one of the company suites. You can stay there for a couple of weeks until you get your own place."

"Thanks, but I don't intend to stay on Luna."

"You haven't even heard my job offer yet. You'd be working directly with Benyawe and her team dismantling and analyzing Formic tech. She told me if I left the clinic without signing you, I was in big trouble."

"I appreciate the offer, but my priority now is to help my family."

"Doing what? Salvage work? You'll help them far more by working for me, Victor. I'd pay you very well. You could transfer what you earn directly to them."

"My family is getting out of the salvage trade. They want to retrofit their ship with mining equipment. Money can't do that. I can."

"Money can do anything, Vico, if there's enough of it."

"What about Imala?"

"What about her?"

"Are you offering her a job as well?"

"My father offered her a job before the invasion. She threw the offer back in his face. He'd never allow me to bring her on after a move like that. And anyway, she's not an engineer, which is what I need."

"I'm not an engineer either."

"You don't have a degree maybe, but you know the principles better than most. I'd rather hire *you* than ten stuckups with Ph.D.s."

It was a tempting offer. Victor liked Benyawe. And it was the kind of work he had always wanted to do. Meaningful, inventive work. Most of the repairs he had made on El Cavador were fairly mindless—putting sprocket A back with sprocket B. But occasionally the work had required him to throw out a part entirely and build something new from scratch. A better part. A more efficient design. A machine that did everything the previous part did but which required less energy or produced less heat. That was the work he had enjoyed: the meticulous disassembly of something to understand how it operated, followed by the careful application of those principles to build something new. It was exactly what Lem was offering.

The only problem: It was Lem who was offering it.

"I appreciate the offer, Lem, but right now I can't."

Lem nodded. "Six months to a year from now, after you've helped your family, maybe you'll change your mind. Contact me then."

"I will."

Lem sat in the recliner by the bed and leaned back with his hands behind his head. "I'm also here to inform you that the charges against you from the Lunar Trade Department have been dropped, including the charge of fleeing from custody, which is a serious felony. Charges against Imala were dropped as well. It wasn't hard to do. We simply showed the LTD how their rejection of your evidence of the invasion was the primary reason why Earth was so unprepared. They locked you up and buried your evidence in red tape when they should have announced you immediately to the world. When we threatened to file suit, claiming that their willful negligence resulted in the destruction of a good portion of our corporate fleet and personnel, they did whatever we asked." He shrugged. "Of course, we'll probably end up suing them anyway."

"Thanks for clearing my name."

"Lawyers are the deadliest of weapons, Victor. Make sure the best ones are always on your side."

There was a knock. Imala stepped into the room. "The nurses told me you were awake."

"Awake and talking nonsense," said Lem. "I offer him a decent job, and he turns me down. Talk some sense into him, Imala."

"He doesn't have any that I'm aware of," said Imala.

Lem turned back to Victor. "We're reinitiating cargo shipments to the Belt. Tell me when you want to leave, and I'll get you passage."

"Thank you."

Lem offered his hand, and they shook. "Keep the sun at your back, space born."

"You too."

Lem walked out.

Imala came and stood by the bed, her expression flat. "So you're heading to the Belt. You've made your decision."

"My family needs me, Imala."

"Your mother doesn't want you to come, Vico. She said as much. She wants you to stay here. To go to a university."

"I can't get into a university, Imala. We've been over this. I have no diploma, no birth certificate, no citizenship—"

"You can take tests to get a diploma, Vico. And Lem could help you acquire the other necessary papers."

Victor scoffed. "Yeah. Illegally."

"Maybe not. Maybe he has connections in immigration. And anyway, so what if he does it illegally? You deserve to go to school, Vico. You deserve it more than anyone. If you go back to your family, you'll end up becoming a . . ."

"A what, Imala? A free miner? Is that what you were going to say?"

"No."

"Then what?"

"I was going to say you'll end becoming a suitor in some arranged marriage. That's what your family does, isn't it? They mix up the gene pool by swapping eligible bachelors and brides among the families."

"We have to, Imala. Families are isolated. We can't intermarry. That would be incest. All of our kids would have twelve toes and a second pair of eyes."

"I'm not advocating incest," said Imala. "I'm saying arranged marriages strip you of your right to choose. I've seen the documentaries, Vico. Newlywed brides bawling their eyes out because they've been forced to marry a stranger."

"It's not always like that," said Victor.

"It is sometimes."

"Why are we even arguing about this?"

"Because you're not thinking about your own future, Vico. Your mother is leading the effort to reconfigure the ship. She says she can handle it."

"And she's wrong, Imala. Installing all of that equipment, making all the necessary configurations, it's far more complicated than she realizes."

"Or maybe she knows precisely what she's getting into, and she wants to try it anyway. Sometimes you have to trust people enough to let them succeed and love them enough to let them fail. You can't fix everything, Vico. If you do, the only lesson people will learn is dependency. Your mother has done fine without you all this time. If you rush to her now, what is that saying? Hi, Mom. I knew you were incapable of doing this task, so I've come to rescue you."

"I love my family, Imala. My mother has been through a nightmare. She lost my father, her home, half her family. Is it a crime to want to comfort her?"

"Of course not."

"I have nothing here, Imala."

"A job, a possible future, friends who care about you. That's nothing?"

"My job offer is from someone who lied to us and

abandoned us. Have you forgotten what Lem Jukes is? The only reason he actually followed through was because of the tech. This was an economic decision for him all the way. Why should I put much stock in any offer from him?"

"You're right, Vico. What was I thinking? Silly stupid me." She walked out before he could say another word.

Lem was alone in his apartment when his wrist pad lit up with messages. He flipped through them and saw that they were all from journalists seeking an interview. He had already received dozens of such requests, and he had erased or ignored them all. He was done with the press, done with the phony theater of it all.

By now the media had interviewed many of the miners who had participated in the final battle. Each of them had given harrowing accounts of the fighting. When pressed about Lem Jukes's involvement, they had all explained how Lem had called them to arms and promised to financially reward the ship that accumulated the most kills. The media had had a field day with the Argentine family who had won. Lem had paid them as promised, and the press was all too happy to stick a camera in the people's faces. Some of the women had cried. Now they could get needed medicine and food. Now they could repair their ship.

One reporter had called it "Humanity among the horrors of war." KINDNESS IN THE CHAOS, read another headline.

Lem wanted to laugh. Didn't the press realize he had done it to save his own skin? The more aggressive the miners were, the better chance they all had of getting out alive. Wasn't that obvious? This was self-preservation, you fools, not philanthropy.

But what did the media care? If the charity angle

resonated with people and generated a high click count and ad revenue, they would milk that cow for all it was worth.

Still, Lem was curious why a rush of reporters would contact him now and request an interview days after the battle. Some new bit of information had been released perhaps. Some little nugget of intel that everyone in the world was hungry for.

Curious, Lem went online to see what scrap of information the press was running.

To his surprise, a vid was playing on all of the feeds. It showed Lem at the helm of the Valas, Lem at his warehouse, Lem in his fighter taking on the Formics, Lem interacting with the MOPs. There was audio as well.

How was this possible? Who had taken all of these vids?

It was Father, of course. Who else? He had been watching Lem with hidden cameras every step of the way.

Lem was so furious, he flew immediately to headquarters. Father's receptionist tried to stop him, but Lem blew by her desk and burst into Father's office. "You used me!"

Ukko was sitting at his desk, head back, a paper bib around his neck protecting his suit. A makeup artist was leaning over him dabbing a paintbrush at Ukko's eyebrows. A man with a holopad was standing off to the side. He wore a finely tailored suit, and not a single hair of his head was out of place. He stepped between Lem and his father, frowned, and put a hand up. "I'm sorry, Lem. Your father is in the middle of something. Now isn't a good time. Can I call you later to set something up? We could discuss a time you two could meet?" He checked his holopad. "How's six this evening?" He offered his hand. "I'm Maxwell, by the way."

Lem almost hit him. "I suggest you get out of my way."

Maxwell's smile faded, and he retreated back a step.

Ukko brushed the makeup artist away. "Maxwell, Natasha, leave us for a moment. My son is in a mood. And he and I have urgent business to discuss."

Maxwell stepped to the desk. "Are you sure, sir? We need to be downstairs in ten minutes. They want to check your audio and the lighting on your face."

"I'm going to look like an old man regardless of the lighting or makeup, Maxwell. Give us a minute, will you?"

Maxwell frowned, regarded Lem with sharp disapproval, then followed the makeup artist out and closed the door behind them.

Lem cocked a thumb at the door. "Who is that idiot?"

"Were you not paying attention? That's Maxwell, my new chief of staff."

"Simona is your chief of staff."

"She was. Unfortunately I had to let her go."

"You fired Simona? Why?"

"I demand absolute loyalty from my staff, Lem. Their devotion to me must be unquestionable."

"Simona *was* devoted to you," said Lem. "Insanely devoted."

"She used to be, yes. Until you returned from the Kuiper Belt."

"What is that supposed to mean?"

"She was clearly in love with you, Lem. I'm disappointed you didn't see it. It was blatantly obvious to me."

It took Lem a moment to find words. "Are you delusional? Simona was a friend. And barely that. Most of the time she couldn't stand me."

"She couldn't stand that you ignored her. You bickered like a married couple. I thought for sure you must have slept with her."

Lem blinked. "With Simona? No. Is that why you fired her? Because you thought she was sleeping with me? Because she wasn't."

"I fired her because she betrayed me."

"How? I can't believe that."

Ukko stood, pulled the bib from his neck, crumpled it into a ball, and tossed it on his desk. "You're going to dislike what I have to say next, Lem." He exhaled and sat on the edge of his desk. "I suspected Simona's love for you was increasing. That poses obvious problems for me. I can't have my chief of staff giving more loyalty to my son than she gives to me. So I gave her a test. I knew you were sleeping with Despoina. And I knew you were trying to pull information from her about my affairs. So I wrote an e-mail to myself as if it were written by Despoina and I let that e-mail fall into Simona's possession. If Simona was loyal to me, she would erase it and never disclose it to you. But if Simona was in love with you, if she was loyal to you *over* me, she would show it to you. Which she did. She went straight to you behind my back. My only option was to fire her."

Lem stared. A sick heavy feeling had gripped his chest. "You wrote that e-mail?"

"Despoina was not my informant, son. I did not ask her to spy on you or extract information from you. Nor was she the whore you took her for. She was a sweet girl. For whatever reason, she seemed to be blind to your faults. Or perhaps she loved your strengths so deeply that she saw past what makes you human. Either way, you let a real catch slip through your fingers, son. Her father has quite the empire. It could have been a lovely match."

Lem said nothing. Words wouldn't come. His whole body felt numb.

"You acted too rashly, son. I found your response revolting. Arresting her in the night, banishing her from Luna, writing a malicious, scathing note. What were you thinking? That was cruel and demeaning, son. Totally inexcusable. And what's especially tragic is that it's evidence that you were clearly in love with her. Only a man betrayed by love would debase and humiliate someone like that. If she had meant nothing to you, you would have come to me. I would've been the one who had offended you. But instead, you spit all of your venom at her. You've made plenty of mistakes in your life, Lem, but this is first time I have ever been ashamed to call you my son."

Lem stared at him. His hands were trembling. His words were quiet. "I am not your son. I can't be. No father would ever do such a thing to his own child."

Ukko sighed. "This defense of yours gets old, Lem. You can't blame me for all of your mistakes."

"You created a lie. You invented a situation and provided proof. You built the justification for my actions in my mind. How is this not your fault? She was kind to me, Father."

"Learn from this, Lem. You can't act rashly. You can't hire thugs to—"

"This is not one of your damn life lessons, Father! Or if it is, it's so twisted and demented that I don't want to hear it. You used me. You used her."

"You used her first, Lem. Don't forget that. We both know why you came to my office and approached her."

"It wasn't like that."

"It was, Lem. Your heart might have gone pitter patter eventually, but you were playing her for your own gain. What's that American phrase? The pot calling the kettle black?"

Lem waved his arms and stepped away. "I am finished with you. Done. I don't know why I ever wasted time seeking your approval. You were never going to give it anyway. It's no wonder Mother left us. It's no wonder she's crazy. How could she not be if you treated her like you treat me."

Ukko stood erect and straightened his coat. "Are you done throwing your tantrum now?"

It was such an infuriating thing to say, so condescending, that Lem couldn't form a response.

"You're upset, Lem. My e-mail tactic with Despoina may not have been ideal from your perspective, but love was the reason for Simona's disloyalty to me. So it was her *love* that I needed to test. Simona would be eager to give you proof that might end your relationship with Despoina. I needed to see if her loyalty to me was stronger. It wasn't. Had I known you would have reacted the way you did, I would have taken another approach. We both made mistakes. As for your mother, yes, I probably drove her to her mental state. You're a little old to be having that eureka moment now, though. You should have reached that conclusion about twenty years ago."

The makeup artist had left her mirror on Father's desk. He picked it up and examined his hair. "As for being done with me, well, that's a problem. Because I clearly can't give the company to you if that's going to be our relationship."

He set down the mirror and faced Lem.

Lem paused. "You'll never give this company to me, Father. You never intended to."

"I'm giving it to you now, Lem. I'll put all my stocks in a blind trust. You have plenty of enemies on the Board, however, so I'd advise you to clean house and set things in motion to remove people. Ramdakan can help. He's an expert at that sort of thing. He can tell you who the snakes are, and I assure you we have plenty. I'm as gentle as a butterfly compared to some. Also, I'd recommend putting Benyawe on the Board. We'll be deemphasizing our mining operations and putting a greater emphasis in innovation and shipbuilding. That's our future, Lem. Lots and lots of military ships. We'll be outfitting most of the International Fleet."

"What's the International Fleet?"

"I'll show you. It's time to make history, son."

Father led them from the room. Maxwell was practically coming out of his skin, he was so worried about the time. He checked his holopad four times during the brief elevator ride down. When the doors opened and they stepped off, they found themselves in one of the holo rooms. The overhead lights had been dimmed. A crew of technicians was making final adjustments to the rig of lights and holoprojectors in the center of the room. Ukko paused to shake hands with the twenty or so reporters on Luna who had come to witness the event. Natasha, the makeup girl, brushed Father's cheeks with a light powder.

Maxwell got everyone into position. Father stood off to the side in the darkness. The crowd quieted. The technicians removed their ladders and disappeared into the shadows. The holofield beneath the projector glowed to life.

The heads of five people appeared in the field. Lem recognized a few of them. The secretary general of the United Nations was in the center, a Brazilian woman named Silva. The others were the heads of China, Russia, India, and NATO, who was an American. Secretary Silva spoke first. She greeted everyone who was watching this historic announcement via holo. She explained that each member of the holo was sitting in his or her own headquarters and speaking to reporters gathered at each site.

Silva then spoke for ten minutes on the need for a united global military consisting of soldiers from every nation on Earth. This International Fleet would be led by two experienced military leaders with a track record of working with international troops and resolving global conflicts. The position of Strategos would be responsible for the overall defense of the solar system.

"This duty would go to Lieutenant Colonel Yulian Robinov, who is currently serving as the chair of a council of international military leaders also known as Strategos, from which this new position derives its name." Robinov appeared in the holo alongside the others, with his name and title suspended in the air beneath him.

Secretary Silva continued. "Robinov's international peacekeeping force known as the Mobile Operations Police, who will serve as a model for the International Fleet, was recently responsible for ending the atrocities in China and bringing this horrific war to a close."

The second position of Polemarch, she explained, would be responsible for the construction, maintenance, and operation of the International Fleet's warships. "That duty goes to Major Khudabadi Ketkar of India, whose careful leadership fostered the alliance of Indian Para Commandos and the Chinese military, and who ended the Formics' gas attacks and helped turn the war in our favor."

Katkar appeared in the holo.

Silva welcomed him and then continued. "Creating and maintaining a defense through the International Fleet is a monumental undertaking that will require the resources and efforts of everyone. All nations must join in a united effort to protect our planet from future attacks while maintaining global harmony and peace. This council therefore proposes the formation of a global Hegemony. This Hegemony would consist of member nations committed to protecting our planet and the human race. Member nations would maintain their current system of government; but in global matters they would counsel with the Hegemony, who knows no borders and whose only interest is the planet as a whole and all of its inhabitants. Hegemony offices would be dispersed around the world so that Formics couldn't destroy one capital and thus our global government. We would move the Hegemon's core staff from city to city but never in the capitals of China, Russia, India, or the USA.

"No man is more qualified for the position of Hegemon than the president and CEO of Juke Limited, Ukko Jukes."

A small holofield encircled Father's head where he stood, projected down from a shelf above him. A large floating holo of his head appeared to the right of Secretary Silva.

"As a citizen of the moon," Silva said, "Ukko Jukes represents all of humanity and not any one nation. His devotion to the people of Earth is indisputable. His dedication to our safety, unquestionable. His vast success and experience in the private sector makes him uniquely qualified to handle the heavy logistical demands of building and mobilizing an international fleet. What we are proposing will be the largest undertaking in human history. To lead that effort, we require a hegemon who has proven he is capable of managing operations on such a massive scale.

"The United Nations will vote on this measure tomorrow during our general session, followed by a ratifying vote within each member nation. It is our hope that all nations of the Earth will join this united effort to prevent the atrocities that occurred within China. Never again should one nation suffer alone."

Silva then gave the floor to Robinov, Ketkar, and Father, who each gave brief prepared statements. Lem barely heard a word they said. His mind was reeling. Father as Hegemon, the supreme leader of Earth. It seemed so obvious now. Father had been orchestrating this from the beginning. That's why he had met with the woman from the state department and other dignitaries and officials since. And of course the United Nations would vote unanimously tomorrow. Father would never agree to participate unless he was certain of the outcome.

The holo ended. Father stepped forward and took questions from the reporters present. When asked if he intended to lead both the Hegemony and the company, Father said, "My new responsibilities as Hegemon will consume all of my time. It would be an injustice to the people of Earth not to give them my complete focus and attention. I have asked my son Lem to function as president and CEO in my stead, a recommendation I am confident the Board of Directors will ratify. My son is the most tenacious, brilliant, and fearless man I know. You saw some of that, no doubt, in the vids and accounts of the final battle. I can't express the terror I felt to see him put his life in such danger. Lem is all the family I have. The thought of losing him was almost too much to bear. My heart goes out to China and every parent in the world who has lost a child or loved one in this horrific ordeal. And I give you my solemn promise, should I be elected Hegemon, I will do all in my power to ensure that we never lose our sons or daughters to an alien threat again."

Father thanked them for coming. Maxwell whisked Father away. Lem followed, and once the three of them were back in Father's office, Ukko began cleaning the makeup off his face.

"You've been choreographing this from the beginning," said Lem. "You knew the drones wouldn't work. Yet you sent them anyway to demonstrate to Earth that you were committed to the cause."

"I wanted them to work, Lem."

"Of course you did. If they worked, you'd become an instant hero. But if they failed, there was still much to gain. You would show Earth that you were willing to sacrifice your fortune to protect Earth. You'd still be a hero in a sense. And you sent the drones when you did because you couldn't have Victor and Imala succeed. You couldn't let *me* have the victory. That would throw your plans all out of whack."

"You *did* have the victory in the end, son."

"Yes, but only after you had showed the world you would do anything to protect us." Lem laughed. It was all so clear now. "Benyawe was right, you don't make mistakes. In fact, as soon as the drones failed, you changed your strategy to ensure that I would win. You told me about El Cavador, for example. You showed me Project Parallax because you knew I needed Victor to get a strike team inside the ship. And you knew that with information about his mother's whereabouts, I could re-enlist him in my effort."

"We didn't know Victor was still alive at the time," said Father.

"You did. Somehow *you* knew."

"I'm flattered you think I have superhuman powers, Lem."

"And Ketkar. He helped Mazer and Wit in India and now he's Polemarch. There's a coincidence. What was it, Father? You and he strike a deal? He helps you orchestrate the alliance with China and India and you ensure his appointment as Polemarch."

Father went to the bar and began pouring two drinks.

"Then there's the vid of me," said Lem. "All the hidden cameras. You did it to increase your appeal. Now the world will see you as the father of a war hero. Or, if I died romantically in battle, you'd be the father of a *fallen* war hero, which might be better. You'd get the sympathy vote. Either way you win."

"Or here's a possibility," said Father. "I wanted my son to have a future leading this company. And by making that vid, I made it impossible for the board to disapprove of you." He handed Lem one of the drinks. "I'm offering you a future, Lem. Take it or leave it."

"Don't act like you're giving me a choice, Father."

Ukko grinned, clinked his glass against Lem's, and took a swallow. "Wonderful. I'll take that as a yes."

CHAPTER 26

Kim

Mazer took a civilian flight to Auckland, rented a car, and drove south to Papakura. It felt good to be on solid ground again. He had been ordered to report to base immediately, but he drove to Kim's office instead. He told the receptionist in the lobby that he was here to see Dr. Kim Arnsbrach.

"Is she expecting you?"

"No, ma'am."

"Who shall I say is visiting?"

"Tell her I'm a friend of Bingwen's."

The receptionist delivered the message, and a moment later Kim stepped off the elevator. She looked the same. Her hair was up in the back with her stylus stuck through it, holding it in place. He had sent her a brief text from Luna to let her know he was alive and well and soon coming back to New Zealand. But he hadn't called ahead today to tell her he was coming.

"I know I should have called first," he said. "But I was worried you might not want to see me."

"Why wouldn't I want to see you?"

He suddenly felt awkward. "Because of how things ended last time. You were angry."

"I was a lot of emotions. Anger might have been one of them. I'm also a big girl, Mazer. I cooled off. Life goes on. Isn't that what you wanted? For me to go on."

This wasn't going well. Five seconds in, and it was already awkward again.

"Sorry," she said. "That sounded snippy. I'm happy you're here. I'm just surprised is all." She examined his face. "You've lost weight. Your cheeks are sunken."

"It's been a rough few months."

She was quiet a moment and nodded. "I'm sorry about Patu and Fatani and Reinhardt. And Wit O'Toole and everyone."

"Me too. Do you have a minute? Can we talk somewhere?"

"The park across the street." She moved for the door, and he followed.

"Do you need to tell anyone?"

She gave a dismissive wave. "You pulled me from a boring meeting. I was about to throw myself from the building to get out of it anyway. They won't notice I'm gone."

The park was lush and green with rows of mature oaks along the paths that created a thick canopy overhead. The walkway was cracked and old and dappled with light. It smelled of flowers and cut grass.

"First off, thank you for helping Bingwen," he said.

Her face lit with a quick smile. "How is he?"

"He's in a military school in northern China. I spoke with the director yesterday. Now that the military is transitioning to the International Fleet, the director was unsure about the school's future, but he assured me that Bingwen was safe and would continue to be of interest to China. A lot is in flux, but I suspect they'll transition the school into a youth training facility for the IF."

"Can I contact him?"

"E-mail only. I'll send you his address. He would love to hear from you."

"This International Fleet," she said, "are you enlisting?"

"I already did."

She nodded but didn't look at him.

There was an old wooden gazebo with ivy growing up the sides. They sat on the bench inside. Mazer positioned himself so he was facing her.

"Everything I said before I left, Kim, about not wanting to be an absent father or husband is still true. I resolved to be single when I joined the military because I didn't want to subject my wife to that life. But I've been living that life every day since, Kim. I've been living it moment by moment, and I hate it. I hate it so deeply it makes me sick."

Her hands were in her lap. She watched his face, listening.

"I hate it because you are not in it, Kim. I know I told you to move on. I know I told you to find someone who could make you happier. And maybe you have. But I am going to fight for you, Kim Arnsbrach. I am going to fight to convince you to forget everything I said before. I don't want a life without you. And if there *is* another man in your life, I am going to scare him until he wets himself and runs away."

She allowed herself a smile.

He waited a moment before continuing. "My mother taught me when I was young that all of us are filled with *mana*. It means 'energy' or 'power,' and it flows into us from the natural world. Trees, animals, the wind. I know that probably sounds ridiculous, especially to a doctor, but—"

"It doesn't sound ridiculous," she said.

He nodded. "Well it sounded ridiculous to me. After

my mother died, the older I got, it all sounded ridiculous. All of it. The dancing, the music, the fish gods and creature guardians. It was laughable, fantasy. My father scorned it, and so did I."

He looked down at his hands and back up at her. "And maybe most of it is fantasy. But this *mana,* this essence, that might be real. There's truth to that. When I crashed in China, when I woke up after the surgery, I felt as if life had drained out of me, Kim. I thought it was my body, the injuries, the weakness I felt. But it wasn't. I had lost it before then."

He took her hands. "You're the *mana* I lost, Kim. When I lost you, I lost life. If that sounds hokey and weird, so be it. If you think I'm crazy, fine. You wouldn't be the first to think so."

"You're not crazy," she said. "Annoying sometimes. Stubborn and bullheaded and a terrible communicator. But you're not off your rocker. Not yet."

"I'm a soldier, Kim. I always will be. That's an imperfect situation for any marriage, I know. But I would rather have that, and do everything in my power to make you happy than to live one more second without you. *Kei te aroha au ki a koe.* I love you, Kim. I love you. I should have told you that a long time ago. And until you tell me to go away, I will tell you that every day of my life."

She didn't speak for a long moment. "Is this a marriage proposal, Mazer? Is that what this is? Because a girl dreams about this, and getting pulled out of a status meeting in the middle of the workday is not how she envisions it. You're supposed to be this brilliant strategic mind, capable of planning every meticulous detail of an operation. Yet you don't even have a ring, do you?"

"I have a ring. My mother's. But it's on base, locked up with my things. If I went to get it, I wouldn't be able to leave again. But I re-created it as best as I could to give you an idea of what it looks like." He pulled out his holopad and extended the antennas. A ring appeared in the holofield, hovering in the air. The gold bands were all braided together, encircling the diamond in the center.

Kim extended her hand and slid the ring on her finger. "I hope you don't expect me to carry a holopad around for the rest of my life."

Mazer set the holopad aside and got down on his knees, taking her hand. "Kim Arnsbrach. Will you be my wife and have my children and teach me to be as strong as you and smart as you and good as you?"

She pursed her lips, as if considering his offer. "I'm not sure. I've never much liked the last name Arnsbrach, but Rackham doesn't sound much better."

His heart fell for a moment, but then she smiled and said, "But we all must make sacrifices, I suppose. I have one condition."

"Anything."

"I want a Maori wedding."

He stood and took her in his arms and kissed her right there in the open for all the world to see.

CHAPTER 27

Belt

There was a line of applicants waiting outside the office when Victor arrived. He had posted a job opening on the free-miner nets the day before, but he had not expected to get such a big turnout. He needed three men, the post had said. All mechanics, preferably with experience retrofitting a salvage ship. They needed to be healthy and fit and willing to commit to at least four months on the job, not counting travel time to the Belt. If they proved themselves a valuable asset, they could possibly earn a crew position, but no promises were made.

He had rented a small office at one of the public docks on Luna. The room number had been included on the post. The interviewing wasn't supposed to begin for another half hour, but there was no need to keep everyone waiting. The office was bare except for a small wooden table—scratched and worn from decades of use—and two metal chairs.

The first applicant claimed to be eighteen years old, but he looked fourteen at the most.

"Have you ever installed a D-class laser or one of higher grade?" Victor asked.

"No, sir. But we had D on our ship."

"What ship was that?"

"Hermes's Wings. The Greek Greats Clan. Do you know the one?"

Victor shook his head. "Where's your ship now?"

The boy was holding his hat in his hands. He looked down at it and wrung it nervously. "Gone, sir. Battle of the Belt."

"You don't have to call me 'sir.' How is it that you survived?"

The boy wouldn't look him in the eye. "The morning we decoupled from the depot and set out, I . . . uh, I missed the ship, sir."

His family wouldn't have left him behind. He had probably run away when they docked, knowing they would soon set off to war. Victor felt sorry for the kid, but he wasn't offering jobs out of sympathy, especially to anyone who would abandon his family. Still, the kid needed work the same as anyone. "I can't promise you they'll hire you, but there's a Juke ship called the Valas. A cargo freighter. They may be looking for hands. I know the captain. You can tell her I sent you."

The boy scoffed. "Work for a corporate? Never."

"Those days are over," said Victor. "Free miners and corporates, we work together now. That is, unless you want to go hungry."

The boy's expression fell, humbled. "I beg your pardon, sir. Very grateful for the help. Yes, I'll visit the Valas. Very kind."

Victor gave him the information and sent him on his way. The other applicants came in one by one, but none of them fared much better than the first. Some were in their sixties. Another kept coughing throughout the interview as if he had some upper-respiratory disease. Several were fathers and husbands and asked if they could bring their wives and children along. Victor took their information and told them he'd contact them if they got the job. The truth was, he needed husbands for the survivors of El Cavador as much as he needed mechanics. If they were going to be a thriving family again, some of the women would have to remarry. He couldn't say that on the job posting, however. Wanted: Handsome men of honest disposition willing to marry one of eighteen widows and adopt all of her children. Spanish speakers preferred.

He was beginning to despair after hours of interviews when Imala came into the room.

"Imala. I've been calling you for days, ever since I left the clinic. I must have left half a dozen messages."

"I've had a lot on my mind." She sat in the chair opposite him.

He didn't know what to say. "It's great to see you. I *want* to see you. But . . . I'm in the middle of something. I'm interviewing people. But maybe I could get another chair. You could help me. I'd like to know what you think."

"I'm here for the interview, Vico."

"What? You mean you're applying?"

"That's what an applicant does. She applies. She gets interviewed. Hopefully she gets a job."

"You want the job?"

"This isn't a difficult concept to grasp, Vico. You're offering a job. I need a job."

"Yes, but . . . you *want* to come?"

"I wouldn't be here if I didn't want to come, Vico."

"But I'm going to the Belt, Imala. That's far out there."

"I know how far it is. We went once before, remember?"

"I'll be going much farther than that, Imala. And once we get out there, it won't be easy to get back. This isn't auditing. This isn't a desk job. It's mining."

"You think I can only handle desk jobs?"

"No, of course not. You can do anything. That's my point. This is grunt work. You've got a college degree, real-world experience. A reference from Lem, and you could work wherever you wanted. Luna, Earth. The International Fleet would take you in a hot second. The Hegemony would as well if anyone other than Ukko Jukes was running the show."

"So you don't want me to come?"

"Of course I want you to come. But . . . I can't ask that of you. You have a future, Imala. The Belt is the last place in the system to find opportunities."

"Maybe I don't want opportunities, Vico. Maybe I want something else."

He was quiet a moment. "What do you want, Imala?"

"To be happy, Vico. I want to be happy."

They left three days later on a cargo ship. Victor didn't end up hiring anyone other than Imala. He'd wait until they reached the Belt, where he might find better applicants. Or perhaps Imala was right. Maybe he didn't need to hire anyone else. Maybe he and Imala and the women of El Cavador could do it all.

"Arjuna has crewmen as well," Imala told him. "This is a partnership, remember? He'll want to invest laborers, too."

Victor frowned. "I still can't get used to that idea. These people aren't my family."

"No, but they took your family in. That counts for something."

One week into the trip, the captain came to call on them. "Mr. Delgado, Ms. Bootstamp, would you please follow me to the cargo hold?"

Victor and Imala exchanged glances and flew with the captain to the hold. "I'm instructed to give you this holo," said the captain, handing Victor a holopad.

"From who?" asked Victor.

The captain smiled and flew off, leaving them alone. The hold was brimming with equipment. All of the bays were packed tight with parts and supplies. Victor turned on the holofield, and Lem Jukes's head appeared. "Hello, Victor. By the time you get this message, you'll be a week into your voyage. I'm not one for longwinded apologies, or any type of apology for that matter, but I owe you one. You and Imala both. I wasn't always as honest or forthcoming as I should have been. I know you still harbor some deep resentment toward me, and I can't say I blame you. Some of my decisions have been inexcusable. I can't make up for those mistakes, but what I can do I will. You will find on this ship everything you and your family needs to retrofit your mother's salvage ship. The captain has a full inventory. I made it as comprehensive as I could. Giving you a completely new mining ship would have been less expensive, but knowing you, I worried you might not take it. So don't salvage crappy parts from derelict ships. That's a recipe for disaster. Take these new ones and save yourself a lot of heartache. You can still have the pleasure of installing them all yourself. And since they're already loaded and you can't turn back, you have no choice but to take them. You'll find quickships, two A-class lasers, suits, helmets, wearable diggers, smelters, hand tools, nav equipment. You're pretty much set for life. If you're going to do this, you might as well do it right. Best of luck."

The message ended. Lem's head winked out. Victor stared at the empty holofield for a long moment. Then he looked up at Imala and began to laugh.

Epilogue

Edimar sat at the bay window of the Gagak and went over the data a final time. She checked and rechecked, calculated and recalculated. Then, when she was certain there were no errors, she went to the helm to find Rena.

The past several weeks had been hectic. Now that the war was over, pirates that had gone dormant were now out in full force. Or maybe they never had gone dormant. Maybe they had continued to raid ships all this time, and it was only because of the interference that nothing had been reported. Either way, a day didn't go by without another report or two coming in. Families killed, ships stripped and gutted. The most notorious of these was a vulture named Khalid. He was a Somali, like Arjuna, and the two of them had some history, though Edimar had never been brave enough to ask what.

Rena had implored Arjuna to increase the ship's shielding, and the two of them had had a rather heated discussion on the subject in the corridor. Rena had suggested adding more metal plates to the hull.

"And where am I to find these plates, Lady?" Arjuna had said.

"Wherever you can," Rena had said. "You could start with the walls between cabins."

"You want me to rip out walls? Take rooms away from my crew?"

"You'd be making one big room out of two rooms. They would still have the same amount of space."

"Yes. And zero privacy. How are my men and women to love each other if they share a room with twenty people?"

"Well, Arjuna, let's prioritize here. What's more important to you? The safety of this crew or having everyone gratify their sexual desires?"

"That is easy for you to say," he had said. "You are a woman without a husband."

"And therefore I have no desires? For a man who has three wives, Arjuna, you know next to nothing about women."

In the end Arjuna had closed himself in his room and roared in frustration so loudly that Edimar had heard him all the way back in the cargo bay. That's where she had been spending much of her days recently, holopad in hand, combing the archives of the Parallax Nexus. Now she had the answers, and she was desperate to show Rena.

She found her in the helm at the nav charts. "I need to speak with you. Immediately."

Rena followed her out into the corridor. "You look upset. What's wrong?"

"The Formic mothership. The one Victor destroyed. It wasn't a mothership at all."

"What do you mean?" said Rena. "Of course it was."

"I've been digging through the archives at Parallax. When you look outward, Ukko could have found the ship years ago. If the satellites had been programmed to identify movement like that, we would have had years to prepare."

"We wouldn't have known what it was," said Rena.

"We would've known it was extraterrestrial. We could've prepared for the worst. That would have been better than getting caught with our pants down."

"Don't use that phrase," said Rena. "It sounds vulgar. Why does this upset you?"

"Because when you look out even farther, you can see when the ship separates from something much, much bigger. This mothership that Victor destroyed, it was a scout ship, Rena. The *real* mothership is still out there."

Rena stared at her. "How certain are you?"

"A hundred percent. The data's irrefutable. Eight years ago the scout ship broke away from the mothership. But we saw it four years ago when the light reached us. The scout ship continued its speed at roughly half the speed of light while the mothership began to decelerate. The scout ship eventually decelerated also, but not until much later. So it reached us first. The mothership is now coming at about ten percent of the speed of light, but it is coming, Rena. I played with the data a hundred times. I tested myself. I looked at this from every angle, and I'm telling you, I know I'm right."

Rena said nothing for a long moment. "How much time do we have?"

"Five years. But that's not what scares me the most. This mothership is changing."

"Changing? How?"

"At first I thought it was breaking apart or something, but the pieces don't move like wreckage. They have order. They move like ships."

"I don't understand."

"The mothership is cannibalizing itself, Rena. It's

taking itself apart to create lots and lots of smaller ships. It's transforming itself into a fleet. An army. And I think it's safe to say they're not intending to apologize. I'm glad we stopped this war. I'm glad it's over. But we have a much bigger problem coming."

ACKNOWLEDGMENTS

There are two names on the cover of this book, but a small army of people made it possible. Thanks to Kathleen Bellamy for all her careful assistance. Thanks also to everyone at Tor for their encouragement and skill and expertise, particularly our editor, Beth Meacham, whose input is always wise and inspired. We owe a deep debt of gratitude to Phillip Absher, for his careful reading of the manuscript and for catching mistakes you will thankfully never see. Thanks also to Amy Stapp, Jordan D. White, Aisha Cloud, Andy Mendelsohn, and Jeanine Plummer. You all know how you helped, and we love you for it. We owe a big muchas gracias to Jorge Guillen, who gave advice on some of the Spanish phrases used in the previous two volumes and whom we failed to mention last time. Adelante, amigo.

Lastly, we thank our wives, Kristine Card and Lauren Johnston, the captains of our two ships. They are our first readers and our truest friends, and without their encouragement and counsel and good humor, this book would not exist. Marry well, dear reader, and your *mana* will never drain.